NW

J. T. Ellison's

TAYLOR JACKSON NOVELS

"Mystery fiction has a new name to watch."
John Connolly, *New York Times* bestselling author

"Tennessee has a new dark poet."
Julia Spencer-Fleming

"J.T. Ellison's debut novel rocks."
**Allison Brennann, *New York Times* bestselling
author of *Fear No Evil***

"Creepy thrills from start to finish"
James O. Born, author of *Burn Zone*

"Fast-paced and creepily believable…gritty, grisly
and a great read"
**M.J. Rose, internationally bestselling author of
*The Reincarnationist***

"A turbo-charged thrill ride of a debut"
**Julia Spencer-Fleming, Edgar Award finalist and
author of *All Mortal Flesh***

"Fans of Sandford, Cornwell and Reichs
will relish every page."
J.A. Konrath, author of *Dirty Martini*

"Fast-paced and creepily believable"
Author M. J. Rose

D0754963

jt ELLISON
Judas kiss

MIRA

All the characters in this book have no existence outside the imagination of the author, and have no relation whatsoever to anyone bearing the same name or names. They are not even distantly inspired by any individual known or unknown to the author, and all the incidents are pure invention.

All Rights Reserved including the right of reproduction in whole or in part in any form. This edition is published by arrangement with Harlequin Enterprises II B.V./S.à.r.l. The text of this publication or any part thereof may not be reproduced or transmitted in any form or by any means, electronic or mechanical, including photocopying, recording, storage in an information retrieval system, or otherwise, without the written permission of the publisher.

This book is sold subject to the condition that it shall not, by way of trade or otherwise, be lent, resold, hired out or otherwise circulated without the prior consent of the publisher in any form of binding or cover other than that in which it is published and without a similar condition including this condition being imposed on the subsequent purchaser.

MIRA is a registered trademark of Harlequin Enterprises Limited, used under licence.

First published in Great Britain 2012
MIRA Books, an imprint of Harlequin (UK) Limited,
Eton House, 18-24 Paradise Road,
Richmond, Surrey, TW9 1SR

© J.T. Ellison 2009

ISBN 978 0 7783 0463 0

60-0512

MIRA's policy is to use papers that are natural, renewable and recyclable products and made from wood grown in sustainable forests. The logging and manufacturing processes conform to the legal environmental regulations of the country of origin.

Printed and bound by
CPI Group (UK) Ltd, Croydon, CR0 4YY

J.T. Ellison is a thriller writer based in Nashville, Tennessee. She writes the Taylor Jackson series and her short stories have been widely published. She is a weekly columnist at Murderati. com and is a founding member of Killer Year. Visit her website, JTEllison.com for more information.

To Del Tinsley,
without whom none of these books
would see the light of day.
And for my Randy,
without whom I would be lost.

Judas kiss

Prologue

Blood.

It was everywhere. The floor, the walls, the body. All over the jeans and T-shirt too. Damn, how was that going to come out? With a grimace, the killer set down the weapon and stood over the now inert body. No more arguments. No more screaming about failure, lost promise, disappointments. The wail of a child built in the distance, drowned out by the fury humming in the killer's ears. A smile broke.

"You horrendous bitch. This is exactly what you deserve."

Ten hours later

"Mama?

"Mama, Mama. Hungy. Cookie, Mama. Cookie.

"Wake up, Mama, wake up.

"Went potty, Mama. Good girl.

"Mama?

"Mama owie? Owie? Boo-boo? Mama fall down?

"Bankie, Mama.
"Bankie. Teddy.
"Mama! Mamaaaaaaaaaaa.
"Night-night, Mama. Bye-bye."

Monday

One

Michelle Harris sat at the stoplight on Old Hickory and Highway 100, grinding her teeth. She was late. Corinne hated when she was late. She wouldn't bitch at her, wouldn't chastise her, would just glance at the clock on the stove, the digital readout that always, always ran three minutes ahead of time so Corinne could have a cushion, and a little line would appear between her perfectly groomed eyebrows.

Their match was in an hour. They had plenty of time, but Corinne would need to drop Hayden at the nursery and have a protein smoothie before stretching in preparation for their game. Michelle and Corinne had been partners in tennis doubles for ages, and they were two matches from taking it all. Their yearly run at the Richland club championship was almost a foregone conclusion; they'd won seven years in a row.

Tapping the fingers of her right hand on the wheel, she used her left to pull her ponytail around the curve of her neck, a comfort gesture she'd adopted in childhood. Corinne hadn't needed any comfort. She was always the strong one. Even as a young child, when Michelle pulled that ponytail around her neck, the unruly curls winding around her ear, Corinne would get that little line between her brows to show her displeasure at her elder sister's weakness.

Remembering, Michelle flipped the hair back over her shoulder with disgust. The light turned green and she gunned it, foot hard on the pedal. She *hated* being late for Corinne.

Michelle took the turn off Jocelyn Hollow Road and followed the sedate, meandering asphalt into her sister's cul-de-sac. The dogwood tree in the Wolffs' front yard was just beginning to bud. Michelle smiled. Spring was coming. Nashville had been in the grip of a difficult winter for months, but at last the frigid clutch showed signs of breaking. New life stirred at the edges of the forests, calves were dropping in the fields. The chirping of the wrens and cardinals had taken on a higher pitch, avian mommies and daddies awaiting the arrival of their young. Corinne herself was ripe with a new life, seven months into an easy pregnancy—barely looking four months along. Her activity level kept the usual baby weight off, and she was determined to play tennis up to the birth, just like she'd done with Hayden.

Not fair. Michelle didn't have any children, didn't have a husband for that matter. She just hadn't met the right guy. The consolation was Hayden. With a niece as adorable and precocious as hers, she didn't need her own child. Not just yet.

She pulled into the Wolffs' maple-lined driveway and cut the engine on her Volvo. Corinne's black BMW 535i sat in front of the garage door. The wrought iron lantern lights that flanked the front doors were on. Michelle frowned. It wasn't like Corinne to forget to turn those lights off. She remembered the argument Corinne and Todd, her husband, had gotten into about them. Todd wanted the kind that came on at dark and went off in the morning automatically. Corinne insisted they could turn the switch themselves with no problem. They'd gone back and forth, Todd arguing for the security, Corinne insisting that the look of the dusk-to-dawns were cheesy and wouldn't fit their home. She'd won, in the end. She always did.

Corinne always turned off the lights first thing in the morning. Like clockwork.

The hair rose on the back of Michelle's neck. This wasn't right.

She stepped out of the Volvo, didn't shut the door all the way behind her. The path to her sister's front door was a brick loggia pattern, the nooks and crannies filled with sand to anchor the Chilhowies. Ridiculously expensive designer brick from a tiny centuries-old sandpit in Virginia, if Michelle remembered correctly. She followed the path and came to the front porch. The door was unlocked, but that was typical. Michelle told Corinne time and again to keep that door locked at night. But Corinne always felt safe, didn't see the need. Michelle eased the door open.

Oh, my God.

Michelle ran back to her car and retrieved her cell phone. As she dialed 911, she rushed back to the porch and burst through the front door.

The phone was ringing in her ear now, ringing, ringing. She registered the footprints, did a quick lap around the bottom floor and seeing no one, took the steps two at a time. She was breathing hard when she hit the top, took a left and went down the hall.

A voice rang in her ear, and she tried to comprehend the simple language as she took in the scene before her.

"911, what is your emergency?"

She couldn't answer. Oh God, Corinne. On the floor, face down. Blood, everywhere.

"911, what is your emergency?"

The tears came freely. The words left her mouth before she realized they'd been spoken aloud.

"I think my sister is dead. Oh, my God."

"Can you repeat that, ma'am?"

Could she? Could she actually bring her larynx to life without throwing up on her dead sister's body? She touched her fingers to Corinne's neck. Remarkable how chilled the dead flesh felt. Oh, God, the poor baby. She ran out of the room, frenzied. Hayden, where was Hayden? Michelle turned in a tight circle, seeing more footprints. No sign of the little girl. She was yelling again, heard the words fly from her mouth as if they came from another's tongue.

"There's blood, oh, my God, there's blood everywhere. And there are footprints…Hayden?" Michelle was screaming, frantic. She tore back into the bedroom. Something in her mind snapped, she couldn't seem to get it together.

The 911 operator was yelling in her ear, but she didn't respond, couldn't respond. "Ma'am? Ma'am? Who is dead?"

Where was that precious little girl? A strawberry-blond head appeared from around the edge of the king-sized sleigh bed. It took a moment to register—

Hayden, with red hair? She was a towhead, so blond it was almost white, no, that wasn't right.

"Hayden, oh, dear sweet Jesus, you're covered in blood. Come here. How did you get out of your crib?" She gathered the little girl in her arms. Hayden was frozen, immobile, unable or unwilling to move for the longest moment, then she wrapped her arms around her aunt's shoulders with an empty embrace of inevitability. Pieces of the toddler's hair, stiff and hard with blood, poked into her neck. Michelle felt a piece of her core shift.

"Ma'am? Ma'am, what is your location?"

The operator's voice forced her to look away from Corinne's broken form. She raised herself, holding tight to Hayden. Get her out of here. She can't see this anymore.

"Yes, I'm here. It's 4589 Jocelyn Hollow Court. My sister…" They were on the stairs now, moving down, and Michelle could see the whispers of blood trailing up and down the carpet.

The operator was still trying to sort through the details. "Hayden is your sister?"

"Hayden is her daughter. Oh, God."

As Michelle reached the bottom of the stairs, the child shifted on her shoulder, reaching a hand behind her, looking up toward the second floor.

"Mama hurt," she said in a voice that made her sound like a broken-down forty-year-old, not a coy, eighteen-month-old sprite. *Mama hurt. She doesn't anymore, darlin'.*

They were out the front door and on the porch now, Michelle drawing in huge gulps of air, Hayden crying silently into her shoulder, a hand still pointing back toward the house.

"Who is dead, ma'am?" the operator asked, more kindly now.

"My sister, Corinne Wolff. Oh, Corinne. She's… she's cold."

Michelle couldn't hold it in anymore. She heard the operator say they were sending the police. She walked down those damnable bricks and set Hayden in the front seat of the Volvo.

Then she turned and lost her battle with the nausea, vomiting out her very soul at the base of the delicate budding dogwood.

Two

A morning off.

Instead of lounging in bed, luxuriating in the crisp sheets and getting irritated with the *Tennessean,* Metro Nashville homicide lieutenant Taylor Jackson was squinting at the ceiling in her living room, a small flutter of panic moving through her chest.

"Baldwin?" she called, stepping closer to the fireplace. "Baldwin!"

"What?" A voice floated down the stairs, tinged with impatience.

"You need to see this. I think the ceiling is wet."

The clatter of footsteps on the stairs assured Taylor that her fiancé was making the trek from their bedroom on the second floor down to her, in the room directly below, posthaste. He appeared at her side, joined her in craning his head toward the living room ceiling. A dark gray stain was moving across the joint, treading a thin line of damp. As they stared, a small drop of water beaded up from the end of the discoloration. Neither of them moved as it grew, larger and larger, then broke off and fell with a muffled *plop* onto Baldwin's shoulder.

They sprang into action, no words needed. Baldwin sprinted back upstairs toward the bathroom to turn off the water. Taylor went to the kitchen and came back with a spaghetti pot. She stood under the dribble, catching droplets of water as they rushed through the surface of the drywall and fell to earth.

God, what next?

Baldwin came back to the living room with a stepladder. "This house is built on an Indian burial ground, Taylor. I swear it. I turned the water off. We can set the pot on this. It might help keep the carpet dry." He positioned the ladder under the leak and took the container from Taylor, setting it on the top. A happy plink rewarded his efforts.

They shared an exasperated laugh. In the month they'd been home from their pseudo-honeymoon, everything that could go wrong with their relatively new house had. A fitting metaphor for their life. No matter what they planned, how they tried, they couldn't seem to get onto the right page and make it official. Taylor was content to remain unmarried. Baldwin was starting to come around to her way of thinking.

"Who do you want me to call? The home warranty place?" He started for the kitchen.

"Yeah. The number is in the folder in the server. They're going to have to send out a plumber now, we can't wait."

He opened the drawer and pulled out an overstuffed file folder. "Okay, I'll make the call. But I've got to finish packing. My flight leaves at ten-thirty."

Taylor gave the ceiling a last hard stare, then joined Baldwin.

"Here, give me that. I'll call. You go on and finish packing. Besides, the plane leaves when you tell it to. Director."

He shot her a look. "I'm not the Director. I'm the Acting Director while Garrett has this stupid surgery. That just means I get to push his pencils around his desk and pretend to look important for two weeks. Seriously, I'd rather stay here, fight with the plumber."

Garrett Woods, director of the FBI's Behavioral Science Unit and Baldwin's boss, had called the previous evening. He'd gone for his routine yearly physical and ended up hospitalized, scheduled for a triple bypass. He needed someone he trusted to hold down the fort. Baldwin was the obvious choice. Taylor hoped it wasn't a play to get him to come back and run the BSU permanently. There'd been quite a shake-up while Taylor and Baldwin were in Italy, celebrating what should have been their honeymoon. The man who'd been leading the BSU, Stuart Evans, had been summarily fired after a personnel issue made headlines. The Bureau wasn't a big fan of having their personal laundry aired in the media. Garrett Woods took the position again, leaving his number three in the bureau spot. He hadn't been happy working at that level anyway, was thrilled to return to the BSU and make things right with his investigative divisions and behavioral analysis unit profilers.

"You need to go tend to Garrett's cases. And make sure he listens to the doctors. I can't believe he's so sick."

"Me neither. He seems so indestructible to me, always has. So you think you can handle this?"

She kissed him, then pulled back and raised an eyebrow. "Uh, yeah. It's just a little leak."

"Okay, then. I'm going to finish packing." With a pat on her rear, he left the kitchen. She smiled after him. God, what a goof she'd become. Fools in love...

And their love nest was falling in around their ears. This would be the fourth time she'd had to call for service since they'd moved in two months ago. There had been contractors crawling all over the place for silly little issues—a broken fan blade on the heater, a squirrel who'd nested in the crawlspace and chewed through some electrical wiring, a faulty thermostat on the freezer. Now a leak in the master bath. They were making their bones with the warranty company. She got the plumber's name and number, left them a message, then went upstairs, determined to make Acting Director Dr. John Baldwin regret that he was leaving for two weeks and prove her point. The Gulfstream couldn't exactly leave without him.

The phone rang as she hit the second stair. What now? She backtracked, went to the kitchen and saw the number on the caller ID.

"Hi, Fitz," she answered.

Sergeant Peter Fitzgerald, her second in command, greeted her brusquely. "I know it's your day off, but you need to come in. We've got a murder that's going to have fleas."

"Who?"

"Some sweet little mother out in Hillwood. I'm hearing words like *Laci* and *Peterson*."

Taylor shuffled her fingers through a notepad that sat next to the phone, ready for an urgent message. *No, thank you. I'm not in the mood for a murder. I think I'll pass.* But she couldn't. She was the homicide lieutenant, and if her team needed her, that meant she would show.

"Fine. Give me twenty minutes and I'll be on the road."

"The fed gone yet?"

"He's finishing packing."

"Well, go kiss his pretty little face goodbye and get your ass down here. We need you."

She hung up and the phone rang again. The plumbers. They greeted her warmly. Of course they would, she'd be sending their children through college if this was more than a simple leak. They said their technician would be out in an hour. She told them where she'd hide a key, then ran up the stairs. Baldwin was zipping his suitcase.

"You ready?"

"As I'll ever be."

"Good, come on. I'll drop you off. I have to go in."

"Who died?"

Ah, the bliss of living with a fellow law enforcement officer. He just *got* it.

"Fitz says it's a young mother. It must be catching on fire for him to drag me in on my day off." She pulled a black sweater over her gray T-shirt and went into the offending bathroom. She brushed out her hair and gathered it into a ponytail, frowned at the toilet, where she assumed the leak had generated, then went to her closet and grabbed a pair of boots. Hitching up the legs of her jeans, she slipped into the Tony Lamas without sitting down and jumped up once, landing softly to set her heels and drop the pant legs. Ready.

Baldwin was standing in the doorway to the master,

watching with a bemused smile on his face. "Thirty seconds flat. Not bad. You look stunning."

Taylor rolled her eyes at him. "Let's go, lover boy. The sooner you get to Quantico, the sooner you can come home."

Three

Taylor met Fitz in the parking lot of the Criminal Justice Center. Clouds scudded across the graying sky. Despite the beauty of spring in Nashville, the weather was wholly schizophrenic. Sunny one minute, stormy the next. She took off her sunglasses and slipped one temple into her sweater collar.

"Yo," Fitz called, pointing to a white Chevy Impala, his official department issued ride. "I gotta run back to the office for a second. Want a drink?"

Taylor nodded her head and started for the car. She took the passenger's side, pushing the seat back to accommodate her long legs. Fitz disappeared into the bowels of the CJC and returned a few minutes later with two Diet Cokes. He slid into the driver's seat, handed over the soda. She cracked the lid and sipped, then put the can between her thighs.

The sun popped out for a brief second, enough to blind her, so she put on her new Ray-Bans, a purchase she made in the duty-free in Milan's Malpensa airport. They were wide and black and made her feel glamorous, a tiny homage to her new European sentiments. Traveling in a foreign country with a native speaker of the language had the tendency to make you *feel* more. She'd been on several trips overseas before, but had never experienced them the way she'd experienced the three weeks touring Italy with Baldwin.

She was having trouble acclimating. She missed the slow easiness of Italian life—the languid drives, the frequent stops for food and wine, the symmetrical beauty of the olive groves and vineyards and cypress-lined drives, the feeling that she was very, very young. And if she were being absolutely truthful, it had been damn nice to have three whole weeks without a single dead body.

The clouds smothered the burgeoning sunlight again, but she left the glasses on. Annoying, that's what these transitional months were. She wanted it to be one or the other, warm or cold, sunny or cloudy.

Fitz pulled out of the parking lot.

"How ya doing?" he asked.

"I have a leak in my bathroom," she pouted.

"I told you not to buy a new house. If you'd gotten one constructed like they should be, something solid, like those great old Victorians in East Nashville, you wouldn't be having these problems."

"No, Fitz, I'd just have termites and gang-bangers. No thanks. Gentrification just isn't my thing."

"Spoiled."

"Not. We just wanted something…airy."

Fitz laughed. "Airy my ass. You wanted something big enough for that damn pool table and a passel of kids."

Taylor turned to him, suspicious. "What in the world makes you say that?"

He looked at her with one eyebrow cocked. It made his face look crooked, like Popeye full of ruddy wrinkles. "You don't?"

"Don't what?"

"Want to have a pack of brats with the fed." He said it so calmly she went on immediate alert.

"Where are you hearing this stuff? I've never said anything about having a baby. We can't even manage to get married, so I'm hardly gunning for offspring. I don't know if that's something I ever want to do." She looked out the window, watched the edge of downtown Nashville slip away like a veil was lifted. Brick and cement became foliage. They were on West End, heading out to Hillwood. A bucolic drive through the suburbs. Was that prompting Fitz's question?

"Okay, girlie, I'm convinced. But I'm hearing this crime scene might be a bit off-putting. If you were fixing to get yourself knocked up, I might encourage you to skip this one, look the other way."

"Jesus Christ, Fitz, tell me what's at the scene."

"Parks is there. Hey, there's a picture in the visor. Grab that, wouldja?"

Good, Taylor thought. Bob Parks was as level-headed a patrol officer as Metro employed. If there was something wild at a crime scene, he would know how to tamp it down so the press couldn't get too insane. She unfolded the sun visor, expecting a crime scene photo. Instead, a picture of a boat dropped into her lap. She turned it around so it faced up. It was pretty, white with tall sails, sliding through impossibly blue water.

"Yes…?"

"Parks said it was a little gruesome out there, that's all."

"No, I mean, what's with the boat?"

"Thinking of buying it."

Taylor looked at the photo again. It was…well, it was a boat. That's as far as she went with sailing. Not her forte.

"When are you planning to drive this boat?"

"Jeez, LT. It's called sailing. And it's for when I retire."

Fitz clamped his mouth shut. Taylor recognized the action—he was finished talking about it. He'd warned her about the scene and lobbed a bombshell about the future; that was as far as he was willing to go. Great.

An ambulance whipped past them, coming from the opposite direction. Going to St. Thomas, she thought. She mentally crossed herself, as she did every time she heard a siren. After thirteen years on the force, five of them in Homicide, she wasn't so jaded that she still couldn't have some compassion for the strangers in this world who might need a little looking over.

She toyed with her new engagement ring. The post-engagement pre-marriage ring, actually. When he'd first proposed, Baldwin had given her a stunning two-carat Tiffany sparkler, with delicate baguettes parading around the platinum band. Gorgeous, but impractical. And since the wedding hadn't gone off—no fault of her own, she'd been unceremoniously Tasered and flown unconscious to New York with poor Baldwin standing at the church waiting for her—the new ring was a representation of a second chance.

He'd arranged to slip away for a few moments in Florence, then shown up for dinner at a little place they'd fallen in love with called Mama Gina's, a flush around the crinkles of his intense emerald eyes. To the delight of their regular waiter, Antonio, and the rest of the restaurant patrons, he'd dropped to one knee and presented her with a new ring. One that held an even deeper promise. The five Asscher cut diamonds twinkled from their platinum channel setting. Baldwin told her each diamond represented the next five years of their lives together, and he'd buy her another in twenty-five years.

Aside from the romantic notion of it, the practicality of the ring touched her. It was flat. It didn't catch on things like the Tiffany. And it wouldn't get in her way if she had to fire her weapon unexpectedly. The gesture was overwhelming, and she'd almost told him to find a church that very moment. He knew what she was thinking, and that had been enough. She hadn't decided whether she was ready to try again.

She dragged herself back to reality when Fitz harrumphed at her. He was turning onto Jocelyn Hollow Road, and Taylor could see the parade of vehicles lined up at the end of the normally quiet street.

The attendance to an unnatural death often seemed a three-ring circus to the uninitiated. The entrance into the cul-de-sac was blocked by a confluence of vehicles. There were five Metro blue-and-white patrol cars. First responders had already left the scene. Whenever 911 dispatched the police, the closest fire engines and an ambulance were actually sent before the squad cars. Standard operating procedure. The clues were apparent; there was no hurriedness, no rush. There was nothing that could be done for this particular victim, so the next steps were being taken.

The *why* had begun.

Fitz stopped the vehicle three houses away and they

exited the car, making their way to the command station at the base of the driveway. A sign on the black mailbox had the name WOLFF in curly letters. Taylor always wondered exactly why people would want to advertise their names on their domiciles. An address she could understand, but the name…it seemed silly. And a safety issue. The last thing in the world she would ever do is publicize where she lived. Of course, she wouldn't know what name to put on the mailbox. Jackson? Baldwin? Jackson-Baldwin? That just sounded like a funeral home.

A crowd of people had gathered directly across the street, standing in the yellowish grass, waiting. Recognizing the authority in Taylor's stride, they started yelling when she came close. One voice rose above them all.

"What happened? We have a right to know what's going on at the Wolffs'." Fear made the man's voice tremble.

Taylor turned, took in the speaker. He was an older man, with black hair that looked suspiciously dyed. Unshaven, thick glasses, pajama bottoms, jean jacket over a dirty sleeveless undershirt. Her immediate thought was *widower* and she stopped, feeling sorry for him.

Realizing he'd caught her attention, he repeated the question. "What's going on in there? Did something happen to Corinne or to Todd? Is Hayden okay? My God, you can't protect us from anything, can you? You and that damn police chief, you've got this all locked up, don't you?" He swiped a handkerchief across his nose.

"Sir," Taylor began, but the rest of the crowd began

in on her. The sentiments turned from fear to vitriol in a heartbeat.

"All you do is give speeding tickets!"

"The gangs are running this town!"

"We live out here in the suburbs and expect to be safe. This is a good neighborhood. I'm going to talk to Channel Five about this. Phil Williams should be checking you out!"

Taylor held up her hands for silence. "People, please. My name is Taylor Jackson, and I'm the lieutenant in charge of the homicide division. I haven't even been briefed on this incident. Perhaps you'd like to give me some time to get acquainted with the scene and determine what's happened before you tear me apart?"

They grumbled, but the logic shut them up.

"Thank you. Please know that we'll be doing everything in our power to solve this case. I appreciate that you're upset, and I can't blame you. But let me get a sense of the scene, and I'll come back and talk to each of you again. All right?"

She stepped away before the crowd could respond. She'd be talking to them. Interviewing them. Trying to ascertain if there was someone in that mix who'd had a hand in the murder she was about to dissect.

"Fitz, can you get their names? Just in case. I don't want to miss anyone."

"Sure," he answered, pulling a notepad from his shirt pocket.

She crossed the street and met up with Bob Parks. He was twiddling his finger in the curled edge of his mustache, ruminating to a uniformed officer about the chances of the Tennessee Titans after a scandal-rocked combine.

"Hey, how's my favorite LT? You happy to be home from your grand tour?"

"Not really, Parks, but thanks for asking. I'd hop on a plane back in a heartbeat. Don't give up on the Titans too soon, my friend. They'll recover. In the meantime, go root for the Predators."

He looked shocked. "Hockey? Are you kidding, LT? I'm a pigskin man, tried and true. I'm a Volunteer. I bleed orange." He thumped his chest with a closed fist. Fervent was an understatement when it came to fans of the University of Tennessee football team.

"Well, our Volunteers need to take the SEC Championship this year or Phil Fulmer will wake up to a moving van in his driveway. Besides, being a good Tennessee fan, you should understand the importance of us having a well-rounded professional sports system to augment the college faithful. We need to sign the UT boys when they graduate, right?"

Fitz crossed the street to their position, waving the notebook. "Got 'em."

"God, a woman talking football is a beautiful thing, eh, Fitz?"

Fitz just shook his head. Taylor spoke again, dispensing with the chatter this time.

"What do we have here?"

The smile left Parks's face and he became all business.

"It's not pretty, I'll give you that. Decedent's name is Corinne Wolff, female Caucasian, twenty-six, married and preggers. We've been really careful about who's gone in the house, there's a lot of latent blood around. I've got everything ready to put in my report, if you want the particulars now?"

"Just run it down for me. Highlights."

"Okay. I got the call around 9:40 a.m., came straight here. Met the sister, who was being attended to for shock by the EMTs. House 37 got the call, they were here first with two trucks and the ambulance at…" He looked at his sheet. "9:38 a.m. Sister's name is Michelle Harris. She was holding the decedent's daughter, Hayden Wolff, who was covered in blood but seemed in stable condition. She relayed that her sister was dead inside the house, facedown on the floor in her bedroom. She didn't recall touching anything, but we printed her for exclusion. First entry was made at 9:48 a.m. by me and EMT Steven Jones. We entered the home, cleared the downstairs, noted the amount of blood, made our way upstairs to check the victim."

Parks had gotten ashen under his normally swarthy skin tone. "It's stinky up there. Looks like she's been dead for at least a day. Got smacked around pretty hard. Jones touched her wrist, just to confirm, and we agreed it was too late for his assistance. We retraced our footsteps and I started the evidentiary procedures. We had three more patrols on the scene at that point, so we got started setting up command and control while we waited for you. Despite the biologicals everywhere, the scene is pretty much contained to the master bedroom. That's where the action took place. The rest is secondary transfer."

"Fitz said there was a little girl. Did the transfer come from her or the killer?"

Parks nodded. "Looks like the kid. You'll see when you get in there. I talked to the sister, got her story. Apparently they had a date to play tennis and she dropped by to pick the victim up. She entered the house, saw her sister, grabbed the kid, called 911 and skedaddled. She's been questioned already, but I knew you'd want to talk to her. I've got to warn you, the victim's parents are here. The sister called her mom after she finished with 911. Everyone is pretty shaken up."

"Where's the husband?" Taylor asked.

"On a business trip. Convenient, huh?"

"I'll say. Can you find out where he is for me?"

"Already done. The mom called him, he was in Georgia and is on the road now, driving back. Should be in this afternoon."

Taylor looked at Fitz, who was writing in his notebook. "Wouldn't you fly home if it were you?"

"Yep," Fitz said.

Parks gave her a wry grin. "I asked the same thing. No direct flights. It was quicker for him to drive. At least, that's what the mom said."

Parks handed over some of the items Taylor would need to enter the house—booties, latex gloves. He offered a blue paper mask, similar to one her dental hygienist wore, but she shook her head once, declining. No sense in that. No matter the precautions, the scent of death would sneak into her sinuses, settling for hours. She slipped her sunglasses into her front pocket; she wouldn't need them inside.

"Is Father Ross here?"

The Metro police department's chaplain was a kind, gentle man who Taylor had relied on more times than she could remember. It was hard enough to inform a family member that a loved one was dead. Having the minister along was not only helpful, it was mandated.

"He's here. The whole group of them, parents, two

sisters and the kid are in the next door neighbor's house, huddled up, waiting for you."

"Anyone know when the victim was seen last?" she asked.

"We're working on nailing that down right now. The sister talked to her Friday. One of the neighbors might've seen her, or something."

"Okay. When did the ME get called?"

"Same time as you, LT. Dr. Loughley is on duty this morning, she's—"

"Right here," a voice called out. Taylor turned to see her best friend, Samantha Loughley, walking up the drive, her kit slung over her right shoulder. Her dark brown hair was up in a ponytail, thick bangs swept across her forehead. The bangs were a new look, and Sam had been bemoaning the haircut for a week.

"Morning, sunshine," she said as she reached Taylor. "What's up, Parks? Fitz, you look well."

Fitz grinned back in acknowledgement of the compliment. He'd been working hard on his weight and now had his formerly oversized belly down to a trim and manageable thirty-eight inches. The weight loss took ten years off his fifty-five-year-old frame, and Taylor knew he'd begun dating a woman he'd met at a barbeque cooking contest. Oh. Maybe that's what the boat was all about. She shook the thought off. They needed to focus on the murder.

"Like the new look, Owens," Fitz needled.

Sam rolled her eyes. "Are you ever going to start using my married name, *Sergeant?*"

"Naw. I like Owens. Loughley's too hard to say." He jostled her with his hip and smiled.

Sam dropped her bag on the folding card table that

had been set up for the field command station. "Fine. Call me whatever you want. Just put that degree in. I spent too much money not to use the title."

"*Anyway,*" Taylor said, getting their attention back from their game. "Sam, we were about to make entry on the scene. I haven't been inside yet. Parks says the victim is a female Caucasian, pregnant and toasting. So let's get this over with, okay?"

Fitz looked over to the neighbor's house. "I think I'm gonna go next door and have a chat. Y'all have fun up there."

Taylor watched him go. Good. Two birds, one stone. "We set, Parks?"

Parks nodded. "Tim's here too, ready to go." Tim Davis was the lead criminalist for Metro Nashville police. He'd started in the Medical Examiner's office as a death investigator, then moved over to Metro in anticipation of their eventual establishment of a crime lab. Taylor always enjoyed working with the young man. He was very serious about his craft.

"No time like the present." Taylor started for the door, Sam right behind her. The videographer was on the narrow porch, camera on the boards between her feet, ready to document their walk through. Taylor didn't recognize her. Tim Davis was waiting patiently, kit in hand.

"Hey, Tim," Taylor said.

"Morning, LT. Dr. Loughley. Have you met Keri McGee yet? She's going to be doing the video feed for us this morning."

A sunny blonde stuck out a pudgy hand. "Good to meet you, Lieutenant. I just moved up here, used to be with New Orleans Metro. Really glad to be here."

Taylor held her hand up. "It's good to have you. I'd

shake, but I'm already gloved. Welcome to Nashville. You just stick to my six and we'll be fine. If you need to boot, try to get back outside and don't screw up the scene, okay?"

"Sure thing, ma'am."

Taylor fought the urge to snap. *Jesus, girl, don't call me ma'am. I'm not old enough to be your mother.* Instead, she smiled and stepped into the house.

Rotten chicken. That's what the first olfactory note identified. Just as quickly, the coppery scent of blood, the stink of putrefaction and decomposing flesh, and a sweet, almost perfumelike scent. Not air freshener. Hmm. Taylor's eyes adjusted as her subconscious mind worked its way through the instinct to flee. It wasn't a natural smell, and her heart raced for a moment. A normal first reaction, borne of self-preservation, would be to get the hell out of there. A couple million years of evolution warned her—there's danger here. She'd felt it before, knew it would pass in a second. She let herself adjust, breathing through her mouth. Sam was by her side, doing the same thing. They were trained to make it go away.

Taylor let her eyes wander the room in front of her. She was standing in a marble-floored foyer. There was a table against the closest wall with pictures in silver gilt frames—happy, smiling newlyweds against a summer-wooded backdrop. The stairs were directly to her right, hardwood covered in an ivory Berber runner. Just past the banister was the entrance into the dining room, loaded with heavy dark oak furniture, silver and crystal, an oversized china cabinet. To the left, a brief hallway that opened into a great room. The floors in the dining room were burnished oak, the great room was carpeted in the same light Berber wool.

Every few inches there were tiny crimson footprints. Little heels here, little toes there. They looked like mouse trails, in and out, back and forth, leading up and down the stairs, into the great room, and Taylor could see they trailed into the kitchen on the far side of the dining room. They were everywhere; some light, barely pink enough to mar the carpet, some outlines or edges. Closer to the stairs, a few were dark, almost seeming they would be wet to the touch. Sam drew in a deep, sharp breath.

Taylor forced her brain to shut off that emotional center which would allow her to acknowledge the desperation the child must have felt to be wandering around the house, her mother's blood on her bare feet.

"This is Homicide Lieutenant Taylor Jackson," she said aloud for the benefit of the video camera. "I am the lead investigative officer at this crime scene, 4589 Jocelyn Hollow Court. I'm going to do one pass through the lower part of the structure." Nodding at Sam, she went to the right, into the dining room, avoiding the blood. Sam picked her way after Taylor. Tim and Keri followed, the group moving as one, silently assessing.

The footprints wended their way through the dining room, under the table, and back into the kitchen. There was no rhyme or reason to the pattern, just a nomadic line of passage, typical of a youngster moving aimlessly about her home. Some areas were just faint impressions, blotches, and some were well formed. That made sense to Taylor. The blood would wear off after enough steps. With a child, her uneven toddling tread would account for the inconsistencies.

The dining room had a door that separated it from

the kitchen, but it was propped open with a stuffed cat doorstop. The door was white, a six-paneled French style, covered with what looked like cherry juice finger-paints. Taylor knew what they really were; the little girl had swept her bloody hand along the door as she walked from room to room.

The kitchen was baby-proofed, with locking mechanisms on all the below counter cabinets. The smell of rot was more prevalent, and Taylor spied a Wild Oats bag with a package of chicken in the deep stainless steel sink. Well, that accounted for the stink downstairs. If the victim hadn't talked to her sister for two days, and the chicken was coming back to life, then there was a good chance she'd been dead at least a day. Taylor only put chicken in the sink if she needed to defrost it and had the time to do so. That would give a convenient timeline—a day to thaw and a day to start smelling. Though it just as easily could be the victim came home from grocery shopping and didn't get all the packages stored before her assailant appeared. They'd need a liver temp or a potassium level from the vitreous fluid for something more accurate, but it was a start. Never assume, that was her mantra.

Fruit in a basket on the granite countertop, an empty carton of organic fat-free milk, an empty yogurt container…if Taylor *was* going to guess, it looked like the victim had just finished eating breakfast before she vacated the room and got herself killed.

An answering machine hung on the wall, the red light indicating new messages blinking.

"Be sure someone gets those messages," Taylor said to Tim.

Sam made a noise in the back of her throat. "I was

planning on shish kebabs for dinner. Guess I'll make a salad instead."

The videographer didn't comment, and Taylor shot her a glance. Keri wasn't fazed, was simply documenting. Excellent. Taylor caught Sam's eye and smiled. Always the jokester.

"Let's head up." Taylor walked slowly from the kitchen through the great room, back to the foyer, the group in her wake. The stair had a landing halfway up and turned to the left. There was blood smudged up and down the stair runner, not the same kind of hit and miss footprints they'd been seeing. Taylor asked Sam what she thought it was from.

"Baby that small can't get up and down with a normal stepping motion. She'd have to drag herself up step by step, on her hands and knees, slide down on her bottom. If she was covered in blood…"

"Oh." The image was vivid in Taylor's mind.

Placing their feet in between the splashes of color, they made their way to the second floor.

"Baby gate isn't up," Sam noticed. "Get a shot of that, would you, Keri?"

"That explains how she was able to wander the house." Taylor took in the setup.

To their right were three doors, all leading to bedrooms. To the left, the hall led away from the stairs. The scene was similar to below, but more intense. Distinctive tiny red footprints, defined smears along the walls. Macabre artistic skills from a young child surely affected more by confusion than anything else.

The rooms each glowed with a different palate, and the hall bath was decorated in a nautical style, reminiscent of a beach hotel. It struck Taylor. The obvious effort that had gone into decorating was apparent. And the trimmings weren't bought at Target or Pottery Barn. The décor was top of the line, custom designed.

A quick perusal showed a guest room, an office and a nursery. Blood smears and light footprints wound in and out. Taylor followed the path. The nursery was painted in various tones of pink and lilac, with a mural of a forest on the western wall. The furniture was bleached oak; there was a mobile hanging above the oversized crib. Sunlight poured through the windows, barely checked by a light pink sheer. There was a small half bath off the nursery. Taylor glanced into the space. The smell of feces and urine was strong—a miniature plastic toilet sat on the floor next to its life-sized companion. It was full of waste. The child was toilet-trained, but without her mother to empty the basin, the little potty was full to the brim.

Nose wrinkled, Taylor walked the length of the hallway to the master bedroom. The door to the room was open wide, wedged against the wall with a small bronze mouse. Corinne Wolff liked her doors open, no question about that. The walls were painted a creamy sage, the furniture dark rattan and rosewood. Island style, a retreat for the owners. Taylor remembered seeing an ad for the same style of room in an upscale design catalogue.

The interior of the room was awash in incongruous colors. The blood had molted into a dark brown stain, except where it cast against the walls and a white shaded lamp in a deep burgundy.

They saw the feet first. The body was half hidden by the king-sized bed. They crossed the room with care. No one wanted to be responsible for mucking up any evidence they might find. The room was at least forty feet in width, the bed in the center of the back wall. There was approximately fifteen feet of space on each side. The body was in the south quadrant of the room. Taylor heard Tim scratching notes as they moved to the far side of the bedroom.

Corinne Wolff was barefoot, her legs drawn to her chest. She was half on her side and half on her stomach, facing them. Her chocolate-colored eyes were open but unseeing, the irises like gummy coffee. Her brown hair was matted with blood from an obvious gash across her forehead. Her jaw was broken, misaligned along the lower half of her face, jutting obscenely toward the ceiling. The body was crooked too; her arms stretched out as if she tried to break a fall then changed her mind. She was dressed in panties and a sports bra, a pink cashmere blanket draped over her midsection. A thick pool of blood approximately two feet in length and a foot wide surrounded her head and her torso, and a small plush toy was tucked into the crook of her arm. Footprints led around the body, away from the body, back to the body. Along Corinne's side, the blood had been disturbed.

Taylor and Sam stepped closer. "Oh, man," Sam whispered. "That poor thing."

"Corinne or Hayden?"

"Both."

Taylor wasn't sure what bothered her more, the teddy bear tucked into Corinne's arms, the blanket draped across her seminakedness, or the plush, stuffed Gund My Doctor kit that sat by her head. Her daughter, unable to understand what was happening, had tried to help. She'd managed to get a large pretend Band-Aid stuck to the top of her mother's hand. Hayden had tried to fix her. And then she'd lain down next to her mother, covering herself in blood.

They got the necessary pictures and videotape, then Sam set to work. She pulled back the blanket and saw the pregnancy.

"Oh, jeez. I hate this." She felt the body. "She's cold and malleable. The blood pool has soaked into the carpet and is tacky to the touch. I won't know an exact time of death until I run the temp during autopsy, but this should give you a time frame to start looking at. Rigor is completely gone. Livor mortis is set, the discoloration consistent with a body lying in one position since death. She's been dead at least thirty-six hours. I'd say she was killed right here, fell in this position and didn't move. How far along is she, do you know? This looks like a four, maybe five-month bump."

"I don't know. Parks said she was pregnant, but he didn't say when she was due. Thirty-six hours minimum? God, that little girl was here in this house with her dead mother all that time. Poor baby."

Sam continued her examination. "With a mother who'd been violently bludgeoned to death. Blunt force trauma to the extremities, the head. Her jaw is certainly broken, she's missing some teeth." Sam was finishing her initial assessment, making notes in a small black reporter's notebook. "This is a mess, T."

"Tell me about it. I don't see any weapon conveniently lying around, do you?"

"No. And this is too much damage to just have been someone's fists. Tim, you hear that? You need to keep an eye out for a weapon."

"Yes, Dr. Loughley."

"Okay, folks. Let's rock and roll." Sam and Tim continued their duties, with Keri filming everything for posterity. Taylor went to the window. The cream-colored roman shades, covered with blood spatter, were at half-mast. She glanced out at the street below. The neighbors were still grouped on the opposite lawn, talking quietly amongst themselves. She didn't see anything out of place, no one who stood out as having a more than neighborly fascination with the goings-on.

Sam stood, leaning over the body, then turned to Taylor. "It's going to be a long day. I need to run out to the van for a couple things. Are you ready for some air?"

"Yeah."

With a last glance at the victim, Taylor led the way out of the master and down the stairs.

When they got back to the front door, Taylor asked the question that had been burning in her mind from the moment she laid eyes on the body of Corinne Wolff.

"Just where is this husband?"

Four

The Harris family had taken refuge with the Wolffs' next-door neighbor.

Fitz nodded to her as she came in. There were five people in the room, sitting, staring, crying. Father Ross, the department chaplain, was holding a woman who looked to be in her early fifties, with reddish hair. The woman was sobbing, nestled into the chaplain's shoulder. The mother. The room was deadly quiet outside of the woman's choked tears.

A dark-haired young woman met Taylor's eye. A mixture of revulsion and longing crossed the woman's face, quickly replaced by a hardness, an implacable blankness. Taylor had seen that look before. People hated to see her; she was the harbinger of death. But she held the answers, the clues, the reason. They needed her. Taylor guessed the woman was twenty-eight, maybe thirty. She could see the resemblance to the victim.

There was something else on this woman's face, but Taylor pushed it away.

She was this woman's polar opposite—where Taylor was tall, honey-blond, gray-eyed, full-lipped and broad-shouldered, this woman was five foot three or four, dark and quite athletic. Her body hummed with health and well-being; her face wasn't exactly pretty, but what men who were being kind would call interesting. She gave Taylor another look, and this time the meaning was inescapable.

Taylor was unsettled. She never enjoyed being the object of another woman's attention. This woman wasn't exactly hitting on her, but she'd made her interest known. Lovely. What was up with that?

"I'm Lieutenant Taylor Jackson, Metro homicide. I'm so sorry for your loss, ma'am."

The dark-haired woman didn't smile, but stuck out her hand.

"I'm Michelle Harris. Corinne is my sister."

Taylor was surprised when the woman spoke; the voice was deep and husky, that sexy, cracked sound that men always flocked to. They sounded alike.

Michelle gestured to the tear-streaked woman standing with Father Ross. "This is my mother, Julianne Harris." She went around the room in turn, naming her family.

"My father, Matthew Harris. My sister, Nicole Harris. Carla Manchini, Corinne's neighbor. We're waiting for my brother Derek, he'll be here shortly. Do you know who did this to my sister?"

"Not yet, unfortunately. We're early into this investigation, Ms. Harris."

"It's Miss."

Taylor cocked her head to the side for a brief instant, then replied, "Miss Harris. Sorry. Where's your sister's daughter?"

The smaller of the two sisters, Nicole, spoke, her voice stronger than she looked. "She's taking a nap in the back room. Poor thing was absolutely exhausted. Once the paramedics said she was fine, we gave her a bath, fed her and got her down. She seemed all right, physically."

"Why, Lieutenant? Hayden didn't have anything to do with this." Michelle Harris was sharp-tongued, challenging. Taylor forgave her, poor girl's sister was dead, but ignored her for a moment. She turned to the other sister.

"Nicole, right?" The girl nodded.

"You gave her clothes to the officer? We're going to need to process them as evidence."

She nodded. "That crime technician officer was with us when we changed her. We did everything just how he told us to."

"That's good. We appreciate your help. Sergeant Fitzgerald will help me gather your statements. Mrs. Manchini, I'd like to speak with you alone. Can we go into another room?"

"You don't want to talk to me first?" Michelle asked.

Taylor met Michelle Harris's eyes. They were as odd as Taylor's own, a blue so clear you would almost say they were transparent. Taylor's were gray as a cloudy sky, one slightly darker than the other.

"I want to speak with everyone who is here. I just need some information from Mrs. Manchini to start. Please, bear with me. I'm afraid it's going to be a long day. Mrs. Manchini?"

The woman stooped when she stood, unable to straighten all the way. She gestured to the hall, and Taylor followed her out of the room. She stopped walking when she heard the deep voice of Corinne's father speaking.

"You okay, sweetheart?"

Taylor edged back to the living room entrance, careful to stay out of sight. Eavesdropping. She could see into the room perfectly; there was a mirror on the opposite wall above a small writing desk that reflected their actions. Fitz had his back to her, was talking to Father Ross.

Michelle Harris turned and grabbed onto her father, the words pouring out of her like a spigot left on during a summer drought. "Oh, Daddy. I don't know if I am. I don't think I'll ever get the image of Corinne laying there on the floor all bloody, with Hayden next to her, out of my mind."

"I know, honey. It must have been horrible." He pulled her in close, and Michelle melted into his arms. Taylor felt a pang of jealousy. Michelle's father was her savior, her protector.

"Haven't you heard from Derek yet?"

"He's in that infernal lab class until noon. I'm going to head over to Vanderbilt now, be waiting for him when he leaves. I don't want him to hear this from an outsider. I'll bring him back here with me. Will you be okay for a little while?"

"I'll be fine, Daddy. Once I talk to the detective, I'll sit with Mom. You and Derek take your time. He's going to be a mess."

"Yes, he is. Thank you for understanding. You always were my good girl. I love you, Shelly. Take care of Nikki too. She's not as strong as you and your mom." He hugged her tight to his chest, and Taylor turned away. A grieving family. Why did that make her feel so empty?

* * *

Mrs. Manchini had led Taylor into her bedroom. Her chintz bedroom. Unlike the coolly decorated perfection of the Wolffs' house, everything here smacked of homemade kitsch.

The master was small, about half the size of the house next door. A four-poster bed with a canopy and frilly lace pillows took up much of the space. Cliché, Taylor thought, then mentally chided herself. The Manchini house did seem a caricature of itself, the woman who owned it a shadow of a real person, insubstantial. Carla Manchini could have been anywhere from forty-five to sixty-five, with outdated wire glasses, thinning blond hair in a partially grown-out perm and slightly crooked teeth. Her parents must have decided that they weren't quite bad enough to invest the money into fixing. As a result, when she spoke, a snaggletooth incisor appeared on the right upper side, and her lips folded around it as if not sure what they were meant to do.

Taylor realized Carla had been talking and focused.

"I'm not sure what you want with me, Lieutenant. I didn't know them next door very well, no, I didn't. I mind my own business over here at Manchini's *casa,* yes, I do. I'm not a spy, don't go looking into my neighbors' backyards, I truly don't."

Taylor looked at the woman, wondering why she was so adamant. She wouldn't meet Taylor's eye, just sat on her bed, her gaze flitting about as she twisted her hands together.

"Actually, ma'am, I'm just wondering if you've noticed anything funny over the past few days."

The woman shook her head solemnly. "I surely didn't."

"Nothing?"

Mrs. Manchini paused for a moment, shut her eyes, remembering. "The lights were on. Mrs. Wolff turns them off in the mornings, but they burned all weekend."

"And that was unusual?"

"Yes."

Ah, another item for the timeline. Perfect.

"When was the last time you saw Mrs. Wolff?"

"Oh. Well, I can't rightly recall. Today's Monday, and Monday is my book club, yes, it is. I don't remember seeing Corinne today, and I usually see her in the back, watering her begonias. Such a pretty garden she has, yes, she does. Just put it in this past weekend. It's a little too early for those flowers, but what do I know? I did see her on Friday. Friday is my garden club, yes, it is." Twist, twist, twist.

The repetition tic was starting to bother Taylor. The woman was going to sprain a wrist if she didn't lay off her hands. "Friday at what time, ma'am?"

"Oh, well, I couldn't be exact. Something around three-twenty in the afternoon, if I had to push myself to remember, but I wouldn't want to be misleading by not being one hundred percent right, no, I wouldn't."

"You're doing just fine."

The woman bobbed her head, a shy smile crossing her face at the compliment. Taylor got the feeling the woman didn't get many and softened her tone.

"What was Corinne doing at three-twenty, Mrs. Manchini?"

"Playing with little Hayden. Such a beautiful child, yes, she is."

"Backyard, front yard?"

"Oh, yes, of course. They were in the side yard,

actually. I believe Mrs. Wolff was putting down some wildflower mix, trying to pretty up the area where their trash cans go, yes, she was."

Didn't keep an eye on her neighbors. Yeah, right. "Did you see anyone with her?"

"Other than Hayden? No, I didn't."

"What about Mr. Wolff?"

This earned Taylor a direct, but fleeting, glance. She was rubbing her hands together now. The conversation was making her nervous. Nervous was always interesting.

"Oh, I don't know him very well. A handsome man, yes, he is, but not very open with the likes of me, no, he isn't."

"Did they have any problems that you were aware of?"

"Why, no. No. None at all. They seemed to be very happy. Very content, yes, they were."

"And you didn't see anyone else near the house. What about Saturday?"

"No, I didn't see anyone there Saturday, no, I didn't. I'd like to get back to my guests now, if I could?"

"Just a few more questions, Mrs. Manchini. Are you here in the house during the day?"

"Yes, yes, I am. I retired from the post office a ways back, yes, I did. I keep pretty much to myself nowadays, yes, I do. I read, and watch television, and go to my book club and do some gardening. I have lots of friends, yes, I do."

"That's good, Mrs. Manchini. Do the Wolffs entertain often?"

"Well, of course. They're young and popular, they are indeed. But no more so than anyone else on this street. I've lived here for forty years, yes, I have, and I've seen neighbors come and go. Everyone seems very happy here, yes, they do." She stopped wringing her hands, set them in her lap. The knuckles were red and gnarled. Combined with the wistful statement, her true age showed through. A lonely old woman, Mrs. Manchini.

"Okay, ma'am, let's get you back with the others. You're very kind to allow your house to be overrun like this. I'm sure the Harrises appreciate your help. I may want to talk to you again. Would that be okay?"

The woman lifted herself slowly off the bed, making the springs squeak in protest.

"Certainly, of course. Any time you need me, I'll be right here, yes, I will."

Taylor followed the mousy Mrs. Manchini back to the great room. The scene hadn't changed much, except Michelle Harris now sat in a flowered chintz-covered armchair, holding a blond cherub in her arms. The little girl had china-blue eyes, a soft rosebud mouth, ivory skin with red apple cheeks. This must be Hayden. The child caught her eye, an unfathomable darkness shifting behind the cornflower depths. She spied Taylor's gun, fixated on it for a moment, then started to cry, burying her face in her aunt's shoulder.

Taylor and Michelle Harris sat at the kitchen table in Mrs. Manchini's house, afternoon sunlight streaming hard through the southerly facing windows. Michelle was handling herself as well as could be expected, considering Taylor was pumping her again about her traumatic morning.

The father of the victim had returned with the

younger brother, who wasn't taking the news of his sister's murder well. Fitz had Derek Harris out on the back deck, talking with an avuncular tilt to his head. Taylor could see the two men over the top of Michelle Harris's shoulder, out the bay windows that were framed with a short, fringed chintz curtain. Taylor couldn't imagine looking at all the busy mishmashed floral patterns and colors day in and day out.

At least she'd identified the unknown scent in the Wolffs' house. It was the perfume Corinne's sister wore, a heady scent overlaid with iris and jasmine. Cloyingly sweet, and too heavily applied, as if Michelle had used soap, lotion and perfume all from the same line.

Nose twitching, she continued the interview. "Okay. Run me through it again. Start with the last time you talked to your sister."

Michelle was pale, looking drained and torn. She kept glancing over her shoulder at her little brother, obviously wanting to comfort him.

"Michelle?" Taylor asked.

"Sorry, Lieutenant. You know how it is with siblings. Sometimes you want to protect them from hurting."

"No, actually, I'm an only child. I wouldn't know. So please, run through it again. You and Corinne had a tennis date?" She sat back in the wooden chair, crossed her arms across her chest and waited patiently.

Michelle toyed with her ponytail, wrapping it around her neck in what Taylor thought was a compulsive gesture. "That's right. We play at Richland. We've been making a run at the championship flight for the past few weeks. We're doubles partners, have been for years. I thought about playing singles once, but Corinne wouldn't hear of it. We are, were, such a great team. Something happens to us on the court, we can just sense each other's movements, I guess."

"And your sister played even though she was pregnant?"

"That's right. She played up until the week before Hayden was born, only stopped when Todd begged her. This time, she's had such an easy pregnancy that she swore she would go from a match straight to the delivery room. She would have, too, I bet. Corinne could always make her body work to her specifications. Give her a sprain, she'd manage to mend in time for the next event and never lose a step. She's a wonder woman."

"When was the baby due?"

Michelle's voice grew thick. "Eight weeks."

"Wow. She wasn't very big for someone seven months along."

"She didn't get big with Hayden either. Only gained eight pounds, and Hayden was seven pounds, six ounces. Her body snapped right back. She was on that road this time, too. The poor baby. What will they do with him?"

Tears sprang to Michelle's eyes. Taylor looked away while Michelle recovered her composure. She didn't especially want to think about fetal death certificates right now.

"Let's talk about that in a bit. Stay with me, okay? So you were coming to pick her up—"

"Actually, I noticed that she hadn't turned off the outside lights. That was unusual. Corinne was very…specific about certain things. She always turned those lights off as soon as she got up, which was usually 5:30 a.m. sharp. It was almost to spite Todd, really. They'd had an argument about the style of lights. That's not important, sorry. She gets up, turns off the lights, starts the coffeepot, does half an hour on her elliptical, then gets Todd up. On the days he's home."

"When does she turn the lights on for the evening?"

"What?" Michelle asked.

"The outside lights. When does Corinne usually put them on?"

"Oh." Michelle pursed her lips and thought. "You know, I'm not sure. I'd guess at dark."

"Okay, so the lights were on when you pulled up. What else caught your attention?"

"I got out of the car and started toward the house. The door was unlocked, but that's nothing new. No one around here locks their doors. It's stupid, but they all feel so safe. I bet they'll start locking them now." Michelle got a dreamy, detached expression, began reciting in an absent tone. "I went in the house, saw the blood, ran up the stairs, saw Corinne, saw Hayden, freaked, grabbed Hayden, and ran."

"You called 911."

"Yes, I did. I'm sorry, Lieutenant, I'm just still so shaken up. Just seeing all that blood, seeing Hayden…." Her voice trailed off and her eyes clouded with tears. "I don't think I'm ever going to be able to erase that moment from my memory. Do you ever have that? I imagine with all the bodies you've seen, that you can just shut it off and not think about it. Me, I'm going to remember that bedroom for a very long time."

"You're doing great, Michelle. Just a few more questions, okay? Tell me about Todd."

"What's there to say? Todd is—"

"What's there to say?" Matthew Harris stormed into the kitchen. "I'll tell you what there is to say. Todd isn't here, and my Corinne is dead. He might as well have beaten her to death himself. Him and all this travel, this desperate need to get his name out there. If he'd been home, protecting Corinne like he should have been, this wouldn't have happened. My daughter and my grandson wouldn't be dead."

Five

Matthew Harris stepped toward Taylor, pointing his forefinger at her chest, making jabbing motions in the air. "I don't want to hear anything from you, Lieutenant, except 'I'm going to nail this bastard to the wall for what he's done.' That's all I need to hear."

Taylor stood, stretching to her nearly six-foot height, only an inch shorter than Corinne's father. He took another step toward her and she put up her hand.

"Mr. Harris. I suggest you take a step back."

"Daddy!" Michelle was on his arm, yanking at him, pulling him toward a chair. "I'm sorry, Lieutenant, this isn't like him. Daddy, what is wrong with you?"

Taylor had a brief, flickering image of her own father's incredulous face, staring at her through the thick Plexiglas of a patrol car, but shook her head to disrupt the thought.

Matthew Harris sat heavily at the kitchen table, lowered his head onto his folded arms, and began to cry.

Taylor caught Fitz's eye and he came in from the deck, the younger Harris boy following on his heels.

"Dad, are you okay?" The boy sat down, his hand on his father's heaving back.

Taylor jerked her head to the right, signaling to Fitz to follow her. They left the grieving Harrises at the kitchen table and stepped outside, closing the French doors behind them. Taylor pulled her sunglasses out of her pocket and put them on.

Fitz had a furrow between his eyebrows. "Anything new?"

"No. Michelle Harris told me the same story twice, with nearly identical details each time. From what I'm hearing, nothing is rehearsed. We have a timeline at least—the lights were on all weekend, and the neighbor saw Corinne on Friday. Michelle Harris said Corinne turns the house lights on at dark, so we can start with the assumption that the murder happened sometime after sunset Friday. The sisters are upset, the father is cracking under the pressure."

"That's understandable."

"Of course it is. The mother refused to be sedated. I'd like to take a shot at her before she changes her mind. I'm anxious to meet the husband."

"The brother pointed me in the husband's direction."

"Really? That sounds promising. I'd like to hear what he has to say. The father just intimated that he felt Wolff was responsible, too. He's pretty upset, I didn't get the feeling he thought Wolff committed the murder. Just that he wasn't around to protect his wife."

"Well, the kid seems to think that Wolff is entirely capable of doing the deed. Says they fought all the time, that Corinne was talking about leaving him."

Taylor looked over the hedge into the Wolffs'

backyard. Nice, open view for Mrs. Manchini. "Funny, the sister didn't mention it. Let's go talk to the mom, if she's ready, then we can talk to the kid."

"Mrs. Harris, could you tell me a bit about your daughter?"

Taylor was back at the table in the chintz kitchen, a fragrant cup of tea steaming at her elbow. Corinne Wolff's mother was doing better than before. Father Ross sat next to her, holding her hand. Her husband was in the other room. Taylor didn't feel like having a confrontation with him. Besides, girls talked to their mothers.

She sniffled into a tissue. "What do you want to know?"

"Did she have any enemies? Was she fighting with her husband? What was she like? I need to get to know Corinne so I can start looking for her killer."

"She was a wonderful child. Gifted."

"Gifted how?"

"She was an athlete. Tennis. She was ranked in the top ten in her age group for most of her career. She wanted to go to the Olympics. But that all changed when she got into high school."

"What changed for her?"

Julianne Harris stifled a smile. "My Corinne discovered boys. And suddenly, tennis was something she could play with *them*. She stopped training, decided she wanted to be normal. It was a huge waste of talent, she was qualified to go out on the circuit. She made the finals at Wimbledon, in the juniors, against the number one seed. A girl from Russia. Nearly took the match. The loss was…difficult for her."

The tone of her voice made Taylor think the loss might have been hard for Mrs. Harris, too.

"So where did Corinne go from there, Mrs. Harris?"

"She got tremendous grades, went on to Vanderbilt. She continued to play, just without the same fervor that she had as a girl. She met Todd, they graduated, and she worked for a time before she got pregnant with Hayden. They were so happy, oh, you should have seen the look on her face when she told me. It was a very easy pregnancy for her. This one wasn't as simple, but she was doing so well."

"How would you characterize her relationship with Todd?"

Mrs. Harris fiddled with her stringy tissue. That was interesting. Taylor could tell the woman was trying to think carefully about what to say. Protecting the husband? Or protecting her daughter? The Harrises weren't unbiased in all of this. They had a granddaughter to think of as well.

Mrs. Harris sighed deeply. "Oh, Lieutenant, what can I say? They were just like any other new family. They had their issues, but they seemed to be superficial. Todd would do something to upset Corinne, she would call and complain about it. I'd tell her how much I understood and she'd attack me, accuse me of hating Todd. It was a very typical mother-daughter-husband situation. As far as I know, Todd didn't do anything exceptional. He is a solid man, a good provider. He works too much, but he's the sole breadwinner. Corinne didn't want to have children only to let a day care raise them. She was adamant that she stay home with Hayden. And Dalton... Did anyone tell you that they'd named the baby Dalton? In my day, it was always bad luck to talk about your unborn child, but nowadays they don't think that way." The tears started again, and Taylor decided she'd had enough for the moment.

"It's a nice name, Mrs. Harris. I'm so sorry for your loss. Thank you for your candor. I appreciate it. I'll let you get back to your family now."

Taylor left Father Ross to it. He was going to be much more of a comfort now than she ever could.

Taylor took Derek Harris outside to chat. They got seated in the chairs on the deck, Fitz and Taylor facing Derek. He was happy to talk badly about his brother-in-law.

"They'd been having problems for a while. Corinne swore me to secrecy. She knew she could trust me not to tell Michelle. Michelle's a little intense. If she'd known they weren't getting along, she'd be badgering Corinne to move out or something."

"Tell us what happened."

"Corinne didn't say what they fought about, only that they had a huge, terrible fight. I remember she came over to Mom and Dad's that night, she looked like she'd been crying. Anyway, we were talking after dinner. She told me he'd gotten furious with her and stormed off. She hadn't seen him for about five days, didn't know where he was.

"But he came home the next day. I went over there after class to check on her, and he was sitting in the living room, drinking a beer. She had this chirpy look on her face, seemed happy that he was home. Do you think he killed her?"

Taylor dodged the question. "What's Todd do, Derek?"

"He's a contractor. Builds housing developments. The Trace, Harpeth on the Walk, those really upscale communities. He has some out-of-state projects too, that's why he travels so much. He's usually gone on the weekends to his off-site developments."

"Wolff Construction? That's him?" Fitz asked.

"Yeah. You know it?"

"I looked at one of the show homes in Harpeth on the Walk. It was very nice."

"Todd's great at what he does. He's driven, always looking for a new deal. He's a decent enough guy. Until Corinne told me about the fight, I didn't know they had problems. I guess everyone does, but all I've ever seen is my parents, and they're stupid in love with each other. Fighting wasn't something we had a lot of growing up."

Must be nice. Of course, Taylor's family didn't fight, they were just icily polite to one another. Lacking passion, one could say.

"Would you say that your brother-in-law was capable of hurting your sister?"

Derek's eyes were huge. He was young, but not young enough to miss the inference. "Jeez, I just can't imagine him killing her. I guess anything's possible, though."

That's what she needed to hear. "Derek, thank you. If you remember anything else, please let me know." She gave him a card. He took it and went back inside.

She and Fitz had just started to compare notes when Taylor's cell phone rang. She took it off her hip and looked at the number. Tim Davis.

She answered the phone. "What's up?"

Tim sounded as excited as she'd ever heard him. "You need to get back over here. I think I found the murder weapon."

Six

Taylor was in Corinne Wolff's lovely walk-in closet, listening to Tim Davis. The scent of cedar was tickling her nose.

"So I was just doing a cursory look-through, and saw a little bit of blood on the corner of the drawer. When I opened it, there it was, lying in the clothes. It was covered up, but you could see the outline plain as day. Blood soaked into the scarf covering it. Guess whoever stashed it didn't expect us to look there."

Tim recreated his actions, pulling open a drawer labeled SCARVES. Nestled into the multicolored silk was a tennis racquet. It was bent and dented, and had visible blood and matter coated along the edges.

Taylor thought about the wounds on Corinne's body. Sam would have to confirm it at autopsy, but she thought that a tennis racquet could do the damage she'd seen. Wielded with enough force, anything could be a weapon. She asked anyway. Tim had seen it all.

"Think this could do that much damage?"

"Sure. It's nice and strong. Head's just like a ripe melon. You hit it hard enough, it'll split open. And you know how head wounds bleed. She had a ton of gashes, that's where all the blood came from. Enough that the poor little girl was able to cover herself in it and track it around. Someone was pretty hacked off at this woman."

"No kidding." Taylor looked back into the room, at the stain where Corinne Wolff had lain on her carpet, bleeding from a dozen wounds. Not the way she'd like to go. She turned back to Tim.

"Great job, man. This is going to help tremendously. Get it photographed and see if there's any prints. Wouldn't that be nice—we'd be able to wrap this thing up today."

"I'll give it a good going over, Lieutenant. I love it when the criminal's dumb enough to leave the evidence behind."

"No kidding. This seems to be a weapon of convenience. Her gym bag was on the bed, the racquet must have been right there. I'm wondering if he got interrupted, stashed the tennis racquet in a hurry to get out of here."

"Could be. Or he didn't think we'd look in here. You know how people are. They don't realize we actually have brains."

"Truer words were never spoken, my friend. Let me know if you find anything else."

Taylor was happy to have so many pieces falling into place. Half her job was done—they had a victim, a weapon, and eyewitness testimony that dissent had crept into the Wolff household.

Now they just needed the husband.

* * *

A dark SUV pulled into the street on Jocelyn Hollow Court and stopped just short of the crime scene tape strung across the Wolffs' driveway. Taylor heard the neighbors buzzing as she walked out of the house, heard the snap, snap of cameras taking pictures. The media had arrived earlier and were reporting from a safe distance. But their long lenses could see quite a bit. And this was grade A, prime time footage. The husband had arrived.

Taylor watched Todd Wolff get out of the Lincoln Navigator, his body quivering with trepidation. He left the door open, the key in the ignition, the V-8 engine rumbling like a purring lion as it idled. He walked around to the passenger side, his steps heavy. His shoulders were bent, his nose red and swollen from crying. He stared at his house as if he'd never seen the place before. It had been six hours since he'd been told his wife and unborn son were dead.

Fitz sidled up beside her. "Wolff must have driven like a bat out of hell to get here so soon. I didn't think he'd be in before six at the earliest."

He handed Taylor a bottle of water, which she accepted gratefully. She twisted the top and drank deep, washing the taste of murder out of her mouth. She put the cap back on and spoke under her breath.

"He certainly looks distraught."

"That's an understatement. Dude looks like shit."

Wolff was still staring at his house, and now took a few faltering steps toward the front porch. Taylor went to him quickly, getting a hand on the man's forearm. He stopped and turned, looking at her with wide, blank eyes.

"Who are you?" he asked in a monotone.

"I'm Lieutenant Taylor Jackson, homicide. This is Sergeant Pete Fitzgerald. Why don't we chat for a minute, Mr. Wolff."

She steered him back toward his truck. He strained against her, pulling away.

"No, I want to go in. I want to see Corinne. I want to see Hayden."

"Mr. Wolff, your wife isn't here. She's been transported to the medical examiner's office. Why don't you come here and sit down for a second."

Taylor looked up and saw that several of the neighbors had come back to attention, grouping across the street, and the newsies had their cameras trained on the grieving husband. Damn.

She looked around for a moment. They needed privacy, and she didn't want to parade him into his house until the crime scene people were through.

"Actually, let's go next door and talk, okay?"

"To Mrs. Manchini's? She doesn't like me." But he tucked his head and changed direction, heading straight to his neighbor's house without additional complaint. Taylor followed after a quick glance over her shoulder at Fitz, who was standing next to Wolff's truck, casually looking through the open driver's side door at the interior. He shook his head and Taylor continued toward the Manchini house. He hadn't seen anything out of place. Yet.

The Harris family had been excused from the scene at three-thirty. They had left directions to the Harrises' house in Sylvan Park, phone numbers and cell numbers where they could be reached. They'd taken Hayden Wolff with them. Taylor saw no reason to make a fuss over that, it wasn't as if they were going to steal the child, after all.

Wolff stopped short at the edge of his lawn, head swiveling, breath suddenly coming in little pants. "Where's Hayden? Where's my daughter?" He started back toward his house. Taylor grabbed his arm again.

"Whoa there, Mr. Wolff. Your daughter is still with your in-laws. Her grandparents. She's just fine, was a little tired and hungry, but she's safe. You don't need to worry about her."

"I want to see her. I want to see her right now. I want to see my daughter!" His voice rose in pitch until the last word came out in a wail. Taylor heard shutters clicking as Wolff dropped to his knees in the grass between the two houses, sobbing. The video cameras rolled, gathering the scene. It was heartbreaking, and would make for a very exciting five o'clock news hour.

Taylor stepped to his side, squatting down to get face-to-face with him. Damn it, she didn't want to be on the news doing this.

"Mr. Wolff," she said as kindly as she could muster. "You need to get up and come with me now, sir. Let me get you situated next door and we can chat. The sooner we can do that, the sooner I can get you reunited with Hayden."

"My son," the man screamed. "My son is dead and you're holding my daughter. This isn't right. This isn't fair!"

Fitz appeared at her side. She caught his eye, gestured with her head. Histronics weren't going to help. They both took hold of an arm and raised Wolff to his feet. He was crying hard, tears and snot mingling into channels running down his chin, but he stopped yelling. A step in the right direction. Without further incident, they were able to get him all the way to the Manchini front door and slip him inside.

Taylor's phone rang, and she pulled away, letting Fitz guide the distraught man to the now familiar chintz couch. Carla Manchini stood in the middle of the great room, watery eyes shining behind her glasses. This was more excitement than the woman had seen in years.

Seeing an unfamiliar number, Taylor decided to let it go to voice mail and joined Fitz, Mrs. Manchini and Todd Wolff in the great room. Probably a reporter anyway.

"Mrs. Manchini, do you think it would be possible if we could have the room to ourselves for a few minutes so we could speak to Todd alone?"

Disappointment clouded the older woman's eyes, but she nodded like a little bird. "It's nearly time for me to leave for my book club, it's going to take me at least thirty minutes to get to Davis Kidd. There's a fresh pot of tea in the kitchen. Can I trust you to lock up for me, Lieutenant? Normally I don't worry about it, but now…"

"Of course, ma'am. We truly appreciate all your help today. You've been a huge asset."

Tickled, the woman gathered her purse, a well-thumbed copy of Tasha Alexander's *A Fatal Waltz* and left. Her book group would be hearing some exciting tales this evening.

Todd Wolff was collapsed on the sofa. He'd stopped actively crying but was sniveling, wiping his nose with the back of his wrist.

Taylor took a seat in the chintz armchair next to him.

She waited for him to gather himself, handed him a tissue from the crochet-covered box sitting on the end table next to her. He wiped his eyes and cleared his throat.

"Mr. Wolff, can I ask where you've been?"

When he didn't answer immediately, Taylor sized him up. He was a handsome, well-made man, with a thick shock of black hair, flashing black eyes, and deep stubble along his cleft chin. Looking at him, Taylor thought about the fair Hayden and wondered, just for a minute. Two dark-haired, dark-eyed parents, and their offspring a blonde with clear blue eyes. Interesting, genetics.

With a huge sniff, Wolff finally began to speak. "I have a property getting ready to open in Savannah, Georgia. I was down there overseeing the last bits and pieces. There's a million things to be done, and I'm the one who has to get the checks written."

"You build houses? Wolff Construction?"

"Yes."

"When did you leave for Georgia?"

"Friday, around noon. I've been going every two weeks now that we're getting close to wrapping the project."

"You normally drive?"

"Yeah. I'm a successful developer, but I'm not made of money. It's cheaper that way."

"Seems like a long trip," Fitz observed.

"I like the drive. It clears my head."

"Did you usually spend the weekend when you made the drive?" Taylor asked.

"Yes. I come back on Monday afternoon."

"When's the last time you spoke to your wife?"

Wolff was quiet for a moment. "Saturday morning."

"That was the last time?"

"Yes."

"Did you try to call her again after you spoke on Saturday?"

"Yes. I wanted to read Hayden a story Saturday night. It was our tradition."

"She didn't answer?"

"No." Wolff's voice wavered, but fresh tears stayed in check.

"Weren't you concerned that you couldn't reach Corinne?"

Todd flinched at the mention of his wife's name. "I wasn't really paying attention, God help me. I was so caught up in the problems we were having on-site that when I didn't reach her, I just left a message. I figured she was out with her sisters anyway. When I went out of town, she usually did a girls' night with friends, or hung out with Michelle and Nicole and watched movies. She'd get a babysitter for Hayden sometimes, take advantage of some private time. I tried to call her again at around ten, but when the answering machine kicked on, I hung up. Tried her cell once, then went to bed myself. She didn't like me checking up on her."

"And you tried on Sunday?"

"I called Sunday around noon, and she didn't pick up. But again, it didn't worry me. She's very independent, doesn't need me around to keep her entertained. Since I have to go out of town so often, she's used to it. How did she, how was she…"

He started crying again. "Who did this, Lieutenant? I love my wife. We got along, had a beautiful little girl, a son on the way. We were happy. This isn't the kind of thing that happens to happy people."

Oh, if it were only that easy, Taylor thought. The good and happy people get to lead normal lives, bad things only happen to bad people. Yeah, right. "Unfortunately, I can't answer that for you right now, Mr. Wolff. Let's talk some more about your interests in Savannah. Where do you stay when you go down there?"

"There's a Hampton Inn down the street from the property. My secretary can give you all the particulars."

"That's where you stay every time?"

"Yes. It's convenient, and clean. And not too expensive. I have to watch the bottom line, you know?"

"Your company has made quite a name for itself. How'd you get into construction?"

"The honest way. I worked summers for my dad, he operated a heavy crane for a guy over in Ashland City. I had a chance to do little bit of everything. I love carpentry, love to see homes rise out of nothing. I've got a decent head for figures. It was a natural extension of my upbringing. Why does that matter?"

Taylor crossed her legs. "We're just talking here, Mr. Wolff. Is the business doing well?"

"Better than I deserve."

"No money issues? You guys were doing okay financially?"

"Lieutenant, I hardly think—" He stopped, the implication of Taylor's question hitting him. "You think I did this."

"I'm just trying to get a feeling for your life, Mr. Wolff. I'm not implying anything. Tell me about your finances. You mentioned that you drive instead of fly because it was cheaper. Is your business having problems?"

He became very still. "Lieutenant, what happened here? What happened to my wife? No one will tell me."

The raw emotion tugged at Taylor's center. She caught Fitz's eye. Either this guy was one hell of an actor, or he genuinely didn't know the manner in which his wife had died.

"Mr. Wolff," Taylor tried again. "Do you and your wife fight?"

He met her eyes, his gaze direct and unflinching, deep pools of pain. "Of course we fight. We're not perfect. We have tiffs, like every other married couple in the world. If you're asking if I killed my wife, the answer is no."

Taylor assessed him for a moment longer. Well, it was always worth judging the reaction to reality. She decided to take a chance. Something about Wolff's demeanor made her believe him. A quick glance at Fitz confirmed her decision was sound.

"We don't have a lot to go on right now, Mr. Wolff. Evidence is being collected, the investigation is underway. What I *can* tell you is your sister-in-law came to pick Corinne up for tennis this morning. Your wife was found in your bedroom, severely beaten. Your daughter seems unharmed."

"And the baby?"

His voice cracked and tears spilled down his cheeks, silent silver tracks. The voice of a man condemned, a man who knew the answer to his question but forced himself to ask it anyway.

"Your son didn't survive the assault, Mr. Wolff. Your

wife had been deceased for some time when she was discovered. I'm very sorry."

Wolff hiccupped, then stood and bolted. Taylor heard him vomiting in the guest bath, then water running to cover the noises.

Fitz had sat silent throughout the exchange. "You think we need to bring him downtown?" he asked quietly.

The water was still running in the bathroom. Taylor shook her head, but answered him under her breath. "I think he's got enough on his plate right now. That was an awfully visceral reaction for someone who knew what was coming. He may be pulling one over on us, but I'm inclined to think he may be telling the truth. Either he's quite the criminal mastermind—arranging to be out of town, hiring someone to kill his wife—or he doesn't know what happened. Let's give him the night with his daughter, and question him again in the morning. We've got a lot of background to go through, need to see what their finances are like, sift through all the evidence Tim collected. I say we write things up and call it a night."

"I agree. I'll get him over to the Harrises' so he can see his daughter."

"Sounds good. I'm going to go into the office, make up the murder book, check in with the captain. I'll see you there."

The toilet flushed and the water stopped running. Wolff came back into the room, his eyes bloodshot, looking chagrined. "I'm sorry for losing control like that."

"It's okay. We understand. I think it's time to wrap things up for today. Your wife's body will be autopsied in the morning, and we'd like to talk to you some more. But for now, we're going to get you with Hayden and your family."

As they left, Taylor couldn't help but look back at the Wolffs' house. What had happened? Was this a home invasion gone bad? It didn't look like anything had been tampered with or stolen. No, this felt personal, and Todd was the obvious choice.

There was something about him. So far he'd shown nothing but the appropriate responses. But Taylor couldn't help but think about Corinne's family, and her father, insistent that Todd was somehow culpable for the murder.

It wouldn't be the first time she'd been lied to.

Seven

Taylor took her time driving downtown, thinking about the afternoon. The murder weapon stashed in the closet, Todd Wolff's seemingly genuine hysteria. It was much too early to dismiss him as a suspect. Violence on this level, in the victim's home, so often was a result of a domestic squabble gone wrong. And there had been plenty of husbands who had duped even the best investigators. Mark Hacking came to mind. He'd gone on television, cried and begged, pleading for justice for his pregnant wife, when in actuality, he'd shot her, dumped her body in a Dumpster, replaced their mattress and nearly got away with the whole crime. Scott Peterson was another classic example. It was a sad statistic—the number one cause of death for pregnant mothers was domestic homicide.

But if he'd done it, he was a cold-blooded bastard. Murder your wife, your unborn child, and leave your daughter trailing around the house alone for days? Jesus. That took some balls. Or desperation.

It was ten after six and Taylor was topping Nine

Mile Hill. She'd made the short trip into Bellevue and gone through the McDonald's drive-through before heading back downtown. The whole day had been lost at the Wolff crime scene and she hadn't stopped to have anything to eat. She munched a chicken sandwich as she drove, feeling virtuous for skipping the fries.

Nine Mile Hill, so creatively named because it was exactly nine miles from the heart of downtown Nashville, the Cumberland River, afforded Taylor a lovely panoramic view of the city. The sun was setting behind her, catching the reflection off the Lifeway warehouse. The skyscrapers and the Capitol building that made up Nashville's skyline were bathed in a rosy copper reflective glow, shimmering like an urban mirage. Taylor had lived in Nashville her entire life, but had never seen this vision. It was gorgeous and filled her, making her feel whole and drowsy. She was tempted to pull over and watch until it disappeared, but the sun did the trick for her, shifting slightly in its evening zenith. The mirage faded, and the downtown Taylor knew reappeared.

The little things were becoming so important. She'd always had a knack for finding beauty in the most unlikely places. When it came to her unbidden, it felt like a blessing.

As she drove through Belle Meade, she thought about Corinne Wolff. This murder was going to seize the attention of Nashville. Always fascinated by suburban crime, the city would rally around a dead mother-to-be. She made a mental note to talk to Dan Franklin, the department's spokesman, to work on some language that would be appropriately somber. If she didn't get a viable suspect right away, a story like this could breed controversy. She didn't need the national news outlets breathing down her neck. She'd had enough of that on her last big case.

Gossip, rumor, innuendo. A homicide detective's best friend was the undercurrent, the shifting of allegiances, the aspersions cast. It took a rare talent to sift through the lies, arrive at the truth. Taylor had always had a sense for accuracy. But when the media got involved, the deceptions became driven by ratings. A brave new world.

She'd only had serious media trouble twice in the past, once several years earlier, the second only a month prior. The Snow White Killer, long dormant in Nashville, had risen like a phoenix and started killing again. She was still uncomfortable with the nature of the media's interest in the case, how easily they dragged her and the department through the mud. There was constant second-guessing and now, with the benefit of hindsight, Monday morning quarterbacking galore. Two months later, Taylor lay in bed at night, watching replay after replay of the case on cable news, wondering if the interest would ever truly end. The national news outlets had camped along the streets of downtown Nashville like hippie jam bands, partying over the leftovers of each family's grief. The slightest whiff of resolution and they'd be back at it.

The earlier trouble, well, she didn't like to think about that.

The thoughts came quickly, whipping through her mind like a breeze. Snow White. His apprentice, the self-proclaimed Pretender, a man with no name and no compunction when it came to killing. Still out there, lurking in the deepest recesses. Which brought her to Baldwin.

Baldwin would have firsthand access to anything new on the still very open case. He'd promised to look into the Bureau's files while he was in Quantico.

If she were being honest with herself, she hoped he would find something fresh, something concrete. Something more than the ephemeral, hair bristling on the back of the neck feelings Taylor had. Feelings were all well and good. She trusted herself, trusted her instincts. Every once in a while, her skin tingled and she felt eyes on her back. She assumed the Pretender was keeping tabs on their investigation into his whereabouts, and sometimes followed her. She could almost sense him when he was near. He set her radar off, though she'd never gotten a real look at him.

They needed concrete evidence. Needed to know the name of the murderer who masqueraded in other killers' emotional garments. They had nothing.

Headlights flashed and she came back, surprised to see she was already at the Criminal Justice Center. Car coma, that's what Baldwin called it. It happened too often; she'd be lost in thought and realize she'd driven to her destination without seeing the path. Too distracted. She needed to be more on her game. The time off had only intensified the need for her to get her head back to Nashville, and on keeping herself safe.

She parked and crossed the lot, taking the back stairs two at a time. She swiped her key card along the access box at the back entrance to the building. The door dumped her into the hallway just outside the Homicide offices. The second shift had already arrived; a noisy buzz emanated from the homicide office.

The hall was blocked by a young patrol officer from the first shift who was bent in half, butt sticking up in the air, her flashlight swinging precariously close to her head as she dug green-colored photocopied paper out of a box. She straightened, shuffled the pages of announcements, meeting schedules, calendars—the normal office detritus. It only took her a few moments to rearrange the corkboard, posting new job listings and notices. When she was satisfied, she stood back and looked to make sure everything was set to rights, then slid the Plexiglas closed and locked it with a miniature key. She noticed Taylor, mumbled "Sorry," and shoved the box out of the way. As Taylor passed her, she went on to the next glass slot, the one with the latest WANTED posters. She unlocked the casing, reached in her little box and pulled out several posters, arranging them in order of priority. The highest priority was an infamous cold case that appeared to have gotten a lead.

The Cold Case team. Taylor didn't envy their jobs a bit. She couldn't imagine working full-time with the lost, spending all her time living other people's pain and agony. Taylor was convinced that in order to heal, a victim's family just needed to know what actually happened. For those who were missing, who were dead with no killer captured, no answers, the waiting was unbearable. Nashville had plenty of cases that fit this précis, and six or seven that were actively being worked.

With a brief wave at two of the B shift detectives, she went into her office and shut the door behind her.

Absolutely astounding. Looking at the top of the wooden desk, Taylor couldn't help but think of a tornado's aftermath. When she'd left the night before, everything was in its place, the in-box and out-box were empty, and the desktop was completely clear. Now, it was overflowing. She spied at least four incident reports from the Wolff crime scene, a couple of red actionable items from upstairs, an empty three-ring binder some kind soul had thought to provide, knowing she'd be collecting all the information for its innards, creating a new murder book labeled Wolff. Several multicolored sticky notes, a full call sheet, a brief scattering of pens and pencils. A shaft of moonlight peeked through the open blinds, illuminating a white sheet of basketball brackets with a hot pink postie reminding her to make her picks before Thursday at noon or else she wouldn't be able to participate in the yearly NCAA pool. Away for a day and the desk bloomed like forsythia, one moment barren and empty, the next full of unruly flowers. With a sigh, she slipped around to her seat and started organizing. She couldn't work in chaos, never had been able to tolerate a mess in her proximity.

Her voice-mail light was blinking. She played the messages. The only one of interest was from Lincoln Ross. Oh, thank goodness. It was good to hear his voice.

She never realized how much she missed being around her team until they weren't there. She'd missed them all while she and Baldwin were away, and returned to the news that Lincoln Ross had been tapped for an assignment. A "Special Assignment." That's all she'd been told. She could guess what cases might be important enough to put a homicide detective on a full-time assignment, had made a few attempts to get information from her captain, Mitchell Price. He'd only smiled and nodded with each guess, not giving her the satisfaction of knowing which supposition was correct.

Setting a sheaf of paper aside, she flipped open her cell phone and dialed the number. Lincoln answered on the first ring, his deep, honeyed voice tinged with irony.

"Thank God it's you, LT. I have a problem," Lincoln said.

"Talk to me. I miss you, by the way. Are you ever coming off this project?"

"I hope so. I think things are about to break. This stupid confidential informant got me in a world of hurt, and I had to push back. That's part of the problem."

"What happened?"

She heard the deep, readying breath. "I had to partake." He spat the words out as if saying them would ease a bad taste in his mouth.

"Oh, Lincoln. You know that's not—"

The despair in his voice broke her heart. "Shit, LT, I know. Trust me, it was drilled into me a thousand times before I got involved in this case. I didn't have a choice. This is getting dicey. I didn't know what else to do."

"What was it?"

"What else. Crack. Messed me up good, too, even though I barely had a hit. God, LT. It was terrible. You don't think they'll fire me?"

Taylor laughed. "No, I don't. My God, Linc, you're one of the finest officers we employ. If you said there was no other choice, I believe you, and so will Price. He'll go to the mat for you. How'd you get yourself stuck?"

"The CI has been meeting me at a skeevy hotel, bringing me the information. Some of his cronies followed him to the meet. There was nothing we could do without blowing the whole thing. Thank God they didn't recognize me, that would have ended it all right there, with me on the floor in a puddle of blood. No, they were all fucked-up and wanted to party some more. I've been feeding the CI drugs to sell to them. They insisted on trying the merchandise. I said no, the head dog said yes. Stuck a revolver in my face. I didn't think I had much of a choice after that. I faked it best I could, but I still had to blow something out, you know?"

It was the bane of undercover work, especially when the target of the investigation was into the drug scene. Balancing being a cop and not blowing your cover was difficult at best. Lincoln wasn't undercover though, and she didn't want to upset him further by telling him that it *was* likely disciplinary action would be taken against him. A suspension without pay, probably. That could wait until he was back with her.

"You need to be careful, my friend. Write the whole thing up and we'll handle it together. Okay?"

"Okay. Thanks. I gotta go. We've got a meet in twenty minutes. See ya."

That just sucked. She hated that Lincoln had been forced into harm's way by someone else's stupidity.

There was another message, this one from Baldwin. Just checking in, he said. He sounded stressed. Well, she could identify with that. She called him back, but he didn't answer. She put her phone away and got to work. She had a suspect to catch.

The sun was setting on Quantico, Virginia.

Dr. John Baldwin stood. He'd been sitting in a chair

that was too low to the ground for his long legs, and it screeched with the sudden movement.

"Damn it, I don't like lying to her."

"I know that, Baldwin. I wouldn't have asked if it wasn't absolutely necessary, you know that." Garrett Woods tried for affable, but Baldwin wasn't fooled. He'd known the man too long to trust such a conciliatory tone.

"You know karma is going to bite you in the ass for faking heart problems."

Garrett smiled, his dark eyes crinkling at the edges. "I could have gone into a diabetic coma instead. Would that have been more realistic? I am diabetic, after all."

"You should take better care of yourself regardless. But be warned, if we find out he's heading anywhere near Nashville, I am out of here. How in the world did you let him slip the net?"

"We're still figuring that out. And don't worry about your princess. She can take care of herself. Don't delude yourself there, my boy. She's managed quite well without you all this time. She's not some weak-kneed little kitten that needs your protection. You'll be back there soon enough. There's work to be done here first."

Baldwin took a lap around the small room, stopping at the window that overlooked the parade grounds in front of the gate into the complex. Garrett had asked to meet him in an outbuilding, outside the National Center for the Analysis of Violent Crime offices, which housed both the Behavioral Science Unit and the Behavioral Analysis Units. It was a smart thing to do; that building was filled with perceptive people. This conversation didn't need an audience.

After spending the past year in Nashville, he'd found himself dreading the thought of the BSU walls closing in around him. He'd always hated being stuck inside, much preferred working in the field. He loved the work, just didn't like having to share his workspace with forty other people.

Garrett's reach had been dragging him back to Quantico more and more often. After hearing this news, he was going to have to stick around for a while. Quantico was the last place he wanted to be right now.

"I could give her a generic warning. Anything funny happens, let me know. Something so she wouldn't be blindsided."

Garrett shook his head, a fine sheen of sweat shimmering along his closely clipped hairline. "No. Not yet. Let's get some confirmation first. This may not happen. We don't need to blow your cover over a maybe. Langley would not like that at all."

Eight

When Taylor was deep in a case, every workday lasted just a bit longer than the last.

She left the office a little after eleven o'clock, planning to forage in her kitchen for wine and cheese, maybe a hunk of bread. It was too late for a real dinner, and after five months living with Baldwin, she'd come to realize she didn't like to eat alone anymore. She dragged into the house at eleven-thirty, yawned and decided to hell with it. She'd just head upstairs and have a decent breakfast instead.

Baldwin had called, leaving a message on the machine for her, one designed to incite a lustful longing for his warmth. She'd smiled at the attempt to solicit dirty thoughts, but was too tired to think of much except getting into the bed and sleeping forever.

There was a bill on the counter from the plumber. God, she'd forgotten all about the leak. It seemed impossible that she'd started her day with such a banal issue. It felt like a week had passed.

Just a cracked cock and ball assembly, allowing the

water to the toilet to steadily overflow. He'd replaced it, and the charge was $150 for parts and labor, but with their new home warranty, their cost was only $42.50. That was a relief. She checked the ceiling in the living room, it had already dried without leaving a stain. Good. Replacing a ceiling wasn't high on her list of things she wanted to deal with. Though they'd had a million little issues with the house, so far they were just that, little. She rapped her knuckles on the cabinet— knock wood they'd stay annoyances rather than something major.

She called Baldwin back and they chatted for a few minutes. She told him about her day and he assured her that Garrett was just fine. After her fourth jaw-cracking yawn, Baldwin suggested she get some sleep. They hung up with promises to talk in the morning.

A dog barked once, sharp and deep, then howled. The sound gave her a chill, and she set the alarm before moving upstairs.

She washed her face, brushed her teeth, and was climbing in the bed when she heard the tape for the first time. Channel Five kindly replayed their ten o'clock newscast at midnight on their sister cable station. The anchor was intoning with horror, preparing the viewers with a warning that was sure to keep them riveted to their seats and the channel tuned in.

"We're going to play the 911 tapes from the Corinne Wolff murder scene. We must warn you, the tape is disturbing, and not appropriate for young viewers."

The screen went blank, then a blue background with a graphic of a white rotary telephone popped up, the headline reading 911 Call. The tape started rolling, static whispering at first, then clearer. The station provided a written transcript on the screen to accompany Michelle Harris's words.

"911 Operator: Nine-one-one, what is your emergency?

Michelle Harris: I think my sister is dead. Oh, my God. [crying]

911 Operator: Can you repeat that, ma'am?

Michelle Harris: There's blood, oh, my God, there's blood everywhere. And there are footprints…HAYDEN?

911 Operator: Ma'am? Ma'am? Who is dead?

Michelle Harris: HAYDEN, oh, dear sweet Jesus, you're covered in blood. Come here. How did you get out of your crib?

911 Operator: Ma'am? Ma'am, what is your location?

Michelle Harris: Yes, I'm here. It's 4589 Jocelyn Hollow Court. My sister…

911 Operator: Hayden is your sister?

Michelle Harris: Hayden is her daughter. Oh, God.

Background noise: Mama hurt

911 Operator: Who is dead, ma'am?

Michelle Harris: My sister, Corinne Wolff. Oh, Corinne. She's, she's cold. [crying, indistinguishable noise]

911 Operator: We're sending the police, ma'am."

Taylor turned off the television. That pretty much guaranteed she wasn't going to be able to sleep for a while. She got out of the bed and went to the bonus room, knowing that a few games of eight ball would help settle her mind.

She snapped on the lamp, took the cover off the table and retrieved a Miller Lite from the small dorm refrigerator that stood unobtrusively in the alcove. She twisted off the top, sent the metal cap arcing toward the trashcan with a nice overhead, then cursed. She'd forgotten to bring home the brackets for the basketball pool. Oh well, she could manage that tomorrow.

She racked up the balls and started shooting, the rhythm of her game helping a quiet calm steal into her limbs. Bend, sight, the clicking smack of the cue hitting the ball, drop. Over and over again, until the table was clear. She racked the balls back up, did it again. The beer was empty now, so she got another, pausing to sip at intervals, focused on the task at hand. Trying to empty her mind.

Taylor got tired of being a stranger to deep, uninterrupted sleep, but at least it helped hone her skills on the felt. She could probably make some cash as a pool shark if she ever needed a career change.

Three-thirty now, and she finally started to feel the slight tug at her eyelids that presaged some REM time. She covered up the table, tossed the beer bottles in the trash, shut off the light and went back to her bedroom.

The sense that something wasn't right struck her, and she went to the windows, lifted the edge of the blind and looked out onto the darkened street. The home-owners association had bylaws forbidding street lamps, which was one of the dumbest things Taylor had ever heard of. As a consequence, some of the homes on the street burned the front lights all night, the yellow pools of safety a warning to any who thought to enter, knowing that light was their best deterrent to crime. Not all the home owners felt the same.

With only three houses' porch lights on tonight, and those farther up the street, the darkness was deep and penetrating. Taylor took in the shadowy brick structures, the trees waving long-boned fingers in the air. In a day or two, they'd be in full bud. Spring generally appeared overnight in Nashville. Taylor wondered if she stood and watched, would she see the coming of the equinox? Instead, there was nothing to observe, no one on the street lurking, staring up at the windows.

"Silly goose," she said, her voice's typical no nonsense tone a comfort.

She got into the bed and stared at the grotesque shadows cast about the room by the night-light's reflection on the ceiling fan. Thought about Corinne Wolff, beaten, alone, unable to fend off her attacker. Rolling onto her side, she caressed the pillow facing her, where Baldwin's chiseled features usually gave her a respite. The emptiness was palpable. Stretching her right arm out, she slid it under the pillow. Her fingers closed around the grip of her Glock. A shiver went through her, and she was finally dragged under.

The lights were doused at last. He wondered how she slept. On her side, or her back? On her stomach, vulnerable and unable to defend herself if surprised? Oh, if that were only the case. But no. He'd watched her walk, the long stride never hesitating, never compromising, and knew she slept on her side, a leg thrown over the man next to her. Confidence. She had that in spades. Oh, what he wouldn't give to teach her humility. Bliss.

A nosy dog scented him and began baying. He moved deeper into the woods, away from the house, away from civilization. The time would come. He must simply bc patient.

Tuesday

Nine

Despite the alarm going off in her ear for a full twenty minutes, Taylor couldn't rouse herself. She finally reached a hand over and stifled the music, glancing with one eye at the clock face. Nearly seven-thirty. Damn it. She needed to be at Forensic Medical by eight to witness Corinne Wolff's autopsy.

She threw back the tangle of covers and went into the bath, started the shower running and brushed her teeth. Fifteen minutes later she rolled out of the garage barefoot, Diet Coke clutched in her lap, jeans and T-shirt on, wet hair smoothed into a coiled bun. She had an awkward crick in her neck from sleeping at an odd angle that the shower hadn't relieved. She could put her boots on when she got to Gass Street, slip into a sweater, too. It was chilly as hell this morning.

She'd made this trek too many times to count in her years as a detective. She felt a strange kind of kinship with her victims—the need to see what was inside, what made them tick. And Corinne Wolff was no ex-

ception. Taylor was interested to see the particulars of
how she'd died, at the very least.

Interstate 40 was packed with early morning com-
muters, and an accident at the Charlotte Pike exit meant
they were crawling slower than normal. The west side
of town was blessed with less congestion, less traffic,
and an easier commute than those people driving into
Nashville from the east, south and north of town. But
an accident could derail that immediately, bringing all
the cars to a snail's pace. Taylor sipped her Diet Coke,
trying for patience. It didn't look like traffic was going
to get moving anytime soon, and she wasn't in the
mood to sit. Damn it, she was going to be late. Another
ten minutes passed before the cars inched forward
enough for her to hop off at Charlotte westbound.
Feeling free, she made an illegal U-turn in front of the
Cracker Barrel, sailed up to White Bridge and got on
Briley Parkway.

The new section of road quickly gave way to the old
four-lane highway, and she started making up time as
she cruised past the defunct Tennessee State Prison, the
site of Robert Redford's film *The Last Castle* and an
architectural dead ringer for Johnny Cash's infamous
Folsom State Prison. It had fallen into disrepair and
was abandoned, left to the ghosts and rats. She tried not
to think of her father, once a brief inmate of those
twenty-foot-high, three-foot-thick crenellated walls.

Now the prisoners were housed at Riverbend, a
maximum-security prison equipped to end the lives of
those fated to die at the hands of the state. She'd been
inside Riverbend's death row cells, with their blue
doors and creamy concrete walls. She never wanted to
return. The overwhelming sense of malevolence

coupled with dread was too much to take. She'd sent more than one of the men housed in that unit to death row and hadn't lost a moment's sleep over them, but she didn't want to experience their last moments first-hand.

Her dad, well, his prison environs were a damn sight cushier than a state penitentiary. The feds were kind to their white-collar criminals.

The Interstate 24 split came, and she passed the exit, driving a few more miles to the Dickerson Road access ramp. Off the highway now, into the run-down streets. This was a sad part of town. A crack whore strolled by, arms swinging wildly as she walked, a timid black man in his forties following some fifty feet behind. Had they made the deal already? They must have, the hooker had the bright, insistent glow in her eyes of a junkie who knows she's about to get a fix.

Taylor shook her head. There seemed to be no legal measures that could stop the pervasive sex trades on the back streets of Nashville. For the pros, a night in jail meant either safety or withdrawal, neither an induce-ment to break free from the life. For the johns, it was just an embarrassment.

She turned on Gass and passed the Tennessee Bureau of Investigations offices on the right. The TBI task force would be furious if they knew Lincoln had broken the rules. Even though he had done something that was life-preserving, they would still punish him. He'd be kicked off the task force at the very least. She wondered if she could keep the situation quiet, then forced the thought from her mind. She was a master at keeping each aspect separate, tackling one thorny issue at a time. It was the only way she could get through the day.

Forensic Medical appeared on her left, shiny as a new penny in the morning sun. Taylor parked in a visitor slot. She jammed her feet into her boots, tucked her sunglasses into their hard leather case, grabbed the sweater and stepped into the bracing morning air. Dogwood winter, that's what her mother had called these chilly spring days. As soon as the trees began to bud, Nashville was nearly guaranteed a late frost, shriveling up the fresh, tender blossoms. Only the most hale of trees and shrubs would stand it; the rest would be shocked back into dormancy for at least another few weeks.

The front of Forensic Medical was lined in clusters of forsythia bushes intertwined with azaleas. The forsythia didn't seem to mind the snap, were rioting in their fervor to spread their rich yellow blooms toward the cool sunlight. The sight made her smile. The mutinous nature of the bushes always lightened her heart. She hated when people trimmed them into balls or squares, felt it killed their wild personality. It was a shame they'd be gone so soon, too. She wished they'd bloom all summer.

Taylor swiped her card and entered the cool offices of Forensic Medical. Someone, probably Kris, the receptionist, was burning a lavender scented candle. Slightly less oppressive than the patchouli incense that sometimes smoked up the foyer, but lavender always made Taylor sneeze. The cacophony of scents that made up Forensic Medical wreaked havoc with her sinuses anyway. Beneath the thick flowering smell was an antiseptic undernote, *profumo della morte.* The scent of death was pervasive and ugly, no matter what Renaissance language she translated it into.

She crossed the lobby, boot heels clomping on the hard floor. The door to the hallway was locked. Taylor swiped the key card again, was rewarded with a resounding click. Making her way toward the autopsy suite, knowing what lay ahead, she resigned herself to the case at hand. All thoughts of spring and happiness left her.

In the locker room, she traded her boots for soft rubber clogs and gowned up. She glanced at her watch. Ten past eight. Not so bad, considering. She pushed open the door of the autopsy suite with an elbow. The aroma of formaldehyde wafted to her nose, mingled with old blood and feces.

"It's about time. I was about to start without you." Sam was ready to go, wired for sound with her headset, standing over the body of Corinne Wolff. She had a scalpel in her right hand, was tapping it impatiently against the table in a staccato rhythm. Skylights set high in the ceilings showered sunlight down on the medical examiner, creating copper highlights in her dark hair.

"Sorry. I had a late night."

"That's okay. I'm just ready to get this one over with."

Taylor glanced around the room. Usually well-staffed and attended, the four additional autopsy tables were empty this morning, a silent tribute to the difficult case that lay ahead. Corinne Wolff lay on the plastic table liner, already prepped and x-rayed, ready for the postmortem. She looked smaller than at the crime scene, more delicate. Fine-boned. Taylor could tell the girl had been beautiful before the beating. The telltale bump on her stomach made the gorge rise in the back of Taylor's throat. Autopsies with fetuses past the twenty-week gestation period always threw her. Oh, who was she kidding? She didn't ever like to see dead women who were pregnant.

"Stuart Charisse will be attending me this morning." Sam had turned on her headset and was beginning her assessment. On cue, a lanky young man with wildly curly hair appeared at her side. He smiled politely at Taylor, started his duties with professional dispassion.

Sam spoke into the headset as she began the external examination.

"Autopsy number T-08-8768, case number T-2008-5389. The decedent is Corinne Elizabeth Wolff, a female Caucasian twenty-six years old, in good physical condition, presenting with multiple injuries. The body is intact, sixty-five inches with a weight of one hundred thirty-four pounds. Body heat is cold, rigor is not detectable, livor is dark, limited to anterior legs, stomach and chest. Hair is dark brown, shoulder-length, eyes are brown, teeth are natural. There is no facial hair. The decedent is clothed in a sports bra and panties. Paper bags are present on the hands. The head, neck and bra are bloody.

"The jawbone is crushed and shows evidence of severe trauma. Accompanying the body there is a small envelope labeled 'teeth found near victim's body.' It contains two bloody molars that belong to the victim as is evidenced by systematic placements in the corresponding sockets. There are fragments that appear to match the additional empty sockets. The teeth are photographed."

Stuart took pictures of the teeth and labeled the jar that held them. The teeth would be released with Corinne's body for burial.

"The bags are removed from the decedent's hands. Examination of hands shows a large plastic Band-Aid partially attached to the anterior of the right wrist. The fingernails are clipped and preserved as evidence."

Stuart and Sam worked well together. Once the nails were clipped and bagged, they began the laborious progression of stripping the body and washing it. Twenty minutes later, Sam was ready to proceed. Corinne now lay naked, even more vulnerable in appearance than before. Taylor felt sorry for the girl. Who did she piss off? Sam's voice dragged her back.

"The body is that of an adequately nourished Caucasian female who appears to be her recorded age."

Sam moved on to a detailed examination of the wound pattern across Corinne's skull and upper body. Blunt force injury number one. Blunt force injury number two. Blunt force injury number three. Avulsed teeth, abrasions, lacerations, bruises, mandible fractures. Because the wounds were so plentiful, Sam began grouping the smaller gashes together. At number eight, Taylor tuned out the recitation.

Rage. Pure, unadulterated rage. Whoever was responsible for murdering Corinne Wolff had been viciously upset with her. Todd Wolff's face rose unbidden, his eyes red and brimming with soon-to-be-shed tears. He had made awfully good time back from Savannah. The trip should have taken at least eight hours; he'd made it in six. Perhaps he was lying after all. But could he have been callous enough to leave his daughter hungry and dirty, crawling through her mother's blood? To murder his unborn son? He'd have to be a pretty cold bastard to do that.

Sam was efficient. While Taylor daydreamed about

suspects and motives, she'd moved on to the internal examination, had weighed and categorized all of the internal organs, removed the fetus, and had taken the saw to Corinne's skull. The high-pitched whine made a shiver flow through Taylor's spinal cord, akin to the feeling she got when someone scratched fingernails on a blackboard, or tinfoil made contact with a filling. And then it was over, and Sam was calmly saying, "The skull is open to reveal extensive subarachnoid hemorrhage of the brain, bilateral and most prominent at the base of the brain. The brain—" A pause here, a squelching noise, then she continued. "The brain is removed to reveal a linear skull fracture occupying most of the posterior aspect...."

Well, Corinne's skull had been cracked, no doubt about that. Taylor's cell phone rang, and she happily excused herself from the rest of the proceedings. She didn't particularly want to dwell on the fetus in situ anyway.

As she turned away, she heard Sam say, "Oh, hoy."

Clicking the button that would send the call directly to her voice mail, she came back to the table.

"What is it?"

"She was strangled."

"Are you telling me the skull fracture wasn't the cause of death?"

Sam caught Taylor's eye. "No, I'm pretty comfortable that the beating was the ultimate finisher. But there is some very subtle bruising around the neck. If I had to guess, I'd say that the killer tried strangling her first and it wasn't working quickly enough. It's harder to strangle someone to death with your bare hands than you might think. If Corinne struggled or fought back, which it certainly seems she did, it would be easy to lose your grip. She was in good shape, pregnancy aside. She put up a fight."

"So the killer loses control of the situation and resorts to beating?"

"Sure. Grabs the most convenient item and starts whaling away. The tennis racquet made a distinctive bruising pattern where the knots of the strings are tied on the outside of the racquet head. The edges could easily create those open gashes. Think about the killer standing over the body, thrusting downward, over and over." Sam was wrapping things up now, tidying as she went, snapping lids on containers, folding closed the flaps of envelopes, handing dissected slivers of organs to Stuart for analysis. "We'll send off the scrapings from under her nails and all the blood work, get you a tox screen as soon as possible. But it's evident what happened."

"There's nothing sexual about this?"

Sam shook her head. "No sign of bruising or tearing, no lubricants. I swabbed for semen just in case, though there was none visible in the vagina or anus, and certainly nothing to indicate sexual assault. This was just a murder, plain and simple."

Plain and simple.

"Were there prints on the tennis racquet, or the body?"

"The racquet was wiped. There were some smudges, but nothing usable. We'll look for some around her neck, but you know how hard it is to lift good prints from skin."

Taylor squeezed her best friend's arm. "Now I just have to figure out who, and we'll be all set."

She left Sam in the autopsy suite, ditched the protective gear in a biological waste receptacle and made her way back to the lobby. The lavender scent still lingered, now joined with the sweet overlay of a familiar, pungent perfume. Michelle Harris stood in the middle of the room, surrounded by her family. Todd Wolff was noticeably absent.

They were talking quietly among themselves, pain radiating from each person, palpable as an aura to a psychic. It didn't take any special powers to know they were hurting; the slumped shoulders, dark circles and red noses spoke volumes.

What were they doing here? Taylor counted five of them: the parents, Michelle and her sister Nicole, and the son, Derek. They were huddled together as if seeking warmth from each other's bodies. Taylor had seen this before. Some families were forced apart by a tragedy; others drew together, working as one to help heal. The Harrises definitely looked to be the latter.

Taylor fidgeted and stalled, pulling at her bun until her hair tumbled down in waves. Annoyed, she whipped it back up into a ponytail. Large families filled her with a sense of dislocation, of longing. She'd never known what it was like to have a support system of siblings. Sam was like a sister to her, but it was different. They didn't share blood, despite their aborted attempt to transfuse each other when they were ten years old. Silly, meaningful, yet neither had the courage to cut deep enough to really get the blood flowing into each other's hands. Being blood sisters wasn't the real thing.

She was about to clear her throat when Michelle

noticed her. The group stopped talking, just looked at her with unfathomably sad eyes.

"Lieutenant," Michelle said. There were a few murmured good mornings from the rest of the group.

Taylor nodded at them, then answered, "What can I do for you?"

It was the mother who spoke up. "We're just here for Corinne. Is it…" She stood a bit straighter. "Is it over?"

Taylor nodded. "Dr. Loughley is finishing up, but yes, the postmortem has been completed. I can't discuss any of the findings, you know that."

"We do. We just wanted to be here for her. It's hard." A deep sniff, but she didn't break. Taylor liked her a bit for it. "Hard to let your child go through something so invasive. If Corinne's spirit is anywhere near, she'll know we're here for her."

"Todd didn't want to come?"

Mr. Harris coughed out a noise of disgust. "Todd took Hayden to his parents' this morning. He didn't even bother to stay, just whisked her away. He doesn't care about Corinne. He's just concerned with himself."

"Daddy, that's not fair." Michelle came to her father's side, touching his arm. "Todd knows you and Mom are too upset to care for Hayden. He's trying to do you a favor."

"Bullshit!" Derek Harris spoke for the first time, his full, thick hair falling over his forehead. He turned to Taylor. "You need to look a little closer at my brother-in-law, Lieutenant. I know he's got something to do with this. I wasn't so sure yesterday when we talked, but he's acting strange. Something is up with him. I think he might be responsible for Corinne's death."

Interesting. The united front for Corinne certainly didn't extend to her husband. Taylor held up a hand. "I will be looking at every angle of this case backwards and forwards, I can guarantee you that. Now, if you'll excuse me, I need to make it downtown for a meeting."

"Lieutenant?" Nicole Harris, raven hair, soulful brown eyes, thin frame bordering on emaciation, put up her hand as if she were a student seeking a professor's attention.

"Yes?"

Nicole took a deep breath. "It's about the baby. What's...we want to know what's happening with...with his body."

"Oh," Taylor said. "Of course. That's going to be up to you. The folks here at Forensic Medical will issue a fetal death certificate, and you'll have the option to bury him separately, or with Corinne. His body will be released with hers."

The relief bled from them in waves. Michelle took her mother's hand and looked at Taylor. "We were afraid he might be...disposed of."

Taylor's stomach flipped at the thought. It was horrid enough to have seen the tiny body, imagining him being thrown away saddened her deeply.

"I understand. That happens sometimes, but usually with indigent women who are early along in their pregnancies and don't have family to claim a fetus. After twenty weeks, though, the baby is treated as a person by the medical examiner. I assure you, the baby was handled with a great deal of care."

"Did you see him?" Mr. Harris spoke quietly, almost as if he didn't want to hear her answer.

"I did." Taylor's voice cracked as she spoke. "I have

to go now. Please accept my deepest condolences on your loss. I'll be in touch soon."

She left them there. As she walked away, she didn't look back.

Ten

Taylor got into the 4Runner. Jesus. She rubbed her eyes hard. Buck up, she told herself. It could have been worse. You could have had to tell them their daughter was raped, or slit open, or stowed away in a barrel of acid. Unfortunately, as bad as Corinne Wolff's murder was, it could always have been something more. Little comfort to the Harrises, she knew, but it made her feel better.

Hoping for an escape from the thought of those accusing eyes, she plugged her phone into the charger, then turned on the speaker and dialed "one" for her voice mail.

Baldwin's deep voice spilled from the little phone, made tinny by the poor quality of the speaker.

"Just checking in, babe. Hope you're having a good day. Call me when you get a chance. Love you."

Taylor dialed him back. He answered on the first ring, sounding a bit distracted.

"I've had a fun morning. Everything good with you?" she asked.

"Absolutely. Everything is fine. Can't say I miss the place, I'll tell you that."

"Is Garrett okay?"

"Oh. Yes, yes, completely. He's going to be just fine."

"That's good. Send him my best, will you? And take care of yourself."

They chatted for a few more minutes, then she depressed the end button, her mind immediately back in the case. Time to go to work.

Baldwin hung up the phone and sighed deeply, running his hands through his dark hair at speed. It made the ends stand at attention, a look he knew Taylor found terribly amusing. My little porcupine, she called him. He rolled his eyes at the silliness of it and wished he were home.

God, he hated lying to her.

No, everything was not okay.

Baldwin had always excelled at compartmentalizing. He was able to stay calm in the face of the most intense scrutiny, could clinically analyze any situation without getting close, then could move on to the next case with precision and no regrets. The FBI knew that when they hired him. The CIA knew that when they called on him.

He'd been with the profiling unit for about four years when Garrett suggested a quick day trip to Washington, D.C. for an unusual case. "It's a favor for a friend, Baldwin. I just need you to look the scene over, go through some of the evidence, and tell me what you think."

He'd gone willingly enough. Garrett had always

been fair, a mentor. He both regretted his acquiescence and thanked God he'd been the one asked to come that day. He thought back to the beginning of this subterfuge, the June morning that altered the course of his life.

Traffic was difficult, as it always was. Garrett hadn't spoken much as they made the drive north. It took them an hour and forty-five minutes to reach the Beltway. Not the greatest time. But once they were on 495, the roads miraculously cleared and within five minutes they were on the George Washington Parkway, heading toward McLean, Virginia.

Just past the Chain Bridge Road exit, Garrett had pulled into a scenic overlook. The Potomac River churned at their feet, the woods beyond the overlook were thick and foreboding. The faintest of paths could be seen. Garrett walked that way, beckoning Baldwin to follow. There was something familiar about the area. It took Baldwin's mind a moment to register that they were very near Fort Marcy Park, the site of one of the most famous alleged suicides in Washington history— White House Deputy Counsel Vince Foster. Talk about a can of worms. Pushing the scandal out of his mind, he followed Garrett deeper into the woods.

About two hundred yards into the thicket, they came to a slight opening among the trees. Baldwin smelled the blood before his mind registered the scene.

The clearing looked like the set of a low-budget horror flick. A makeshift drying rack was strung between two trees: flayed skin, pieces of genitalia, a severed head with wild, staring milky eyes, all were precisely tacked to the wires. There were at least five women in various stages of decay, their bodies no longer attached by the normal seams. Flies buzzed heavily around the torso of one obviously fresh kill.

Baldwin felt the bile rise in his throat, a completely unnatural reaction for him. Something evil lurked in these woods. He could feel it oozing through his pores, and fought the urge to run back to the car.

"Holy mother of God. What is this, Garrett?"

Garrett's answer came out as a sigh. "That's what I need you to tell me."

Later that first day, his face white and pinched, Baldwin had sat in the upstairs room of Mr. Henry's, a noisy bar in the District. Garrett sat beside him, silent.

Garrett had insinuated answers would be forthcoming from this meeting, but so far, there was nothing. Baldwin drank draught Sierra Nevada Pale Ale, desperately trying to wash the taste of decomposition and fear from his tongue.

He looked out the window, watched people moving past, happy that they were unaware of the horror he'd experienced. How to keep them safe?

When he turned back a large, bald-headed man sat across from him, assessing. Shrewd eyes bluer than cold ocean water, a thick neck and fingers, he gave his name only as Atlantic, a moniker obviously befitting his appearance.

Atlantic said he would become Baldwin's handler on these gruesome, silent cases. Baldwin listened attentively, mesmerized by the icy eyes, trying to place the older man's nationality. He'd narrowed it to a Balkan state, could detect some touches of British influence in the drawn-out *A*'s, but couldn't get a precise fix. It annoyed him.

Atlantic talked in his odd accent for what seemed

hours, though Baldwin knew it could only have been a few minutes. When he finished, Baldwin asked, "Why me?"

"Because you are the best we've ever seen. Because you're a natural polyglot, can assimilate to any country. How many languages are you fluent in? Eight? Nine?"

"Thirteen."

Atlantic tipped his head in respect and tapped the edge of the table like a snooker master. "Because you have the compassion to give these victims closure but the brains to keep silent. And because we ask."

It had been enough of an answer at the time. Baldwin agreed to take on the position of profiler to the setup Atlantic called Operation Angelmaker.

His first assignment was to track the Forest Killer. Baldwin had blown the case wide open in a matter of days. The killer was a legal attaché to Zambia. Baldwin stopped him before he killed his sixth victim. The man had been summarily deported with a stern warning to his government to never let him set foot back in the United States. The killer's flashing grin as he boarded the jet home to Lusaka haunted Baldwin's dreams.

That was the first. There were more. Rarely on U.S. soil, the cases he worked were quiet, involved and deadly. Different killers, different MOs. Killing zones and sprees that needed to be kept as quiet as possible, that needed to be solved through back channels. These weren't the men who made it onto *Court TV*, or even made it to court. These killers were protected.

The governments of various countries kept silent assassins on the payrolls. Men and women paid to kill, trained to be sociopaths, sometimes broke from their proscribed paths, headed out on their own to satiate their burgeoning needs. Developed a bloodlust that their government targets couldn't sate. Tracking these assets was a vital function, one not left to everyday agents.

Operation Angelmaker had a real name, "The Joint Preparedness Task Force on the Convention of Potentially Dangerous Assets," but TJPTFOTCOPDA just didn't work as an acronym. So OA they became, a covert group so secret only the immediate members knew it existed. There was no congressional oversight, no Presidential discretion, just the head of the CIA and people on a purely need-to-know basis.

The arrangement Atlantic made with Garrett Woods was for Baldwin to be borrowed, from time to time, to oversee "projects." What Baldwin actually did was profile these international serial killers, men the United States government would normally seek to put in jail. These killers were valuable to their country's government, or valuable to the United States in some capacity. Men with unnatural proclivities, as Atlantic so aptly put it. Baldwin's job wasn't to keep them out of trouble, or keep them hidden, so much as predict where they might strike next. If the Angelmakers knew where a killer would hit, they could arrange for bait to be delivered, usually in the form of a contract hit that needed the assassin's immediate attention. It kept the innocents from too much risk, and allowed them to keep closer tabs.

If he were honest with himself, the cross-cultural analysis was fascinating. Nature versus nurture didn't exist in the Angelmakers. Evil superceded all.

The program went against every grain of his being, but he understood the necessity of wet work. Baldwin had always been a good soldier. He agreed to work with the group with one condition. The United States government wasn't much in the habit of using their assassins in their own backyard. If any of these men ever stepped foot on U.S. soil again, Baldwin would be notified. He knew what these maniacs were capable of. He insisted on the stipulation, and Atlantic agreed.

He'd been working with the group for ten long years. They had at least fifty men and women in their sights at all times.

Garrett's sudden heart problem was a fallacy. Baldwin had been pulled to Quantico so Atlantic could honor their agreement. He was being warned, and given the tools to suss out his enemy. A nemesis had disappeared from the OA's radar screens. The killer had cleared out his home, taken all his papers, all his false IDs, and disappeared. The chatter on the circuit was he'd contracted a job in the States, but so far, no one would own up to the hit.

The assassin was an American, at least by birth. He'd been brought up all over the world, the brilliant, prodigal son of a career diplomat. He'd started killing early, sanctioned by the government. His extracurricular activities were hidden well, he had worked hard to be quite discreet. But he wasn't quiet enough. Once he'd gotten the OA's attention, they knew he needed to be watched. And now, all the field reports agreed. The killer known simply as Aiden was making a transatlantic journey.

Baldwin had danced with Aiden many times. He could recognize his signature anywhere. Aiden liked to be thought of as an old-school assassin, an artist who used a silver garrote to strangle his victims. He had at least forty kills to his name that they knew of; the actual number could have been much higher. He played the game, knew about the OA team, knew he was fed targets. He was an indiscriminate sort—he didn't need a type, just needed a neck. That made him especially dangerous.

If the reports were right, if Aiden was truly in the States, Baldwin needed to keep a very close eye on him. If he could find him.

Eleven

Taylor and Fitz sat at a patio table in the back of Las Palmas. The front room was filled with giggling Vanderbilt co-eds and migrant workers on their lunch break, a testament to the quality of the restaurant as well as its reasonable prices. Taylor was nibbling a steak fajita quesadilla, Fitz was plowing through a taco salad. A pitcher of sweet tea separated them.

"So what did Price say?" Fitz asked.

"He understood, for starters. He'll fight any disciplinary action taken against Lincoln. So Linc will feel a lot better about that. Poor guy, he was completely rattled. I don't know if it was the dope or the sheer terror of having to report that he'd been smoking it. Can you imagine Lincoln with a few toots in him?"

Fitz laughed. "No. Mr. Fancypants has always struck me as the one scotch before dinner because it looks good, rather than enjoying it type. He isn't much for losing control."

"Well, that's to be expected, if you think about his background. Damn, it would be nice to have him back to work this Wolff case. I'll bet there's a ton of financial discovery, right up his little computer-literate heart's alley. Marcus is back tomorrow, right?"

Marcus Wade, her youngest detective, had been out for four days doing his in-service training rotation. Without the two detectives, the squad had been too quiet.

"He'll be in bright and early tomorrow. We can get him up to speed with the Wolff case, let him go to town. Media's having a field day with the 911 tape."

"Yeah, I'll bet. I heard it last night. It's gut-wrenching."

"Wish they wouldn't do stuff like that. Makes our life harder."

"No kidding." She took a bite of quesadilla, wiped her mouth off with a napkin. "When we finish here, I want to take a run out to the Wolff house. The second interview with Todd Wolff is scheduled for two o'clock. Corinne's whole family came to Forensic Medical this morning, did I tell you that?"

"No."

"Yeah, well, they were all in the lobby when I left the autopsy. It was miserable. They told me Todd took Hayden to his parents' house. Do you know where they live?"

"Not offhand. Did they say it was far?"

"Didn't say. I haven't gotten a call telling me he isn't going to make round two, so I assume it's close by. Think he'll show up with a lawyer?"

Fitz rolled his eyes. "If he knows what's good for him, but with any luck, no."

"We can tag team him, see if he's come up with anything else. The autopsy was pretty straightforward.

Someone beat the living hell out of Corinne. There were signs of strangulation too. I want to look closer into Mr. Wolff's days away." She set her fork down on the edge of the plate, suddenly not hungry.

"So, tell me. Do you know what case Lincoln is on?"

Fitz dunked a tortilla chip in the spicy salsa and crunched before answering. "No, but I can guess. While you and the fed were off gallivantin', he had several calls with that confidential informant he'd been wrangling, the kid working as a deejay?"

Taylor nodded that she remembered, and Fitz continued. "Well, the CI started talking big that he would be willing to distribute drugs through the club. He needed a dealer. Lincoln was the behind-the-scenes guy for a week, and then he dropped off the radar. I think Vice decided to keep him on it. Linc's a smart kid. He can land on his feet. But couple all that information, and I'd assume it's something to do with our good friend Terrence Norton."

Taylor groaned. Terrence Norton had been a fly in the department's ointment for years. A hoodlum, a generic neighborhood thug, he'd risen through the ranks of the underbelly of Nashville with meteoric speed. Drugs, shootings, assaults—the kid had a rap sheet fourteen pages long but skin like Teflon. None of the charges would stick. With each hung jury, each dismissed case, Terrence grew stronger. He was the main conduit of heroin and cocaine into Nashville, running the drugs up I-24 from Atlanta. But Terrence reported to someone, wasn't high enough to be running the operation himself.

Taylor desperately wanted to see him nailed and

out of her hair. She'd thought the chance was there—
two months earlier, the Tennessee Bureau of Investigation had taken over a case of possible jury tampering.
The final report had been on top of Taylor's files when
she returned from Italy, finding no apparent wrongdoing. The TBI had happily dumped Terrence squarely
back in the locals' lap, but kept the task force open, just
in case something broke.

Terrence had been relatively quiet in the time since
she'd been back, hadn't killed anyone that they knew
of.

A thought hit her. "It can't be Terrence. He'd recognize Lincoln, wouldn't he?"

"Well, he kept that cue-ball look after you left, and
grew a beard." Fitz laughed. "Scruffy, moth-eaten curly
shit, too. He looks like a hood, not at all like his usual
dapper self. And Terrence only dealt directly with you
and me. So he'll fit in okay. Besides, until his little
foray onto the wild side, he was only working with the
CI. Terrence wouldn't have ever seen him."

"I worry about him. I'd never forgive myself if we
lost him. He gave me the sense things would be
breaking soon, so hopefully we'll have him back."

"Amen to that, sister."

Taylor pushed away her plate, let the companionable
silence build. She hated to drag everyone into her
paranoia, but she knew she needed her back watched.

"Someone's watching me."

Fitz met her eyes, didn't blink, or shake his head, or
pat her on the arm. She appreciated that. He knew her
well enough to know if she felt she was being watched,
she was.

"Think it's Snow White's apprentice? Sorry, the

Pretender?" He made little quote marks with his fingers. "Why would he call himself a pretender, anyway? Seems derogatory to me."

"I think he's shooting for something like a pretender to the throne. Someone who should rightfully rule, but circumstance has taken their monarchy. A self-anointed king of serial killers. No one said he wasn't cocky." She took a drink of her tea and shifted in her chair, glancing around as she settled back in.

"No, I don't think it's him. I don't know why, but this feels different. Wrong, somehow. The hair on the back of my neck stands on end and I can feel it, you know? Like electricity. It's so strange. Ah, hell. I'm just getting spooky. I'm sure it's nothing."

"Now who's kidding who?"

She smiled. "I know. It will be fine. I'm aware of it, so that's nine-tenths of the solution right there. So. You want to go to the Wolffs' house with me? Do a run-through before the interview?"

"Why not. I don't have anything better to do. Let's go."

The Hillwood neighborhood that the Wolffs lived in was quiet on this Tuesday. Much less frantic than the day before. The crime scene tape was still strung across the Wolffs' driveway, a patrol officer was sitting quietly in his cruiser in front of the mailbox to discourage any thrill-seekers from coming by and messing with the scene.

Until the scene was officially released, they needed someone to keep guard. Taylor hoped that would happen today, there was no sense in wasting resources that could be used elsewhere.

Taylor pulled in behind the cruiser. The officer left his vehicle as she and Fitz climbed out of the Impala. Official business, they needed to have department vehicles on the scene. Taylor had never been fond of the Impalas, but what could you do? Couldn't exactly ask the new chief to assign Porsches to the troops. The Chevy had some get-up-and-go at least, could haul ass if needed, unlike the Mercury she'd been forced to drive as a junior grade detective. She always felt so conspicuous in the white sedans, figured it was from too many years driving an SUV in a town where bigger was always considered better and a GMC Suburban was *de rigeur* for any class.

Fitz had started talking regional barbeque contests with the patrol, so Taylor took the opportunity to examine the Wolffs' house. On the face, it was no different than yesterday—a handsome two-story tan brick colonial with a narrow white picket front porch, blue shutters, four curtained windows symmetrically set on either side of the front door, up and down. A chimney rose from the left side, the great room's fireplace.

Taylor had noticed that both the Wolffs and Mrs. Manchini had converted to gas fireplaces. It was difficult to find newer homes in Nashville with the traditional wood-burning style, and Taylor had warned Baldwin that no way, no how was she going to go with gas. Pretty, convenient, easy, yes, they were all of those, but Taylor liked the real deal—the smell of smoky maple or popping oak hardwood, the action of piling in the kindling, stuffing the paper, stacking the wood. She'd much rather spend some time and effort to have a fire than stare at glowing coals and fake flames.

A closer look at the house revealed the slightest difference in the color of the brick between the top and bottom of the house. It would only show in the most perfect of light. Well, that made sense. This section of town, with its stunning one- and two-acre lots and trees, had undergone its own renaissance. The allure of having a little land was popular in Davidson County. Most of the original homes in the development were like Mrs. Manchini's one-story rambler, tiny in comparison with new houses recently built.

An army of architects had moved through Hillwood in the recent years, helping new and old residents add on. Some people took the carport or garage, made it into a living room, built a new portico, cut in some skylights and were thrilled with a simple renovation. Others, with more grandiose plans in mind, put entire second stories on their homes. That's what had happened with the Wolff house. Now that she knew what to look for, she could see the lines well. It was a beautiful job, but Taylor could see the bones of the rambler beneath its stately new persona.

Those extensive renovations would have been as expensive as buying a brand-new home, but the schools, the land, and the country club nearby were excellent enticements for a young family like the Wolffs. She had wondered why they didn't live in one of his developments, but decided that perhaps it was the same reason she and Baldwin had opted out. No trees and no privacy. The houses Wolff's company built were stunning, but the lots were close together and the land had been cleared entirely, which meant every tree was newly planted by a landscape designer. Regardless of size, they didn't have the stately beauty of the real deal. This neighborhood, on the other hand, had a homey, genuine feel. And much more privacy.

She signaled to Fitz, who broke away from the patrol officer and met her in the driveway.

"You ready to go in?" she asked.

"Yeah. Sorry. Junior over there was all excited about the Memphis Bake, but he had it confused with the Huntsville Social Club. Got him straightened out."

"Very generous of you. I assume you feel he wouldn't be any competition?"

"That kid? Ha! He wouldn't know pepper from paprika. Doesn't have a chance against old Pops here." He tapped his chest. "Pops has got it going on, I'll tell you for true. I've found the most subtle nutmeg, comes from this little back alley store in Bombay, doesn't taste like anything out there. They won't know what hit them."

Fitz was a world-class amateur barbeque enthusiast, winning all the regional competitions with his amazing rubs and slow-cooked Boston butts. He traveled to various contests most weekends, racking up the awards and bringing lunch for them all every Monday.

"You put nutmeg in your barbeque? Isn't that illegal?"

Now it was Fitz's turn to laugh. "Only in Texas, darlin'. Only in Texas."

He took off for the house, Taylor following him closely. The seal was intact on the front door. Fitz slit it open with a pocketknife and they went in.

The scent of death was still strong, lingering in the bloody carpet, the walls. Taylor wondered if Todd would try to sell the place or go on living there. Though he hadn't had the same shock as Michelle Harris, seeing Corinne in a pool of blood in their bedroom, there was no question a life had ended under this roof. Violence stayed, steeping in the walls, regardless of the abilities of the professional cleaners. They could clean the surface, but the malevolence could never be fully exorcised.

They moved in a pattern similar to the prior morning, through the dining room into the kitchen, then into the tastefully decorated great room. *Architectural Digest* magazines were stacked with precision on the coffee table, three crystal clocks each told the same time, and a honeysuckle scented candle with one half inch of pristine white wick showing sat in a rose marble holder. The mantle over the fireplace held three espresso colored vases in various heights, each filled with a slightly different shade of cream silk orchid. The walls were done in faux Venetian plaster in an ecru tint. The furniture was soft chocolate leather. A forty-inch flat screen television was mounted on the wall across from the sofa. The Wolffs certainly appeared to be living the good life.

And considering the fact that the Wolffs had an eighteen-month-old child, the only real evidence was the understated nursery, the baby gate and the baby-proofed cabinets. It was astounding, really. Taylor had seen homes like this before, knew people who just didn't become gaga over their children, buying every plaything on the market, turning their formal living areas into romper rooms. Hell, she'd grown up in a home like that, and she'd turned out just fine. It was her parents who were royally fucked up. Not that she was lumping the Wolffs in with her parents, of course.

"What's this?" Fitz asked. He was standing next to a short cognac-colored smooth leather chair, which sat beneath a hanging tapestry at least seven feet in length depicting a leaping unicorn being speared by a group of men. He fingered the cloth.

Taylor joined him. "It's a reproduction of one of the Unicorn Tapestries. *The Unicorn Leaps the Stream,* I think."

"Are you sure it's not the real deal? It's pretty heavy."

"No, it's just a nice reproduction. If I remember, the originals are in The Cloisters, part of the Metropolitan Museum of Art in New York. They're French, fifteenth century or so, made for Louis XII, I think. They probably bought this at the Met's Museum bookstore, or out of the catalogue. Why, what's the matter?"

Instead of speaking, Fitz's mouth quirked up in a tiny half smile and his blue eyes twinkled in amusement, then he turned back to his task. He sometimes gave her that face, half-proud, half-bemused, looking right through her in that odd way that made her pull at her ponytail with self-conscious embarrassment. It wasn't her fault that her parents had dragged her to every museum known to mankind and she remembered this shit.

"I feel a draft coming from the wall." He started running his hands along the tapestry. Taylor was struck by a thought.

"Pull the tapestry aside, I think there's something here. Manchini's house, next door? She had a door on this part of the living room wall, must be a basement."

Fitz wrestled the heavy cloth away from the wall. "Bingo." The draft was coming from the hole where the doorknob should have been. That made sense; in order for the tapestry to lie flat against the wall the Wolffs had to remove the knob. Instead of struggling to get behind the heavy tapestry, Taylor and Fitz lifted it gently from the wall and laid it on the leather chair. The door opened inward, revealing a set of stairs that led to darkness. Sure enough, a basement.

"Did anyone pick up on this yesterday?" Taylor asked.

"Not that I know of." He went down the first three steps, then charged back up, swiping at his face.

"Argh!"

"What?"

"Spiderweb."

Taylor laughed so hard she had to lean back against the wall to keep herself from tumbling down the stairs. The spiderweb in question was swinging merrily to and fro as Fitz sputtered and scratched at his head. She nearly bit her lip in two trying to stop the giggles.

"It's not a spiderweb, you old fool, it's the pull for the light." She reached around him and tugged on the string. The naked hundred-watt bulb came on with a snap, blinding both of them for a moment.

Blinking as her eyes adjusted, Taylor stared down the stairs, the light illuminating only the immediate stairwell. Fitz was grumbling behind her. She unlatched the snap on her holster, slipped her Glock out of the creaking leather. Holding it at her side, she started down. There was a landing, and she stopped, cautious, sticking the gun and her head around the corner at the same time, just in case. She saw nothing to alarm her, and returned the weapon to its holster as she went down the remaining steps. There was a light switch at the base of the stairs. Taylor flipped on the overhead fluorescent.

It was a standard basement: cement floor, unfinished walls on three sides, one painted, as if the owners had contemplated finishing the room and wanted to see what it would look like. The barest whiff of stale air indicated a minor mold problem; the floor was cluttered with stacks of cardboard boxes, bicycles, sleds. All the material that wouldn't fit nicely in the garage was placed haphazardly down here. It was just a storage space, probably only four hundred square feet: twenty feet deep and twenty long. Certainly nothing exciting.

She returned the weapon to its holster. They did a pass through, looking behind boxes, but Taylor didn't see anything out of place.

"Let's get Tim back out here to go through all of this, okay? Just in case."

"Will do." He froze, then spoke, dramatically sotto voce. "You hear that?"

She stopped moving and listened. Yes, she did hear something. Footsteps. There was someone in the house with them.

There was no hesitation. Her weapon was drawn and pointing up the stairs before she took another breath. Fitz had his gun palmed too. Using hand signals, Taylor indicated that she was going to go up the stairs and he was to follow.

The steps creaked as Taylor tread on them, and the footsteps above stopped abruptly at the noise.

"Shit," she whispered. The element of surprise was gone. She got to the top of the stairs in a heartbeat. Leading with her gun, her eyes swept the living room. No immediate threats. Fitz was bumping up against her back. She nodded at him, then took three quick steps out into the room and turned left, into the foyer. Fitz went right, into the kitchen. Nothing, nothing, nothing. They met again in the dining room, and Taylor pointed at the ceiling with her Glock. They listened carefully. There they were again, the footsteps. Whoever had invaded the house was upstairs.

Standing at the base of the staircase, Taylor was just taking the first step when a shadow crossed the hallway. Holding her breath, she aimed her weapon at the banister. Step one, step two, step three, no one in her sights yet, step four, step five, there, the shadow was getting closer, closer, step six…

"Police, don't move! Hold it right there," she shouted.

The shadow jumped and screamed. Taylor's finger tightened on the trigger, and she took one more step.

"Lieutenant, don't shoot!" the silhouette yelled, and Taylor, recognizing the voice, eased the pressure off the trigger, just a fraction. A young woman appeared at the top of the stairs, hands up.

Taylor lowered her weapon. "Christ almighty, Page, what the hell are you doing, trying to get yourself killed? I almost shot you!"

Fitz was laughing, the eerie tension forcing emotion to the surface. He and Taylor slumped together on the stairs, guns at their sides. Julia Page, the assistant district attorney, stood at the balcony, her arms now crossed on her chest, chin-length curly chestnut hair sticking out in every direction as if it had been frightened and was trying to get away.

"What the hell are you doing creeping around here with your guns drawn?" Page demanded.

"What the hell are you doing here without calling me first?" Taylor snapped back.

"I did call you. Left you a message and everything. Said I was coming over to meet you. God, Taylor."

Page came down the stairs, ashen. Taylor whirled and went into the kitchen. Her hands were quivering, and she jammed them into the front pockets of her jeans in an effort to hide the fact. Page and Fitz both followed a moment later, but Taylor could tell Fitz had said something to Page. She was bristling, her hair looked like she'd stuck a finger in a socket. Page's hair was a dead giveaway to her every emotion. The sight made Taylor want to laugh, and the effort it took to hold the bubbling mirth down helped her regain her composure.

"That was a close one, Page. You should have called out when you came in."

This time Page looked at the ground, chagrined. "I know. Sorry. I didn't see either of you and just assumed you'd gone around back or something. I thought I'd get a look, form an impression without bothering you. Sorry," she repeated.

"It's okay. But now you know why we ask for nonessential personnel to get clearance before they enter a scene. Didn't the patrol outside tell you to announce yourself?"

The pointed chin raised an inch. "I'm not exactly nonessential, Taylor."

"Yeah, but you almost got forcibly made redundant, so next time…." Her hands had stopped shaking, the adrenaline coursing through her system ushered back to its home.

Page nodded. "Okay, okay. I just wanted to see the place. I didn't talk to the officer outside, I waved at him and he waved back. How is the investigation coming?"

"We don't have much to go on yet. We're supposed to be meeting with the husband at two."

"Well, it's one forty-five now, you'd best get going if you want to make it."

Taylor looked at her watch and cursed. "Yeah, we'd better go. We can talk after, okay? Meet me in my office at three or so. Will that work?"

Page nodded. "I'll see you then."

The three exited the house. Fitz slapped a new label on the door. He peeled off from the two women and made his way to the patrol, and Taylor knew the young man was going to get a tongue blistering. He should never have let the A.D.A. in the premises without alerting the two officers inside. It was sloppy work. While the situation never got entirely out of hand, it had been close. That was a story that would have made the national news—A.D.A. shot by lead investigator of case. Taylor shook her head at the mere thought. Besides, she liked A.D.A. Page. Would have hated like hell to kill her.

Todd Wolff was waiting for Fitz and Taylor in the lobby of the CJC, alone. This cheered Taylor to no end. No lawyer meant they'd be freer with their questions. She had to give Wolff credit, it was a good trick. Show up without a lawyer, make yourself look innocent. After some essential paperwork, they'd gotten him signed in and made comfortable in a blue interrogation room simply furnished with a table and four chairs, two on either side of the table. Sodas all around, video and audio rolling, Fitz led him through the particulars.

"You know you have the right to legal representation, don't you Mr. Wolff?" Fitz scratched at his ear with a pen, doing his damnedest to look disarming.

"I didn't think I was under arrest," Wolff said.

"You're not. We're just talking. But I'd be remiss if I didn't say it. You know how that works. So, if we're all good, tell me your full name, please."

"Theodore Amadeus Wolff. Todd for short."

"Your date of birth?"

"August 4, 1979."

"Place of birth?"

"Clarksville, Tennessee."

"Social?"

"413-00-8897."

"Address?"

"4589 Jocelyn Hollow Court, Nashville, 37205."

Taylor nodded at Fitz, and he leaned back in his chair, gesturing for her to go ahead.

"Okay, Todd. Thanks for that. Let's get started, shall we? You have everything you need?"

"I do. Let's get this over with. I want to get back to my daughter."

Taylor tapped her pen on the table. "We heard you took Hayden to your parents. Where do they live, Todd?"

"Clarksville."

"Any particular reason you didn't leave her with your in-laws? They're a bit closer. Wouldn't it be more convenient for you?"

"Do I have to answer that?"

Taylor didn't say anything, just raised an eyebrow. After a moment, Todd reached some kind of decision. "Okay. I'm not a fan of saying anything ugly about my in-laws, but I just felt my parents might be better equipped to deal with Hayden right now. The Harrises are great, and we get along fine, but Corinne was…special to them. The favorite. Hayden is the light of their lives. They're mourning, and I didn't want a constant reminder of what they'd lost running around their house. You know?"

He looked so forlorn that Taylor believed him. She eased back in the chair, adopting a more casual stance. "That was a kind thought. Tell me about your wife, Todd."

Wolff nodded, gathering himself. When he finally spoke, it was with a quiet strength, as if some font of internal fortitude had opened a wellspring in his heart.

"Corinne was, well, a force of nature. We met in college, and I fell hard immediately. We went to Vanderbilt, you know? She was a cheerleader, I was warming the bench with the basketball team. She was perfect, all bubbly and sweet, this crazy smile that just shot through me. Everybody loved her. She was the president of her sorority, captain of the tennis team, a straight-A student. We were together for a week when I told her I was going to marry her. She said yes."

He smiled to himself, eyes gone fuzzy at the memory. "We were sitting on the deck at San Antonio Taco Company, drinking too much beer and eating tacos, and I just leaned over and said 'I'm going to marry you, you know.' She smiled and said, 'Well, when you ask, I'll say yes.' It was perfect. She's, she was amazing. I can't believe I'm never going to see her smile again."

Taylor gave him a moment to gather himself, watched him wrestle with the memories. He was a handsome man, jet black, wavy hair, eyes so brown they looked black, a wide, firm mouth. Ropy muscles in his forearms implied strength. Taylor could imagine any one of a thousand sorority girls who would say yes to marriage material like that.

"So tell me how you got home from Savannah so quickly yesterday."

His head snapped back as if she'd struck him.

"I...I told you. I broke every speeding law on the road."

"And managed to cut two hours off an eight-hour drive."

"That's right."

"I don't believe you."

The silence hung heavy in its accusation. Todd didn't speak, just set his lips and shook his head. Taylor came at him again.

"Do you have a life insurance policy on Corinne?"

Todd sniffed a few times. She could see the internal debate, the realization that he'd been careless, should have known better than to come without an attorney.

"Todd, I asked you a question. Did you have a life insurance policy on your wife?"

"Yes. Of course I did. We've got a child. We've got policies on both of us in case something happens."

"For how much?"

He mumbled a number.

"Say that again? I didn't hear you."

"We each have policies worth three million dollars. I think I'd like to talk to a lawyer now."

"Did you murder your wife, Mr. Wolff?"

He stood suddenly, the chair scooting back with a screech. "No, damn it. But you're going to try and pin this on me, I can see it. And I don't intend to be made a fool of, Lieutenant. I didn't kill my wife. Am I under arrest?"

The room was thick with tension. Taylor stared into Wolff's black eyes and saw the first vestiges of fear forming. It just served to pique her interest.

"No. You're not. Yet."

Twelve

Taylor was sifting through the afternoon's events in triplicate when her phone rang. She recognized the number as Forensic Medical, Sam's extension. She glanced at the wall clock. Five. Too early for toxicology reports. She answered on the second ring. There was no greeting, just Sam's overt enthusiasm spilling out of the receiver's speaker.

"You are a lucky woman."

Taylor tipped her chair back and put her feet up on her desk, crossing them at the ankle. "Why would this be?"

"Because you are going to go home, take a shower, put on something fabulous, and join me as my date for the evening."

"Oh, hell no. I've got a shitload of work to do, and I am definitely not in the mood."

"You don't even know what it is and you're turning it down?"

"Yes."

"Oh, Taylor, you're a stick-in-the-mud. I insist you accompany me. I've lost my date for the evening, he is head over heels in love with some microbe growing in a petri dish in his office. I need an escort. It's not acceptable for a young lady such as myself to be out on the town all by her lonesome. So get your shit together, go home and get yourself in something elegant."

Taylor groaned. "Elegant? What, pray tell, are you planning to drag me to?"

"The American Cancer Society Dinner. I'm the keynote speaker."

"No, Sam. Absolutely not," she said with more enthusiasm than she felt.

"Great. I'll pick you up at six forty-five. You should wear that red dress we got you in Barbados."

"There's no place for me to carry my weapon on that dress."

"And that, my darling friend, is the point. I don't think you're going to have to shoot anyone at the Frist Center."

"Famous last words. I remember the last time you told me I wouldn't need a gun, I ended up being kidnapped."

"Well, no one is going to do that tonight. I promise. Just some rubber chicken and a bunch of free champagne. You need a break. I bet you've been after the bad guys all day."

"Of course I have. It's my job." But Sam had already hung up. Taylor rolled her eyes, put the phone back in the cradle, and dropped her feet to the floor.

Choices. Sit at her desk, filling out paperwork, listening to the B-shift detectives fart and tell bad jokes while they waited for a case to break, or get dressed up in something hideously uncomfortable and make nice all night. She really didn't know which option would be worse.

Taylor eyed the red dress dubiously. She was already in a strapless bra, thigh-high sheer black hose and three-inch black pumps. Sam and Simon had brought the dress back from a Caribbean vacation, Sam gushing over the clingy style, declaring it would be gorgeous on her figure. Taylor had thanked her, but never tried it on. It was a postage stamp as far as she was concerned.

Well, bottoms up. She slipped the fabric over her head, surprised at how heavy it felt, considering how little of it there was. She shimmied until the dress stopped, hitched against her hips, and she tugged at the hem. Suddenly it was on, flowing, draping, hitting her curves in all the right places. She looked into her mirror. Holy shit. Sam was right. It was pretty. Delicate spaghetti straps, deep across the bust, showing off her décolletage to perfection, an empire waist that let the clingy fabric float around her knees. She was going to have to put on this getup for Baldwin, he'd enjoy it.

She left her hair down, and it swished full and thick against the middle of her back. She put on a touch of eye shadow and mascara, and feeling risqué, painted her mouth with a deep crimson stain, then topped it with some Carmex. Done. A stranger in red.

A horn beeped and she snapped off the light, rushed down the stairs, grabbing her purse and a wrap as she exited the front door. The small clutch was a concession she'd been required to make. She hated carrying a bag, dragging one around was counterintuitive to her lifestyle. Normally, as long as she had pockets for her Chapstick and a belt to attach her holster she was all set.

But there was no good place to stow a weapon in this outfit. She could have tied a blade in her garter, slipped a one-shot revolver into her cleavage, but they were too impractical. So she settled on a black satin evening clutch that was just big enough for a Taurus 941 .22 revolver with a nice, short two-inch barrel, one of the many "fun" guns she had in her safe. Her normal ankle weapon was a bit larger, a .22 Beretta that she kept inside her right cowboy boot in a custom-made leather pouch, but the Beretta was just heavy enough to be a pain to carry in this purse.

Sam whistled at her from the open top of her BMW, a construction worker catcall.

Taylor flipped her the bird, then yelled, "Put the damn top up. It's way too cold out here to be buzzing around like this." She locked the door behind her and walked to the car, a tiny bit unsteady on the unfamiliar heels.

Sam just smiled. "Fine, grump. I figured you'd like the fresh air." The top whirred into place and snapped closed. "You look nice."

"So do you." Sam was wearing a midnight-blue Grecian styled gown, strappy gladiator sandals on her feet, her hair piled on top of her head in a messy knot, the bangs thick and stark across her forehead. As usual, she looked chic and together. Taylor pulled down the mirror as Sam put the car in gear and backed out of the drive, feeling a bit garish with the red lipstick.

"Don't touch it. You look fabulous."

Taylor put the mirror back into place and smiled at her best friend. "Thanks."

"You're welcome. So, how's everything?"

They chatted during the fifteen-minute drive, catching up on non-law-enforcement issues. Sam scooted through the light traffic and when they pulled up in front of the Frist valets, Taylor felt as relaxed as she had in days.

They dropped the car, went inside the stunning museum's outdoor tent. The fête was underway. Black-tie-clad men and elegantly gowned women strolled, drinking champagne and nibbling hor d'ouevres served on silver trays. Sam and Taylor each accepted a flute from a waiter and toasted one another, clinking glasses softly. "*Salut,*" Taylor said, the word making her miss Baldwin.

They circulated through the room, greeting people they knew, which was most of the crowd. Several of Taylor's mother's friends came up and complimented her on her dress, asked how Kitty Jackson was faring these days. A few deigned to ask about Win, her father.

She answered both with equal insouciance—Kitty was fine, she'd met a Swiss banker skiing in Gstaad over the winter and had elected to stay in Europe for the remainder of the spring. Win was in a minimum-security prison in West Virginia, a guest of the federal government.

Most people didn't know all the facts behind the Win Jackson case. The feds had managed to keep his role in a huge money-laundering and human trafficking ring relatively quiet. Win wouldn't be testifying against his former boss. The man known eponymously as L'Uomo was in a Brazilian jail at the moment, most likely chained to a wall. Good riddance, Taylor always thought. He was human scum.

Taylor felt like her brittle smile was pasted on. The allure of these events had long ago lost their charm. She'd been a good soldier for a long time, attending the parties and the charity events that made up the bulk of Nashville's social calendar at the behest of her parents. She'd even gone through a ghastly coming-out season when she was eighteen—a year of heavy drinking and petting that culminated with a curtsey at the white tie debutante ball, Sam and Simon snickering at her side.

She supposed the companionship made it that much easier for her to rebel against her parents' well-borne intentions for her; Sam hadn't wanted a Junior League life either. Knowing it was just a matter of time before they'd be out on their own, in Knoxville at college, away from the prying eyes of Nashville's glitterati, helped them get through the events.

They both gave back to their parents' world, but in their own ways. Taylor did her best to protect them. Sam uncovered their darkest secrets. It was a fair trade, really. As long as every so often, they paid the piper.

This early spring evening, they did just that. And Nashville society was its always polite self, happy to see both Taylor and Sam playing along for a night, at the very least, and didn't make too much trouble. Instead, the topic of conversation was the Corinne Wolff murder. Tongues wagged; the Harrises weren't unknown on the circuit, though they weren't invited to the best parties either. Corinne ran with the athletic country club set. New money, Taylor heard one Botoxed and plumped woman whisper. The ultimate sin.

The prevailing opinion was a drug addict had broken into the home to steal money for a fix. Taylor didn't have the heart to tell them that most junkies were at heart gentle souls who would be more likely to steal a purse than beat someone to death, but hey, let them have their fears.

The Nashville press was in attendance; she and Sam posed for countless photos. She knew she'd be razzed at work tomorrow, but didn't care. She had a nice chat with Amy Hendricks, a *Tennessean* reporter and former classmate at Father Ryan. All in all, it was a typical Nashville cocktail party, pleasantly benign, bordering on soporific.

After a half an hour of inaneness, the chairwoman of the event, Linda Whaley, came to steal Sam, leaving Taylor cruising the room by herself. She wasn't alone for long. Within a few minutes, three different men had asked if they could buy her a drink. Though she was gracious and appropriately flirty, she'd started drinking the champagne with her left hand as a hint. The ring wasn't scaring off any potential suitors. A couple wore wide gold bands themselves. Dogs.

She glanced at her watch. The dinner should start anytime now. On cue, she heard a tinkling. The dinner bell. Tossing off the last of her champagne, she handed the glass to a passing waiter and started for the tables. Linda had told her she'd be seated at the front table with Sam. Great. Just what she wanted, to be at the center of all this attention.

A gentleman done up in full evening kit, white tie gleaming against his black satin lapel, held the door to the dining room open for her. She nodded her thanks and entered the room. She stopped for a moment to get her bearings and a voice spoke softly in her ear, making her jump and clutch at the snap of her bag. Jesus, didn't people know better than to sneak up on a cop?

"Heya, Tawny."

She turned and took in the speaker. A heavyset man in his late forties, graying at the temples, loose jowls, buttons on his shirt strained as if it had been seen one too many times at the dry cleaner, or one too many trips to the buffet. Leering at her as if he could lap her up. She had no earthly idea who he was.

"I'm sorry. Have we met?"

The man glanced over his shoulder, leaned in conspiratorially. "Tawny, Tawny, Tawny. My God, I never imagined I'd see you in the flesh. Yet here you are, an angel in red. Or a succubus, I should guess. What do you say you and me split out of here, go have ourselves a little private party?"

Taylor did her best not to laugh at the egregious pickup. "I'm sorry, I haven't got a clue who you are." She started to walk away and he grabbed her arm, pulling her back to him, pressing his body against hers in a much too familiar way.

"Hey there, girlie, I'm talking to you."

Wrong thing to do. Taylor kept her tone measured, her voice low. "Let. Go. Of. Me. Now. Or I *will* break your arm."

He unhanded her, and she whirled away. He followed on her heels.

"Where the fuck do you think you're going?" he snarled at her.

Instead of speaking, Taylor just stopped, casually opened her purse and showed him her gun. The man smiled. His bottom teeth were shaped like pegs and stained brown. She repressed a shudder.

"Oh-ho, aren't you a little tigress. Keeping a concealed weapon, are you? I've got some friends who I'm sure would like to know about that. You should probably give me the gun, little lady, you wouldn't want to hurt yourself." He started to reach for the weapon. Taylor snapped the purse closed, grabbed the man's hand and twisted, hard. He was forced to spin away from her and she used that momentum to get him moving back toward the door.

"Hey!" he said, loud enough to get the attention of a passing waiter, who looked on in shock as Taylor maneuvered the boor right back out into the hallway.

She tossed him up against the wall face-first. He landed with a thud, grunting, then turned on her. She had her badge in her hand. His eyes bulged at the gold shield.

"Listen," he started, but she cut him off.

"No, you listen to me. I don't have the first clue who you think I am, but let me introduce myself. I'm Lieutenant Taylor Jackson, homicide. Now who the *hell* are you?"

His little pig eyes got smaller. "Tony Gorman."

"And why did you call me Tawny?"

She could see him calculating. "It's your hair," he said finally. She knew immediately that he was lying. She hissed in his ear.

"You're a liar, Mr. Gorman. Tell you what. Why don't you just slink out of here and I won't arrest you for assaulting an officer. And maybe you'll think twice the next time you decide to lay your hands on a woman. Some of us bite."

She heard him call her a bitch under his breath as he walked away. Fat bastard. She rubbed her arm. She was going to have bruises just the size of Gorman's meaty fingers. Some men just didn't get it.

Taylor went back into the room, feeling like all eyes were on her. The salad was being served. She sat next to Sam, who gave her a look of concern, but she shook her head. "Later," she mouthed.

She ate, and made polite conversation with the couple to her left, and drank a fine glass of Bordeaux. She clapped the hardest at the end of Sam's speech, and was more than relieved to see the evening draw to a close. Her feet hurt. She just wanted to get out of her clothes and into the bed.

She told Sam what happened on the way home. By the time they'd arrived at the house, Taylor was laughing about it and Sam had graced her with a new nickname, Miss Tawny T. She drove off with a wave and Taylor bolted the door behind her. She went into the kitchen, turned on the alarm system and dumped her shoes with a clatter on the hardwood. She'd retrieve them tomorrow. It was eleven-thirty. Too late to bother Baldwin, he was on Eastern time and probably already asleep. She envied his ability to drop off as soon as his head hit the pillow. She poured a glass of Chianti and went upstairs to the office.

She booted up the computer and walked to her bedroom to change. She shed the dress and accoutrements like a chrysalis, feeling better the instant she was naked. She walked back to the computer, set the wine on a coaster and started Googling *Tawny*.

What's in a name? Tawny seemed to be a favorite pseudonym for porn stars and wannabe actresses. The Tawny Frogmouth was a bird, a family pet rabbit named Tawny had its own Web site, lots of flora and fauna that got the tawny designation, even a port. Nothing that looked like her, though. She tried Tawny Nashville, got a few live sex operators and a Greek restaurant, but still nothing with ties to her life. Obviously it was a case of mistaken identity.

But Taylor was uncharacteristically unnerved. She'd seen the look in Tony Gorman's eyes, the twist of lust in his features. This was a man who'd thought of sex when he saw her, and that made her more uncomfortable than anything she'd felt in some time. If she'd been weaker, or another woman entirely, the situation would have gone a different way.

She erased Tawny from the browser and plugged in the name Tony Gorman. Too many hits to count. She tried variations—Anthony Gorman, Tony Gorman Nashville, Anthony Gorman Tennessee, but the results were just too numerous. She was damned tired, and figured she'd have better luck using the police channels to track the bastard.

Taylor closed the Web browser, leaned back in her desk chair. Thought about the quick glimpse into Tony Gorman's soul. She had been familiar with the concept of desire from a relatively tender age. Her parents, for all their failings, had treated her as an adult from the time she could be expected to make a few of her own decisions, and as a result she'd ended up being rather precocious.

When her body developed, her gangly height and tomboy attitude turning into a lush ripeness at age fifteen or so, she'd found herself the recipient of plenty of unwanted attention. Most came from older men; boys her own age had no idea what to do with her. She'd gone from being a favorite colt to a sleek thoroughbred in the span of weeks, and was somewhat shunned among her male playmates, who had always treated her as just another one of the boys. She'd felt that was unfair and from then on stuck to dating boys older than her.

She'd lost her virginity to a friend of her father's in a torrid affair when she was seventeen. She was head over heels in lust with the man, a classics professor at Vanderbilt. Dr. James Morley was sexy and urbane and taught her many things about life and love. The relationship was the final nail in the coffin for Morley's crumbling marriage, but he'd remained friends with both Taylor and his wife. He had a fatal heart attack a few years later, and Taylor had grieved for him.

Over the subsequent years she'd had a few short-term affairs, lovers her age who were frightened by her intensity, older men who wanted to protect her, to keep her. She had a knack for getting involved with men she could never love but who loved her, and that had forced a few nasty breakups.

Baldwin was the first man she'd ever truly loved, loved in a way she'd thought she was incapable of. The giving and receiving of hearts was something she had always scoffed at. It was wonderful and scary at the same time. But if she were honest with herself, Baldwin had some of the same characteristics as her first lover— the cosmopolitan attitude, the intelligence, the striking looks. But Baldwin was different in all the good ways; he was an honest man. No need to worry about infidelity; he'd never tried to hide anything from her. No late-night cruising through his e-mail or wallet would be necessary, she'd simply ask and he would always answer.

And maybe, deep down, knowing he'd always be

truthful was the most important part of her feelings, the reason she'd been able to give herself fully to him.

Taylor shook off her emotions, shut off the computer. As the light sputtered out on the screen with a snap, she bade farewell to the ghosts lingering in the room with her. She finished her wine and turned off the light.

Her bed was warm and soft, and she felt sleep tug at her immediately, probably as a result of all the alcohol. Groaning, she got up and took two Advil, sucked down five Dixie cups of water, hoping to alleviate what she assumed would be a killer headache in the morning. She didn't get hangovers from wine anymore, but could be struck with a migraine if she didn't prepare her body for the process.

She climbed back in the bed, this time nearly boneless. Images from the evening spun through her head, the ugly twist to the strange man's mouth, the whirling waiters, the pouty-lipped social mavens with their identical face-lifts and overinjected foreheads. She was asleep within moments.

The ringing phone woke her. It was still dark. Somewhere in her consciousness, she palmed the Glock from under Baldwin's pillow as she answered the phone.

"What?"

There was nothing. A deep silence filled the room, static and bottomless. She wondered if she were dreaming. Then she heard the breathing.

She slammed the receiver down. It rang again immediately. The backlit caller ID said UNKNOWN NAME UNKNOWN NUMBER in a ghostly green.

Of course. She answered it anyway, this time more awake.

"What." It wasn't a question.

This time a man's laugh filled her ear. It wasn't Tony Gorman, that much she knew. This was a different tone altogether. And then he was gone.

Taylor continued to grip the phone for another minute, listening to the soft bonging of the dead line. She set the phone back on the cradle carefully and sat up, slipping a pillow behind her back. She wouldn't turn on the light—if the caller was anywhere near, he'd see that and know he'd rattled her. There would be no more sleep tonight. She caressed the Glock, comfortable in the knowledge that she was safe enough. She'd just like to know who was trying to spook her.

Thirteen

Sometimes Baldwin just wanted to kiss the bureaucracy he worked for.

Not that he was a fan of all the measures put in place since 9-11, but the upside was when the FBI, or the CIA, needed to find someone, they could.

It was late. A glance at his watch showed two in the morning. He wondered if Taylor was asleep, or playing pool. This was her witching hour, the time she was most likely to start awake and begin thinking. That woman thought too much. He toyed with the idea of calling, but didn't want to risk it.

He decided on a cup of coffee instead.

The lights were still burning through the outbuilding where he and Garrett had quietly set up shop. Garrett was on the phone in the office next door with yet another international agency, getting cooperation from all sides in the hunt for their killer.

The short hallway opened into a galley-style kitchen.

Two fresh pots of coffee were already made, and he poured himself a cup, sipping it as he went back to his desk.

Baldwin vowed that he would find Aiden, sooner rather than later. The hunter had become the hunted, and Baldwin was the master. Though his eyes were crossing at the multitudes of miniature lines of data, he felt like he was getting closer. Instinct dictated that Aiden would follow a somewhat set pattern for his trip to the United States. The trick was simply figuring out the start point for his journey. Italy, Germany, and England had already been ruled out. All the South American countries were off the initial lists as well—if Aiden had been in Europe as recently as a month ago, it was possible he'd been called to another continent for a hit they weren't aware of, but unlikely. He wouldn't blend in as well as he did in the European nations, didn't work in that region very often.

Aiden was a rare beast. On the OA radar for six years now, he'd started life as an intense loner who traveled the world on the heels of his diplomat father. At some point they had a massive falling-out, so Aiden rebelled and went into the service. He'd done well in the Army, qualifying as a sniper, but something went south. After only three years on his tour of duty, he was discharged for conduct unbecoming.

Aiden disappeared for a while, then emerged as a freelance assassin. Some of his more unsavory ex-Army buddies got him into the game. He became an assassin of stature, one that could be counted on for a clean hit at long range. Very valuable. But Aiden got bored. He began contracting for the more personal hits.

He was used by nasty characters who wanted to send a message when they assassinated someone. And Aiden's silver garrote was unmistakable.

Yet the professional assassination game still wasn't enough for him. Aiden liked to go off the reservation. The OA monitored him as best they could, using eyes and ears to let them know when he skipped off plan.

Baldwin knew all this, knew how dangerous Aiden was. Knew that he must be traced, at all cost, or innocent people would die.

Baldwin had compiled a list of known aliases and sent it to the International Air Transport Association. The IATA in turn kindly filtered all of those names through their eTARS database, the names coursing through the Aviation Management Systems Departure Control System, or eDCS, popping up matches that met Baldwin's parameters. Typical of the overcomplicated governmental structure, it was a fancy way to say they were combing the passenger manifests.

Coffee half finished, Baldwin went back to stacks of pages, scanning the names, departure flights, dates, numbers in the party. He was looking for a man traveling alone, buying one-way tickets, or tickets with extended return dates. This was Aiden's usual standard operating procedure. Baldwin was a fan of Occam's Razor, figured all things being equal, starting with the most obvious answer was generally the best approach.

It was 4:00 a.m. when he finally saw it. He flipped open the file of the eighth report and the name practically jumped off the page.

"Gotcha," he whispered.

Wednesday

Fourteen

Taylor stretched. She'd fallen asleep despite her intent to stay awake for the remainder of the night. The malice from the previous evening was lost in the warm sunlight streaming through her shades, and she wondered briefly if she'd dreamed the whole thing. But no, the Glock was still in her hand.

The television came on, the morning news blaring. She tuned it out, rolled around in the sheets for a few moments, having her usual morning debate. Get up or play hooky. The former always won, unfortunately.

Groaning, she secured the weapon and pulled on a pair of yoga pants. She thought about washing her face, and made five steps toward the bathroom but drew up short when she heard the now familiar words.

"Nine-one-one, what is your emergency?"

"I think my sister is dead. Oh, my God."

Michelle Harris's tear-stricken voice drifted from Taylor's television. She sat back on the bed and listened to the rest of the tape, following with the visual on the television screen, the lines scrolling slowly.

Taylor shut her eyes and rubbed her knuckles against the closed lids. The media would make hay out of this as long as they didn't have something more sensational to cover.

Michelle Harris's voice, sharp and immediate, made Taylor sit up. Live, or recently taped, the words were unfamiliar. This was a new interview.

Taylor reached for the remote and turned up the volume.

Michelle Harris was wearing a white button-down shirt that washed out what little color she had left in her face. Her cheekbones created dark hollows, her lips were bloodless, her hair lashed back in a ponytail so tight it seemed to pull the hairs from their roots. She looked like absolute hell.

"Miss Harris, when was the last time you saw your sister?"

"On Friday. We grabbed a Starbucks after tennis."

"And you never saw your sister alive again?" The anchor's eyes were misty, she obviously felt every word's impact.

"Yes. The next time I saw Corinne, she was, she was...dead." Michelle's voice was breaking, rich with emotion, but her eyes remained dry.

"And you," the anchor began, but Michelle interrupted.

"Whoever killed her needs to know that we won't stop until he is caught. We will hunt you down, and kill you ourselves. You can't do something like this and not get punished. I just can't believe that someone could do this to my sister. It's not fair." Overcome with emotion, she began to cry. The anchor threw it to commercial.

Taylor punched the power button with her thumb, and the television snapped off. Damn it. Just what they needed, Michelle Harris on national TV, playing the victim.

Morning soured, she went downstairs, rubbing sleep out of her eyes. She was famished, so she poured a bowl of cereal. Checked the milk, yes, still fresh enough—the organic stuff Baldwin had talked her into lasted at least a week longer than regular. Dropped a tea bag and some honey in a cup, splashed in a little milk, then filled it with boiling water from the in-sink tap. Stood at the kitchen sink, gazed out into the backyard. Spooned crunchy wheat biscuits into her mouth slowly, watching the woods, thinking.

A huge rabbit was in the back, nibbling on the clover. Taylor could see another farther back into the thicket, on alert, watching over his mate as she foraged for breakfast. The knowledge that she'd soon be sharing mornings with baby bunnies made her smile. She watched the creature hop slowly forward, just a few inches at a time as it grazed. Then it stopped, ears alert, nose twitching.

With a suddenness that made Taylor's heart race, the rabbit fled, scared by something. A dog, most likely, Taylor could hear the faint echoes of barking bleeding through the air. She looked closer at the spot in the lawn vacated by the panicked rabbit. What was *that*?

She set the bowl in the sink and made her way to the back door. Stepping out onto the deck, she heard the alarm buzz its warning tone. Shit. She'd forgotten to turn the damn thing off. She dashed back inside and punched in the code. It squawked and the series of lights turned green. Disarmed.

She went back to the yard, bare feet cold as she picked through the still dew-wet grass. A lump of dark was thirty feet to her right, in line with the kitchen window.

She drew closer, scenting the murk of decay, heard the buzzing of the flies. A furry pile, red and slick. She recognized the cottontail of a rabbit, the body skinned, turned inside out. Poor beast. There was a thin line of wire digging deep into the animal's neck, the ends wrapped around each other like a twisty tie on a loaf of bread.

She felt exposed, her T-shirt too thin, and she rubbed her arms up and down for warmth. She wasn't an idiot, knew this was a message. The who wasn't the important question, she assumed it was from her nocturnal stalker. Why she was being targeted, that's what she wanted to know. Was this the work of the Pretender? He seemed too subtle for gross displays, but perhaps they'd misread him.

She didn't want to touch the carcass. She needed to secure it in some way, keep it intact and safe from the multitudes of predators that would surely come to scavenge. Preserve the integrity of the message so a tech could come collect it as evidence. She went around the side of the house. The lid from the trashcan wouldn't work, it was too flat. There was an empty flowerpot, a good-sized one that held a dead hydrangea. Perfect. She dumped the flower and the dirt onto the ground, then went back to the dead rabbit, carefully placing the pot over the body. That should keep for an hour or so.

Feeling eyes on her from every corner, Taylor left the makeshift shrine in the yard and went back inside. Her morning's peace shattered, she abandoned the cup of tea on the counter, dressed quickly and headed into the office.

There were news vans lining the streets in front of the CJC, receiver satellites pointed toward the heavens. Taylor decided to park in the adjacent lot so she wouldn't have to run the media gauntlet. She walked the cement ramp, spiraling down toward the street, her boot heels echoing with each step. The repetition calmed her, the pattern resonating through her mind.

She managed to slip in the side door unnoticed. The building itself was humming, noisy, aware. She stopped for a Diet Coke, feeding her dollar into the machine, the can dropping with a clatter. Normally the noise thundered through the halls; today it was barely heard. She entered the Homicide office, saw Lincoln Ross sitting with one butt cheek on the edge of his desk, holding court. It looked like half of headquarters had jammed into Homicide.

A few people acknowledged Taylor, polite "Loot's" and "Morning, LT." She nodded back, caught Lincoln's eye.

His face lit up when he saw Taylor. He jumped off the desk and greeted her with a hug. She hugged him back, hard, thrilled that he was out and obviously okay. She stepped back and took him in. More than okay. Lincoln had a gap-toothed smile that spread from ear to ear. His new look made him seem vaguely like a pirate—bald head, curly beard, eyes flashing with charm and intelligence. Toss him a cutlass and he'd be ready to rapier his way through downtown Nashville.

"Girl, you look great. Whatcha been doing while I've been away? You and the fed have a good trip?"

"It's damn good to see you, Linc. First things first. What's happening?"

He smirked and waggled his eyebrows. "I got Terrence Norton for you, all tied up with a pretty little bow."

They bumped knuckles, her generation's version of a high five. "Really? That's great news, Lincoln. But why is every newsie in town camped on our doorstep?"

"Got his boss, too." He said it with such nonchalance that Taylor instinctively knew it was someone visible that no one would ever expect.

"Okay, you've got me. Who's been running this train?"

"Our very own Sidney Edgar."

She drew back in surprise. "Kong?"

"Yup."

"Sidney Edgar, wide receiver for the Tennessee Titans. You are shitting me."

Sidney "King-Kong" Edgar had been a first round draft pick, a rainmaker for the Titans, a young man out of Atlanta who had more brawn than brains. He was six foot four inches of lean, hard muscle, devastatingly dangerous when his hands got within five feet of the pigskin, and a gangster thug to boot. Since he joined the team, Kong had rushed for over one thousand yards and been arrested no less than eight times, always skirting the edge of felony territory. He ran with a bad crowd, a posse of ruffians who traveled between Nashville and Atlanta, lawless men who were regularly picked up for weapons and drug-related charges.

Though as far as Taylor knew, they'd never been

connected to Terrence Norton's gang. She said that, and Lincoln nodded.

"We didn't know that either until last night. I have to say, I can act. After Sunday night..." He gave her a meaningful look she understood immediately. He'd smoked crack with them, so they'd accepted him.

"Anyway, my CI told me the big dog was coming in. He very kindly left his cell phone on so I could hear the deal being made, and I called in the cavalry. It was too sweet. Caught Kong and Terrence Norton with their hands full of crack baggies."

Lincoln was obviously still riding the adrenal train. Taylor thought he was probably putting a good face on the situation; she knew it must have been dicey, moment-to-moment danger.

In that inevitable way with men who'd had street violence bred into them before they were weaned, Edgar had always seemed a little too close to the edge. It was a sad thing. So many of those boys pulled themselves up by the bootstraps, got straight, made something positive happen. And some were just a little too weak, too easily seduced by the illusion of power.

Lincoln was wrapping up his tale. "We brought him in, got him processed. King Kong and Terrence, plus fifteen others, will be arraigned this morning. That's what the news is here to see."

Taylor squeezed his arm. "Have you been debriefed?" When he nodded, she said, "You take the rest of the day off. Go get some rest. You must be completely exhausted."

"You sure, LT? I hear you've got some stuff on your plate."

"I'm sure, Lincoln. Whenever you're ready, no rush. But yeah, I need you sharp, so you go do what you need to do to get yourself back in the real world. We'll pick up with you tomorrow. Deal?"

"Deal, Loot. Thanks."

She left him to his adoring crowd and went into her office. Marcus Wade joined her after a few minutes.

"Morning, Marcus. How'd in-service go?"

"I still have a badge, and a gun. My fifth day is scheduled for June." He rolled his eyes. In-service, while required, was generally considered one of the most boring weeks out of the year. Cop school, four days of repetition of items they already knew by heart. Inexplicably, the gun qualifications came a few months later, a single day of shooting to requalify.

"Mine is too, I think. We must be on the same testing day. Well, that's good news. Fitz bring you up to speed on the Corinne Wolff murder?" He nodded. "Good. I want you on that case, but I need you to do something for me first."

She leaned over, spoke quietly so no one enjoying the Lincoln Parade could accidentally overhear.

"I met someone last night who I think may have something shady going on. I'd like you to do a quick run-through of his background. Anything and everything you can find on the guy, okay?"

"No problem, LT. What's his name?"

"Tony Gorman. I'd assume the full name is Anthony. I don't have much more than that, and it's a generic name, but if you pull the DMV records, I can ID him. Then you can dive in, see what his story is."

"I assume I'm doing this quietly."

"You got it, puppy. He's tied-in somewhere, was at

a charity dinner last night, so he's got some money. I didn't recognize him, but he knew me. Only he called me Tawny. When I challenged him, he thought I was being coy. And that makes me uncomfortable."

"Tawny? That sounds like—"

Taylor blushed. "Exactly. And that's about how he treated me. Look at this." She shrugged out of her cotton sweater, pulling her right arm out to show the underside of her bicep. There were four distinct round bruises. Marcus's eyebrows disappeared beneath the shock of bushy brown hair that flopped over his forehead.

"Why didn't you arrest him?"

"I thought about it, but if he was truly mistaking me for someone else, I had no cause. He was just an over-zealous jerk. Not a prison offense, you know? But he won't forget meeting me anytime soon. I got him in a forearm lock and he tried to get away. Another few seconds and I would've snapped his arm in two. I bet he's got a nice bruise this morning too." She slipped her arm back into the sleeve of her sweater, pulled it down.

"I'll find out what his deal is, Taylor. You can count on it."

"Thanks, Marcus. Let me know when you find something. I'm sure it's nothing, just a mistake." Her words were stronger than her mind. Gorman had looked at her like he knew her intimately; she had the distinct feeling that there was more to the sexy moniker than met the eye. Either she had a doppelganger out there plying her wares, or something was up. Combine that with the dead rabbit from this morning....

Marcus was just outside the door. She called after him. "Marcus, one other thing?"

He turned back. "Sure, what?"

"Have Tim Davis take a run out to my house. Someone left me a present in my backyard this morning, a dead rabbit. It had been garroted. I secured the remains. Ask him to run some forensics on it for me, okay?"

Marcus came back into the office, eyes filled with concern. "Someone killed a rabbit and left it in your backyard? Are you sure it wasn't caught in a snare and flailed into your yard?"

Taylor saw the desecrated creature in her mind's eye, gray and red commingled, the wound ends of the silver wire thrusting out of its neck. A shudder ran through her.

"Yes, I'm sure."

Marcus was eyeing her. She could see the speculation rampant behind his gaze. He shut the door and sat opposite her.

"Is everything okay, boss? You seem a little…"

She pulled the rubber band from her hair impatiently and slung it back up. "I'm fine. Really. It's just been a long couple of days, and someone is playing a sick joke on me. That's all. It's nothing to worry about." She gave him a winning smile, but he didn't smile back. He just nodded and rose, looking at her with obvious concern.

"I'll let you know what we find, okay?"

"Thanks, Marcus." She hesitated a moment. "While you're at it, put a trap on my line. I've been getting hang-ups. I'm sure it's just someone trying to make me uncomfortable." When he started to speak again, she just shook her head. He stared at her, but kept his mouth shut.

After he'd left, she looked at the phone. She really should call Baldwin, let him know everything that was going on. She toyed with the phone receiver, her hand tracing figure eights on the smooth black surface. The phone lit up, the caller ID indicating the call was from Forensic Medical. There was plenty of time to call Baldwin and play damsel in distress. Later.

"Lieutenant Jackson," she answered, her voice strong once again.

"Taylor, it's Sam. I've got something you need to hear about Corinne Wolff."

Fifteen

Taylor listened to Sam, writing down the words to make sure she had the record in front of her, then hung up the phone. She toyed with the cord for a moment, wondering. On its face, the news wasn't anything significant. But considering the victim's previous delicate condition, it was...interesting.

More questions for Todd. Taylor glanced at her watch. Ten thirty-five.

"Oh, shit." She scrambled up from the desk, bringing along the yellow notepad with her scribbles. She was already five minutes late to her third interview with him.

Taylor met Fitz outside interrogation one. He gestured for her to follow him into the printer room where they had the camera feed from the interrogation rooms. The antiquated television monitor was on, the cameras rolling, capturing the movements of the two men ensconced in the room. Todd Wolff had brought a lawyer this time, not willing to make the same mistake twice. They were sitting side by side at the table, each man sitting with his arms crossed across his chest, not speaking. They looked impatient, slightly annoyed, and worried. Perfect.

Taylor watched for a moment. "Look at Wolff. He looks nervous, don't you think?"

"He doesn't look happy, I'll give you that."

Taylor pulled her hair down, reworking the ponytail. "I just talked to Sam. We've got some interesting items to discuss with Mr. Wolff."

"Well, the hotel he claimed to have stayed at said he wasn't there over the weekend. So he's got one whopper of a lie in the bank already."

"Really? That's interesting. Can the cell phone company triangulate where he was when he got the call?"

"There's a warrant being drawn up as we speak." Fitz looked at the monitors again. "Think he's responsible?"

"I don't know. I want to gauge his reaction to this information Sam just gave me, see what he gives us."

"Then let's get this over with, shall we?" Fitz gestured toward the door. Taylor nodded and knocked, rapping her knuckles along the wood for effect, then entered the close room.

The lawyer jumped to his feet, hand out expectantly, a broad smile across his swarthy features. He had thinning salt-and-pepper hair and a thick bridge of a nose that amply supported a pair of horn-rimmed glasses. His eyes were slightly bulbous, irises blue but whites bloodshot, whether from too much alcohol the night before or stupendous allergies, Taylor couldn't tell. He pumped her hand, asked if she was well, greeted Fitz, all in a capable, no-nonsense way. Then he sneezed, ah…ah…ah-chooing with gusto into a white embroidered handkerchief. That explained the eyes, Taylor thought.

"Miles Rose. Good to meetcha."

Todd Wolff barely acknowledged their presence. She studied him. Was he grieving, and too distressed to play nice? Or was he upset to be treated like a suspect? Taylor couldn't tell. Wolff had completely shut down since their last conversation.

They got situated, Fitz and Taylor on one side of the table, Rose getting resettled in his makeshift office on the other side with Todd staring silently at the wall. Taylor watched Rose decant his briefcase onto the table, waited patiently while he chose a particularly fine ballpoint from his collection of pens, placed the pen on a yellow legal pad, then grinned.

"Ready," he said.

Amused by the display, Taylor asked, "Are you sure?"

"Oh, yeah. Got everything I need right here." He tapped the pen to the legal pad, then touched it to his temple. She heard Fitz sigh through his nose with the utmost derision.

"Okay then." She turned to Todd. "Mr. Wolff, I'd like to continue where we left off yesterday. We are concerned about the time frame on the day of your wife's death. You were notified of her death while you were in Savannah, is that correct?"

Todd looked at her, as if seeing her for the first time. "Why does that even matter? Do you have any more leads on who killed my wife and son?"

"We're working the case from every angle, Mr.

Wolff. Trust me. Now, back to your drive home. You were in Savannah when you got the call, that's correct?"

Wolff looked away. "That is correct."

"And you made the trip home, an eight-hour drive, in just under six hours. That right?"

"Yes."

"Any reason you didn't fly? Wouldn't that have been quicker?"

"You already asked me that." Wolff crossed his arms.

Rose leaned into the table. "My client called the airlines, but there was nothing that didn't connect through Atlanta. I don't know if you've ever flown through Atlanta, Lieutenant, but I'm sure you'll understand that my client didn't want anything interfering with his return to the Nashville area."

Taylor gave Rose the briefest of smiles, then turned back to Wolff.

"No chance you got pulled over, is there? Something to give us an actual time and place to go from? Because I've made that drive, Mr. Wolff. It takes the full eight hours, even traveling at eighty miles an hour."

Todd shook his head, glancing at Rose before he spoke. "No, I didn't get a ticket. I was going faster than eighty, I'll tell you that. I nearly got myself killed more than once."

"How about a gas receipt? Big truck like yours, there's no way you could possibly make it home from Savannah on a single tank of gas."

"I could give you that, but I don't save those receipts. I rely on my bank statements to tally up my gas costs."

When Taylor didn't respond, Wolff quickly filled the silence. "I've got a gas card. That way I can keep those charges on one card to keep it all straight. I can get deductions on my taxes, you know. So yeah, I stopped in a little town…I can't remember the name of it now. But I'm sure I can find the information once my statement comes." He smiled for the first time, satisfied with his answer.

"That's great, Mr. Wolff. We've already pulled all of your financials, so we'll be able to get that answer right now." She leaned back toward the corner, where a small table sat with a phone. She stabbed at a button, then hit speaker. Marcus's voice rang through the room.

"What can I get you, LT?"

"I need the bank statements for Mr. Wolff analyzed. Please look for charges specific to his gas card so we can see the stops at gas stations on the day in question. He says he stopped in a little town, but can't remember the name. Any chance you could ID the place for me, so we can check that out?"

"Sure thing, LT. I'll get back to you in a minute."

She clicked the speaker off and looked at Todd Wolff's vividly white face.

"Was it something I said?" she asked.

"I just, I didn't realize, I…" He trailed off.

Rose jumped in. "This is highly irregular, Lieutenant. I don't believe I've ever seen—"

"Stow it, Mr. Rose. This is hardly irregular. Mr. Wolff is lying to us, and I'd like to know why." Taylor ignored Rose sputtering and hand-wringing, instead focusing on Todd.

"Todd, when was the last time you had sex with your wife?"

Todd's eyes got round. "What does that have to do with anything?" He stopped, and Taylor could see his mind whirling along the process. He became rigid in his chair.

"Oh, my God. Are you saying she was raped?"

Taylor didn't react, just sat back in her chair and glanced at Fitz. He gave her a barely perceptible nod. "Mr. Wolff, all I'm asking is when you last had sexual relations with your wife."

Miles shot up a hand. "I'd like a moment to confer with my client, please."

"It's really not that difficult a question. Mr. Wolff, how about it? When did you and Corinne last have sexual relations?"

Todd's head was on a pivot, swinging rhythmically between his lawyer and Taylor. She could almost hear each distinct turn.

Rose got to his feet. "Don't answer that. Lieutenant, we need the room, please."

She gave it a moment, then nodded. She clicked the remote, turning off the audio and video feed. They stood and went into the hall. Rose closed the door quietly behind them.

"The monitors?" Fitz asked.

"Oh, yeah." They went into the printer room, stood shoulder to shoulder and watched the show. Too bad it was illegal for them to listen in; the sound mike remained off, the tape wasn't rolling.

"Why's he balking about answering the sex question?"

"Fitz, that is an excellent question. I'd like to know the answer myself. Shouldn't be such a big deal, they were married. Granted, according to the kid brother, they'd had that huge fight, but that was a month ago. They'd probably made up. Unless…"

Taylor could tell that Rose was doing all the talking. Todd just sat, head in his hands, shoulder hunched in misery. After a few moments, Rose threw up his hands in exasperation, then looked straight into the camera, motioned for them to come back.

Taylor raised an eyebrow. Rose knew the score.

They went back into the room, got settled, and Taylor hit the button to restart the tape. Rose spoke first.

"I have advised my client that unless you intend to arrest him immediately, he should no longer participate in the interrogation. My client does not agree. He wants to continue talking to you. I've warned him that this isn't a good idea, but he is quite insistent. So. The floor is yours, Todd."

Todd's eyes were rimmed in red. He met Taylor's gaze. "I didn't kill my wife."

"That wasn't the question, Mr. Wolff. I asked when you last had sex with your wife."

Taylor crossed her arms and waited. Todd was obviously wrestling with something. Finally, he took a deep breath. "Corinne and I hadn't had sex for at least a week before I left town."

"Would you be willing to take a DNA test to confirm that statement, Mr. Wolff?"

"Why do you need DNA from me? I just told you I didn't have sex with her."

Taylor glanced at Fitz. He read her gaze and made a note on his paper.

"Because you may or may not be telling the truth, but the tests don't often lie. The autopsy showed that Corinne had engaged in sexual relations recently."

Todd stared at her hard, a muscle in his jaw working furiously. Gritting his teeth. He was trying not to react, and it was difficult for him. She found that response more interesting than denials and lies. What if he did kill his wife? Lying about the sex would be a great starting point for their evidentiary investigation.

So far Todd had displayed little emotion outside of his initial despair at the loss of Corinne. But some people are natural actors. He obviously had a temper, that much was apparent right now. She decided to push a little harder, see what broke free.

"Was your wife having an affair?"

Wolff flinched. "No. Of course not. You've obviously made some sort of mistake. We did have sex before I left. I forgot."

"You just told us that you hadn't had sex for a week."

"I was mistaken. It was the night before I left. I'm very upset, Lieutenant. Surely you can understand that. Details aren't perfectly clear in my mind."

"Okay, Mr. Wolff. That's fine. We'll arrange for that DNA test as soon as we wrap up here. Let's talk about something else for a moment. Was your wife taking any prescription medication that you were aware of?"

The subject change caught him off guard. He sat back in his chair, eyes squinted in distrust. Then he answered.

"As far as I know, she was taking a prenatal vitamin, and some extra folic acid. She might pop some Tylenol if she had a headache or a sprain. My wife was extremely healthy. She was very careful with what she put in her body, even when she wasn't pregnant. But if you've been through the house, you'll have noticed that already."

The organic milk carton sitting on the counter popped into Taylor's head. Okay, so that much was consistent, at least.

"Then would it surprise you to learn that she had a large presence of benzodiazepine in her system?"

"A benzo what?"

"A benzodiazepine called lorazepam. It's a prescription anti-anxiety medication. Ativan is the brand name. We found a therapeutic level in her bloodstream."

Todd was shaking his head dismissively. "There's no way."

"Unfortunately, there is a way. She'd been taking it for several weeks at least, according to the medical examiner's office. Are you sure you don't remember anything about it? She never mentioned feeling anxious, calling the doctor, getting the prescription?"

"No. There's no way she was taking anything like that. Hell, she wouldn't even drink a cup of coffee since she found out she was pregnant. There's no way she knowingly took any kind of prescription drug. God, not without telling me first."

"Who is her obstetrician?"

"Katie Walberg. At Baptist. She's been going to her for years. They're big buds. You can ask her, she'll back me up. No way Corinne would do anything to jeopardize the pregnancy. If she was anxious, she would have told me. Trust me on that." He crossed his arms again and clenched his teeth. Taylor recognized the signs. He was getting defensive, and that meant he was hiding something.

"We'll be sure to contact Dr. Walberg this morning as well. It seems, Mr. Wolff, that your wife was doing a few things outside the scope of your knowledge. Is there anything else you'd like to tell us before we tear your life apart? Because trust me, the more you lie, the worse this gets. There's nothing I can do to help you if you keep lying to me. If you tell me the truth, I'll be able to fight for you. But if you're being dishonest with me, I won't give you a second chance. Do you understand what I'm saying?"

Todd looked her in the eye and nodded. "I'm not lying."

"The hotel you supposedly stayed in doesn't have any record of you over the weekend."

Todd looked wild-eyed at his lawyer. Rose put his hand down on the table. "We're done here, Lieutenant. Charge him, or we're leaving."

Taylor let a silence settle on the room before she answered. "All right. You guys sit tight. I'll have one of our crime scene techs come take the DNA sample, and then I'm going to go talk with Dr. Walberg. Make yourselves comfortable. I'll be back."

She and Fitz rose and left the two men behind.

"Wow," Fitz said. "Nice bombshells."

"He's changing his story. Let's give them some time, see if he changes it again."

They split in the hallway, Fitz to go handle the DNA collection, Taylor to talk with Corinne's doctor. Taylor went back to the homicide offices. Marcus was sitting at her desk, the phone to his ear. She dropped in the guest chair opposite him and waited. He was muttering into the phone, writing rapidly on a sheet of paper. After a few moments, he thanked whoever he'd been talking to so intently and hung up. He gazed at Taylor for a brief second, then handed her a sheet of paper.

"We need to arrest Todd Wolff."

Sixteen

Taylor read the sheet Marcus handed her twice, chewing on her lower lip. Damn. Marcus was right. She needed to arrest Todd Wolff. Suspects lie about the stupidest things, and Wolff had been telling some whoppers. But not enough to push her over the edge into believing without a doubt that he'd actually killed Corinne. But this was evidence that she could use for an arrest warrant.

"Who found this?" Taylor asked.

"Tim Davis. He just faxed the report to us a few minutes ago. I called him to double-check his findings. He's back at the Wolff residence right now, combing through the house again. He said he'd call immediately if anything else popped up."

Taylor read through the report a third time, focusing on the line Marcus had highlighted in pink.

Blood drops found in two areas of decedent's husband's vehicle. The first grouping of .20 centimeter diameter blood drops are collected from the gearshift column of a 2006 Lincoln Navigator, black in color, registered to Theodore Wolff. The second grouping of .5 centimeter blood drops appears on the inside left corner of the silver built-in tool box custom made to fit the rear of the Navigator. Both areas have been collected and submitted for DNA testing, but initial examination show them to be A positive, matching the blood type of the decedent, Corinne Wolff.

Well, wasn't that just the shit. Corinne's blood in her husband's truck. They would need to do further testing to prove that it was actually Corinne's blood, and there was always the chance that the blood was old, unrelated to the murder. But that would be awfully convenient. On its face, this was enough to both secure a warrant, and to convene the grand jury and to seek a true bill indicting Todd. The first step in any solid investigation, physical evidence collection, so often cut through the bullshit the criminals were spewing.

"What do you want to do?" Marcus asked, leaning back in her chair. He looked good behind her desk, she'd give him that.

Taylor drummed her fingers along the edge of frayed wood. She rarely saw this side of her desk anymore, though she'd spent years in this very chair, reporting facts to her superiors. The wood was splitting in two areas, the new damage most likely from a chair being scraped along the edge of the desk. She fingered the gashes. She liked the change; this old perspective made her feel like she was back in the trenches.

"Well, we already have Todd here. Fitz is setting him up for a DNA test. We'll have to ask the lab to do a quick blood typing on the sample, make sure Todd isn't A positive, then we can get the warrant prepared. Julia Page will be able to convene the grand jury session once we've got the blood type established. I need to do some follow-up on the drug found in Corinne's system. You say Tim is still at the house?"

"Yes. He was going to fine-tooth everything again, just to be absolutely sure he hasn't missed anything before we release the scene."

The phone on Taylor's desk rang, and Marcus read off the caller ID to her.

"Well, speak of the devil. This is Tim Davis calling you right now. Here." He picked up the phone receiver and handed it to Taylor.

"Lieutenant Jackson," she said into the phone.

"Hi, Lieutenant. This is Tim Davis. I'm at the Wolff crime scene, and I've got something I think you need to see."

"Marcus just gave me your report on the biological evidence you've found in the husband's truck. Is there more of the same in the house that we missed?"

"Oh, no ma'am, I've collected every bit of biological evidence that is relevant to this case. I've gone through the house several times, on my hands and knees in the appropriate sections. I've got all of that. This is something…well, you just need to see it for yourself, ma'am. It's in the basement, ma'am."

Tim wasn't a fly-by-night kind of guy. If he felt that strongly that Taylor needed to attend him at the scene, that's what she was going to do.

"I'm on my way, Tim. Hang tight." She hung up, stood and stretched.

"Okay, Marcus, do me a favor. I need you to call

this Dr. Katie Walberg while I go out to the Wolff house. See if you can get me in to see her, today. I'll talk to you in a bit."

Taylor grabbed an unmarked Impala and headed toward West Nashville. She crossed the Woodland Street Bridge and took the highway. It would be faster that way. As she drove, the sun disappeared, roiling black clouds building on the horizon.

Traffic was light, a pre-rush-hour reprieve. Her cell phone rang and she answered. It was Marcus.

"I've got a couple of things for you. First off, I talked to Dr. Walberg. She couldn't stay on the line, she's in the middle of a delivery. She confirmed that Corinne Wolff was a patient, but can't release any of the records without a court order. She was real nice about it, just needed to cover her ass. I've put in the request. She said she'd call back after the delivery, as long as she knows the papers are in the works she's happy to talk to you."

"Okay. I'll just plan to swing back by her office when I finish here."

"You know, LT, I can do that for you. There's no need for you to be running around doing all the legwork on this case. That is why they gave you the title, you know."

She grinned. Marcus always knew just the right thing to say. "I know you can, Marcus, and I appreciate the offer. It feels good to be out and about, you know?"

"I know. Management definitely puts a crimp in your style. No worries, LT. I'll handle the warrant and let them know you're coming in, then I'll get back to your mystery man from last night. I haven't found anything yet, but I'm early into it. This Wolff stuff derailed my morning. I'll let you know. Now, there's something else. About the rabbit."

"Oh yeah. Tim can go do it later."

"He sent Keri McGee. She just called me. There's no rabbit."

"Of course there is. I saw it. I put a flowerpot over him. Did she go to the right house?"

"Yeah, she did. The flowerpot is on the side of your house, and the rabbit was gone. Maybe one of your neighbors cleaned it up thinking they were helping?"

Taylor thought about that. A logical explanation. So why was the hair on the back of her neck standing on end?

"You're probably right, Marcus. I'm sure that's the deal. I'll ask around when I get home. The folks next door have a couple of dogs, they were probably making a ruckus, smelling something dead. Tell Keri thanks for trying for me."

They hung up. Taylor took the Charlotte Avenue exit and cut through Hillwood into the Wolffs' neighborhood. She pulled into the cul-de-sac and parked behind Tim's Metro Crime Scene truck.

Tim was sitting on the front porch swing, unmoving, his back so straight that it didn't make contact with the seat back. He hopped to his feet as soon as Taylor exited her vehicle.

"Hey," she said.

"Hey, yourself. Sorry to drag you back out here, but you need to see this in person before I start disassembling."

"Disassembling what, Tim? Now that I'm here, clue me in."

He blushed and looked away, eyes cutting to the

right. Oh, good grief. Old-fashioned Southern men, they actually believed in respecting women. Her curiosity won out over teasing him. "Fine. Just show me if you're too embarrassed to talk about it."

He nodded once, then whipped around and headed into the house. Taylor followed. He went directly to the basement stairs, headed down without a word. The air smelled cool and musty, similar to the day before. When they reached the bottom, Taylor saw Tim's light rigging set up, the five-hundred-watt beam pointing to a spot on the wall.

He was talking again, his words jerking out of his mouth rapid fire. "I was moving some of the boxes, looking for anything I might have missed. A box fell off the stack here." He pointed to a cardboard bankers' box, the contents spilled on the concrete floor. Plastic jewel cases, the kind that house music compact discs, were spread across the floor, the flash of the silver contents catching the light from the stairwell.

"Were they bootlegging CDs? Let me guess, there's cartons of cigarettes too. The Wolffs are working for Al-Qaeda." Taylor threw Tim a smile to let him know she was kidding. Poor boy was so serious all the time.

"It's worse than that, LT." Tim walked around the spilled box and went to the back wall, the one that was painted. He knocked on the cement. Instead of making no noise, a sharp clang rang out. Raising an eyebrow at Taylor, he pushed. The entire wall swung away, opening into a dark gap.

"A secret chamber. Cool."

Tim just shrugged in answer and disappeared into the wall. Taylor followed him. The air changed in this room, there was no must, no humidity. It smelled of Clorox.

Tim hit the lights, and Taylor sucked in her breath. Her first impression was medieval torture chamber. The second was film studio. Tim stayed quiet, giving her a moment to process. There was a double bed in the center of the twelve-by-twenty-four-foot space made up with white sheets and a white down comforter. Fluffy pillows completed the ensemble. To the right was a peg board, filled from top to bottom with various…well, the only thing she could think to call them was *accessories*. Sex toys, whips, a dominatrix hood and rubber merry widow, gag balls, dildos, vibrators. It was a veritable sex store, all tucked neatly away in the basement of the suburban family home. Taylor had seen plenty of these accoutrements on various crime scenes. What she hadn't seen was a sex chamber equipped with two professional video cameras, a boom, four different mikes and strategically placed lights.

"They're making pornography?" Tim asked, the tremor in his voice belying his normally staid demeanor. Tim was horrifically discomfited, that much was evident. A good churchgoing man, he wouldn't be a big fan of the Wolffs' sideline.

Taylor walked around the space, looking. "Good assumption. One of them was, at least. It's certainly possible that Todd was running the show and Corinne didn't know, or vice versa. But I doubt that. Something this elaborate, it would be hard to hide from your spouse. I'd like to look at the boxes out there again."

She left the room, made her way back to the boxes. She started to reach for one, then stopped. "Tim, have you printed this stuff yet?"

"No, ma'am. I just backed out and called you."

"Are they labeled?"

"Only with dates. They go back a few years."

Taylor sighed. "Well, we're gonna have to process this entire setup. I'll poke at a couple of these discs, see if I can find anything recent." She looked around the basement one more time. "I daresay you'll find both Todd and Corinne's prints down here. I want to know if you find anyone else's."

Taylor picked through the CDs with a pencil, selected a few at random with dates that ranged from 2005-2008, waited for Tim to print their jewel cases, then took the contents with her and started for Baptist Hospital. Tim had called in backup; it was going to take all afternoon to process the sin den, as Taylor had named the Wolffs' playroom.

In the meantime, she still needed to speak with Corinne's doctor.

What in the name of hell was Todd Wolff doing with a mini movie studio in the basement of his house? And just how many more secrets could there be, hidden behind the façade of the Wolffs' perfect life?

Seventeen

Taylor pulled under the portico entrance to Baptist Women's Health facility, flashed her badge at the valet. He pointed to a spot at the front, and she left the car there.

The directory listed Dr. Walberg's office on the seventh floor. She pushed the up button on the left side of a bank of elevators, the doors to one opposite her slid open. Once inside, Taylor glanced in the smooth, mirrored wall surface and cursed. She pulled her hair out of its ponytail and shook it, turning upside down and running her fingers through as a makeshift comb. The humidity coupled with the threat of rain had created a riotous mass of baby curls around her face, which caused her hair to get wavy and stick out in all directions. She flipped back up, gathered the mess into her left hand and wound the holder back into place. She was swiping on Burt's Bees pomegranate lip balm when the doors clanged open.

A hugely pregnant woman appeared, her belly distracting Taylor from noticing anything else about the woman. Well, *she* was in the right place. Taylor held the elevator doors for her. The woman waddled in and gave her a tired smile.

"Damn Braxton Hicks. I thought this one was for real."

Taylor tried for sympathetic as the doors slid closed, then grimaced. Not her idea of a fun day, that. She hadn't felt the tug, the desire for motherhood yet. And pushing thirty-six, she was going to have to think about it. But not right now. She'd had a scare a few months prior, and that had been enough to convince her that she was not, by any means, ready.

On the seventh floor, she went a few feet down the hallway and entered Suite 702. The door opened into a large space full of comfortable chairs and baby magazines. Dual receptionists looked up in unison.

Before Taylor could say a word, the woman on the right stood and waved her toward a door that said PRIVATE. Taylor crossed the waiting room, ignoring the looks from the curious. She opened the door and the receptionist greeted her.

"You must be that policewoman the doctor said was coming over."

"How did you know?" Taylor asked, shaking the woman's hand and handing her a card.

"Honey, I know all our patients. We aren't scheduling new clients these days. Dr. Walberg's practice is full up. And the gun is a bit of a giveaway. Who do you see?"

"Oh, um," Taylor started, and the receptionist just smiled.

"Make sure you get your annual and a Pap, dear. And don't forget your monthly breast exam."

"I did. I won't. I mean, I will." Taylor shook her head. "Is Dr. Walberg—"

"She's waiting on you right now. Here you go."

The receptionist knocked once on a wooden door, then opened it. A small woman with dark gray hair and wireless glasses sat behind a massive mahogany desk.

"Dr. Walberg? Lieutenant Jackson is here."

The doctor popped out of her chair with a litheness that belied her age, came to the door and shook Taylor's hand. "Thank you, Darlene." She nodded in dismissal at her receptionist, then closed the door behind her.

"Hello, Lieutenant. I'm sorry to meet you under these circumstances. Most of my work involves happiness, not murder. Can I get you anything?"

"I'm fine, thank you."

"Good. Here, let's sit. I have Corinne's file. Your colleague faxed over the warrant, so I'm free to discuss anything you need to help solve this case."

"I appreciate that, doctor." Taylor sat, crossed her legs and rested her hands in her lap. "My first question is, did you prescribe lorazepam for Corinne? We found therapeutic levels in her bloodstream."

"Yes, I did."

Taylor was taken aback. "Really? I thought that it wasn't good for pregnant women."

"Considering some of the alternatives, lorazepam is the best choice for pregnancy. Especially in the third trimester. Corinne was having episodes, panic attacks. She asked for something benign to help take the edge off. I also gave her the name of an excellent psychologist who was working with her on some behavioral therapies. Panic disorder is something that can be conquered, and Corinne was making great strides."

"Did anyone else know about this? Her husband?"

"I doubt it. Corinne was horrifically embarrassed by the...lack of control, she called it. She'd always been a major overachiever. She was an athlete, a world-class one for a while. Ever since she was a teenager she had a presence of mind about her that I don't usually see in women twice her age. Everything she set her mind to, she accomplished. Excelled. Grades, sports, boys. The panic attacks were not on her game plan. Of course, I don't think getting murdered was on her agenda either." Sadness crept across the doctor's features. She cleared her throat, and Taylor got the impression Walberg was holding back tears.

"You've been treating her since she was a teenager?"

"Yes. Though her mother probably doesn't know that. She started coming to me right after her sixteenth birthday, before she became sexually active with a boyfriend. She wanted to go on birth control pills and get instructions in the proper way of handling condoms. I nearly laughed that first time. She was so matter-of-fact outwardly, but you could tell that inside she was scared to death. That was Corinne, though. She would never let anyone see anything but the calm, cool, rational, successful side."

"Except you."

Dr. Walberg nodded. "I was frank with her, treated her with respect, then told her not to go to bed with the boy. That she'd have plenty of time to get to the physical side of life. She lost her virginity that weekend." The doctor's face softened, and she smiled. "That girl was more stubborn than any mule. Tell her not to do something, tell her she couldn't do something, and she'd do it just to spite you."

"You liked her."

"Yes, I did. I'd like to think we were friends as well as doctor and patient. She was a lot of fun. Girl like that, so driven, so composed, she reminded me of myself at her age. I took that sass to medical school. Corinne could have done anything she wanted, instead decided to go the marriage track. Not that there's anything wrong with that. I just saw her changing the course of humanity with her drive. It was a shame that she settled."

"And the lorazepam? What was giving Corinne panic attacks?"

The doctor looked out the window. "She wouldn't tell me," she said softly. "Just described the symptoms, said it was getting to be more than she could control, and was there something that could help. She wouldn't tell me a thing. And now we'll never know. Damn her." The doctor took off her glasses, wiped a hand across her eyes.

"The therapist?"

She put the glasses back on and raised an eyebrow. "You're welcome to try. I sent her to Dr. Ellen Ricard. She's downtown on Broadway, by Arby's. In the same building as Dr. Wang's LASIK enterprise." She scribbled a number on the back of a card, then handed it to Taylor. "Here. Call ahead. Ellen's usually booked all week. You'll have to see her after hours. Tell her I sent you."

"Thank you."

The doctor was tensed in her chair, obviously ready to get back to her patients. Taylor paused for a moment, then asked, "Doctor, you said Corinne started coming to you at sixteen. After that first sexual partner, did she confide in you about any others?"

The doctor stared at Taylor, brows knitted as if she were making a great decision. Taylor waited her out. There was a battle raging behind the doctor's eyes. She finally smiled, the gesture not reaching her eyes.

"Lieutenant, I'll tell you this. Corinne liked sex. That was another reason I was surprised she settled down so young. Once she had it that first time, nothing could stand in her way. She was hyperactive sexually all through high school and college. She wasn't giving it away, mind you, she just practiced an overly healthy version of serial monogamy. Before she married Todd Wolff, she'd had dozens of sex partners. Though according to her, when she did marry Todd, that was it. She didn't cheat. Said it would be tacky. I hoped it meant she'd grown up."

Taylor stuck out her hand and the doctor shook it, her own cool and dry to the touch. "Thank you, Dr. Walberg. You've been a huge help. And I'm so sorry for your loss."

"You're welcome, Lieutenant. If you need anything else, you know where I am."

Taylor left the woman standing at her plate glass window overlooking downtown, lost in thought.

Taylor called the number on the psychologist's business card the moment she exited Walberg's office. She let the number ring and punched the down button on the elevator. If she could reach Corinne's therapist, she was only two minutes from her office. After four rings, an answering machine came on with instructions to leave a message. Taylor did, asking for Ellen Ricard to call her back as soon as possible.

She stepped in the elevator and glanced at her watch.

If Walberg was right, Ricard wouldn't get back to her until after five or six at the earliest, when her normal day's schedule ended. It was four o'clock now. Plenty of time to get back to the office, go over her mental notes about Corinne's background, check in on the Wolff crime scene and secure a warrant for Dr. Ricard's records. Then she could start combing through the home movies she'd brought from the Wolffs. Joy.

The sun was back out, the storm clouds dissipated. It had rained while she was inside, hard, from the looks of it. The air had a bite to it; the temperature must have dropped twenty degrees in the wake of the storm. She shivered as she got into the Impala. Crazy weather.

She'd left the radio tuned in to JACK FM and when she turned the ignition, one of her old favorite Duran Duran songs, "Hungry Like The Wolf," spilled from the speakers. Singing along, she turned right on Charlotte Avenue, crossed under I-40, then exited onto James Robertson Parkway. The roads were still wet and slick. There would be plenty of accidents clogging up the highways tonight.

Five minutes later, she pulled into the parking lot of the CJC. Streams of workers were exiting the doors, the day shift over. At least it would be quiet in her office, for another hour or so. She might even have a moment to make a call to Baldwin, see how his day was shaping up. She could bet that he hadn't seen some of the items she had today.

Smiling to herself, she took the back stairs, slid her keycard through the mechanized device and pulled on the door as soon as she heard the lock disengage. She stopped at the soda machine for a Diet Coke, then walked the thirty steps to the homicide office.

Marcus and Lincoln were sitting quietly at her desk, their heads bent together at a conspiratorial angle. They didn't hear Taylor enter the room, didn't move. Their eyes were locked on a laptop placed on top of Taylor's desk.

"Lucee…I'm home." Both men jumped in surprise. Taylor smiled at them. They didn't smile back. Taylor felt her heart do a quick shuffle. She'd never seen the two of them look so serious. Or bleak.

"What's wrong with you two? Lincoln, why are you here? I thought I gave you the rest of the day off."

Marcus looked at her, face distorted as if he were in pain. "I called him in, LT. I needed his help. It's…" He trailed off, bit his lip.

Lincoln took a huge, deep breath. "Tell her."

"Tell me what? Did I get fired while I was out? C'mon, you guys, you're freaking me out."

Marcus turned the laptop around. He whispered, "I'm sorry," then left the office.

Lincoln walked around the desk and put his hand on Taylor's shoulder. "This is my personal laptop from home. Hit play. Don't turn the sound up. When you're done, we'll be here." He stepped out of the office, pulled the door closed behind him.

Taylor stared after him for a brief moment, then sank into her chair. She pulled the laptop onto her lap. The screen was frozen on a black background. A large white box was centered on the screen with a smaller black arrow indicating "play." She clicked on the arrow.

The video buffered, loading. Fifteen percent, forty-five percent, seventy percent, one hundred percent. Taylor's heart was hammering in her chest. What the fuck was this?

The screen stayed black for a moment, then she saw…people. The video wasn't clear by any means; it was dark and grainy, in black and white. But she could easily make out two people. A woman and a man. Naked. Obviously having sex. The man was on his back, the woman on top. The shot was from a slightly downward angle, about twenty degrees right of center. A thick fringe of blond hair hid the faces of both participants. They rocked together, fitting well, neither one frantic, a seductive dance as old as mankind itself. There was subtle shifting, the pace quickened. The woman arched, then stopped moving. The man's arms slid around her body. Taylor saw what looked like a tattoo on the man's right wrist. Her hand went to her forehead, then to her mouth. She knew that tattoo.

The woman moved slightly, shifting to the left. The man's profile came into view. Taylor realized she was looking at her old partner and lover, David Martin. What in the…

"Oh, my God," she whispered.

The woman who'd climbed off David Martin was Taylor.

Eighteen

Taylor fought back a wave of nausea. Her thoughts collided rapidly, a centrifuge of denial. There was no way the woman on the tape was her. But of course it was. As she looked closer, she recognized her sheets, her lamp and the windowsill. This was her bedroom in the cabin. And David Martin was alive. The video had to be at least two years old.

Oh, Jesus. She forced herself to watch it again, then again. All three times, the video ended with a clear shot of Taylor's face and naked breasts as she passed the camera. Taylor knew the path she was taking, she was on her way to the bathroom. The first thing she'd done every time she finished having sex with David Martin was take a shower. Something deep inside her was never happy with their encounters, and she always wanted to wash him out of her as quickly as possible after their interludes.

She took a huge, gasping lungful of air, realizing she'd been holding her breath so long she was starting to see spots. Lincoln and Marcus had seen this. Her team had seen this. Dear God. Where had this tape come from? And how in the world did it get posted to the Internet?

She stood abruptly, knocking the laptop off her lap. It clattered onto the floor. She whirled around and went to the door. She opened it and gestured to Lincoln and Marcus, who were sitting, waiting. They came in the room silently, Lincoln shutting the door on them.

Taylor was trying to keep her cool.

"Sit down, both of you." They sat.

"Where did you find this?"

Marcus raised his head. He looked utterly miserable. "I was looking for the man you had the run-in with last night. I'd been trolling most of the afternoon, plugging in various names, cross-referencing his with Tawny. There was a site that had a match, deep down into the Google file directory. I clicked on the link, tried everything, but I couldn't get to it. So I called Lincoln. He guided me through. We saw rather quickly that it was a partnership site, one that the members have to join to access the videos."

"It's sophisticated as hell, Taylor. I had a bitch of a time hacking it. But I got in. And we pulled up the link that matched." Lincoln looked at her. "You should sit down."

"What?" she asked.

Lincoln swallowed and Marcus looked like he was about to burst into tears.

Taylor gritted her teeth. "What, God damn it?"

Lincoln looked her in the eye. "There are eight more videos like this one. All with you and David Martin. People pay to download them, one hundred dollars a pop. The site is called Selectnet.com."

Taylor felt the world shift the tiniest bit on its axis. Her chest closed and she couldn't breathe. She shut her eyes and willed her body back into action. She would be damned if she was going to faint in front of them. It took a moment, but the vertigo stopped, and she opened her eyes. They were both watching her carefully, as if readying themselves for a defense in case she whipped out her weapon and started firing at them. It was a thought. Jesus. She carefully laid both hands on the desk, well within their sight. They both relaxed fractionally.

"Who else knows?" Flat, girl. Stay emotionless. You are in control.

Lincoln looked at Marcus, then back at her. "Just us. We thought about disabling the videos, but then they'd know we were in their system. They might shut the whole thing down and disappear. There are…other items that we may need to look at in addition to yours. We figured it would be better to wait, show you, and create a plan of attack. We assumed that you didn't know that you were being taped." He said it in such a matter-of-fact manner that Taylor fought the urge to come around the desk and hug him. No matter what, they'd believed in her.

"No, I didn't. I…" Oh shit. She heard the crack in her voice. Do. Not. Cry. You are not allowed to cry. Fury and frustration clogged her mind. She wanted to scream. She wanted to hit someone. She wanted David Martin to come back to life so she could strangle him. She cleared her throat, tried again.

"David Martin is the last person in the world that I would want to keep for posterity." She tried to smile, knew her lips were crooked. Holy shit. What were they going to do? Something like this could ruin her. Think, girl. Her mind felt like sludge, all she could see was the image of her getting off the bed and David Martin's smug, dead features as he watched her walk away.

"We've been running backtraces all afternoon. I think I found the name of the company that manages the site, though they are buried, and I mean deep. It's a firm out in California."

Her head was clearing a bit. "Okay. What was the connection to Tony Gorman?"

Marcus took over. "He's a member of this online club. From what we can tell, the members pay a fee, go through a background check, and are then voted into the membership. Once they are in, they can upload, download, watch anything. There are five levels of membership, each with its corresponding site archives. The more money you put in, the deeper you can go. These videos were in the third level of membership. We looked at some of the others. The first two tiers are all homemade, poor quality kind of stuff. The third was better quality, but still not fantastic. We assume that the higher up the chain you go, the better the footage."

"My God." Taylor sat back in the chair. "Are all these videos labeled Taylor Jackson?"

"Well, there's the good news. They don't have your real name. They call you Tawny from Nashville. So that's where Gorman saw you, no question about that."

"Have you found the son of a bitch?"

Marcus finally smiled. "Yep."

Taylor's cell phone rang, making her jump. She glanced at the caller ID, saw it was Corinne Wolff's therapist. She held up a wait a minute finger to Marcus and answered. A crisp British accent greeted her.

"This is Ellen Ricard. I understand you're looking for information on Corinne Wolff."

The no-nonsense greeting wrestled Taylor's emotions back into place. "Yes, I am. Would you be willing to talk with me?"

"Yes. I can't until day after tomorrow. I can see you in my office at eight o'clock Friday morning."

Taylor glanced at her watch. "Are you sure we can't do it tonight?"

"Yes, Lieutenant, I'm sure. I have a speaking engagement this evening, then a late flight out of town. I'll return too late tomorrow evening to meet. I will see you Friday morning. You know where to find me, I presume?"

"I do. Thank you. I'll try not to take too much of your time."

"Until then, Lieutenant," and she was gone.

Taylor hung up the phone. "Leads on the Wolff case. I need to bring you both up to speed." She ran her palm against her forehead, making decisions. "Okay. First things first. Where is Tony Gorman?"

"Antioch. He lives on Blue Hole Road. We can go pick him up, if you'd like."

"I think the sooner we get tapped into this underworld, the better we're going to be. I appreciate you guys trying to insulate me. I don't know if that's going to work for long. We have to find out how these tapes were made, who uploaded them, everything. I don't know if we can keep it quiet, it's going to take man hours. I will cover you as long as I can without Price catching on." The nausea returned with a vengeance. "Has Fitz seen this?"

"No," they both answered in unison.

"Thank God for that. I don't know if I could ever look him in the eye again. You two are bad enough." She stood and turned her back on them. How in the world was she going to work this?

"We didn't watch them, Taylor. As soon as we realized it was you, we stopped, and started digging. I promise." Lincoln was reaching for her now, his arms around her in a massive bear hug. The urge to weep was overwhelming, but she bit the emotions back again. Crying wasn't going to accomplish anything. She hugged him back.

"Well, it wasn't much of a show, if I remember correctly. You guys are wonderful." She broke away from Lincoln and squeezed Marcus on the shoulder. "Go get that fat fuck and let's have a little discussion with him."

Nineteen

Taylor kept on her feet after the boys had left. She was overwhelmed with the urge to pace, then had to stop herself from calling Baldwin. Despite wanting the reassurance of his voice, that was a conversation she would rather not have. *Hello dear, how was your day? By the way, there are some videos of me having sex with my old partner on the Internet.* No, she didn't think Baldwin would be too thrilled. She'd never gone into any detail about the David Martin shooting, much less disclosed that they'd slept together. Great. This was going to be a huge mess. Damn him! And wasn't it just typical of David, fucking her from the grave. The bastard.

Think, she commanded herself. She cued up the video again. How had David done this?

David Martin had been an uncharacteristic series of mistakes. They worked together, that was mistake number one. He was a dirty cop and Taylor hadn't known until she was deep into the affair. He oozed Southern charm, called her names that annoyed her like *sugar britches* and *sassafras*. He wasn't formally educated, was ex-military like so many others on the force. He didn't call his mother on Sundays, drank too much, and as she found out later, dabbled in recreational drugs. She wondered for the thousandth time why she'd ever slept with him in the first place. Even Sam had raised an eyebrow when Taylor admitted to the relationship.

It was destined for failure from moment one, and that, she decided, was why she'd entered into the affair. She didn't want a husband. At the time, she just wanted to have some fun. David was attractive, there was no doubt about that. There was a base chemistry between them from the beginning. The affair had begun after an intense night where they'd been shot at, narrowly escaping being hit. The two of them had been holed up in an improvised bunker, completely pinned down in a weak defensive position behind a series of metal trashcans, taking fire from some stupid gang-banger they'd been pursuing. They'd barely made it out alive.

That first encounter was a pure adrenaline rush. The result of coming close to death, the urge to reach out and feel something, anything. Common enough among law enforcement.

Then David had seduced her. Cheesy attempts at romanticism—flowers, candy, dates at nice restaurants— the whole she-bang. And she'd let it happen because she was bored. When she realized he was starting to have feelings for her, she broke it off immediately. Soon after, she was promoted to Sergeant, then just as quickly, Lieutenant. David remained a detective. The resentment began there and continued to grow.

When Taylor uncovered David's role in an operation that was highly illegal, found out he was working with a couple of vice detectives who were running methamphetamines through the city, she'd been ready to take him down. David knew it, came to her house and confronted her. Taylor had been forced to shoot him to save her own life.

Now he was finding yet another way to screw with her, this time in the most literal of senses. He'd been dead for more than a year. How had he managed to upload videos of them having sex to this Web site?

She hit play. This time, she turned up the sound fractionally. Nothing came through the speakers. Clicking the stop button, she thought for a moment. She needed to hear the tapes as well as see them. Offsite was the only safe way to do it, but she couldn't leave at the moment. But she did have her iPod. She opened her top drawer, disconnected the earplugs from her Nano, and plugged them into the jack on the side of Lincoln's laptop. Then she stood and did something she'd never done before. She locked the door to her office.

Relatively comfortable that she was safe, she returned to her chair, put the earbuds into place, and hit play.

An hour later, she was exhausted, embarrassed and furious. She'd watched all nine tapes of herself shagging David Martin. She was disgusted at the mere thought of other people watching these intimate moments. It was horrifying to contemplate. Why anyone would purposely allow themselves to be taped having sex was lost on her.

She closed the laptop. One thing she'd learned from the tapes, there were two cameras in the cabin. One was solely focused on her bed. The other pointed from her bedroom into the loft where she used to house the pool table. That camera hadn't been used much, only to show them playing pool, then transitioning into the bedroom. By the angles, she could only assume that the cameras were hidden in the air vents.

That son of a bitch. She scoured her mind for a time when he would have had the opportunity to install the cameras. She never left him alone in her house, rarely let him stay over. Having sex with him was one thing, actually sleeping with him was another matter entirely.

As she fumed and seethed, racked her mind, Taylor never entertained the thought that David wasn't solely responsible for the tapes. That was a grave mistake.

"I haven't done a damn thing. I don't know where you get off having me arrested. Stupid bitch!" Tony Gorman was locked in an interrogation room, spitting mad. He was alone, but yelling at the camera mounted on the wall. Taylor, Marcus and Lincoln were in the printer room, watching him on the monitor while the boys brought her up to speed. Gorman continued to scream, but Taylor simply clicked off the mike. Silence crowded into the small space.

"How do you want to handle it, LT? Want us to talk to him first? He's been pretty feisty since we brought him in." Lincoln was spoiling for a fight. The weeks working on the Terrence Norton case hadn't entirely worn off. His normally urbane exterior had shifted, allowing the strong emotions he usually kept in check to surface.

"I want to talk to him alone."

"Is that such a good idea, Taylor?" Marcus tapped the television screen. "You don't know what he might do."

Taylor stared at the stranger. "I want to talk to him alone." The tone in her voice stopped them both. She felt them shift away from her, trying to respect her space. She turned and looked at them.

"Don't take it like that. While I'm talking, I want you to listen. See what he isn't telling me. Because a jerk like this isn't going to start spewing gospel just because I ask him nicely. Can you do that for me?"

"Of course," Marcus said. Lincoln nodded his acquiescence as well.

"Good. Let's do this." Taylor left them, went to the interrogation room. Shit, she needed to get this resolved, and fast. The media would catch wind of Todd Wolff's arrest any time. The last thing she needed was this bozo taking her away from a murder investigation. But she had to know the truth.

When she opened the door, Gorman practically roared at her. "What took you so God damn long?"

Ignoring him, she got settled in the chair across from Gorman, the small desk separating them.

"I said, what took you so fucking long? And take these handcuffs off of me. I haven't done anything wrong. I don't know why I'm even here. I want my lawyer now!"

"Give me a break. Listen, pal. You're here to answer some questions for me. If you quit your blustering and shut up, you'll be out of here in no time. Assuming you haven't done anything illegal, that is."

Gorman's round face was leaking sweat. His close-set eyes flashed with disdain, and something darker. He had the common look of a bully—little eyes, pug nose, reddish skin and thin lips. Put him in a wife-beater and he'd look like every other piece of trailer trash, a baseball cap and he'd look like a million other ex-fraternity boys gone to seed. She often wondered about the genes that produced this same look over and over. If a defective chromosome could produce mongoloid features in children with Down's Syndrome, perhaps that same kind of genetic anomaly could produce the generic bully facial features. Taylor could see the cruelty in his face. She watched him have an internal debate, then nodded when he settled for giving her a belligerent glare.

"Good. We can be friends now." She lowered her voice, playing up the huskiness, and leaned forward in the chair. "Tell me, Mr. Gorman. Do you like watching strangers have sex?"

He didn't answer, but his eyes gleamed. He licked his skimpy lips and Taylor felt the gorge rise in the back of her throat. Ugh. This guy was even less appealing than she'd first thought. No wonder he needed to watch.

"I'll take that as a yes. I'd appreciate you giving me some information about this Internet club you belong to. Selectnet.com, I believe it's called?"

Tony Gorman was an excellent liar. He was a champion liar. He looked Taylor straight in the eye and told her all about Selectnet.com. He never looked away, never flinched. The skin around his eyes didn't tighten, he didn't move his hands or shift his eyes. His body language alone could have won him an Oscar. He talked and talked. What he didn't realize was the entire time he spoke, his pupils dilated and contracted as he thought up his falsehoods. All in all, she had to give him props. He was a very creative fake.

Taylor was better. She'd known men like this her whole life. Men who felt the woman's place was in the kitchen, cooking gourmet meals, shaking up a martini and making sure their man was serviced properly.

So she let him talk. She didn't listen so much to what he was saying. She wondered, though, why he felt he needed to create such an elaborate fabrication to cover his true intent. After fifteen minutes of his bullshit, she yawned and stretched.

"Well, that is absolutely fascinating stuff, Mr. Gorman."

"I've told you everything I know."

"And it was all crap. If you'd like to get out of these handcuffs, get out of this room, I suggest you start telling me the truth about Selectnet.com."

He sputtered, and she let him go through his denials. Taylor stared at her nails, and nodded. Then she tried again. She only hesitated a moment. Desperate times called for desperate measures. She sat back in the chair, casually draping her arm over the back.

"Tell me the truth now, Mr. Gorman. You'll notice that you haven't been booked. You've just been brought in for questioning in a very informal environment. No one knows you're here. I haven't turned on the cameras. I can do whatever I want to you, and no one will ever be the wiser." As she spoke, she used her right hand to slip her Glock out of its holster and set it on the table between them. Gorman's eyes popped open.

"Are you threatening me?"

"No. I'm giving you options. You can talk to me

now. Or you and I can slip out the back door, without a single person knowing where you are." She ran her fingers playfully along the slide of the weapon. "I'd sure hate to have any accidents with you, you know. We'd have to go on the news and explain your role in today's little charade, explain how we picked you up for…hmmm…child pornography sounds good." She raised an eyebrow at him, smiled.

"I bet we could make that stick, too. You look like the type that might just get curious every once in a while. Am I starting to make myself clear, Mr. Gorman? I hold the reins here. You start telling me the truth about this little club you belong to, or things can go very badly for you this afternoon. Got it?"

He got it. In typical bully fashion, the moment Gorman was presented with real strength from the opposition, he caved. The story he told Taylor made the fury rise in her stomach all over again.

Twenty

The conference room was warming under the mid-afternoon sun despite the dark curtains that covered the windows. Baldwin sat at the rectangular table, Garrett Woods by his side. Atlantic's round moon face was superimposed on the wall, the plasma screen that they used for secure video feeds connected to Berlin, his home base for that day.

Baldwin was bleary-eyed. He needed sleep. Soon. He ran his hand through his hair and yawned, then rubbed his eyes for a second before he continued.

"Sorry about that. Just a little tired. Didn't get the whole story put together until breakfast."

"Not a problem, Baldwin," Atlantic assured him.

"Okay, let me continue. The first name I flagged was Ali Fatima, traveling from Lisbon to Paris three weeks ago. He stayed there for a week, we've got hotel records for him under the alias Andre Guigernon. He flew under the Guigernon name from Paris to Montreal, where he also stayed for a week. It's going to take more extensive searching to determine what he was up to, but we can revisit that. You may want to notify the French and Canadian authorities, see if they have any unsolved murders from those two weeks that our boy might be responsible for."

"I'll take care of that," Garrett said.

"Okay. In Montreal, he became Alexandre Cadoc, flew to Seattle. We had a bit of luck there, SeaTac has a convenience corridor for international passengers which allows people to move more quickly through customs. The cameras in the corridor got a beautiful shot of him. He exited to baggage claim, left the building, and returned two hours later, checked in as Arthur Bleheris, flew to Denver. We have him renting a car there, and that's it. BOLOs are out on the rental, but there's been no trace of him since he started out from Denver. The rental agency has GPS in their cars standard, he specifically requested one without the device. The clerk remembers him saying he preferred to get lost, that was the only way to truly see the country.

"That's it. That's all I've got. I don't know where he is, what he plans to do. There's still no word on who's contracted a hit in the States." He slumped in his chair, stared Atlantic dead in his cold eyes. "Where was his tracker? How could Aiden have engineered all of this so quickly without our knowledge?"

"The tracker is dead."

Baldwin narrowed his eyes. "When?"

"Florence, four weeks ago."

Florence? Baldwin and Taylor had been in Florence four weeks ago. He'd bought her a new ring, they'd giggled like teenagers. And then it hit him. Aiden. Taylor. Both in the same city, with Baldwin as the common denominator. He exploded out of his chair.

"You knew. Damn it, you knew. Why didn't you warn me?"

"We don't know his intentions." That was all Atlantic would say.

"We don't know them," Baldwin said. "Right. He may be on a job, a hit that no one has a record of? Come on. A few weeks ago, he just so happens to be in the same town where my fiancée and I are on vacation. His tracker is found dead, and he comes to the States. What the hell do you think his intentions are? He's after me. He vowed to take me down after the debacle with his family. And here I am, in Quantico, insulated as hell, when I should be back in Nashville making sure he doesn't blow up my life like I blew up his."

Atlantic merely tipped his chin down and said, "We need you to find him, Baldwin."

Baldwin was too tired to fight. Arguing with Atlantic was fruitless, he'd learned that long ago. He turned to Garrett. "I can't believe you didn't tell me this. You know that I need every ounce of information to find this fool. You held back the most important piece of the puzzle. Jesus, Garrett. I thought I could trust you."

Atlantic cleared his throat. "He was acting on my instructions. We didn't want your judgment clouded. If you thought he was targeting you, you wouldn't have been of any use to us."

"Of course. Because that's all that matters to you, isn't it? That I give you what you need. Screw you."

Baldwin stormed out of the room, went back to his makeshift office. Damn them all. They were going to get people killed, and for what? To preserve their gravy train of illicit activities? It hardly seemed worth it.

He put it aside for now. Somewhere out there, Aiden was driving a car toward a certain destiny, and Baldwin could only pray that he'd find him in time.

Twenty-One

Using the information Tony Gorman gave her, Taylor set Lincoln to verify his story. Gorman didn't realize just how valuable the information he'd provided was. Taylor immediately recognized the makings of a massive federal case, and knew she didn't have much time.

She'd let Gorman go; Marcus escorted him to the front doors and found him a cab. She didn't think he'd be back for more any time soon. He wasn't a player in this operation, just a willing voyeur. As long as they were of age, there was nothing blatantly illegal about watching other people have sex. He'd be a good boy and stay quiet, Taylor was sure of that. The child porn threat had been a good guess, he looked like a man ready to get home and erase his hard drive as soon as humanly possible. Score one for her talent of reading people. If he got caught up in arrests later, she wouldn't mourn for him.

Drumming her fingers on the desk, she thought about her next steps. She needed to get to the cabin.

The scene of this humiliation. She'd kept it as a rental property—her first home, there was no way she was going to sell it to a stranger. Instead, she'd rented it to two girls from Belmont University. Which meant that one of them had a camera pointed at her bed.

Baldwin. She knew she needed to tell him what was going down. Knowing she was just stalling, she promised herself that she'd call as soon as there was more time to actually talk. She couldn't just call him in the middle of the day to cry on his shoulder about what was turning into the most colossal bad day she'd ever had. Worse than having her throat slashed by a suspect. Worse than being kidnapped on her wedding day. Worse than having to arrest her own fucking father, for the sweet love of Christ.

Stop that, she commanded herself. She bottled up her own emotions, tossed in a liberal dose of the thought of Baldwin's disappointment in her and put in the cork. There was work to be done.

Despite everything happening, her number one priority right now had to be the Todd Wolff case. It felt like she'd been divorced from the process for years instead of an hour. Not trusting herself to make the walk down to central booking to see how things were coming along, she called Fitz's cell phone.

"Heya," he answered. Blessed man. He knew nothing of the craziness that had just ensued upstairs. If Taylor couldn't face Baldwin's disenchantment with her, how was she going to handle things when Fitz found out? She swallowed hard at the thought and put on her brave face.

"Heya back. How's the processing going?"

"Wolff isn't a happy camper. But that's to be expected. It's Miles Rose we need to watch out for right now. He marched out of here about ten minutes ago, swearing high and low that he was going to call a press conference and let the world know how his client is being railroaded."

"Funny, Miles doesn't strike me as the press conference type."

"Me either. But he and Wolff had their time to confer after we did the DNA swab. They both came out of it looking like the cat who ate the canary."

"He doesn't know we have his wife's blood in his truck. He won't be feeling too great when we clue him in about that. What else is going on?"

"I don't know. He didn't give us anything different, no new alibi, nothing like that. He's making all the right noises about being booked. But I got a feeling something's up."

"When's the press conference supposed to be?"

"I don't know."

"Okay. Thanks for handling this. I'll talk to you later. If you hear anything, and vice versa."

"Sure thing. Later."

They hung up. Taylor blew her breath out hard. Lawyers. They could always find a way to get into the fray.

She started to get up but her telephone rang again. The D.A.'s office. Uh-oh.

"This is Lieutenant Jackson."

"Hey, it's Julia Page. I see that we're filing against Todd Wolff as we speak. The general sessions warrant was issued already and the judge is going to set the date for a preliminary hearing, see if there's enough to take it to the grand jury. We'll go for a quick hearing date. Do you have any more new evidence?"

Taylor resisted smacking herself in the forehead. Oh man, the videos. She completely forgot the five discs she'd brought back to the office.

"I might. We've got some new evidence to run. I think you're moving a bit too quickly, don't you? We don't have this case sewn up by a long shot. It's definitely not ready to get to the grand jury."

"It's a piece of cake. He's accused of murdering his pregnant wife. You know how low the threshold for probable cause is in a preliminary hearing. They'll bind him over to the grand jury in a heartbeat."

"Wouldn't you rather have all your ducks in a row first?"

"Slam dunk, Lieutenant. Complete slam dunk. Trust me. We'll get him arraigned and you guys can present the rest of your evidence as it comes in."

"Will he get bond?"

"Maybe. I don't know who's up today. If it's Judge Harrison, no way, no how. But if it's that new chick, Bottelli, she might just spring him. Either way, it'll cost him an arm and a leg."

"Fine. Whatever you want, Page. You're the legal eagle here, not me. Just make sure it all sticks. I don't want to be answering questions on the news about how we fucked this one up. I will drop the blame squarely in your lap."

Page laughed, and not in an entirely unfriendly way. "I know you will. I never doubted that for a minute. Bye." She was gone before Taylor could say goodbye herself.

God, Page sounded like a tiger with a juicy hunk of steak. She could almost hear the girl growling in territorial fervor. Even the most jaded lawyers could get caught up in the glitz of a big murder case.

Too much to do, too little time. The cabin, her feelings, the violation of knowing her naked body was on display for any stranger willing to pony up the cash would have to wait for a little bit. She needed to do some movie analysis.

"Marcus!" she yelled. He came to the door of her office. His dark hair was mussed, making her long for Baldwin. She stowed her feelings.

"Nothing yet, LT. We're—"

"It's not about that, puppy. I've got five items I took from the Wolff crime scene that need to be looked at. In the mood for some more movie screening?"

The look on his face actually made her laugh, which poured from her mouth like a waterfall. Oh, that felt better. She had a brief moment of peace, knowing it was all going to be okay. She wasn't quite sure how, but she'd make it through. It wasn't like she'd been responsible, or willing, for that matter.

"Don't worry, they aren't of me. I don't think. The Wolffs have a rather sophisticated movie studio hidden in their basement, and I believe this is the by-product. Since we're overwhelmed with smut today, let's go see what they've been up to."

Marcus had the good taste to look chagrined. "Okay."

"Hey, do me a favor? Order a pizza or something, I'm starving."

"Sure thing. Pizza sounds good. I'll meet you in the conference room in a minute."

Taylor went into the conference room, popped the first of the five discs into the DVD player. She used the remote to fast forward to the first scene. Marcus came in, seated himself and nodded. She hit play.

Unlike the grainy feed from the Selectnet.com Internet site, the television screen filled with a warm, soft light, the camera clearly focused on a bed. Taylor recognized the setting. It was the Wolffs' basement, no doubt. The movie was certainly homemade, but the quality was fine and the camera operator obviously had some training. A music track, new age jazz, played unobtrusively in the background.

The camera panned in. There were two women on the bed, passionately kissing, writhing together. They were mostly naked, though one was wearing a bra without cups so her full breasts showed, jutting up at an absurd angle. The other had a jeweled belt around her waist and nothing else. Taylor started to look away, then saw a man enter the picture. Todd Wolff came to the bed. The women greeted him, taking off his clothes, begging him to join them.

"This is just plain old homemade porn." Marcus was shaking his head

"With our murder suspect doing…jeez, what *is* he doing? Oh." Wolff's back was to the camera and he spanked one of the women with the palm of his hand, a loud slap. Taylor hit pause, swallowing her distaste. By God, she wasn't a prude, but she was tired of watching people have sex.

Marcus took the remote from her hand, hit play, then fast forward. Wolff became a comic figure parroting the act of love, bucking and rolling around the bed with the two women. Marcus left the DVD running and turned to Taylor.

"It's a nice setup. We need to find out if they're distributing it, or using it for their own entertainment."

"I assume we can arrest them if they're distributing it?"

"Well, that depends. If it's done without the knowledge of the participants, of course. But they look rather willing, and from your description of the scene, it would be hard for them to pretend they didn't know exactly what they were doing. No, they might be making legitimate movies." Now he turned red, but plowed ahead. "Have you ever been to the Hustler store on Church Street?"

She gave him the most sardonic of grins. "I take this to mean you have?"

He gave her the same smile. "You're telling me you haven't?"

Taylor shook her head. "No. I've driven by it a million times, of course, but I've never had occasion to go in."

"Well, I think a field trip might be in order. There's a whole section of this kind of homemade stuff. *Naughty Neighbors*, *Slutty Soccer Moms*, that kind of material. There's a big trade for it. Wolff might have been trying to break into the market."

"I think I'll let you do the background for this one." She looked at the screen again. "Maybe he's just a sicko who likes to tape himself having sex with women other than his wife. No wonder she was having panic attacks. I would be too."

She turned back to the television, and Marcus started to hand her the remote. Something caught his eye and he hit play, ending the fast forward.

"I will be damned," he said.

"What?"

"I think we know who was operating the camera."

"Back it up." Taylor sat back in her chair heavily, watching. Marcus obliged her, hitting rewind, then play at the moment that caught his attention.

Corinne Wolff danced around the lens of the camera. Her hair was done up in pigtails. She wore a Catholic schoolgirl plaid skirt and a lacy pink bra with the nipples cut out. Sucking suggestively on a lollipop, she danced in front of the camera, her husband and the two women watching appreciatively from the confines of the bed. Corinne did a slow striptease, easing out of the skirt, unhooking the bra, then worked her way to the edge of the bed. Todd reached for her, pulling her to the center, where mouths and hands surrounded her body until she disappeared beneath them. The shot faded to black, the music ended, and Corinne's moans of ecstasy lingered until the credits rolled. After a brief fade to black, another scene queued and started running. This one was similar to the earlier shots.

"So much for panic attacks." Taylor didn't know what to make of this new information. Corinne wasn't visibly pregnant in the video, so chances were it had been shot several months earlier.

There was a knock at the door. Marcus opened it; their pizza had arrived. He smiled at the young receptionist who'd been kind enough to bring it to them. When she blushed and backed away, Taylor realized the sound from the video was still on. As she hit the stop button, she made a mental note to explain later.

Marcus shut the door and brought the food to the table. They started eating, both thinking for a moment while their stomachs filled.

Marcus talked through a mouthful of cheese. "You realize that blood drops aside, our suspect pool just grew a deep end, don't you?"

"Oh, yeah. We're going to have to find every person the Wolffs entertained in their basement. There's bound to be a few disgruntled actresses running around Nashville. You weren't kidding about the amateur porn at the Hustler store?"

"No, I wasn't. There's a wide selection. I think it would be good for us to find out if Wolff was at that level or if it was for his own personal use."

"This is turning into a very strange day, Marcus. Tell you what. How about you run through the rest of these tapes and see what you can glean. There're more boxes back at the Wolff house, Tim was processing the basement when I left him. It's going to fall to us to go through all these discs. What fun. I'm going to go see if we can have another chat with Mr. Wolff."

"No problem. I'll let Tim know to get me any additional discs he's processed." He looked at her, caught her eye. "What are you going to do about, uh, your tapes?"

Taylor shook her head. "I'm just not sure, Marcus. From what that toad Gorman told us, that operation is larger than we have the capacity for. I think we're going to end up calling in the TBI, at the very least." She picked at the crust of her slice.

"What about Baldwin?"

"What do you mean?"

"Why not let him handle it?"

"FBI instead of TBI?"

"Yeah."

She tossed the remaining crust back into the box. "Aside from several looming conflict of interest statements I could make, I don't think he'd be inclined to be subtle about it. He'd hunt down whoever did this and make them pay. Or shoot me dead. If we can handle this quietly, I'd prefer that." She gave him a pointed look.

"You haven't told him yet, have you?"

"Hell, no. I'd rather eat ground glass. Not exactly the conversation I want to be having, if you know what I mean. I think I'm going to have to talk to Price though. And that may not go so well for me. You do realize that."

"Which is exactly why you should talk to Baldwin. He could shield you from some of this."

"No, he can't."

And I wish that he could.

Twenty-Two

Taylor went next door to the sheriff's office and arranged for yet another meeting with Todd Wolff.

Everyone in the office looked peaked. She guessed it had been quite an afternoon for them. A murder suspect, a famous footballer and fifteen of his cronies, that would be enough to tax any county jail.

Within ten minutes, Todd Wolff was escorted to an interrogation room. He was already dressed in a tan jumpsuit that said Property of Sheriff's Office and wearing handcuffs. Taylor had waved off the leg irons; there was no need to get him more riled up with that indignity. Taylor shook hands with Miles Rose, nodded to Wolff.

"Please, have a seat. Things have moved quickly, Mr. Wolff. I've got a few more questions, then you can head back to your cell."

"I've advised my client not to talk to you, Lieutenant. God knows what you have up your sleeve this time. Fabricating more evidence?"

"Miles, I appreciate your help. Really, I do." The

sarcasm dance. She was used to this part of the procedure—anything the lawyer said would be tinged with
mocking, her response would be scornful, then they
could all go home. Bit players in a nationwide legal
drama, repeat performances daily at the matinee and
evening shows.

Niceties done, Taylor watched Todd Wolff. She held
a manila file folder in her lap, his mug shot paper-
clipped to the front. His face was gray, his eyes bloodshot. His lips held the ghost of a smile, unlike his
photo, which showed his teeth bared like a pissed-off
dog. The congenial college boy was gone, replaced by
a world-weary construction worker. An interesting
transformation. Handcuffs did that every time. Money
might change the outside, but a person's soul was
intact, regardless of the spit, shine and polish a little
cash could bring.

She opened the file folder, brought out two still pho-
tographs. Holding them to her chest, she said, "We've
made some discoveries this afternoon, Mr. Wolff. I'd
like to talk to you about your movie studio."

Wolff raised his hands and used a fingernail to scratch
his eyebrow. His finger trailed off to his temple, and
Taylor could see him massaging it slowly. He didn't
answer.

"Do you have a headache?"

Wolff snickered. "Wouldn't you?"

Taylor nodded. "Probably. Answer my questions
and I'll make sure you get some aspirin before you go
in for the night."

"Whatever." He looked away, already disengaged.

"As I was saying, the movie studio."

"What about it?"

She laid the pictures on the table. Wolff barely glanced at them. Miles, on the other hand, dropped his pen on the floor. The photos were stills from the first video Taylor had seen, the two girls and Wolff. She held back one photo.

"I'd like to know who these fine ladies are, Mr. Wolff."

He grinned at her then, a lupine smile that tore away the handsome, collegian jock and made him look dangerous.

"No."

Taylor glanced at Miles, who was leaning over the table looking at the stills. Getting his rocks off, probably. His face was alight with something akin to joy. Men and porn. What was the attraction? She tried again.

"Mr. Wolff, be reasonable. We need to talk to the women you videoed. At the very least, we need to make sure they did it of their own volition. Surely you can understand that."

"Trust me, they did it of their own volition." He was mocking her openly now.

"Then let me talk to them and find out for myself. Satisfy my curiosity."

"No. I'm done here, Miles. I'd like to go back to my cell now." Slight emphasis on the word *cell*. This was a man who'd suddenly made peace with the fact that he was going to be incarcerated, and Taylor wasn't sure why. She wasn't completely convinced that he'd killed his wife. Yes, circumstance and evidence told her otherwise, but he just didn't feel right for it. Couple that with the sex room in the basement, the fact that Corinne participated in the movies, and Wolff's slightly mordant pride, and something felt off.

"Mr. Wolff, we've found your wife's blood in your truck. I think it's time you start telling us the truth about what happened."

She laid a still of Corinne Wolff on the table. It was one of the early crime scene photos. Todd stared at it for a moment, then started to cry. Rose held up both hands.

"That's it, Lieutenant. We're done here."

She grabbed Rose's arm as they left the room.

"Talk to him, Miles. This will all go easier if he cooperates. You know that. Have him name the actresses and let's be done with this. Have him explain the blood in his truck. If he hasn't done anything illegal, this will go away."

Miles nodded. "I'll do what I can. You know that you'll have to get me copies of those tapes during discovery." The tone made Taylor's skin crawl.

"You can talk to the D.A. about that." She left him standing there, ignoring the smile on his thin lips.

Taylor went back to her office and sat at her desk. She turned on her computer, waited for it to boot up. She let her fingers drum a staccato rhythm against her temple. Tap, tap, tap. Names, names, names. Where could she find the names of the women in Todd Wolff's films?

Jasmine.

Taylor flipped open her cell and scrolled for the number to Castle Salon and Day Spa.

Twenty-Three

"Taylor Jackson, it has been too long!"

"Hi, Jasmine." Taylor greeted her friend with a smile, was enveloped in a lilac-scented hug and left in a dark room to strip. She did, then nestled herself under a luxuriously soft sheet, lying on her stomach, face haloed in a round sheepskin pillow with a hole in the middle. Her nose poked out, which left her feeling exposed and vulnerable. Something in the air, the cacophony of floral scents mingling with cocoa butter and antiseptic that marked the murky interior of the spa, made her feel like she was hallucinating.

Like her name, Jasmine Allôns was dusky and exotic. The woman bled sensuality, as if she were in a constant state of karmic sexuality—a living, breathing kama sutra pose. She made Taylor feel frumpy and prudish, things she certainly wasn't. At least they were the same height. Taylor liked being able to look in Jasmine's sloe eyes while she lied.

Now, Taylor, she chided herself. Jasmine didn't need to lie any more.

Taylor was one of the few people who knew that Jasmine Allôns used to be called Jazz and spent her days and nights sliding up and down a silver pole for a living. Underage when she went to work for an unscrupulous club owner, Jazz became a headliner almost immediately. Taylor had busted Jasmine for solicitation when she was fifteen, turning her hard-earned dance lessons into a profit in the back seat of her car. Not a story that was terribly unknown in Nashville. Jasmine's tale just had a different genesis.

Jasmine's parents were immigrants who'd lost their downtown store in a racist firebombing. A block of businesses and their home went up in the conflagration too—they lived above their 2nd Avenue poster store— leaving them homeless and a vulnerable target of derision and hate. Jasmine's Iranian mother had a degree in molecular biology from the American University in Baghdad, her Iraqi father was a former nuclear physicist who sought and received asylum during the first Iraq war in the early nineties. Which qualified them to open a poster store and drive a cab through the streets of Nashville, respectively. They were both taking the necessary classes to become American citizens when they lost the store. It was the last straw for an impressionable teenage girl who'd been uprooted time and again over the course of her tender years.

Jasmine had always been too radical for her parents' taste. She hated that her parents weren't allowed to follow their academic pursuits in their new country. She fought with them constantly. She forsook their surname and adopted Allôns; her new American friends accepted the name at face value, simply believing Jasmine when she claimed she was French. Foreign was foreign in the south, especially for people of European origin. Unless marked heavily by discernible accent or specific, predisposed-for-recognition features like head scarves for Muslims, not too many locals had the international experience to argue a nationality declaration.

When the store was gone and her family's future uncertain, Jasmine had lashed out, ultimately committing the cardinal sin. She fell in love with a white boy. She left her parents to deal with their newfound problems and ran away with her brand-new boyfriend.

Of course, like her parents warned, the young man turned her on to things she shouldn't have had access to—sex and drugs, mostly. It was an age-old story, a cliché of teenage want and wantonness. She became addicted to crack, started listening when her boyfriend said she could make some money to buy more drugs if she plied her wares on the street. Too smart to become a whore, she'd gotten an "interview" at a strip club, lied about her age and her drug problem, and was hired on as a featured dancer at the Deja Vu on Demonbreun Street. She shook what God gave her five nights a week and one weekend matinee mere blocks from her parents' gutted life.

Jasmine's quick and slippery slope ended when Taylor caught her blowing both a crack pipe and a patrol officer who knew better on his lunch break in the parking lot behind Deja Vu.

There was something about Jasmine's eyes that haunted Taylor. She'd ended up vouching for the girl when it came time for her sentencing, managed to get her supervised probation. She helped Jasmine get back into school, got her a job washing dishes at a restaurant, and watched the girl get off the drugs. Applauded her when she graduated college with a degree in kinesiology. Jasmine was her success story. She didn't have many.

Jazz used to make three thousand dollars a night bending herself around the stage in Lucite platform sandals. Now, Jasmine cost one hundred fifty dollars an hour as a massage therapist. She did Taylor for free.

And she had her slender finger on a spiderweb of silk back into her old life. Taylor knew Jasmine did very quiet volunteer work with girls she identified with, tried to get them out of the life, show them a better way. Jasmine's parents, newly accepted as citizens, had a new home and a new vocation too, operating an off-the-books halfway house for the girls Jasmine thought would be receptive to a new life.

Taylor didn't go to Jasmine for information often. She respected the changes the younger girl had made to her life, that she never played herself off as a victim. Taylor wasn't fond of people who wouldn't take responsibility for their actions. Jasmine did, and didn't apologize for the mistakes she made.

On the verge of sleep and drowsy with memories, Taylor didn't hear Jasmine come into the room. She jumped slightly when Jasmine ran her hand down her naked back, adjusting to being touched by a woman. There was nothing sexual in the grazing, just a masseuse getting in tune with her client's rhythm, but it always took Taylor a moment to relax. Jasmine knew this, didn't rush it. When Taylor's shoulders slumped and her buttocks unclenched, Jasmine started in on the trapezoid muscles, digging her thumb pads deep into Taylor's stiff neck. She sighed. God, that felt good.

After about fifteen minutes, Jasmine finally asked, "So?"

Taylor didn't insult her by pretending she was just there for a rubdown. "I need some information."

"What kind of information?"

"Your kind. I'm looking for a couple of girls. They showed up in a video at a crime scene. Homemade, good quality stuff."

"Sex or just strip?"

"Sex. Bisexual group sex as well as hetero. They didn't exactly seem like they were doing it against their will. But they're young. Couldn't be more than eighteen, maybe younger."

"You gonna bust them?" Ah, Jasmine, always the protector.

"No. Just talk. I need to get some answers, see if they know the brains behind the operation. I've got a suspect who's going to go to trial for murder, and I'm not sure he did it."

There was silence for a few moments, then Jasmine said, "Flip." She raised one edge of the sheet and Taylor, groaning, scootched over onto her back. Once she was settled, Jasmine silently started working on her right hip flexor, kneading the muscle into submission.

Taylor waited. Jasmine knew something already. Even in the dark, waves of intensity came off her body, as readable as smoke signals.

They didn't speak again until Jasmine got seated at the head of the table, stuck both hands under Taylor's shoulder blades and started sliding her fingers into the muscles along the back of Taylor's neck.

"This is about Todd Wolff, isn't it?"

Taylor nearly jumped off the table, and Jasmine laughed. "Relax. I think I can help. For what it's worth, as far as I know, he's harmless."

"I hardly think a man who tapes himself having sex with women other than his wife is harmless."

"And his wife being dead may controvert that impression, but he is. From what I know, he pays well, doesn't ask for anything kinky. All the models are at least sixteen. It's not parochial sex, but it isn't the weird shit."

"Home use only?"

"There I can't help you. I don't know. But I can get you a face-to-face with one of the girls I know who may have done some modeling for him."

"That's what the kids are calling it these days?"

"Oh, Taylor, where have you been?" Jasmine was finishing up now, and patted Taylor on the shoulder to indicate she was through. Taylor sat up, wound the sheet around her torso and cracked her neck with an audible pop.

"What do you mean, where have I been?"

Jasmine slipped the lights up a notch. The gloom in the room went away, replaced by a soft, relaxing glow. The bulb was coated in freesia aromatherapy oil, and the warmth helped the scent disperse throughout the small room. Jasmine pulled her stool from the head of the table and sat, facing Taylor. Her deep black eyes did a ballet of sadness.

"Sex is in, Taylor. These girls are doing film because they want to, not because they're being exploited. It's a status symbol now."

"A status symbol?"

"Yeah. Used to be when you were coming up, having sex with your boyfriend was something only the slutty girls did."

"Well, the slutty girls were the ones who didn't care if people knew they were having sex. The rest of us just kept our mouths shut."

Jasmine smiled. "Now, these high-schoolers are made fun of if they don't have at least three or four partners. You've heard of 'friends with benefits'? Kids who have sex but don't date? This is the next step. I've heard of a club, a secret society that's making the rounds of the private schools. Home movies. They get points for every act—man, woman, oral, anal. The goal is to sell the tape, get it on the Internet. One even made its way to a legitimate commercial distributor, but got yanked when they found out the actors were underage. There's enough of a draw for good amateur porn in the industry to support these foolish actions. Sad, but true.

"And these stupid kids, they see Paris Hilton's sex tape and think they'll get famous if they can score a slot on YouTube. They don't realize how pervasive this industry can be. How dangerous the life can be. I'd be willing to bet most of them don't realize that their parents could probably buy their tapes off the Internet."

Visions of the scenes from Selectnet.com crowded her mind. Taylor shook her head, unable to imagine an underage girl doing this actively and willingly. "I had no idea. Why didn't you tell me?"

"No offense, but it's just not my problem. I need to focus on the girls who actually need help, not worry about some little brat who's driving Daddy's BMW out on Friday night to go blow Todd Wolff so she can get into the club."

"Jesus." Taylor felt sick to her stomach. Kids were so fucking stupid sometimes.

"Yeah, well. I don't think he's going to be much help with this. Let me get the number of the girl I think will talk to you. She's been ostracized from the pack, is quite busy turning her life around. She might be willing to tell you some back-story. I can't promise anything."

"Thank you, Jasmine. I appreciate it more than you know."

Jasmine left her, and Taylor dressed quickly. As she pulled on her boots, Jasmine came back in and handed her a slip of paper with a phone number and a name. Thalia Abbott.

"Treat this as fruit of the poisonous tree?"

Jasmine laughed. "You can use my name. She's a good kid. Got back on the right track, is trying to help get other girls out of it."

"How old is she?"

"Seventeen."

"God, I had no idea," Taylor repeated. It took a lot to shock her. This qualified.

"Well, now you do. I've got another client. Will you be okay?"

"Yeah. Thanks again, Jasmine."

"You're welcome."

Taylor hugged her briefly. She dressed, then stepped out into the hallway. She looked at her watch. The day was bleeding away from her. She still needed to get to the cabin, check and see if there were cameras in the vents stealing nudie shots of her renters. She was hungry, the few bites of pizza hadn't satisfied her. She missed Baldwin. She was covered in slick massage butter, her hair sticking out in all directions. Man, she was a mess.

Out in the parking lot, she got into the truck and stuck the key in the slot. She could slip on a baseball cap and grab a bite at Jonathan's, call the cabin, see if the girls would mind her coming by. They didn't have a choice; she was their landlord and had a key, and contractually could go over any time she wished, but she tried to respect some boundaries.

She flipped open her cell phone and caught Sam, who agreed to meet her for a drink and a quick bite. She flipped the ignition and started west, knowing that she was close.

Twenty-Four

Baldwin woke, disoriented. He looked around and remembered where he was. He was on the cot in his office. Anger bubbled in his chest, he jumped to his feet. There was work to be done. The ways of the OA often made no sense as far as logic went, and bristling about their decision-making process would get him nowhere.

He stretched, went to the bathroom and brushed his teeth, then sought out his boss.

Garrett was standing in the middle of his office, a landline glued to his ear. He nodded at Baldwin and gestured to the sofa, uh-huhing into the receiver the whole time. Right after Baldwin sat, he hung up.

"Well, some good news, at least. The rental car from Colorado was dropped off in Missouri. Looks like our boy spent the night in St. Louis. Problem is, we've got nothing on him since. None of the names we have on file have shown up within one hundred miles of St. Louis in any direction. Photos have gone out to all the law enforcement folks, but for the time being, we've lost him."

Great. St. Louis was less than a day's drive to Nashville, an hour by plane. If Baldwin's gut was right, and it always was, Aiden could be closing in already.

"You said he was in Europe at last count, and the tracker was found dead in Italy. Do we have any proof that he saw me there? That he saw us there? Has he been communicating with anyone?"

"Atlantic hasn't found anything substantial over there, just the timing. Without the tracker's information, it's worthless. It would make sense that he picked up your trail while you and Taylor were there, don't you think?"

"It does." He was quiet for a moment. "I need to go back to Nashville, Garrett. I can't let him get any closer to her. He's too unpredictable, too dangerous. I don't know what his agenda is, but if he's planning some sort of revenge…I refuse to let that happen. I won't lose her."

"Just give us some more time, Baldwin. We're going to track him down. If we don't have him by tonight, you're out of here. Fair enough?"

"I don't know what more I can do for you, Garrett. I don't know where he is."

"There are still sources that haven't checked in. We may be off entirely, he may be on a job. Give us a little more time to see what shakes out. Okay?"

Great. Just great. He was stuck here, looking for a man who might be headed right at his lover. Perfect.

"Fine," he said, voice tight and controlled. "Let's go find the bastard."

Twenty-Five

Taylor sat on her back deck, watching the lightning bugs. This was her perfect time of day, the heartbeat moments between evening and night. She drank beer from the bottle absently.

This had to have been the most fucked-up day she'd had in a very long time.

She and Sam had shared quesadillas and chips, then Sam shot off to pick up the twins and Taylor called the girls renting her cabin. The roommates wouldn't be home for another two hours and had agreed to meet her at nine. She decided to go home, grab a shower and think.

She needed to talk to Thalia Abbott about this teenage sex club. She needed to ascertain whether Todd Wolff was simply a sex fiend or if he'd gone over the edge and killed his wife and unborn son.

Friday morning she'd meet with Corinne Wolff's therapist and find out what drove a totally healthy, strong woman into amateur pornography, psychotropic drugs and psychotherapy for panic disorders. She was fascinated by Corinne's opposing personalities.

She needed to decide what to do about her own videos.

She was exhausted. The massage had been both a blessing and a curse. In the quiet moments between Jasmine's questions, she'd had time to think about what she'd done with Tony Gorman. Once the adrenaline had faded from the afternoon, Taylor wasn't exactly proud of herself. Gorman didn't give her a choice, but she'd never actually threatened a suspect before. Shit, he wasn't even a suspect, just someone she knew would give her answers. She must have been desperate. What if he came back and accused her of something?

No, he wouldn't. He was a putz. She was fine on that account. What she didn't know was how much longer she could hide the information from Price. Or Baldwin.

Lincoln had tracked down the offices in California that were listed on the billing statements for the Select-net Web site. But the trail had ended there. Despite Lincoln's raw talent for ferreting information out of the ether, even he was stymied. Notwithstanding Gorman's information, most of which they already had, he needed bigger resources. Which of course meant escalating the investigation.

She was tempted to let Lincoln simply wipe her videos from the system. More than tempted. That would cover her ass. But how many other women were in those video files unaware? Could she in good conscience walk away from them too?

She knew the answer to that. She didn't have a choice, not anymore. She took another swig of beer, set the bottle on the deck railing, lining up the bottom of the container with the wet ring its condensation created on the dark redwood. The evening still had some lingering warmth from the afternoon sun, a nice counterpoint to the chilly start to her day. She rubbed the back of her neck, then dialed the phone. Baldwin answered on the first ring.

"Hi, babe. How are you?"

She took a deep breath. "I've been better. Do you have a minute?"

"Actually, yes. What's wrong?"

"I need some professional advice." She laid out the facts in as cool a voice as she could. When she finished, she could hear him breathing in the background.

After a moment, she heard him mutter, "Son of a bitch."

Yeah, you hit that one on the head.

He continued, his voice strained. "Jesus, Taylor. This isn't the best timing."

"Trust me, I'm a little perturbed myself. But that's not the big problem. My embarrassment aside, I don't know how many more videos are up there of other unsuspecting women. From what we could access through their firewall, the vast majority of the videos are just like the ones of me. Dark, grainy, low quality. Hidden cameras. Lincoln hasn't busted through to their higher echelons yet, the better stuff might be hidden up there."

He was silent.

"For God's sake, say something."

"What do you want me to say, Taylor? This is a bit overwhelming. Are you sure there aren't more of you?"

"No, I'm not sure. I'm not sure of anything. All I know is there was a slew of videos of me fucking some guy I can't stand. Some guy I fucking killed." She couldn't help raising her voice. "What is this, Baldwin? Are you jealous of a fucking ghost?"

"Don't start attacking me. I'm—"

"You have absolutely no idea how humiliating this is. My team saw the video. Lincoln and Marcus *saw* me. And God knows how many other people. So yeah, I'm a little upset. And you're not helping."

He was quiet for a moment. When he spoke again, his voice had a dangerous edge.

"I'm just not exactly thrilled with the idea of my fiancée on the Internet, *fucking*, as you so crudely put it, another man."

Taylor caught her breath. "It's not like I arranged for this, or gave my consent. Come on, Baldwin, what the hell?"

She was just about to hang up on him when he said, "I'm sorry. You're right. That was cruel of me. Are you okay?"

"Of course I'm not okay," she snapped. "But I don't have a choice. I need to figure out what to tell my boss."

"Don't do that just yet. God, Taylor. You landed in it this time. Let me look into this. It sounds a lot like a case we had a few years back. We busted an amateur porn ring, a group of motorcycle freaks who were posting videos of unsuspecting women showering in their homes. I'll make a couple of calls, see what I can find out."

"What, now you're sorry about it all and you want to help?" The snide edge to her tone surprised her. That wasn't fair of her. He sighed deeply then, and she wished she could take it back.

"I didn't mean it like that. I just meant—"

"I know what you meant," Taylor said. God. She shouldn't have told him. She *knew* she shouldn't have told him.

"Stop, okay? Trust me, I've got about fourteen different emotions running through me right now. I'd like to kill David Martin, but that's not an option. I'd like to kill you, but you're too far away." She heard something odd in his voice. Jesus, what was happening? Was her whole life going to collapse because of David damn Martin?

"Yeah, well, then I'm kind of glad you're there and I'm here. I'd like to go on appreciating my life, at least as long as I can." She reached for her beer.

"Let me go and start checking this out. I…I'll talk to you later."

The abruptness of his desire to stop talking to her hurt her feelings more than his coldness. She said goodbye and hung up, wishing she had an old-fashioned phone so she could slam the receiver down and he could hear that she'd hung up on him. The button to turn the phone off wasn't nearly as emphatic, or satisfying.

Darkness had descended. Taylor glanced at her watch. Not quite nine yet. She had a few more minutes before she had to head out to the cabin. She went inside, careful to lock the door. The beer was making her sleepy. She sat down on the couch, flipped on the television. He hadn't said I love you before he hung up. She'd never fought with Baldwin before, not like that. It made her nervous. It made her realize that she loved him. She cared what he thought about her. And that was the scariest part of it all.

An unfamiliar calm settled over her, and she fought the urge to fall asleep. Too much to do.

But the room was warm, and she was comfortable. Though her mind was unwilling, her body, deprived of a decent rest for days, won the battle.

* * *

He stood on the back deck, watching her through the blinds. She was deeply asleep, her arm thrown up over her head, a cowboy boot propped on the coffee table. How he longed to enter the house. For now, he was content to watch her sleep. Watch the faint rise and fall of her chest, watch the spot in the hollow of her neck that flashed with each beating of her heart.

She was lovely.

Perfect.

His.

Thursday

Twenty-Six

Taylor was shocked when the sunlight streaming in her southerly facing front windows woke her. She looked at her watch—6:00 a.m. How in the hell? She'd slept for almost ten hours. She was a stranger to deep sleep, much less an entire evening and night's worth at once. She felt sluggish, but when she sat up, she realized how rested she was. Goodness. If she could do that every night, she'd be in heaven.

She got up, pulled off her boots, and went to the kitchen for a drink of water. Looking out the window, she saw her next-door neighbor striding across her back lawn. Knowing he'd be on his way to the back door, she went to greet him. She realized she hadn't turned on the alarm the night before.

Don Holmes knocked a moment later, rattling the blinds, a manic grin spread across his features. To say Don was more of a morning person than she was would be an exercise in understatement. She opened the door, prepared herself for the torrent she knew was coming.

"Morning, Don. How are you?"

"I'm okay, Taylor. Beautiful morning, isn't it? Just wanted to let you know, you had a dead rabbit in the backyard, I took care of it. Someone had killed it, then put a flowerpot over it. Crazy. The dogs were barking at it, so I cleaned everything up, disposed of the carcass. You know it had a wire across its neck? How do you think that happened? Probably some kids playing back in the woods. Anyway, just wanted you to know. I'm in a bit of a rush, need to get to work. Have a good day!"

And he was gone. Her neighbors were very nice, but sometimes a little nutty. Well, that explained that. Getting forensics off a rabbit carcass was a long shot anyway. At least now she knew she hadn't imagined the whole thing.

She went upstairs to shower. Jeans, cowboy boots and a black T-shirt on, she came back to the kitchen, strapped her weapon to her belt, made a cup of tea. Don should be gone by now. She decided to brave the morning outdoors and drink it on the deck. She took the phone with her. She needed to know what had happened with Baldwin while she slept her life away. She knew they needed to clear the air.

Sitting in her favorite Adirondack chair, she returned Don's wave—he was pulling out of his garage. She had all the privacy she'd need.

Baldwin answered on the first ring.

"Good morning," she said, wanting something neutral, not sure how it was going to go.

"Hi." He was short, and said nothing further.

"You can't seriously still be mad at me?"

"Who says I'm mad?" he said.

"You sound pretty pissy. It's not like I asked for this."

She heard him sigh. "Truce, okay? I reacted badly. I wanted to rush to your aid, and I couldn't. And I'm not used to hearing your snappy side."

She thought about that for a moment. He'd wanted to come to her, to help. He was right, she had been snappy. Though she still felt justified in that.

"All right. I'm sorry. I shouldn't have yelled at you."

"What about hanging up on me? Are you sorry for that?"

She squirmed. Being repentant was not in her nature. "Yes. I was being childish. Fair enough?"

He was quiet for a second, and she knew she'd been forgiven. "Fair enough. Why do you sound so chipper, anyway?"

"You'll never believe this. I just woke up. I completely crashed last night. All this shit aside, I feel great."

"Maybe we should invest in some sleeping pills, get you rested like this more often." He was teasing her, and her mood lightened. Everything would be okay.

"Don the motormouth was over here…" She trailed off. She hadn't told Baldwin about the rabbit, or the stalking, or the overwhelming creepiness she'd felt for the past few days. Time to change the subject.

She took a sip of tea. "So, any progress on your end?"

"Yes, actually. We—"

She didn't hear him. Over top of the railing, she saw a man standing in the forest that edged the back of their property. Her heart skipped two beats, then came back with a vengeance, showering her body with adrenaline. Her vision became pinpoint, every detail stood out. She knew immediately, without a doubt. It was him.

The man who left the rabbit, who'd been calling, who stalked her dreams. He saw her looking at him and smiled, then turned and disappeared into the woods.

She looked wildly to the east. Don was long gone, disappeared out of his drive into the neighborhood, his garage door just finishing closing behind him. She was alone. And either hallucinating or in danger.

"Baldwin, I…I need to call you back."

"What is it? What's wrong?" Obviously she hadn't disguised her concern when she spoke—she could hear the alarm in his voice.

"It's nothing. I've got some wacko hanging around, making obscene phone calls, that kind of crap. I'm pretty sure he just came to the edge of the lawn, stared right at me. I'm going to—"

"Are you armed?"

Baldwin sounded distant, a voice she didn't recognize, and the note of menace sent a chill down her spine. She froze, then slipped her hand to her waist, unlocking the flap to her holster and unsheathing her Glock. She palmed the gun and set her finger along the trigger.

"Yes," she whispered.

"Listen to me very carefully. I want you to go inside the house, hit the alarm, then get on your cell phone and call for backup. Do not hang up the phone, Taylor, do you understand me?"

She didn't argue. Stepping inside, she locked the door behind her, went to the panel in the kitchen and pressed the button that would send a silent alarm to the security monitoring system. The call would let them know that she was in imminent danger, needed cops rolling her way immediately with lights and sirens off.

She'd never had cause to use it before, simply pushing the button made the hair raise on the back of her neck. When she and Baldwin had the system put in, he'd insisted on the feature. She wondered now if this was the reason why. He knew something.

"Baldwin. I've tripped the silent alarm. Tell me what's going on."

"I can't, not entirely. This person you saw, describe him to me."

"Hey. Tell me what is going on."

"Taylor, please, I'm asking you to trust me. Just tell me what he looked like."

Taylor conjured the man, feeling her pulse race as he reappeared in her mind's eye.

"Tall, at least six-two. Brown hair, longish, falling over his right eye. Tan slacks, a cream sweater under a blue windbreaker. I couldn't see any more than that."

"If I faxed you a picture, could you ID him?"

"You know who this is? What the hell?"

"Just…go grab this fax. I'm sending it now. I think I might know who it is. And if it's him, you're in danger."

"I can take care of myself, Baldwin. Unless he can stop bullets—"

"Not from him. No one is safe from him, gun or no. Just go look at the fax, Taylor."

His voice was strained and coupled with a note she'd never heard before. Fear. It scared her. She climbed the stairs two at a time and went into Baldwin's office on the second floor. The paper was printing out of the fax machine. She picked it up and glanced at it.

"Yes, Baldwin. It's the same guy."

"Oh, God." Baldwin was breathing heavily into the phone. "Where the *hell* are the cops?"

"Uh, babe? I am a cop, unless you forgot." Her doorbell rang. "Hear that? They're here."

"Check before you open the door." She started down the stairs, listening to Baldwin screaming at someone in the background. Wow, she'd never heard him get this rattled before. This character must be quite the creep.

The doorbell rang again, and she saw movement through the glass insert. She reached for the knob. It felt slightly hot, but she knew that was her imagination. She turned the lock and swung open the door.

The vision before her looked like something out of the apocalypse. Surreal. B-movie cinematic. Two burly men, one blond, one redhead, both crumpled in a bloody pool at the top of her steps. She could see an early-model generic gray Ford Taurus parked on the street in front of the house, knew they were the undercover unit the alarm company had sent. Their throats gaped at her, slit wide from a sharp blade. The redhead was still alive, barely. She could see him mouthing the word *sorry* over and over, his eyes blank, emptying. His mouth stopped moving as she watched.

Her peripheral vision registered the man who'd been at the edge of the woods standing in the grass of the front lawn, hands in his pockets. She looked up and time stopped. They stared at each other, eyes locked. He didn't move toward her, didn't threaten. Then he nodded, puckered up his lips and blew her a kiss. Taylor blinked, hard, not believing what her mind was telling her was happening, and he was gone. Not more than two seconds had passed.

"Oh, my God," she yelled. She slammed the door shut and threw the bolt. Jesus, she'd had a clear shot at him. She'd never raised her weapon. What in the hell?

Had she frozen? Had he been a figment of her imagination? Her training was unconscious at this point, she should have leveled her weapon and taken a shot. Why hadn't she? Confusion flooded in; she came back when she heard yelling.

"What, what?" Baldwin was roaring in her ear. She ignored him for the moment, ran upstairs and secured a second and third magazine for her gun. She came back to the top of the stairs, sat on the step. Putting the gun in her lap, she opened her cell phone, called in to dispatch. Two phones, one gun, and one suspect who was playing tricks with her head. She didn't like the odds.

"Hold on," she said to Baldwin as dispatch came through the line.

"Nashville dispatch."

"This is Lieutenant Jackson. Code three, 10-51, 10-54. Repeat, 10-51, 10-54! Officer needs assistance code three. I need bodies at my location, my home address immediately. I have a suspect on my property, armed and dangerous, repeat, armed and dangerous. He's just killed two security guards on my front step. I don't have him in my sights—I am locked inside the house. I need you rolling now!"

"Oh, dear, sweet Jesus." Baldwin was cursing in her right ear. Dispatch was moving, incredulous at her call.

"Lieutenant, confirm that for me again. You've got a 10-51, 10-54, code three, officers down. We are rolling, lights and sirens, Lieutenant, ETA three minutes. You all right?"

"Confirmed, off-duty officers down. I am uninjured, but I'll be better when y'all get here. Tell them the suspect is six-two, brown on brown, wearing tan pants, cream sweater, blue windbreaker."

"Will do, LT. Be careful."

She hung up. She could hear the faint screams of the sirens already, knew she'd be fine, but her hands were shaking. She slipped the cell back into its belt hook, palmed the Glock. He couldn't unlock doors and get inside that quickly, and even if he did, she had her weapon trained on the stairwell, locked on the front door. Sweat beaded on her forehead, in the small of her back, between her breasts. She took a couple of deep breaths, trying to force the adrenaline back into dormancy. Anger replaced the physical rush. She hissed at Baldwin.

"What in the name of all that's holy is happening here? And how do you know this person? Talk fast, the cavalry is coming."

"Oh, Taylor. I am so sorry. I should have trusted my own judgment. I knew you were in danger, I just didn't realize he'd move so quickly. I'm getting on a plane. I've already got the pilots gassing up and revving the engines. I'll be wheels up in fifteen minutes. When they clear the scene, get out of there. Go to the office, make sure you've got a guard on you. If it makes you feel better, it's me he wants."

"Who wants? Baldwin, you are making no sense." There was banging on her door. She looked out the front window, there were four police cruisers and multiple people milling across her front yard. "They're here. I need to go deal with this. You're coming now?"

"I'll be there in an hour."

"Who is he, Baldwin?" She walked down the stairs, listening to his struggle on the other end of the phone.

Knowing he was coming somehow gave her the courage to open the door, allowing the sight of the two dead security guards to fill her with horror again. Weapons were everywhere, black and dangerous, bristling with unvented fury. Officers surrounded her house, scattering like quail into the backyard and the forest beyond. The scent of blood was strong in the air; the dogs across the street were baying in frantic unhappiness.

"Who is he?" she asked again.

"His name is Aiden," Baldwin answered. "It might as well be Death."

Twenty-Seven

Taylor was sitting in the break room at the CJC, toying with a Styrofoam cup. She looked at the fat industrial wall clock for the thousandth time. Damn it, it was nearly noon. When were they going to come talk to her? And where was Baldwin?

This sense of doom, of not being able to do anything, was worse than anything she'd ever felt. Waiting wasn't exactly what she was built to do. Kick ass, take names, and worry about the ramifications later, that was her job. Sitting around being protected, that wasn't on the menu when she check-marked the box and signed up to be a cop. She was the one who was supposed to be doing the protecting.

Instead, she sat in this overly bright room, away from the nexus of communication. Hell, she hadn't even been allowed to drive herself to the office. Baldwin must have called in to Price, because a burly patrol officer named Bud had bodily taken her from the house and thrown her into his cruiser. He screamed off into the quickening morning with her in the passenger seat, slightly dazed at the ferocity of his action. She wasn't accustomed to being pushed around.

Price had met her at the doors to the CJC, his mustache drooping. Fatigue, anger, hunger—all showed up in the man's facial hair. Taylor had learned to read the twitching of his lips before looking into his eyes long ago. When she realized he was worn-out, she did look him in the eye. What she saw there worried her. More was happening than she was being told.

She'd been debriefed, escorted to this room, handed a cup of coffee and told to sit tight. Price had shut the door behind her and she'd half waited to hear the sound of the lock being thrown. It hadn't, but she decided she'd listen to her boss and sit still. The minutes ticked by, ten, fifteen, thirty, forty-five, fifty-five. Nearly an hour passed with no word. The clock slammed into the top of the hour and she couldn't take it anymore.

Oh, screw this, she thought. She stood, tossed the cup in the trash and got her hand on the door. She opened it to see Baldwin coming at her like a heat-seeking missile. He had dark circles under his eyes, but he smiled. There was still a tiny bit of lingering tension after their fight, but when he put his mouth on hers, all was forgotten. She luxuriated in his kiss, in his nearness. She wrapped her arms around his body, wondering if he was always this warm. She didn't want to be the one who ended the kiss, waited for him to pull back. When he did, she stepped away, breathless, slammed the door and crossed her arms across her chest.

"That took more than an hour. Talk," she commanded.

"Wait a minute," he replied. "Price is—"

The door to the break room opened again and she jumped out of the way. Price entered the room. He didn't speak, just helped himself to a cup of coffee. He sat at the table, took a healthy gulp and grimaced.

"God, that's bad. It must be old." He reached over his shoulder and tossed the remains in the sink, set the cup down on the table with a soft plop, then sighed heavily.

"Captain, what is going on?" Taylor's words were measured. She was starting to get highly annoyed.

Price and Baldwin shared a look. Price's nod was barely perceptible. Baldwin gestured to the chair, indicating Taylor should go ahead and have a seat. With a glare at them both, she did.

"What?" she asked.

"Okay." Baldwin pulled out a chair with a scrape, and sat. "There are two things happening right now. We're searching the woods behind our house for Aiden. He is exceptionally dangerous, and pissed off at me, which makes him even more frightening."

"Baldwin, who is he?"

He scrubbed his hands through his hair. "That is a very long story." He looked at Price. "This guy is on our wanted lists. He's international, which is why you aren't familiar with him. We don't know why he's in the States." Price nodded, and Baldwin turned back to Taylor. "We have something else going on that you need to deal with first."

"Just tell me what's happening."

Both men grew silent. Taylor waited for a moment, doomsday thoughts spinning through her head. When neither spoke, she threw up her hands in frustration.

"For God's sake, I can handle it. Did my dad break out of prison, or my mother die?"

"No," he answered.

"Then the world isn't at an end. Just tell me already. You know I hate this kind of shit. Stop protecting me."

Baldwin looked at Price, then back at Taylor. "The media has your videotapes."

Taylor didn't move, but her heart fluttered. She'd spoken too soon. The apocalypse *was* upon her. "No," she said.

Price cleared his throat. "Yes. It gets worse. There is a tape circulating of the night David Martin died. It shows you shooting him."

"I know I shot him. I was there, remember? He was chasing me through the cabin, trying to kill me. I had to shoot him. It was him or me." Her voice sounded weak, and she sat straighter in the chair. "It was him or me," she repeated more firmly. "Everyone knows that already."

Baldwin nodded. "We know. But the videotape that's been released doesn't exactly show that."

"What are you talking about? If it's off the cameras that took the shots of us having sex—sorry, Captain—then it will show exactly what happened. I've seen the sex tapes. The angle would have been perfect."

"The angle was perfect. But it doesn't look like self-defense. He was begging you not to shoot him, and you take a step closer and plug him." She started to interrupt but Price raised his hand. "I know you didn't kill him like that. Your version of what happened stood up in court, and I know you wouldn't lie. But someone has made it look like that's exactly what happened, and it's been fed to the media. We have a bit of a problem, as you can imagine."

"What's the problem? I'll go on television and tell

them what happened. That whatever they've been given is a fake."

Baldwin and Price exchanged glances again.

Price spoke first. "Taylor, I can't stop this immediately. We have to go meet with the Office of Professional Accountability. They are making some serious noise."

"Now?"

"Yes."

She looked at Baldwin.

"Don't worry, babe," he said. "It will all be fine. Go with Price. I've got some calls to make. We'll figure it out, I promise. Okay?"

Taylor stared at him, recognized that he was barely holding it together. Things must be worse than she could imagine. She licked her lips and gave him a tiny smile. She realized he'd been holding his breath.

"Okay." She turned to Price. "But Captain, tell me one thing. How did this tape make it to the media?"

He had the good manners to look embarrassed. "I got an anonymous phone call around seven-thirty this morning, saying you were filmed in a compromising position. The caller assured me that it was going to air on the midday news. But whoever did this coordinated their attack, Taylor. The sex tapes haven't broadcast yet locally, they are on the national cable news networks. Damn media fuckers didn't bother to confirm the source. It was out before I had a chance to stop it." His voice broke. "And I did try, Taylor. I did try. We could demand they take down the story, but that's going to add fuel to the fire. The sex tapes and the subsequent shooting video, all of this has been carefully planned to take you down. We'll figure out another way to fight it, I swear to you."

Oh, this was not good. This was not good at all. The word *national* replayed itself in her mind a few times, giving her a real flavor of the exact type of shit she was in. Taylor shut her eyes, tried to remember the last time she'd been called in front of the OPA. It was still called the Investigative Services Division then, and it hadn't gone well. There were new people involved now, new management. Maybe this would go smoothly. A knot in her stomach gave way to a fiercer, gnawing pain. She winced, swallowed hard, then opened her eyes.

"Fuck," she said.

Twenty-Eight

Metro's Office of Professional Accountability was freezing cold. Someone had turned the air-conditioning on full, complete overkill considering the still moderate temperatures outside.

It took all of Taylor's self-control not to shake. She didn't want to give the wrong impression, didn't want Captain Delores Norris to think she was scared. She figured the air-conditioning was a trick they used. Anything to make themselves feel more powerful. Price didn't seem affected, just crossed his left ankle over his right knee and sat quietly, obviously lost in thought.

Taylor hadn't had much contact with the OPA since David Martin's death, only a standard investigation a month ago when she'd been forced to discharge her weapon into the killer called Snow White. That was fine by her. The officers of the OPA weren't ever very popular with the rank and file. They couldn't afford to be chummy, had to keep themselves separate, above reproach. No fraternization.

When the ISD became the Office of Professional Accountability, Fitz had immediately christened them the Oompas. Homicide had gotten a good laugh out of that, the name drifted through the ranks until it was almost second nature. Taylor figured everyone called the OPA crew the Oompa-loompas. Behind their backs, though. Never to their face.

When the new OPA captain had been tapped three months ago, the unit's nickname became more prescient, and Taylor often wondered if their Chief of Police actually had a sense of humor. The new captain's name was Delores Norris, and she couldn't have been more than five feet tall. She beat Metro's minimum height requirements by being black and a woman, moved quickly through the ranks and ended up as the head of the most hated department on the force. Her diminutive physical presence only perpetuated the nickname, and it didn't help that she had slightly bowed legs that forced her body into a swaying walk. As she waddled down the halls, a faint strain of *Oompa, Oompa* could be heard. Taylor didn't know how the woman stood being the center of so much derision.

Especially now. At the moment, Taylor was the target of the Oompa's derision, and she didn't feel at all amused by the situation.

Delores Norris sat high, back straight as an arrow, the cloth of her starched uniform jacket not touching the back of the chair. Her hair was cut short, close to her head, with wiry gray curls around the temples. She read a report in front of her, tapping her pen along the manila edge. Every third second, she looked up at Taylor over bright red plastic half-moon glasses and shook her head slightly. After what felt like an hour of this scrutiny, Norris closed the file, set the pen alongside.

"So, Lieutenant. I can't tell you *how* disappointed I am to see you in *my* office today. You've *had* an exemplary career with Metro, one worth watching. I've been keeping my *eye* on you, young lady." Her accent was odd, not foreign, but strange, like she was covering a severe lisp. She put emphasis on the wrong words, making the cadence of her voice grating.

Taylor felt like an errant schoolgirl. Making fun of the Oompa was easy when you weren't face-to-face with her principal's scowl. Taylor just nodded weakly, not sure what the woman wanted her to say.

The Oompa stared at her a moment longer and Taylor swore the woman's lip twitched. Damn her, she was enjoying watching Taylor's discomfort. The realization simply served to piss her off. She sat straighter and looked the Oompa in the eye. She'd done nothing wrong, she wasn't going to be made to feel she had.

"You *realize,* Lieutenant, that these are extremely *serious* times for you. The videotapes of *you* having—" she stopped here, sniffed as if smelling an exceptionally foul turd "—having relations with your fellow officer are one thing. We're going to have to *deal* with these *charges* separately. What's most germane to *this* particular discussion is the video of you shooting *your* fellow officer. In cold blood, I *might* add. This is looking very *bad* for you, my girl."

God, the woman's ridiculous enunciation and emphasis made Taylor want to scream. Instead, she spit, "Oh, sure, let's just skip over the fact that we all know that isn't the truth and that I shot David Martin in self-defense. He was trying to kill me. Might I add the grand jury agreed with that assessment, as did your office?"

"Taylor," Price warned.

Taylor clenched her teeth together. When she didn't speak, the Oompa jumped in.

"Well, Lieutenant, I *must* say that the video is quite *damning*."

Taylor didn't ungrit her teeth. "The video has obviously been doctored."

"So you *claim*, Lieutenant, so *you* claim. But that's not *such* an easy thing, now is it? Stepping on *your* peers on your way up the *ladder* wasn't enough for you?"

"What?" Taylor swung her gaze to Price, who was sputtering with indignation.

"Captain Norris, I resent that implication. Lieutenant Jackson's record is spotless, she earned her way into the position. You are completely out-of-bounds here."

"Am *I*, Mitchell? You've had this girl's *back* covered for years. Perhaps it's time to let her *stand* on her own, spread her wings, and see if she can *actually* fly."

"I don't see that this is the time for metaphor, Delores. We're talking about the career of one of the most decorated officers in the department, a woman who has the respect of the troops *and* her management."

There was no question of the implication of Price's statement, and Taylor fought to keep the smile off her face as the Oompa's head began to explode. The painfully proper elocution vanished.

"How *dare* you imply that I don't have the respect

of the troopsss! Why, I'll have you know that I've been commended no lessss than four times for *my* devotion to this department—"

"Delores." Price leaned forward, his eyes narrowed. "I'm not implying anything about your career path. I'm just saying that in addition to being an excellent officer, Lieutenant Jackson has forged the respect of her peers through exemplary fieldwork, as well as years of investigative practice. She's an asset to this organization. She tells me that the video was doctored, that she did not shoot Detective Martin in cold blood, and I believe her. I'll fight you to the death on this one, Delores. Trust me on that." Price's fury was barely contained. He ran a hand over his bald head, where beads of sweat were starting to form.

Taylor was shocked. She couldn't remember ever hearing her boss tell a superior to fuck off, but he'd just done it. And the Oompa knew it. She darkened to an unhealthy puce and returned her red glasses to her face to cover her discomfiture. She finally cleared her throat and looked at Taylor again.

"Well, my girl, that *was* an impassioned plea on your behalf. Suppose you *tell* us what happened that night." She flipped on a tape recorder that sat at her elbow. "For the *record*, of course." The Oompa smiled, and it was a nasty thing to behold. Still four shades of angry, she looked like a possessed Potato Head doll. The Mister version, not the Missus.

Taylor shook that image from her head and looked to Price, who was frowning, obviously still upset. He nodded, twisted a finger through his thick mustache. "Taylor, tell us exactly what happened. Don't leave anything out."

Taylor sat back in her chair and blew out a breath. She had a few choice things to say to Delores Norris, but she'd have to bite her tongue. No sense getting into a pissing match with the woman who had a say in her eventual sentence. She nodded at Price, took another deep breath, and began.

"Okay. Trust me, every single detail of that night is etched on my brain. It's not like I could forget." Taylor brought up that evening from her memories, forehead creased as she recited the story.

"I was trying to decide how to tell Captain Price what I'd discovered. I must have picked up the phone ten times in ten minutes. I knew how bad this looked, knew it was going to ruin careers. But it had to be stopped."

Taylor hit redial, heard the call connect and start ringing, then clicked the off button and returned the phone to her lap. If she made this call, there was no going back. Being right wouldn't make her the golden girl. If she were wrong… well, she didn't want to think about what could happen. Losing her job would be the least of her worries. She was damned if she did and damned if she didn't.

She set the phone on the pool table and went down the stairs of the cabin. Stepping into the kitchen, she opened the door to the refrigerator and pulled out a Diet Coke. She laughed to herself. Like more caffeine would give her the courage to make the call. She should try a shot of whisky. That always worked in the movies.

She snapped open the tab and stood staring out of her kitchen window. It had been dark for hours, the moon was gone and the inky blackness outside her window was impenetrable, but in an hour the skies would lighten. She would have to make a decision by then.

Taylor turned away from the window, eyes unfocused. There was no other way. She couldn't, wouldn't compromise herself for that fool. An unfamiliar sound brought her back to the moment. It sounded like the transformer at the base of her driveway, a deep electronic humming. A fraction of a second later there was a loud crack, then the lights went out. Her heart pounded and she chided herself. Silly girl, she thought. In this section of Bellevue, the lights blew out all the time. Nashville Electric Service had a crew on call for this area twenty-four hours a day. It sounded like a simple power surge had caused the lights to blow. Now stop being jittery. You're a grown woman, you're not afraid of the dark.

She reached into her junk drawer and groped for a flashlight. Thumbing the switch, she cursed softly when the light didn't shine. Batteries, where were the batteries?

She froze when she heard a different, softer noise. She went on alert, all of her senses going into overdrive. She strained her ears, trying to hear it again. Yes, there it was. A scrape, just off the back porch. She took a deep breath and sidled out of the kitchen, keeping close to the wall, moving lightly toward the back door. Her hand went to her hip and found nothing. Damn it. She'd left her gun upstairs.

The tinkle of breaking glass brought her up short. The French doors that led into the backyard had been breached. It was too late to head upstairs and get the gun. She would have to walk right through the living room to get to the stairs. Whoever had just broken through her back door was not going to let her stroll on by. She started edging back toward the kitchen, holding her breath, as if that would help her not make any noise.

She didn't see the fist, only felt it crack against her jaw. Her eyes swelled with tears and before she could react, the fist connected again. This time, her teeth exploded into her mouth and blood sprayed from her lips. She spun and hit the wall face-first. The impact knocked her breath out. She felt the intruder grab her as she started to slide down the wall.

He moved fast, lightning quick. Now that he had his hands on her, she had the advantage, she knew exactly where her attacker was. She started to turn and duck, but a hand on her shoulder pushed her face-first into the wall. Fuck, that hurt.

She fought back with everything she had. She could tell it was a man, not just because of his strength but also from the telltale hardness pressing into her lower back. Great, he wasn't going to be satisfied with just beating her up, he wanted to get his rocks off too.

Not if she could help it.

She twisted hard, coming face-to-face with his chest. She threw a punch but he grabbed her fist, wrestled her back against the wall. He got his hands around her throat. She struggled against him, quickly realizing that he wasn't there for a rape and a beating. He was there to kill. Since he was overpowering her, she went limp. She lolled bonelessly against him, surprising him with the sudden weight. She took that moment to push off the wall with her right leg and shove with all her might. It created some space between them, enabling her to slip out of his grasp. She fell into the living room, crashing into the slate end table, opening a bloody gash on her shin.

Her attacker lunged after her. Taylor used the sturdy table to right herself and whipped out her left arm in a perfect jab, aiming lower than where she suspected his chin would be. She connected on target and heard him grunt in pain. Spitting blood out of her mouth in satisfaction, she kicked him in the stomach and felt the whoosh of his breath as it left his body. He fell against the wall as she spun and leapt to the stairs. He jumped up to pursue her, but she was quicker. She pounded up the steps as fast as she could, rounding the corner into the hall just as her attacker reached the landing. The lights snapped back on, blinding her for a brief second.

The gun was on the edge of her pool table, next to the phone, right where she had left it when she went downstairs for a soda. She was getting careless. With everything that was happening, she shouldn't have taken for granted that she was safe in her own home.

Her hand closed around the grip of the Glock. She palmed the nine-millimeter, spinning around to face the door just as the man came screaming through it. She didn't stop to think about the repercussions, simply reacted. Her hand rose. Using instinct instead of taking aim, she put a bullet right between his eyes. His momentum carried him forward a few paces. He was five feet from her when he dropped with a thud.

She heard her own ragged breathing. She tasted blood and raised a bruised hand to her jaw, feeling her lips and her teeth gingerly. Son of a bitch had loosened two molars. The adrenaline rush left her. She collapsed on the floor next to the lifeless body.

The throbbing in her jaw brought her back. The sky outside was brightening, the morning light highlighting the horrible mess in front of her. She must have been out for a while. Rising, she took in the scene. The man was collapsed on her game room floor, slowly leaking blood on her Berber carpet. She idly eyed the stain.

"That's going to be a bitch to get out."

She shook her head to clear the cobwebs. What an inane thing to say. Shock, she must be going into shock. How long had they fought? Had it been only five minutes? Half an hour? She felt like she had struggled against him for days; her body was tired and sore. Never mind the blood caked around her mouth and the gaping slash across her shin. She put her hand up to her face. Her nose was broken again. Damn.

She eyed the man. He was facedown and canted slightly to one side. She slipped her toes under his right arm and flipped him with her foot. Maybe there was some adrenaline left in her system. The shot was true; she could see a tiny hole in his forehead. Reaching down, she felt for his carotid pulse, but there was nothing. He was definitely dead.

"Oh, David," she said. "What were you thinking?"

"I still have the scar on my leg from the coffee table." Taylor brushed tears out of her eyes and swallowed the lump in her throat. She shifted, coming back to the present, shaking the past away. She stared at Delores.

"The grand jury heard this story. They felt I'd acted in self-defense. I did act in self-defense. Your office cleared me of any wrongdoing. Whatever you've seen on this tape is a lie. It's been doctored. The electricity had cut out during the attack and came back on. Surely that would give a gap in the tape. It would be easy to fill in the blank."

The Oompa squiggled off her chair. Standing, she was the same height as Taylor was sitting. She looked Taylor over.

"*We'll* be the ones who determine that, Lieutenant. There has *also* been a complaint filed *against* you for harassment and unlawful detainment. It seems *you* had an unpleasant conversation with a possible *witness*. He says you *drew* your weapon. Is *this* true?"

Crap. God damn Tony Gorman. She'd underestimated him.

"That's not exactly what happened."

"We'll see. I think you've crossed *one* too many lines, *Miss*. I'm sorry, but while we investigate, *you're* going to have to turn in your badge and gun. We have to do *this* by the book. *You* are on an unpaid suspension as of this moment, and the *investigation* into your *actions* will tell us what *really* happened the night of your fellow officer's murder. It's *hard* to manipulate a videotape, despite what television might tell you. *And* we'll be looking into the harassment charges as well."

"What?" Taylor asked, as Price said, "You can't suspend her for this! She's done nothing wrong."

The Oompa smiled her crooked smile and held out her hand. "Oh? I think *killing* a fellow *officer* in cold blood qualifies as *wrong*, Captain. I think threatening *witnesses* qualifies as *wrong*. I *can* suspend the lieutenant, and I just did. The public would have *my* head if they thought we were covering *this* up. Your weapon and badge, *Lieutenant*."

Taylor struggled to shut her mouth. She wasn't going to help herself by reacting any more than she already had. The Oompa had it in for her, she realized that now. And that could be deadly for her career. Without looking at Price, who was shouting curses at Norris, she stood. She towered over the Oompa, who didn't blink, just raised her hand higher.

Taylor unsnapped her Glock from her hip holster and set it in Norris's tiny little palm. Then she removed her shield from her belt and set it gently on top of the service weapon. She swallowed and the roar sounded in her ears. Her heart started to pound, and she heard nothing else. She turned smartly on her heel and marched from the OPA offices.

Twenty-Nine

Taylor didn't stop. She ignored Price calling her name, ignored the snickering coming from Norris, just walked straight out of the administrative offices, and out of the building. The sun was preparing to set, the darkness of early spring supple in the sky.

Suspended. And here she'd been worried about Lincoln. That was fine. She didn't care. All she knew was she needed to get far away from the sneer of the Oompa, from Price's indignation on her behalf, from her own memories. She kicked it into high gear as soon as she was down the stairs, her cowboy boots ringing out on the pavement as her steps got faster and faster. She hit full speed, legs stretching out, her stride lengthening as she crossed the parking lot. She went to the first available car, a cream-colored Caprice. The door was unlocked, the keys tucked into the visor. She barely slowed, just threw herself into the seat, slammed the key home, turned the ignition and peeled out.

"Damn, damn, damn, damn." She repeated the word over and over, the mantra helping her calm a bit. The fury boiled over as she pulled out of the parking lot. She never looked back, just focused on the road ahead. She had no idea where she was going, she didn't see anything outside the windshield. She just drove. North, south. It didn't matter. Her cell phone rang. She reached into her pocket and turned it off without looking.

Downtown bled away. Noise and dirt and memories slipped away. She drove and drove, unaware.

She exited the highway when the full moon captured her attention. She'd been driving in circles around Nashville, delving into the backroads would be her escape. She got on a windy, two-lane road heading west. She knew the area well enough to realize she was well south of Franklin, somewhere below Leiper's Fork. She knew her way home, she could drive straight west until she hit the Natchez Trace, then drive north. The back way home. Fitting really. She'd never been able to take the easy path through life, but always ended up somewhere that she could find her way.

The night sky was deepening, the moonbeams stalking the trees, making them look like men lining the road. Ghosts in this area, she knew. So many battles fought, so many lives lost. The trees were silent soldiers, a path of sentries allowing her passage.

She came to a railroad crossing and slowed, making sure there wasn't a train coming. The railroad tracks were deserted, and as she drove over the bumps she looked left, then to her right. Something was on the tracks. She slowed more and looked closer. It didn't fully register until she was across the tracks.

A dog. A beagle, from the looks of it, slowly trotting away from her, alone on the moonlit tracks. The sight broke something inside her. She pulled the car over, safely out of the way of oncoming cars and trains. She got out, hiked back up the little hill to the crossing, and started after the dog.

"Hey, puppy. Stop, sweetie. You're going to get hurt." The dog, hearing her voice, did stop. He turned and lolled a doggy grin at her, cocking his head to the side. Like he was saying, hey, lady, whatcha doing on the tracks? *You* might get hurt.

She snapped her fingers and whistled low. He wagged his tail and grinned his doggy grin. He didn't come to her. He just stood and watched her come closer and closer. He wasn't wearing a collar. He wasn't terribly scrawny, but he wasn't fat and glistening as if he'd recently escaped from a backyard. He looked like a traveler, one who knew the shortest routes, the easiest cut-throughs. A vagabond dog, out to see the world. To confirm her feeling, when she was close enough to touch him, he reached forward with his snout, touched her hand briefly, then turned and trotted away. The tracks arched to her left, going around a bend, and Taylor watched his wagging tail fade away around the curve. He didn't want to be helped. He belonged in his little doggy world, knew where he needed to be and what he was supposed to be doing. Unlike her.

She realized she was crying only when the dog disappeared.

Baldwin had worked himself into a state. Taylor hadn't answered her cell phone for hours, Aiden was still on the loose somewhere local, and the television spewed rumor and innuendo about his lover on every channel. If faced with an opponent at this moment, he felt fairly sure he'd be able to wring his neck with little trouble.

It was near midnight when his cell phone finally rang. Thank God, it was her. He answered the phone, short and sharp.

"Jesus, Taylor, where have you been? You scared the hell out of me."

He heard the thickness in her voice, like she'd been crying recently. It broke his heart. Not a characteristic that was common to his woman. Weakness wasn't her style.

She spoke softly. "Don't yell at me, okay? I'm fine. I'm heading home. I need sleep. I need to figure out what I'm going to do. I'm tired. Are you there?"

"I am." He softened his tone. "Have you eaten?"

"I'm not hungry," came the flat reply. "I could use a cigarette, though."

He gave a half laugh. "Okay. I can probably arrange that, you have a pack stashed around here somewhere. Just drive safe, all right? I'll see you when you get here."

"Bye," she said, and she was gone. All the breath left him in a hurry. He hadn't realized just how worried he was for her until he knew she was okay.

Damn. How could things have gone so far south so quickly? It was barely twenty-four hours since she'd called and told him of the sex tapes. Now they were all over the news, in addition to the one showing Taylor shooting David Martin. He felt certain he could discredit that video easily, he had people working on it already. It seemed an audio track had been added that made it sound like Martin was begging for his life. Easily proven. But the damage of Taylor being forced to hand in her badge would take longer to undo.

He saw lights angle into the front window. He snapped off the television midreport, went to the garage and opened the door. He smiled when she came into the warmly lit room. Her hair stood on end, her nose was slightly red. Her gray eyes were stormy, a furious tempest raging in their depths.

"Who's the porcupine now," he asked, taking her into his arms. She sighed, not rising to the tease. Her back was ramrod-straight, her muscles clenched. He ached for her, wondered if he should try to talk or take her straight to bed. Instead, her stomach rumbled loudly.

"Let me make you something," he said.

"No, really. I'm okay." Her heart wasn't in it, she sounded decidedly absent. He released her. Ignoring her protestations, he went ahead and opened a can of soup, warmed the oven for bread. She stood woodenly at the sink, staring out into the backyard.

The soup heated quickly. He poured a cup, set it and half of a sliced baguette on the table, then prodded her to the seat. He was struck by a memory of his mother, easing him into a chair after appendix surgery in junior high. Her cosseting had upset him, so he took the lesson to heart and stepped away, allowing Taylor to reach for the spoon without condemnation.

A few more moments passed. He let the silence linger, then poured a cup of soup for himself and sat across from Taylor at the table.

She finally spoke. "I keep trying to build a future, and the past won't let me. Martin, L'Uomo, my idiot parents. Every time I take a step forward, something happens to slam me back. I don't get it."

Her tone had changed to quiet resignation. Arguing

her success was fruitless now, he knew that. He decided to try a different tack.

"Do you want to hear what's going on, or would you rather not?"

She looked at him, a fine spark of curiosity crossing her features. That's my girl, he thought.

She sighed deeply, then dipped her bread in the soup and began eating. "Oh, it's hot." She dropped the bread back on the plate, laid the spoon down. "You might as well tell me. It's not likely to go away just because I'm avoiding it."

"No, it's not. But I think I can help."

"I don't know about that, babe. I might've just fucked things up for good." That uncharacteristic note of fragility was back, and Baldwin longed to comfort her.

"Hardly. I have a friend working on the tape of David Martin's shooting. She's already found several dubbing marks, so we should be able to discredit that accusation by morning. As for the others, I spent some time with Lincoln after you left. He wants you to call him, by the way." He gestured toward his cell phone, but she shook her head.

"Later," she said.

"Okay. He gave me all of his data and I fed it to another friend, the one I told you was working on a similar case. He's already tracked down the owners of the Web site and had it pulled from the Net. No new tapes will show up."

"Oh, crap. The girls!"

"Huh?"

"I was supposed to go over to the cabin, look for any cameras that might be there. I fell asleep last night, and forgot this morning, with all this…mess." The bitterness in her voice was unfamiliar.

"They called. They went through everything and found a couple of minicams, right in the vents where you suggested they look. Your crime scene tech, Tim Davis, has already collected them and taken them back for analysis. I'm having them sent to Sherry Alexander, she's the friend I mentioned who's working on the tapes. If anyone can find a route back to their owners, it's her."

Taylor nodded, her hair swinging forward to cover her face. Impatiently, she started to wind it back into a ponytail, then stopped. Her arms dropped to her side as exhaustion overcame her.

"Still want that cigarette?" he asked.

Taylor shook her head. "Hon, I need to go to bed. Take me?"

"Of course." He stood, pulling her to her feet. He intended to be tender, to gently raise her to her feet, brush her lips with his, but the proximity of her body coupled with this strange vulnerability was too much for him. He kissed her roughly. She responded, arms wrapped around him like a vise, and for a moment he wondered if they'd even make it upstairs. The kiss deepened and he felt himself harden. She grabbed his hand and led him from the kitchen. He turned off the light as they went.

Friday

Thirty

Taylor woke at 5:00 a.m. The barest hint of light nudged at the blinds, day trying to force its way into their bedroom. She glanced at Baldwin—he was lying on his back, naked, arms flung over his head. She rolled toward him, snuggling in to his bare chest. His arms came round her body automatically, their warmth and safety allowing her to close her eyes again.

She was just drifting back to sleep when the phone rang. They both jumped. She glanced at the clock, more time had passed than she thought. It was now six-forty.

"You get it. I don't want to talk to anyone," she said.

Baldwin groaned, then unhanded her and reached for the phone. She curled up on her side, strangely happy. After everything that happened yesterday, the knowledge that he was here with her made the bad stuff seem less important.

Baldwin rumbled hello into the phone, sounding so hoarse and male that it warmed her insides. A few seconds later he stiffened, then sat up, pulling the sheet with him. He reached for the television remote, clicking it on and turning the station to MSNBC. He nudged her in the back. She rolled to him, and he pointed at the TV. He turned the sound up, and her heart sank. A blonde wearing a well-cut cream suit and a New York newscaster bob was in a split screen with Michelle Harris. Concern was etched across her artificially smooth forehead.

"Miss Harris, you're telling us that the Metro Nashville Police have mishandled your sister's murder investigation? It was our understanding that a suspect has been arrested in the case, your brother-in-law, is that correct?"

"That's true, they have arrested Todd. But after the situation yesterday, I can't be sure that he was the right person to arrest. If the police can't be trusted not to kill their own, how could they possibly arrest the right man?"

"Oh, God," Taylor said.

The blonde pursed her lips and tapped a pen against them, looking pensive. "Ms. Harris, is there something that you've discovered that questions the *veracity* of the arrest?"

Michelle looked confused for a moment, and Taylor realized she didn't know the meaning of the word veracity. A moment of pity overcame her and just as quickly fled when Michelle spoke again.

"All I know is that this investigation has been a mess from the word go. And to top it all off, the woman leading the charge has been on the news here because of her sordid private life."

A malicious smile spread across Michelle's face. Taylor thought *don't do it*. Michelle ignored the silent plea.

"It was all over the news last night, those disgusting tapes of her having sex with her partner, then shooting him to death in cold blood. What kind of person does that? And how can the Nashville police leave her on the job?"

"An excellent point, Ms. Harris. Representatives from the Metro Nashville police have confirmed to MSNBC that Lieutenant Taylor Jackson has been relieved of duty pending an investigation into her actions."

Taylor's stomach turned. "Oh, Jesus. I think I'm going to throw up."

Baldwin started to turn the television off. His face, unguarded for a moment, was contorted with anger.

"We will sue the living shit out of them for that, babe. Don't worry for a minute. They have no right—"

"Wait, shhh. Stop, stop, don't turn that off. What's she saying?"

The blonde had finished her character assassination of Taylor and gone back to the matter at hand. "Now, tell me, Ms. Harris, what did you find last night that convinces you that this investigation is being mishandled?"

Michelle Harris gleamed. She held up a sheaf of papers and shook them. The rustling was amplified, she'd gotten the papers directly next to the mike that was clipped to the top of her blouse. "That detective on the case, the lieutenant, she's got a history of brutality. I have a friend who told me she has been cited several times in the past for over-the-top violence against suspects. She's killed more people than anyone on the police force. It's all right here."

The anchor was beside herself with glee. "We need

to take a break, please stay with us." The screen went to commercial and Baldwin hit mute. Taylor already had the phone in her hand.

"Whoa, who are you calling?"

Taylor stopped, then set the phone back in the cradle.

"Work. Fitz. Someone. I don't know. I can't believe she'd go on the news and say that. Where is she getting her information?"

"That's an excellent question. Mischaracterized as it may be, that's damaging."

Taylor started to pace. "I figured she was a fame seeker the second she started doing the talk shows. Corinne was the favorite, Michelle was the one in the family who always felt outcast. I've assumed this is her way of getting some attention—first going on everywhere to talk about finding the body, the 911 tapes, and now this. Something isn't quite right with Miss Michelle, I'll tell you that right now. No way, José." She grabbed the phone again.

"Taylor," Baldwin said.

She continued dialing, setting the phone between her shoulder and her ear, looking for a pad she kept on the night table to write some quick notes.

"What?"

"Babe, you can't do that. You need to let me handle it."

"Of course I can. What do you—" The realization hit her. She stopped short, nearly fell back in the bed with the weight of it.

She had no badge. She was suspended. Without her shield, she couldn't do a damn thing to stop this. Anger rose to the surface. That damn bitch Norris.

The phone was answered on the other end. Taylor

murmured, "Wrong number." She hung up the handset, looked at Baldwin.

"I can't just sit by and let this slide, Baldwin. I have to do something. What do they expect, I'll sit here like a good little girl while they submarine my career?"

"Honey, you're going to have to do just that. Let me handle this. We'll be able to prove your innocence in no time, but while that's happening, you need to keep out of it. Keep your nose clean. Though I admit, I'm not comfortable letting you sit here unguarded. Aiden is still out there. He's not happy with me."

Great. An international psycho camped in her backyard, her shield and gun confiscated, a case breaking wide open, and she needed to keep her nose clean. Right.

Baldwin climbed out of the bed. "I'm going to take a shower and head downtown. Let me think about how to keep you protected."

"I don't need protecting, Baldwin. For God's sake, I'm a cop. I have weapons. We have the alarm. Aiden isn't going to get anywhere near me again."

He turned to her, sat back down on the edge of the bed. She slid closer, rested her head on his shoulder. She didn't want someone else protecting her. Between the two of them, they could handle anything.

"Babe," he started again, softer this time. "You need to understand my position. Aiden is a cunning bastard. He's been killing with impunity for years, practically sanctioned by my own actions on his behalf. He doesn't lie down, and he doesn't give up. He has a real vendetta against me. I had him banned from the States. He had a mother, a wife, if you can imagine that. He tries to get home to…see them, and so far I've been able to head that off. Five years, actually, that I've kept him from his family. Now that he's here, I have to get them protected."

"See them. You mean kill them."

"Not exactly. His mother is still alive, but in a mental institution in Rhode Island. His wife, that's more complicated. His wife was the one who turned him in originally, back in 2006. She caught him up to his elbows, literally, in the stomach of a prostitute in Berlin. Didn't know what to do, so she ran. Went to the consulate, told them about it. I was called in soon after that—once the information filtered up the chain, my contact was made aware of the situation. Aiden had gone off our grid, was 'working on his own,' as they like to say." He was silent for a second, and she started to talk, but he squeezed her arm.

"I know what you're going to ask. Why would he come after you?"

She nodded.

"There was nothing for him to prey upon with me. As an adversary, Aiden has always had a level of, well, let's call it respect for me. And I, him. He's one of the most complex killers I've ever profiled. He makes Ted Bundy look like a charm school dropout. But now…I have you. I'm finally vulnerable. Prevailing wisdom is he may have seen us in Italy, that's the only way we can imagine he would have known the level of emotion at stake for me now. Killing me doesn't serve his interests. Killing you would make me suffer in unimaginable ways. That's how he works. Problem was, we weren't sure of his intentions, not all the way, until he showed up here."

He squeezed her arm again. "There's more you

should know." He got up, slipped on his boxers and sat in the chair across from the bed. The fact that he'd severed physical contact was disconcerting. Taylor had the feeling she was playing confessor to his sins. She was right.

"I killed Aiden's wife."

Taylor felt her eyes widen. "What do you mean, you killed his wife?"

Baldwin sank his head into his hands for a moment, hiding his face. He ran his fingers through his hair and met her eye.

"It was an accident. A terrible accident. She came after me and I shot her. It was self-defense. At least, that's what Garrett called it. I think I could have handled things differently. She was a woman, weaker than me. I should have been able to fight her off. But she blamed me for Aiden's issues. Accused me of making him into the monster he'd become.

"After she caught him with the prostitute, she decided she wanted help. I managed to slip her out of the country, right under Aiden's nose. I knew he was going to come for her, he'd promised me he'd kill her. When he came to her we'd just gotten her out. We had her stashed in a safe house in Vienna, and he found the address. I got the warning just before he showed up, got Lucy out of the house no more than five minutes before he arrived.

"And then it went all wrong. Without telling us, Lucy had arranged for Aiden to come. She wanted to be with him, was helping conspire to take us down. I can't imagine what she was thinking, she'd just seen her husband slaughtering a woman. Aiden got to her somehow.

"We forced her out of the house. She didn't want to

leave. Was making excuses we ignored. In the car, she pulled a knife, attacked me. I was caught by surprise, reacted. I shot her in the leg, trying to stop her. Hit an artery. She bled out before I could get her to a hospital."

Jesus. "And Aiden hasn't forgiven you."

"No. I took her from him. She was buried here in the States and he hasn't been able to see her grave. He swore he would make my life as big a living hell as his. That's why I've never gotten so close to anyone before. Now, there's you. I couldn't help myself. You became my world. And he knows it." He looked like he wanted to say more, but he stopped, searching her face. Taylor could feel the waves of frustration coming off him.

She went to him, knelt in front of him, took his hands in hers. "Oh, Baldwin. I'm so sorry. I had no idea what you were up against. What can I do?"

"You can let me keep you safe. I failed Lucy. I refuse to fail you, too."

He reached for her, and they both stood up. He kissed her fiercely, with a hunger that made her stomach clench and her head swim. The stubble on his chin scraped hers, she didn't care. She wanted more, raked her nails down his back. He pulled his boxers off with one hand and they were on the bed in a flash. He thrust into her with a single stroke and the world shrank away. No tragedies, no serial killers, no failures. There was nothing but him, filling her, claiming her, crushing her in his arms with brute strength, their frustration and hurt bringing them both to a climax within moments.

Getting up for the second time that morning, Taylor made a decision.

Baldwin had showered and left her blushing in their room. Good grief, that man was insatiable. There was something so joyous in their passion; even when their mutual moods were down they could always find solace in each other's arms. He'd given her strict instructions not to leave the house, left an armed guard at the door and had patrols rolling through the neighborhood.

Fuss, fuss, fuss. She was no stranger to dangerous criminals, knew she could hold her own if need be. Being aware was nine-tenths of the law when it came to being hunted. Not being where you were expected to be also helped. And that's exactly what she planned to do.

No one knew about the conversation she'd had with Jasmine on Wednesday. Thalia Abbott was at St. Ann's. She could swing by there after she went to see Ellen Ricard, who was expecting her to come by at eight.

She invited the guard in for coffee, explained her intentions. She made it clear that he had no choice and made him swear not to tell Baldwin she had left. Give me two hours, she told him, then I'll be back and be a good girl.

When she rolled out of the garage, she was whistling. They may take her badge, but damn it, they weren't going to stop her investigation of these crimes.

Her conscience kept trying to get her attention, but she ignored the little voice in her head that said to go back home, nestle in with a good book, and let Baldwin handle things. When had she ever trusted a man to take care of her? Never. It wasn't that she was thumbing her nose at him, but somewhere, she subconsciously wanted to prove to him that she was the tough girl he thought her. And what he didn't know wouldn't hurt him.

She watched for cars following her, but saw nothing that gave her the slightest bit of concern. So far, when Aiden was around, she'd always been able to tell. He set off her warning systems; all her antediluvian adrenaline caches pushed into the red zone whenever he was in proximity. She trusted that wouldn't change.

His wife's grave. Baldwin had said that Aiden had a twofold plan—ruin Baldwin's life and see his dead wife. She'd forgotten to ask where Lucy was buried. Maybe Aiden had decided to slip off and commune with her spirit before garroting Taylor's throat.

The drive downtown was uneventful and she pulled in to the parking garage under the building. It was dark and gloomy. She wondered briefly if she should go ahead and park at the meters on the street. Deciding that would be the smart thing to do—see, Baldwin, I'm not a total idiot—she wound her way back up the ramps and onto West End. She found a spot on a meter that had a sign saying she could park there starting at 8:00 a.m. She looked at her watch. Seven forty-five. Close enough. What would they do, give her a ticket?

Glancing over her shoulder, she saw nothing out of the ordinary. Baldwin had her spooked enough to watch her back, that was for sure. The thought that Aiden had taken off once he knew Baldwin was in town came back, stronger than before. It made sense. Wishful thinking, probably, but hey, a girl could dream. What would life be like if they weren't chasing madmen? Boring and staid, definitely.

In the lobby, a black lacquered sign listed Dr. Ellen Ricard's office on the eighth floor. There was a

communal bustle toward the elevators—patients, receptionist, the odd nurse in blue scrubs coming in with
coffee from the nearby West End Starbucks. Taylor
moved into the scrum and took her place in the elevator.

Dr. Ricard's office was at the end of the long
hallway on the right, next to an emergency stairwell.
Taylor entered, a discreet ding announcing her
presence. The office was finely decorated—a red and
gold patterned Aubusson rug took up almost all the
floor space, making the matching textured impression-
ist oils by local artist Jennifer Wilken stand out against
the creamy walls. The furniture was thick, square and
suede. A glass coffee table held *Town and Country*
magazines, and the place smelled slightly of Chanel
perfume.

Alerted by the door's subtle chime, Dr. Ricard
emerged from an interior room. She had shoulder-
length silver hair that didn't match her youthful face.
Square black glasses, minimal makeup, black knit
pants with a deep-cut black-and-white silk top—Ricard
was an odd mixture of hippie and hip. She couldn't be
more than forty, but Taylor wasn't very good with ages.

Ricard crossed the room and held out her hand.
Taylor shook it, then followed when the doctor
gestured, leading the way into her inner sanctum.

The room was filled with sunlight—facing east, the
early morning sun spilled through the windows,
lending an air of good cheer to the surroundings. Two
heavy couches faced one another across a second art
deco glass coffee table; a large wing chair covered in
black velvet bore the markings of frequent use. Sure
enough, Ricard crossed the room, curled like a cat with
her feet tucked under her, laid the notepad and pen on

the coffee table and indicated Taylor should sit with a nod of her head. Taylor did, amazed at the control the woman exuded without even speaking. After a moment, the doctor spoke, her accented voice making Taylor feel like she was on a museum tour in Great Britain.

"I'm Ellen Ricard, but you already know that. How can I help you, Lieutenant?"

Straight to business. All right. "Corinne Wolff. She was a patient of yours. I was hoping you'd tell me why."

"If you know she was a patient, then you know that I'm not bound to tell you anything about our private sessions. But, I am sorry that we've lost her. Corinne was a magnificent girl."

"Then help me find out who killed her, Doctor."

"Isn't that readily apparent, Lieutenant? Two days out and you already had a suspect in custody."

"That's true, but I don't think it's a foregone conclusion that Todd killed Corinne. Yes, he's been arrested because there's evidence condemning him, but the investigation into his actions is far from complete. That's not why I'm here. I understand that Corinne and her husband were…open with their sexuality."

"Be that as it may. It's you who isn't sure. You don't want to be responsible if he is innocent."

"You're right, I'm not convinced. I'm not careless with people's lives, regardless of their choices. And stop psychoanalyzing me. I'm not a patient, I'm trying to get some answers."

Ricard finally smiled, and relaxed in the chair. "All right, Lieutenant. I'll stop playing games if you will."

Taylor wasn't sure what to make of the good doctor. Was this going anywhere, or was she just spinning her wheels?

"What's that supposed to mean?"

Ricard steepled her fingers, tapping her two forefingers together. "It means I saw the news this morning. That you'd been suspended. Is this true, or did you get reinstated five minutes ago?"

Taylor slid farther into the sofa cushions, miserable. Damn.

Ricard waved a hand dismissively. "I don't care, Lieutenant. I've seen the tapes."

Taylor blanched, but Ricard continued, not warmly, but with a certain sense of shared camaraderie.

"Don't worry. It's blatantly obvious that someone is upset with you and trying to ruin your reputation. I've been through that kind of crap myself. Intimidation, coercion. Don't let them get you down. But in all honesty, none of that matters here. I see that you're true in your desire to find Corinne's real killer. The fire in your eyes is unmistakable." She smiled, the first kind look that had crossed her face since Taylor entered her sanctum.

"This will have to be off the record, though. Surely you understand. If I'm going to divulge secrets of a patient to an unfrocked police officer, I can only speak hypothetically."

Taylor searched Ricard's face for signs of mocking, and found none. What did she have to lose? It wasn't like she could march into headquarters and announce she'd solved the case anyway. No, better to take the doctor at her word, listen to what she said, glean as much information as possible.

"I understand. That's fine. I'm just curious why someone as controlled and secure as Corinne Wolff would fall apart like she did. For her to be taking prescription anti-anxiety medication during a pregnancy seems wholly out of character, and if it's a clue that will help me discover if it's her husband, or someone else, who killed her…"

Ricard was nodding, so Taylor stopped and let the woman gather her thoughts.

"You know a lot about her already. A thorough victimology, I presume?"

"I'm trying to build an *accurate* victimology. Corinne seemed to be a woman with two distinct personalities. On one side, the suburban housewife and mother, the former tennis wunderkind, the short-lived businesswoman. The other side was apparently out of control, desperately searching for happiness and pleasure. I'd like to find out why this woman had two sides that were so extreme."

"We all have two sides, Lieutenant. The persona we adopt for our fellow man, and the self that we keep hidden, the real part of us that allows the core to make judgments and derive pleasure from our actions. You can't tell me you're the same person at home, in private, that you are in public. Simply being a woman in a man's position would preclude you from showing any normal weakness or vulnerability on the job."

"I'm hardly a woman in a man's position, Doctor. And yes, I am the same woman at work as I am at home. What you see is what you get."

Ricard smiled, her lips thinning. The woman didn't like being challenged.

"Really? How many female lieutenants are there in the police force these days?"

"Plenty."

"And do they have field jobs or administrative posts?"

"In Metro? Administrative. I'm the only lieutenant in the field."

"And I bet you have the respect of your team. That you never show them how deep down you wish you could relinquish control and allow them to care for you."

"Oh, you're wrong there. We are a team. We work together, and I surrender to them all the time. If I didn't they'd never trust me."

"And you have a man at home?"

"Yes."

"What does he do?"

"He's with the FBI. He's…"

"Yes?"

"He's in the middle of an investigation and keeping certain aspects of the case from me. He wants to protect me, and I don't need protecting." Shut *up* already, Taylor. This chick was good.

Taylor continued. "But that's neither here nor there, Doctor. It has nothing to do with Corinne Wolff."

"Oh, but that's where you're so very wrong. Corinne also operated under the misapprehension that she was in complete control of her life. That the choices she made were her choices. That she engaged in distasteful behavior because she *wanted* to. But in reality, there's always a part of a woman that wants to be cherished and protected, not subjected to multiple sex partners. Much less have those most intimate moments sold to the highest bidder."

Taylor looked at Ricard. Behind the glasses, the

mask of cool reserve, Taylor saw a shrewd woman. Taylor made sure her own face revealed nothing but cool interest in Corinne Wolff.

"So you're saying Corinne is a victim?"

"In a way. Corinne, unhappily, is no longer with us to verify that she felt abused by her husband's proclivities. You, on the other hand, are early enough in the game that you can steel yourself to the accusations against you, knowing deep in your heart you've done nothing wrong. Corinne didn't have your fortitude, I believe. She was easily led. Instead of fighting, she acquiesced. Allowed herself to be used."

"I'm not a victim, Dr. Ricard. That's where Corinne and I differ. I'd appreciate you keeping this discussion strictly about her, please. Was she being used by her husband?"

Ricard looked amused for a moment, then nodded and continued. "Corinne was being used by many people. Husband, family, siblings, lover. You'll hit upon the truth soon enough, Lieutenant. Let's talk for a bit about the anxiety a young mother might feel if she were in a position similar to Corinne Wolff."

"Okay."

"Think of the difficulties facing an exceptionally talented child. A completely controlled existence, a world structured around said child's genius. Constant work, attention, adulation and expectation. Until the one day the child wakes up, literally and figuratively, and decides she doesn't want to be a prodigy. She doesn't want to work so hard to live her life. She sees the people around her taking the easy road, sleeping in on the weekends, having plenty of time to date and do homework, and suddenly, she decides that is the life she wants. Someone who is so driven might actually pursue that simple life with the dogged determination that made her such a gifted athlete."

"Corinne's mother mentioned that her drive for tennis dissipated when she got into high school," Taylor said. When Ricard didn't comment, she asked, "Would small things that normally wouldn't be a big deal to you or me set this kind of person off?"

"Certainly. Someone so in control would have great difficulty in letting others take the reins. Unless she was compromised, to a point. Something that wouldn't be rational. Like being in love."

Well, that made sense. Taylor thought back to the first video she'd seen, with Todd and the two girls. Corinne was manning the camera. Perhaps she enjoyed the sex play, perhaps not, but by taking control of what the audience saw and felt, she took control of her situation with her husband. She was directing him, a thoroughly nontraditional role.

"Was there something in Corinne's life that presaged this need for control?"

"Ah, sadly, Lieutenant, since we are only discussing a hypothetical situation, I can't answer that. But someone with this level of need for stability might have a past that saw some sort of abuse, self-inflicted or external. With many young phenoms, their manifestation comes out in their talent. Once that talent is taken away, even something as simple as a parent telling the child he or she must go to bed now instead of studying their art could send a child of extreme gifts into a tailspin. They use their talent for control, just like an anorexic child uses starvation to whittle away her body. It's all perception.

"Take that away, by force or necessity, and you'd have a child who couldn't, or wouldn't be able to survive without some sort of mechanism to control the behavior and desire."

"Sexual promiscuity?"

Ricard gave a ghost of a smile. "Very good, Lieutenant. You're catching on. Monogamous sexual promiscuity, another example of how distasteful anything indiscriminant could be to a child like this."

"But that child would grow into an adult. I take it that she wouldn't grow out of it?"

"Some do. Some don't. Some follow their art, some, when separated from the one item that controls their identity, decline rapidly. They shrivel up, and ultimately end up institutionalized or dead. But that is only extreme cases. Most go on to lead productive, if not happy, lives."

"Would there need to be a catalyst? Something that would send a person like this over the edge, make them do things they otherwise wouldn't?"

"Yes, I believe you could say that. A life-changing event." Ricard spoke pointedly, and Taylor began to understand.

"Was this pregnancy unwanted?" she asked.

Ricard nodded, but said, "I couldn't say one way or the other about that. Corinne was a very regimented, controlled person."

So, that was the problem. She had gotten pregnant and wasn't thrilled about it. That was strange, for a young mother who was seemingly happy.

"Would an unplanned pregnancy be difficult for a woman who has to have control over everything? To the point that it would spark a pathological issue?"

"Nicely deduced, Lieutenant. In some extreme cases, an individual would have difficulty relinquishing control over their body in order to carry a baby. The individual might feel that the fetus is a foreign being and experience moments of hatred so profound that the only comfortable resolution is termination. Or, the individual may seek counseling to better handle the claustrophobic tendencies they are experiencing. High-level anxiety, overwhelming desire to escape, to effect a separation, yes, those things would need to be dealt with using extensive cognitive therapy, regression, relaxation and biofeedback."

"Was Corinne having these problems? Claustrophobia about her pregnancy?"

"Now, Lieutenant, you're treading too close to our hypothetical line again."

"All right. What about medication?"

"Well, in the case of a pregnancy, the client would certainly be encouraged not to use medicinal means to handle the situation."

"But Corinne chose the medicinal route. Why?"

Ricard glanced at the clock. "Oh my, Lieutenant, I'm afraid we need to wrap things up here." She stood.

"One last question." Taylor got to her feet too. "Would Corinne Wolff have been a danger to herself?"

Ricard straightened her glasses and pulled her tunic down so it lay tight across her hips. "She may have been. But I think it highly unlikely that she wielded the murder weapon and beat herself to death."

Thirty-One

Taylor left the doctor's office, head spinning, full of ideas and theories. A better picture was emerging of Corinne Wolff. Taylor knew that the best way to solve a murder was to know the victim. Chances were the murderer was someone in the victim's sphere. The deeply personal nature of the beating, the accessibility to the house, all pointed to a killer bent on revenge and punishment. Ergo, someone Corinne knew. If Taylor could get to know Corinne intimately, she would find the person who killed her. It may have been Todd—the evidence against him was certainly damning—but it could have been someone else.

Since she didn't have anything better to do, she decided to go ahead with her illicit day. She wondered if Julianne Harris would accept a phone call from her? Michelle Harris had obviously checkmarked the box that said Taylor wasn't on their side, but if the mom hadn't shut her out yet… She pulled out her notepad and flipped back to the first few pages. Yes, there was the number for the Harris house. She dialed it, fingers crossed on her knee. Julianne Harris answered on the second ring.

"Do you have news about my daughter?" she said without preamble.

"Mrs. Harris, thank you for taking my call. I appreciate—"

"I don't want to talk about what's been happening to you, Lieutenant. What do you need?"

Short and snappy. Taylor knew she was only going to have one shot at this. "Mrs. Harris, were you aware that Corinne was taking medication for anxiety?"

There was silence, then Mrs. Harris sighed deeply. "Yes," she said.

"Do you know why she was so…anxious?" Taylor asked.

There was silence again. "Let me ask that a different way," Taylor said. Mrs. Harris interrupted.

"No, Lieutenant, you don't need to do that. Yes, she was anxious. She was having panic attacks about the baby. She wouldn't tell me why, but I had my suspicions."

"Which were?"

"I don't want to defame my daughter, Lieutenant. I think it would be best if we stopped now."

"Was Corinne having an affair, Mrs. Harris?"

Mrs. Harris gave an anguished whimper. "Oh, God. How did you find out?"

I guessed, Taylor thought. "Who was she involved with?"

"That I don't know. I don't even know for sure that she was having an affair. She was acting so strangely before she died. Erratic. Obsessed. I've only seen her like that one other time, over a boy she had a crush on in high school. They dated briefly, very briefly, and when he broke up with her, she collapsed. Sank into a deep depression, began writing letters to the boy, begging him to take her back. It was a phase, we snapped her out of it after a few weeks. Lately, though, she's had that air about her. A mother always knows when something's wrong with her daughter, Lieutenant. I don't know any more than that."

"Thank you, Mrs. Harris. You've been a huge help."

They clicked off, and Taylor tapped her fingers on the steering wheel. Todd Wolff changed his story about when he had sex with Corinne the last time. He initially said they hadn't had sex that week. An affair would explain the semen. The DNA wasn't back yet, that would confirm or destroy Wolff's claims. If Corinne was having an affair, who was her lover?

She made her notes, thought for a few minutes, then decided to keep pushing. Thalia Abbott was next on her list.

The bright morning sun created a glare off the midtown skyscrapers. Lost in thought, shielding her eyes, Taylor didn't see the dark-haired man watching her from across the street.

Back in the truck, Taylor pulled the piece of paper with Thalia Abbott's name and number on it from her wallet. She dialed the number, was pleased when a soft voice answered on the first ring.

Taylor introduced herself as a friend of Jasmine's. She didn't identify herself as a cop. It would serve two purposes: first, not chasing Thalia off; second, that bitch Delores Norris wouldn't be able to say she'd been false with a source. Thalia didn't ask what Taylor wanted, said she'd be happy to meet with her, and Taylor asked if now would be inconvenient. The girl agreed, asked Taylor to meet her at St. Ann's Catholic Church off Charlotte Pike in forty minutes. Taylor clicked off the phone. Plenty of time.

She put the 4Runner in gear. Taking advantage of a brief lull in traffic, she pulled a U-turn and headed back toward Vanderbilt. As she passed the stone entrance to the campus, her cell phone rang. Damn, this better not be the kid changing her mind. She glanced at the screen. Baldwin. Composing her voice, she turned down the radio, better to fake the quiet of home.

Prepared, she answered with a chipper, "Hey, babe."

"Taylor, why aren't you at home?"

Man, that was quick. How did he find out? She debated. Lie, say she was at home, or cop to it? Knowing Baldwin, he had cause to believe she wasn't at home—either the guard had blabbed or she had silent, quiet followers. She opted for the latter, she'd laid it on pretty thick with the guard. Might as well stick to the truth.

"I couldn't stand to sit there and not do anything. You of all people should respect that."

"And you of all people should understand how dangerous this situation is." But she heard the resignation in his voice. He was only annoyed, not fully angry with her. He did know her, and the realization made her smile.

"I do. I assume you've got someone on my tail?"

"You weren't checking?"

"Like I said, I assumed."

"Sloppy, Taylor. It could be Aiden, not a service detail."

"If it were, you wouldn't be calling me, you'd be here brandishing your sword. I don't need protecting, babe."

"You need it more than you realize. But that's neither here nor there. What exactly are you up to?"

"Ummm…following a lead."

"I wish you'd let me handle the tapes. Sherry has gotten more information, we're ready to go after them."

"That's great news. No, I'm following up on an interview related to the Corinne Wolff case."

"Taylor, do I need to remind you—"

"No, you don't. I know. I have no badge. I have no authority. I will endanger the investigation if I get involved." The bitterness in her tone surprised her. The anger at being suspended was closer to the surface than she'd like to admit. Damn the Oompa!

"Okay, okay. Listen, when we finish, do me a favor. I'm going to text message your detail and let them know you're aware of them and they don't have to hang back as much. Your job is to let them stay with you. From what I hear, you drive like a bat out of hell."

Taylor drove up Murphy Road, turned north on 46th in front of McCabe golf course. She wended her way through Sylvan Park. Crossing over Colorado Avenue, she began mentally plotting the geographical location of all the states as she went by their street names. It was a game she and Sam had played as little girls riding from Belle Meade through Sylvan Park to get to Bobbie's Dairy Dip on Charlotte Avenue. They tallied points—one for each state capital named, one for each neighboring state identified. Sam's parents were forced to take different routes each time so the girls could have new challenges. The winner got to choose their ice cream treat first.

Taylor remembered the intensity with which they played, the fervor, the laughter when they were wrong. The triumph of sometimes beating Sam, who at seven already possessed a weird, encyclopedic knowledge of useless trivia. It would be nice to go back to a time when the most important thing in her life was getting her ice cream first.

What the hell. She turned left onto Charlotte, past her goal of St. Ann's to the next block. She pulled into the Dairy Dip, open for business with a line at nine in the morning. There was never a bad time for a good juicy burger and some ice cream.

Taylor returned to the 4Runner with a chocolate-dipped twist cone, sugar, not cake. She climbed in the truck, locked the doors, then licked and ruminated. Maybe she should have signaled that she was taking a break, offered to buy her detail ice cream. Then again…

When she was finished, she crumpled the paper napkin, thin even by fast-food standards, wiped her mouth and started the truck. She backtracked a couple of blocks to St. Ann's, swinging around behind the building. She parked with the nose of the truck pointing out to Charlotte, counted off a full minute to allow her shadows to get into place, then exited the vehicle.

Following the mounted signs, she walked toward the school. An eclectic Catholic church, St. Ann's ministered to the local community, holding mass in English, Spanish and Korean throughout the day. The school had a popular K-8 program for both parishioners and non-Catholic parents looking for a solid private parochial education for their children.

Taylor stopped, wondering for a moment. Thalia Abbott was seventeen at a minimum. She wasn't going to school here.

Taylor entered the sanctuary, the cool, incense-perfumed air greeting her. Unconsciously, she dipped her fingers into the small stone bowl of holy water by the door and crossed herself. She gazed at the altar, a peaceful warmth stealing through her. She always loved churches, though she rarely attended services anymore. It was funny, inside a sanctuary, she promised herself she would find a way to attend a service. Once outside, in the hard glare of reality, she never did.

"Are you Catholic?"

The voice surprised her and she jumped. A thin girl, late teens, with long, straight brown hair and deeply soulful brown eyes stood at her left elbow. She smiled, showing even white teeth. Her skin was creamy, unlined. Taylor had the feeling she'd seen the girl before, then just as quickly placed her. The girl looked like Noelle Pazia, a victim of the Southern Strangler she and Baldwin had caught the previous summer. Something about Noelle had always haunted her, and Taylor felt the goose bumps rise as she looked at the dead girl's younger mirror image.

"Lieutenant Jackson, I presume?"

"I, uh, how, um, yes." Impressive elocution there, Taylor. She cleared her throat. "How did you know?"

"I saw the news," Thalia said simply, nonjudgmental.

"Lovely."

"I wouldn't worry about it. No one in their right mind will believe that you killed someone without reason. It's in your eyes. You're a guardian, not an avenger."

Oddly pleased, Taylor smiled at the girl. "Some would disagree with you. You're Thalia Abbott, I presume?"

"And you aren't Catholic, I'd presume."

"You're right. I was raised Episcopal. My dad was Catholic, though. How did you know?"

"You don't have that guilty look on your face. Though you crossed and blessed yourself, you walked right past the confessional without a second glance. Most nonpracticing Catholics couldn't do that." She smiled, and Taylor felt herself smiling back. This was not what she'd expected from her morning. Grace from a seventeen-year-old ex-porn star.

"Let's walk," Thalia said. She guided Taylor out of the sanctuary, into the sacristy. She held a cloth in her hands, Taylor realized she was dusting as they went.

"You're too old for school here."

"Yes. I'm working as a sacristan. I keep things nice for the priests and nuns while I decide what to do with my life. I'm thinking of taking orders, becoming a novice in the fall. I've felt a…calling."

There's a turnaround. Wow. Normally Taylor would encourage a young girl in Thalia's position to look for other ways to deal with life; becoming a nun, sectioning herself off from the world seemed quite dramatic. But something about Thalia Abbott made Taylor bite her tongue. This was a young girl who knew her own mind; to talk to her about her own choices would be tacky. Taylor decided to ease in.

"Thalia is such a pretty name. Is it Greek?"

The girl looked at her in surprise. "Very good, Lieutenant. My mother is from Athens. Thalia was the Muse of Comedy. She also worked part-time as one of the Graces—Thalia the Flowering. It's a nice history. I'd like to think that I inspired some creativity at some point in my life. I'd like to teach art, so perhaps it was prophetic of my mother." They had moved through the nave of the church now, and Thalia pointed to a door.

Taylor followed her out into a small garden, fully enclosed by the surrounding buildings. A pebble path wound through small patches of grass. A few carved statues sat unobtrusively in the four corners, a stone bench sat next to a burbling fountain. They took a seat, Thalia with her back straight and the same beatific smile she'd had on for the past five minutes.

"This is my favorite place. It's easy to think here."

A calm had stolen over Taylor, similar to the feeling she'd had inside the church. "I can understand why. Can you teach art if you're a nun?"

"Of course. Especially in our fast-paced world, where people don't take time to read. Art can play a huge role in communication, especially to the young. There are certainly centuries of religious works to study."

They sat in silence for a few moments, then Thalia spoke again, her voiced tinged with sadness. "Jasmine called me. She told me to answer your questions. I don't know everything about the secret society, but I know some. I'll help in any way that I can."

"I appreciate that. Jasmine told me that there is a club of girls who are making sex tapes to be posted on the Internet. What can you tell me about them?"

Thalia contemplated her hands, which were nestled in her lap. "It's not what they make it out to be, for starters. It's supposed to be this glamorous, exciting club that everyone wants to be a part of, and only the most beautiful and popular are tapped. You know what being tapped is, right?"

"Yes. You're chosen by the group, have to go through some awful ritual, then you're a pledge of sorts."

"Sounds like you've been through it."

"I have," Taylor said. "I don't think it was quite what you've gone through, though."

"Not unless your first task is to fellate the captain of the football team."

Trying not to show her shock, Taylor answered lightly. "Definitely not. That was your initiation?"

"Yes. I got a note in my locker telling me to go to the Pergola immediately. That's what they call this small building off the football fields where some of the kids go to smoke. I followed their instructions. They blindfolded me the moment I walked through the door, pushed me to my knees. Explained that they were tapping me and to prove myself worthy, I had to suck off this guy. So I did. Things took off from there. It was sick, and twisted, and the longer I was involved, the more ashamed of myself I became. Blow jobs became sex, the sex became fetishistic, then they started in with the cameras. Fifty points for getting a video up on the Internet, one hundred for selling it to a production house. When I dropped out, they ostracized me. I stopped going to school, got my GED, and started working here. I needed to find a new path, forge a future that I could live with. To find some forgiveness for my stupidity." She waved a hand in the air, swatting away the memories.

"That's not what you need to hear. Jasmine said

you're looking for names of the girls who were actually on film."

"Yes." Taylor withdrew a folded still shot of the two girls from the video from her pocket. She smoothed it open. "Can you identify either one of them?"

Thalia took the photo. "Both. The one on the left in the pigtails is Tracy Civet, the one on the right is Jere Beisman. Both seniors last year. Both a little nuts, if you want my opinion. They want to do porn full-time. These little movies are going on their résumés."

"And do Tracy and Jere work solely with Todd Wolff?"

"That's what this is about, isn't it? You think they killed his wife."

Taylor didn't miss a beat. "Did they?"

Thalia shook her head. "I don't know. I doubt it, though. They didn't care about her, she was just the cameraman."

"She didn't participate?"

"Not that I knew of."

Taylor had seen tapes with Corinne as an active participant. She must have started off behind the camera, then decided that wasn't enough. Evolution.

"How did she feel about her husband having sex with the girls?"

"As far as I know, she was fine with it. She was very professional, always telling you where to be, where to place your legs, your hands, your mouth. 'Spread those cheeks, girls.'" Her face fell. "This is just what I heard, I never filmed with them. I backed out before it got to that."

"Let me ask you this. Do you know where they were trying to sell the tapes?"

"Todd Wolff should be able to tell you that. That man is a braggart, always claiming to have an in with this major production house. He took possession of the tapes, sent them on to his boss. When one sold, I mean sold into the stores, he'd split the money with the actresses. It got to be much more than an accumulation of points for Tracy and Jere."

"How many girls participate, Thalia?"

She'd rewrapped her hands in her lap, wasn't meeting Taylor's eyes anymore. "Upwards of ten, probably. I only know of two others who are at this level. It's kind of like the Masons, you only get to know who is at the higher levels as you progress through them."

"So you don't know who the ringleaders are?"

"No. Tracy and Jere were my friends. So I thought. The other two girls were seniors this year. One was killed in a car accident right after graduation. Remember last year, when five girls were killed when they ran into a truck?"

Taylor nodded. It had been a horrific accident, on the news and in the minds of Nashville for weeks.

"The other, her name is Ginny Englewood, she graduated and went to school in Georgia somewhere. 'Ginny Loves Wood,' that was her star name. Classy, I know. She didn't continue her career in film. And unfortunately, that's all I know. I'm sorry I couldn't be more help. I should probably get back to work now." Thalia's voice was cracking, bitter tears spilling from her eyes. Taylor knew it was time to stop. She had what she needed anyway.

They stood, and started back toward the door. "You were a huge help, Thalia. I appreciate your honesty. I know it wasn't easy."

Thalia left the tears unchecked, shook Taylor's hand with a firm grasp. "God gives us challenges, Lieutenant. It's how we deal with them that matters."

Seventeen, and already imbued with the wisdom of the world. Taylor felt strangely empty when she left the girl behind.

Thirty-Two

Taylor sat in the truck and wrote up the information Thalia had just given her. She needed to get the names of the additional girls to Fitz, let him and Marcus go to work on tracking them down. And Todd Wolff had new charges that needed to be filed against him, for child pornography. With any luck, they'd be able to parlay the charges into a confession, find out who he was selling the tapes to and shut down the operation.

Fitz answered his phone on the first ring. She talked quickly. It only took a few minutes to relay the appropriate information, and he was off. They couldn't run the risk of him getting caught up in the Oompa's ire. He'd follow the tracks of her morning's legwork, legitimizing the information Taylor had received so the case wouldn't be compromised.

Something didn't feel right about the secret society. The thought of a group of high school honeys trying to break into the porn industry and recruiting their friends seemed a bit much. Taylor suspected there was an outside force, someone professional who was manipulating the girls. Calling it a secret society, preying on the girls' insecurities, their fears, their teenage ambitions to be special, famous. Making them think they wanted this life, making it glamorous, fun, a game. Todd Wolff certainly fit the bill.

Taylor hadn't seen any incidence of other men on the tapes, but if Corinne had been having sex with some unseen participants, maybe that could explain the pregnancy jitters. Her mother suspected an affair, Dr. Ricard had said Corinne was being manipulated by everyone and had used the word *lover* in the list. Sam needed to test the fetus for paternity. She made a note and went back to her thoughts.

Thalia had mentioned Todd Wolff had a boss. She wouldn't be surprised if money had changed hands that had nothing to do with the profits of a sale. Wolff was a pimp, plain and simple. Now they needed to focus on finding who he worked for.

Oh, she should have asked Thalia about drugs. She flipped open the phone and called the girl.

The voice mail came on and Taylor left her a message.

She felt good. She could tell things were about to break. That's the way it was with these cases, either they latched on to a thread that quickly unraveled, or they were stymied for months. Though it sure as hell would be nice if she had a fucking badge so she could do her job.

Her anger spilled over and she slammed her fists into the steering wheel, imagined Delores's pug face. There, that was better. She calmed herself, breathing deeply and letting her shoulders relax. Nothing could be done now. She just needed to persevere, know that the truth would come out soon.

Feeling like her morning was well spent, she lingered in the car, trying to decide what to do next. Damn, this sucked. Couldn't go to work, couldn't go home and sit. Maybe she'd take a ride out and see Sam. Always a safe antidote to whatever ailed her. Long before she had Baldwin, Sam was her first sounding board.

Just to be safe, she called Baldwin and told him where she was headed. He told her he was just down the street from Sam's office at the Tennessee Bureau of Investigation offices, and would meet her up at Forensic Medical in an hour. He reminded her to watch her back.

She started the truck and waited a moment, giving the followers time to get into place. Turning left on to Charlotte, she took a quick right on 46th and got on the highway. Within fifteen minutes she was at the ME's office. She didn't see anyone following her, figured they were playing possum out on Gass Street. If Aiden were anywhere around, she couldn't see him either. She wondered briefly how they were going to find a killer who managed to drift unseen through countries and jurisdictions, then pushed the worry from her mind. She left the truck, locked it with a double beep and walked to the front doors. She slid her pass card through the monitor and was let into the building.

The front desk was manned by Kris, smiling a genuine welcome as usual. She waved at Taylor. "Hey, LT. How's it going?"

Was it possible that Kris hadn't heard the news? Taylor walked over to the desk, fiddled with a pen laid out on the counter.

"Hey, Kris. I'm fine. Do me a favor, will ya? Be sure

you don't let anyone you don't know into the building while I'm here, okay? I've got a creep following me and I'd rather not run into him."

"Your boyfriend already warned me. He called a few minutes ago. I'm telling you, Taylor, I don't know why you don't marry that boy. He is one fine piece of man, if you know what I mean." Kris leered. Taylor blushed and rolled her eyes. She didn't bother answering, just waved and scooted through the second security door that led to Sam's office.

Good grief. Kris's taste in men ran toward the bad boys. Taylor had bumped into her at a local watering hole once. Kris was half in the bag, playing pool and drinking whisky with two guys who looked like Hells Angels. She'd introduced one of the bearded men as her current fling. It made her wonder if Baldwin put off that vibe and she just didn't see it because she knew him so well. She took a seat in Sam's office, propped her boots on the corner of the desk, and waited.

She was deep into a daydream about what Baldwin would look like on a motorcycle when Sam appeared five minutes later, wiping her hands on a paper towel. She took one look at Taylor and her face changed from sunny to stormy.

"You okay?" she asked without preamble.

"Not really, but I don't have much of a choice."

Sam gave her a swift, strong hug, then settled into her chair.

"Do they have any idea what's going on?"

"Baldwin is working on it. He's got a friend who can prove the tapes of the shooting have been faked. The rest is taking longer to sort out. Whoever owns that

Web site is well insulated. And I'm stuck out here in the cold, unable to do a damn thing."

"So where have you been all morning?" Sam's eyes sparkled, and Taylor couldn't help but smile back.

"Okay, I've been doing some digging. I can't just sit on my ass and do nothing. I've tracked down the names of the girls on the videotape with Todd Wolff. Turns out they're high-schoolers in a secret society, making amateur porn. Can you imagine?"

"Ambitious," Sam deadpanned.

Taylor's cell rang, Thalia Abbot's number came up on the screen. "Sam, hold on a sec. Hello? Hi Thalia…Yes, illegal drugs…Okay. Thanks again for all your help." She hung up, took out her notebook, and spoke aloud as she wrote.

"Ecstasy, cocaine and pot. Not necessarily only provided by Todd Wolff. Shocking."

"Kids these days. I worry about the twins. What am I going to do when they reach that age? When they want to know about sex, and drinking, and drugs? I'm sure these girls' parents taught them right from wrong. But look at them."

"I can't answer that. My mother gave me as much attention as a she-cat in the wild, and I turned out okay."

"That's debatable," Sam said.

"Ha, ha."

This time it was Sam's phone that rang. She held up a finger and answered. She listened for a minute, then hung up. "You're going to love this."

"Let me guess. You're being suspended for being friends with me."

"Better. We've got confirmation that the semen that

was present in Corinne Wolff's vaginal vault was viable for DNA."

"Really? So whose sperm was it?"

"Now she asks the smart questions. I had the samples sent off for DNA analysis."

"That's going to take months." Taylor slumped back down in her chair.

Sam pushed her bangs off her forehead and gave Taylor an apologetic smile. "Well, maybe not. You know how they've got the lab proposal on the ballot again? They needed some samples to work with to show the legislature how it's all done. So I slipped Corinne's slides in the stack. Not only was there discernible DNA, we should have the results back by late today. The whole point of the exercise was to show how much faster everything would work, how much quicker crimes could be solved if we were running our own labs. Todd Wolff's DNA is in the system now, so if there's a match between them, we'll know. If there's not a match, we'll know that too."

"Let's hope for a match. If it doesn't, that would confirm another suspect. Someone who was sleeping with the victim. Like we need it to be more complicated." A thought nagged her, but she couldn't access it.

"Look at it this way. The results might answer some questions. If the DNA isn't Wolff's, it could be the killer's. Though I must admit, Wolff certainly looks good for all of this. Did you hear that we matched the blood on the tool chest to Corinne Wolff? There's still no definitive test we can do to establish *when* it was left, which a decent defense attorney will pounce on, but it is her blood."

"No, I didn't. Damn it. How can that bitch idiot Norris do this to me? I just want to work the case. All these tidbits are breaking and I don't have the full picture. How am I supposed to solve a case if I'm not allowed to work it?"

"I know, sweetie. The Oompa is an old, shriveled-up hag who is desperately jealous of your success. The beauty of it is you're innocent, Baldwin is about to prove that, then they'll have to let you back. So keep laying low and wait it out. I know that's easier said than done, but you can't run off half-cocked like you did this morning. What were you doing anyway?"

"I met with Corinne's psychotherapist. After you found the benzodiazepine in her system, I went looking to see who'd prescribed it. Her obstetrician gave her the lorazepam but sent her to counseling too in the hopes she'd be able to conquer her issues that way."

"What was the issue?"

"It seems Miss Corinne might have been dallying in someone else's pool, if you know what I mean. Any chance you ran DNA on the fetus? She was having some sort of freak out about the baby. Was having full-blown panic attacks."

"Of course. We'll get all the results back at the same time. That's interesting about Corinne's pathology. I heard of a case like that in medical school. Woman was convinced she was carrying the anti-Christ, they had to keep her sedated because she kept trying to carve the fetus out of her stomach."

"She was having an affair with the devil?"

"Not that I know of, unless the devil lives in New Jersey and is named Dave. They were a completely normal couple, she developed this pregnancy psychosis after it came to light that she'd been sleeping with her husband's brother too and didn't know who the father was. I think the case study concluded that she was just bonkers."

"Nice, round catch-all medical term, that. Bonkers."

"Well, I'm a pathologist, not a psychiatrist. Speak of the devil."

Taylor turned. Baldwin was standing in the door, his tall frame filling the space completely. Arms crossed, he rested his right shoulder against the door frame. She smiled at him. He grinned back.

"You are a very bad girl. Hi, Sam."

"Aw, how come I never get to be the bad girl?" Sam pouted and tossed a balled-up piece of paper at Baldwin, who caught it and expertly shot it into her trashcan in one sweeping motion.

"Show-off," Taylor and Sam said in tandem, sending them both into gales of laughter.

Baldwin joined in, his good-natured laugh reverberating through the room. When they'd finished their giggles, he took a seat next to Taylor.

"Good news. Sherry has reengineered the tapes, found the splice that was put in. It was a rather sophisticated voice track, not something your everyday hump could do. Whoever did it is an expert with cameras and editing, for sure. The evidence was just couriered to your buddy Delores Norris, with copies sent to Price and the Chief of Police."

He settled farther into his chair and crossed his legs. Taylor noticed his socks were mismatched—one had small clocks and the other minute diamonds. She bit back the laugh; he had been pretty shaken up when he got dressed. Maybe he'd make it through the rest of the day without noticing.

She looked back up and saw he'd been watching her, a crooked half smile on his face. He knew about the socks. He made a gesture with his right hand she'd come to recognize as his nonverbal rendition of "not important."

"A couple of copies might have slipped the Net, may show up on the local and national noon broadcasts."

Taylor felt the relief bloom in her chest. "Thank God."

"Don't be thanking Him, thank me."

"You know what I mean. Thank you, of course. Do you think they'll reinstate me?"

"They don't have a choice. If they don't get in touch within the hour, I've scheduled Sherry for a live interview on Channel 5."

Taylor squeezed his hand in gratitude. "So we just have to wait?"

"Yep. Whatcha talking about?"

"The Wolff case. Sam has pulled a fast one, slipped some DNA slides into the system. Corinne Wolff was having sex with someone, and hopefully we'll find out who. The husband first said they hadn't had sex for a week before her death, then remembered they did right before he left town. But looking at the timeline, if there was active enough sperm for a DNA run, she must have had sex with someone after he left on Friday morning. Think the timing works, Sam?"

"Well, if she died Saturday morning and we pulled motile but nondiscernible sperm at the post Tuesday morning…it'll be hard to prove an exact time, but I'm guessing she had sex with someone superlate Friday night or right before she died on Saturday morning."

"And Todd Wolff left early Friday."

"Ask Baldwin about the pregnancy psychosis," Sam said.

"I need to run it down for him first—I haven't talked about the case with him yet. He was in Virginia until yesterday." A current ran through the room as if they'd hit a fuse box. Aiden. God, she'd forgotten he was out there. She didn't elaborate, and neither did Baldwin. Sam picked up on the uncomfortable silence, but was wise enough not to ask.

Taylor turned to Baldwin. "Let me give you a quick précis of the case. Corinne Wolff, twenty-six, seven months pregnant with a son, her second child. Husband allegedly out of town. She was found Monday morning, beaten to death with a tennis racquet in her bedroom. She'd been dead two days." She looked at Sam, and saw the shadows in her eyes. The Wolff crime scene still bothered both of them. Taylor continued.

"Dead two days with her eighteen-month-old daughter wandering around the house, tracking blood everywhere. The husband left Friday, didn't talk to her all weekend. Temp shows she was killed early Saturday morning.

"Second round of look-sees into the house uncovers a sex basement where the Wolffs were making amateur porn. The reports I've gotten indicate that Corinne was a relative latecomer to participating, she'd always run the cameras. I just found out the girls on the video are underage, part of a pretty twisted secret society that's running through the private schools around town.

"Corinne had high levels of lorazepam in her system, and now the news comes that she had viable semen in her. Wolff left her blood on his truck and in the basement, so we arrested him. Her sister is on the news screaming about our idiocy in investigating the case. Thanks to Miss Sam here, DNA is being run as we speak."

Sam took a bow from her chair.

"I interviewed Corinne's OB and her psychologist, and had a chat with her mother. The mom thinks she was having an affair, the docs claim she was having a hard time with the pregnancy, was suffering from a sort of claustrophobia about having the baby inside her. It was so bad that they needed to prescribe benzos to keep her calmed down. It's an incongruity in the case. By all accounts, this woman was a health nut. She was seven months pregnant and still competing in her local tennis tournaments. The house was filled with all-natural foods and cleaning products. The basement, on the other hand, was this crazy sex den, full of camera equipment and sex toys. Corinne was leading two lives, no question about it."

"Do you think her husband committed the murder?" Baldwin asked.

"It seems like the most logical place to turn. At least in the beginning. Now there are all these complicating factors. He got back from his trip a little too quick for my taste, and he's been awfully nonchalant about things so far. Now that we can charge him with a couple of additional sex crimes, I'm thinking that might loosen his tongue. He insists he didn't kill his wife, but there's some pretty decent evidence to the contrary."

"The baby isn't his," Baldwin said.

Taylor looked at him. "What?"

"The baby. It wasn't her husband's. I'd bet anything that she was pregnant by someone else. That explains the erratic behavior, the sudden dependence on psychotropic medications, the psychosis-based claustropho-bia. It all fits. And if I'm right, her husband might have caught her, either in the act with her lover or just after, and killed her in a fit of fury. Pretty classic scenario, actually."

Taylor smiled. "That's exactly where we've been going with our theories. When I interviewed Corinne's psychiatrist, she mentioned that Corinne may have had a lover. For all I know, we might have two bodies. Wolff might have caught her in the act with another man, beat her, killed the lover, then transported his body somewhere. It would explain Corinne's blood in his truck, that's for sure."

Baldwin was nodding his agreement. "You're on to something, Taylor. Did the crime scene techs find more than one type of blood?"

Taylor looked at Sam. "The DNA won't be back on that immediately, I assume?"

Sam shook her head. "Only threw in the autopsy slides, not the evidence collected at the scene. Sorry."

Taylor shrugged. "So no idea. I've been out of the case for over twenty-four hours. Fitz might have solved it already."

"You'd have heard," Sam said kindly. Taylor shot her a dirty look.

Sam's intercom buzzed. Kris's disembodied voice filled the room.

"Dr. Loughley, the Chief of Police is looking for Lieutenant Jackson. Can I put him through to your line?"

Shooting Taylor an *I told you so* look, Sam said, "Sure thing."

The phone beeped twice, then rang. Sam picked it up and handed Taylor the handset.

"Lieutenant Jackson," she answered. She was greeted by the deep, heavily Southern voice of the chief. In a few short words, she had her life back. He'd even thrown in an apology. She hung up the phone with a smile, winked at Sam and turned to Baldwin.

"Let's go. I've got work to catch up on."

Thirty-Three

Taylor didn't expect a hero's welcome. She didn't want one. She just wanted to slip into the CJC and bust open the Wolff murder. And she wanted Aiden to disappear from their lives.

Instead, news vans lined the streets. Reporters jostled with cameramen looking for the best angle. The national news trucks were parked nose to tail along 2nd Avenue, their remote satellites like a string of herons, balanced on one leg and pushing their crests into the noonday sky.

"Well, at least we know you've got the sympathy of the people," Baldwin said.

"Yeah, that's great. I want the media on my side. This is just going to piss Delores off more. And when the Oompa gets mad, she gets even. I'm sure she's in there plotting all the ways she can make my life miserable. I think we're going to have to circle around, sneak in through the parking lot next door."

"No. I think you should walk the gauntlet."

"Are you kidding?"

"No. Walk through there like a queen, smile, wave, and say 'no comment' in your most gracious Southern style. It's a nice PR move on your part."

"I don't particularly want to be on the air anymore. And it will give Aiden a target. Surely you don't want that."

"You've been maligned, and they want to make it right for you. Let them. He's not going to do anything in the middle of this crowd. Trust me."

"The media wants to make it right for me? Are you high? They'd just as soon cut off my leg as paint me in a favorable light."

But she parked in the gravel by the back door. The scrum grew, microphones growing out of the crowd like black mushrooms. They stepped from the car and she was blinded by the flashbulbs. For one insane moment, she thought of what a celebrity's life must be like, and decided that all this constant attention would suck.

She waved, smiled, ignored the shouted questions, and Baldwin held the door for her. The inside was pleasantly quiet. They followed the green arrows in the linoleum floor to the homicide office. Fitz, Marcus and Lincoln were all there. Hugs and claps on the back were exchanged, then Fitz pointed toward her office.

"The Oompa was here a few minutes ago. She wants you. Hurry up, wouldja? We've got loads to go over with you. Lincoln's about to blow this wide open."

"Okay, okay." With a smile, she ducked into her office. On her desk was a handwritten note on a Post-it, the writing surprisingly crabbed.

Please see me immediately. Captain Norris.

Taylor raised an eyebrow at Baldwin. "Let's go see what the wicked witch wants."

Delores seemed taller in her chair and Taylor wondered if she was sitting on a phone book. She'd been talking for the past five minutes, but after she said they were discounting the allegations of witness intimidation, Taylor had tuned her out. There was nothing she could do to her now—Taylor had been cleared of the charge of murder publicly, privately and everywhere in between—but she was still droning on about professional responsibility and taking precautions in life, blah, blah, blah.

Taylor didn't start listening in earnest until she heard the word *shield,* then focused on the Oompa's ridiculously tiny hand. She took the gold with grace, but didn't feel complete until Norris had returned her Glock as well. Not that she'd been cruising around unarmed, but having that particular gun on her hip meant something to her.

She turned to go, but the Oompa cleared her throat viciously. Taylor looked down at her expectant face.

"Yes?"

"Don't you want to say something?"

Taylor was thrust back in time. Her mother had said that to her when she was a child, the tone readily recognized as a mild scold when she hadn't said thank you to a stranger showing a kindness. She would be damned first.

Taylor stared Norris down for a moment. Carelessly, she replied, "No," and walked out of the office.

Baldwin was waiting in the hall, his face a question

mark. She just tapped her waist, where she'd already secured her weapon and her shield. She didn't speak, just kept walking down to the stairwell. Once they were inside, Taylor started to laugh.

"Dear God, that woman's patronizing looks just get me every time. She really thinks she's the bee's knee."

"You should still be careful around her. She's got a stinger."

"Well, she can take that stinger and shove it up her ass. I know she's got it in for me, but I can't change who I am or how I work just to stay on her good side. I've dealt with women like her before. They are so all-fired busy trying to prove themselves that they lose the respect of everyone around them. She'll screw up. I'm just going to stay out of her way from now on."

They had settled in to work, comfortable and secure, when the call came.

Taylor was in her office, the door open, getting briefed by Marcus on what he and Lincoln had uncovered about the Wolffs thus far. The films, the money, the double life. When she looked past Marcus, she could see Lincoln's leg jumping with nervous energy. He had Corinne Wolff's computer on his desk, Todd Wolff's laptop on the desk next to him. He was flying through the files, nodding, saying yes, yes aloud every couple of moments.

Fitz had been called out on a murder, but promised to get back as soon as possible to help. Marcus had just started going over the gas receipts that Wolff had been so shocked to hear they could easily trace when her outside line rang. Taylor answered the phone, was surprised to hear Fitz calling. He'd only been gone twenty minutes, couldn't have had time to do much at the crime scene.

"Hey, what's up?"

His voice was as grave as she'd ever heard it. "I need you."

She didn't question why, just asked where he was.

"The Parthenon. Bring Baldwin. I've got something you both have to see. Someone's sending you a message."

Thirty-Four

Taylor and Baldwin were screaming up West End, a flashing, blaring siren latched to the roof of the car above the driver's side door. Baldwin was driving. It was too loud to talk, which suited Taylor fine. She knew what this was, why Fitz had called her, his normally boisterous voice filled with dread. Aiden. Aiden had killed. Fitz said someone was sending them a message. The moment she'd hung up the phone, Baldwin had looked at her, his eyes full of questions. He knew too.

"Might be a trap," he said.

She shook her head. A message.

She let the memory of Aiden standing in her front lawn fill her. Scant moments after killing two men with his bare hands, he was so damned nonchalant, so…unfazed by what he'd just done. A sense of failure, of loss for the two men who'd answered her summons for help, died trying to protect her, crept down her spine. She'd been so wrapped up in her own troubles, she'd neglected to even find out their names.

The urban spread became Vanderbilt University, a sedate greenness signaled they had arrived. Taylor had always relished the dichotomy that was Nashville; there was something so joyous in downtown's diversity from block to block. Vandy was always a favorite destination. The hopes of the guileless college students, the ornate buildings teeming with knowledge. Before she could get reflective for her own lost years, Baldwin took a fast right into Centennial Park, narrowly missing the ubiquitous jogger panting down the sidewalk.

The grounds of the Parthenon were filled with squad cars. Blue lights shimmered in the midday sun. A knot of officers stood at the base of the Parthenon steps, looking highly out of place. During the day, this was a tourist destination as well as a favorite walking mall. People brought their dogs to run in the grass, ate picnics at the base of the gigantic oak trees, stared in wonder at the perfect replica of ancient Greek architecture and tribute.

The chill spread deeper into her body. Aside from the cops, Centennial Park was strangely empty. The sight of the Parthenon usually filled her with nostalgia; it was never a complete school year without a visit to one of the most recognizable landmarks in Nashville. She mentally reviewed the information that had been parceled to her on every field trip: built to impress travelers visiting Nashville for the 1897 Centennial and designed to reflect the city's reputation as the "Athens of the South," the building was originally meant to be a temporary structure. The sophisticated citizens of Nashville left it standing and by 1931 it was rebuilt as a permanent monument. The massive bronze doors guarded the largest indoor sculpture in the

Western world: a replica of Phidias's colossal statue of Athena, goddess of wisdom, warfare and the arts, sculpted by Nashville artisan Alan LeQuire. The Parthenon art museum was respected worldwide; Taylor had visited an exhibit only last month.

Now the columns held up a roof covered in friezes that seemed much too prescient. The structure stood lonely and bereft, defiled by unsanctioned death, the site of a modern day sacrifice. Taylor could barely force herself out of the car to meet Fitz, who walked quickly to the car when they pulled up.

He was carrying something.

She stepped from the vehicle and faced Fitz. "Who?" she asked.

She caught a glimpse of the photo he was carrying. It was a close-up shot of a naked torso, she could just see the outline of a collarbone above…

The temperature hadn't risen a degree, yet Taylor felt the sweat break out on her brow. She turned her attention to the gathering of police officers twenty feet away. She forced herself to walk slowly, to seem indifferent. Inside she was paralyzed with fear.

The body was naked, artfully arranged to lean against the top step, so a passerby paying little heed might not take notice, would think that it was simply a scantily clad person taking a brief rest.

Closer inspection showed a shock of brown hair, eyes open yet unseeing, glazed already covered with the slightest tint of white. A silver wire, the ends twisted elaborately, was buried deep in the dead man's neck. There was a flourish on the end of the wire that made Taylor think of leftovers dressed in tinfoil worked into the shape of a swan from a fancy restaurant her parents took her to when she was young. She fought back the bile rising in her throat.

Nailed to the naked, hairless chest of the killer she knew only as Aiden was a piece of paper. It was a scroll of parchment, aged and yellowed, a single trickle of crimson blood streaming down the paper. The handwriting was spidery, old-fashioned. As she read, she sucked in her breath in shock.

Dearest Lieutenant,
The world is a better place with you in it. Consider this minor service a token of my appreciation and everlasting admiration.

The Pretender

Fuck.

"How long has he been here?" she asked, impressed with the steadiness in her tone. She didn't dare look at Baldwin, could feel the thoughts churning in his head from three feet away. She didn't have to look at him. She knew he was stunned too.

"Not long," Fitz replied. "The ME's office has sent a team, should be here shortly. First officer on the scene reported that he checked the wrist for a pulse, said he was still warm. He's been in the sun, but it couldn't have been much more than an hour ago. Jogger was going to run up and down the stairs a few times and saw him. Called it in immediately. I've talked to her." He pointed at a squad car, where a young woman in running gear stood shaky and pale. "Didn't see anything. The park's quiet today, she says she saw nobody around."

Baldwin had been silent up to this point, and Taylor

looked at him. There was a bizarre mixture of revulsion and relief on his face. He answered her unspoken question.

"I don't know whether to be thrilled or horrified. Aiden was a terrible person, and I'm not upset that he's dead. But Christ. The Pretender."

"Staying with the program, I see. Copycatting. You said Aiden killed with a silver garrote, right? Seems our serial killer has turned vigilante." She gave a shaky laugh. "Maybe we should hire him out."

The forced bravado was costing her. The mere thought of a killer she failed to catch being back in her town, killing in her name, for her honor, for God's sake, was terrifying.

Baldwin just nodded. The ME's van pulled up, Fitz spoke to her, his voice low.

"You okay?"

"Yeah. Go deal with the ME." The youngest ME on staff, Dr. Fox, jumped out, eyes bright. The word was leaking out. Sure enough, her cell rang, Sam's name popped up on the caller ID. Taylor took a few steps away and opened the phone.

"I heard. Is it true?"

"Yep. Seems our boy has resurfaced. Did quite a number on Aiden. Why aren't you here?"

"I was in a staff meeting with the board. Couldn't break away. Fox can handle the scene, can't he?"

"Don't know why not. It's a bit cut-and-dried. The nails in his chest are a first for me though."

"Well, I haven't done a garroting in a while, so it should be fun. I'll make sure everything is handled well. Don't worry. I've got to run, we're going back into session. Watch your back, okay?"

"Will do. See you later." She hung up, turned to Baldwin, who was on his phone too. Talking to Garrett, she guessed. Calling off her tail.

She went back to Aiden's body, the feeling of being watched making her shiver. Good grief. This had been one hell of a week. She was starting to get a complex; just how many serial killers could the city of Nashville have in one day?

Aiden's gummy gaze seemed to look directly into her soul. Fitz and Fox joined her.

"It's time to let them do their magic," Fitz said. Taylor nodded. Fox was circling the body, making low clucking noises in his throat.

"Jeez," he said. "This is going to be a fun one."

"You ME folks sure are sick. C'mon, LT, let's get you out of here." Taylor let Fitz walk her back to her vehicle. "I'll take care of this. You go back and work the Wolff case. You don't need me for that, Lincoln and Marcus are handling things just fine. I'll meet up with you later."

She nodded again, numbly, and got into the sedan. Baldwin snapped his phone shut and came around to the driver's side, sliding in beside her. He turned over the engine and Fitz carefully shut her door. She didn't know why she was letting everyone pamper her. *Snap to, girl.*

Baldwin pulled away, eyes on the road. She could tell he wanted to talk. That was good, because she didn't.

"I need to talk to you," he said.

"I gathered. You're practically humming."

He cleared his throat, turned left onto West End. "There's more to the Aiden story than I told you."

She waved her hand in a circle. "Tell."

He signed deeply. "What I'm about to tell you is highly classified."

"What, am I about to get assigned to *Mission: Impossible?*"

"Funny girl." He pulled into an open parking space on the street and turned the car off.

"What's this?"

"I'm not kidding." He took off his sunglasses, looked deep in her eyes. "I'm going to get in serious trouble for doing this. But I can't go on without you knowing the truth."

Taylor's heart skipped a beat. A thousand thoughts ran through her mind, beginning and ending with staccato abruptness. She crossed her arms across her chest, better to shield her from whatever deluge was coming. "Can't go on without me knowing what?"

"It's about me. About what I do. My...past."

"You've fathered a love child."

"Damn it, Taylor, I'm serious."

The outburst startled her, she jumped. He'd never spoken to her harshly.

"Jesus, don't bite my head off. It can't be that bad. Just tell me what's up." She sat back against the door facing him, girding herself for the worst, though she couldn't imagine what that could possibly be.

"I do some work on the side. Profiling work."

"That's it? That's the big confession? You're a profiler. Of course you're called in to consult—"

"For the CIA."

That stopped her.

"You're telling me you're a spy?"

He ran his hand through his hair. "No. Not a spy. A consultant."

"I didn't know the CIA did profiling."

"They don't. That's where I come in. It's a covert group called OA. A task force. Operation: Angelmaker. We follow the bad guys who work overseas. Predict where they might hit, give the people who watch them ideas about how to follow their moves, things like that."

"And this is classified? It doesn't sound like that big a deal to me."

"It's the nature of who we're following that's sensitive. The killers we track…they don't get arrested."

"Why not?"

She watched him struggle for an answer, and felt his intensity. The realization that he was worried that she would judge him for whatever role he played in this shadowy organization made her reach over and take his hand.

"Hey," she said, the challenging tone gone. "You can tell me. It's okay."

He smiled at her. "You may not think so when I finish. We let them go. We track their moves, predict where they will strike, hell, even send them assignments to satisfy their desire to kill. All in the name of national security. If we were to arrest them, it would have a lasting effect on whatever political shit is going down. These people do bad things for us, and for other governments. I try not to get too far into the details, I have a hard enough time with it already. It goes against everything that I am."

Honesty. She knew she could always count on him to tell the truth, whether she wanted it or not. Better late than never, she supposed.

"I can see that. How in the world did you get involved?"

"Garrett. He runs our side of the program. He set me up with a cut-out agent that I've worked with for over ten years. Sometimes they ship me overseas to have me track these guys down. Multiple countries, all over the world. We've always had a standing deal, though. If one of them comes here, I'm alerted immediately."

"This is how you got involved with Aiden?"

"Exactly. He's always had a hard-on for me, but I've never been vulnerable until now. Killing me wasn't what he wanted. He needed to take everything from me, like he thought I did to him." He squeezed her hand. "At least, that's what I'm thinking. I told you we're assuming he saw us in Italy, the timing is right. He killed his tracker and hightailed it over here. Just so you know that Aiden was capable of anything to get what he wanted. That's why I had to go to Quantico, to try and track him down. If they'd told me the truth from the start, that he'd murdered the tracker in Florence, I would have never left your side. I've seen what he can do."

"So have I." The image of the dead security guards stood out in stark clarity as if they were right there in the car with them. She shook the thought off, then another crossed her mind.

"Your Italian is perfect. Is that where you learned, watching some Italian psycho?"

He grimaced. "My Italian, and other languages. It was part of why they wanted me."

"Other languages? What, like German and French?"

He was getting visibly uncomfortable.

"More than those three?"

"Uh, yeah."

"Jeez, Baldwin, how many languages do you speak?"

"Thirteen."

She caught her jaw before it hit her chest. She thought back a few moments. Honesty. Omissions weren't lies, were they? Creative lies, white lies that were meant to protect, those didn't count, right? She shoved that thought away. He was telling her now. Lord knows she'd held a few things back about her past.

"Garrett's heart?"

"Fine." He looked like he expected her to fly off the handle. She didn't like that he'd been forced to lie to her, but that's how she saw it. He wouldn't have done it voluntarily.

She grinned. "Okay. Prove it."

"Prove it?"

"Tell me you love me. In…Polish."

Now he was smiling with her. "It's not one of my best, but okay. *Kocham ciebie,* Taylor. With all my heart." He kissed her, leaving her breathless. When they stopped, her fingers were entwined in his hair and her ponytail had come down. Shit, the top button of her jeans was even undone. Making out in public, just so classy.

Setting herself to rights, she said, "I see we're going to have a lot of fun with this little talent of yours."

"You're not mad?"

"About the OA? I'm not thrilled, but I know you. If you think it's the right thing to do, I'll stand by you. Just don't be dragging any more of these wackos home with you, okay? I have enough to deal with."

The thought sobered them up. "You realize that the Pretender is following your moves now. He's calling himself an admirer, but he's more of a danger to you now than ever."

"Yeah, I gathered that. There's nothing I can do about it at the moment. Fitz will work the case. We just have to see if there's any evidence that can help us put a face to his little pseudonym."

"We haven't heard the last of him." He turned the car on, put it in gear.

"No, we haven't. But we've got bad guys aplenty to deal with this afternoon. Let's go solve the Wolff case."

They were quiet, following West End into Broadway, passing a rollicking crowd of tourists at Tootsie's. When they got back to the CJC, she saw Baldwin scoping the parking lot before pulling in. The threat from Aiden may have been past, but the realization that he dealt with more people of the same ilk made her uneasy, regardless of the assurances she gave him.

Thirty-Five

Marcus and Lincoln had evidently heard the news, because they were both wide-eyed when she walked back into the homicide office. Captain Price was sitting with them, a bushy red eyebrow raised in expectation.

She covered the basics as quickly and as vaguely as she could. Baldwin came in and sat down, handed her a Diet Coke and let her tell the story.

"The Pretender seems to be back in Nashville. I don't know what this means, but he's just killed someone from the FBI's wanted list. The man's name was Aiden. Baldwin worked a case that involved him, and Aiden was seeking retribution. He was responsible for the killings at my house. But he's dead now, and we've got bigger issues."

She showed them the Polaroid she'd borrowed from Fitz. Lincoln passed it to Marcus, and they both got stern looks on their faces.

"So the Pretender thinks he's your personal body-guard now?" Lincoln asked. "What the hell?"

"Aiden was looking to hurt me. He went after

Taylor, and the Pretender seems to have a sense of chivalry," Baldwin said.

Price listened, then got up. "That's it. There's entirely too much bullshit flying around. I'm having a private security detail put on you, Taylor."

"I've already done that," Baldwin said. "I've had them on Taylor since yesterday. We'll just keep up with the watchers, let them know what we know about the Pretender. They're a good team, I trust them."

So he wasn't calling off the dogs while they were at the Parthenon, he was adding more.

"And how long are we planning to keep this up?" Taylor was shaking her head. "No. I don't want them."

"You're going to have to live with it, sugar." Baldwin's stance told her arguing was fruitless.

"I agree. We can't afford anything happening to you, LT. Lincoln and I will start looking for more clues with the Pretender case. We'll find the bastard. In the meantime, we need to keep you off his radar," Marcus said.

"I can take care of myself," she grumbled, but when faced with four glowering men, all intent on keeping her out of harm's way, she decided discretion was the better part of valor and acquiesced. For the time being.

"Can we at least get back to work?"

Price patted her on the head and she narrowed her eyes at him. "I've got a meeting. Fill her in. You should be proud of your boys. And be careful, wildcat."

"Yes, Dad," she said.

"I'm going to join the captain for a moment. Be right back." Baldwin left the room with Price, their conversation quickly moving out of earshot.

Taylor rolled her eyes, then turned to Marcus and

Lincoln. "Good grief. This has been a day. Let me have it. What's the news on the Wolff case?"

Lincoln waved his hand to Marcus. "You go," he said.

"Okay. To start with, we checked on the underage actresses. They've both split town, ostensibly for California. They had auditions today at Vivid Video, and we've got a call in to their 'agent' to get them to call us immediately when they get finished."

"You mean when they come up for air?" Taylor said, making all of them laugh.

"Yeah. Then. So in the meantime, we've been looking at Todd Wolff's files. We've confirmed he wasn't in Savannah when he said he was. He used his gas card to fill up the day before the murder, Sunday, in Crossville. So Wolff was definitely in the state of Tennessee at least one day after the murder."

"Doesn't prove he did it."

"No, but it does verify that he's lied about several things. They're arraigning him this afternoon, so we should get an opportunity to question him again late this evening. Julia Page and Miles Rose have already been informed that we want to have a chat."

"If he was in Crossville Sunday, where was he Saturday?"

"That's the question. We don't know. He wasn't in Savannah. His receptionist caved pretty quick when she realized we knew he was lying. She said he hadn't been to the job site in over a week. The maestro here—" he gestured to Lincoln "—has been working his mojo on their computers. Corinne Wolff was a very bad girl."

"Really?"

Lincoln handed her a sheaf of papers. "She was definitely getting some nookie on the side. Here's her little love notes, courtesy of her private e-mail. They are all from a separate address, a different provider, and password protected. The whole nine yards. We assume she didn't share it with Todd, they have another couple of addresses that are obviously for his work, her friends, and another that's solely smut related. This one was tucked away in a hidden folder."

She knew it. Taylor glanced through the first few sheets. The usual online lovey-dovey stuff, typical of any relationship. "I don't see a name. You're sure this wasn't between her and Todd?"

"Positive. I traced the IP address. It's registered to a completely different person. The same person, by the way, that owns the IP address for Selectnet.com." His smile was nonchalant, but his eyes burned with the knowledge that he'd done something remarkable.

Taylor nearly fell out of her chair. "What? What do you mean? The California company that's putting up the sex videos? My sex videos? Corinne's involved in that?"

"They both are, though in completely different ways. Todd Wolff seems to be the purveyor of both fine art and the lowbrow stuff. He's working for the Select-net company, providing them with high-quality film. That's his big sideline money-maker, the porno flicks he's making in his basement. But we've gone through his finances with a fine-toothed comb, and we found some interesting purchases. Specifically, he bought forty of the cameras we found in the vents of your cabin."

It took Taylor a moment to wrap her head around that little tidbit. "Todd Wolff was responsible for putting the cameras in my house? How in the world is that possible?"

"Not just your cabin. Here's our theory. We've tracked down more of the uploaded videos to the Selectnet site. A huge number come from Nashville. Todd's the head of Wolff Construction. It's as easy as pie—when he builds a house, he places the cameras. The owners have no idea they're there, and he gets to parlay all that unedited film into home movies on the Web site."

Taylor gave a long, low whistle. "Do you realize how many houses he's built? There could be cameras in all of them."

"Well, forty of them that we suspect, at least."

"But he didn't build my cabin. How did that happen? How would Wolff have gotten into my house?"

"Here's the genius part. Before he started Wolff Construction as a home builder, he was a renovator. He did contract jobs for insurance money. Say, for example, a person has a leak in their shower, has to file a claim on their home-owner's insurance to get it fixed. The insurance company contracts with certain construction firms to do the work. We checked, and Wolff Construction was one of those companies. It's how he made enough money, on the books at least, to graduate to the home building company. And the camera purchase is recent, only last year. He could have bought many, many more and we just haven't found the records yet."

Taylor let the thought gel. When had she had work done on the cabin? She didn't remember…oh, yes, she did. She'd done a minor kitchen remodel a year after she moved in. But that wasn't an insurance claim, and she didn't remember working with Wolff Construction. She racked her brain trying to remember the name of the company she'd used, but it wouldn't come. She told Lincoln that.

"I already thought of that," he said. "Even before he started the work with the insurance companies, he worked for his dad. His dad owned several firms, one of which was—"

"Remedy. Remedy Remodelers. Son of a bitch."

"Exactamundo."

"Wow. Lincoln, this is fantastic work!"

"Aww, it wasn't just me. Marcus did some of it."

"Gracious of you," Marcus said.

"Think nothing of it," Lincoln jibed back.

Taylor tuned out their banter. The tendrils of Wolff's multiple illegalities would have serious ramifications. They needed to talk to the press, to get the word out. Which also meant rolling up the Selectnet shop. Even though the site had been pulled from the Internet, they still needed to bring in the ringleaders. For that, she needed Baldwin's help.

"We need to have a press conference, among other things. I'm going to call Baldwin. How much information do you have that we can use to indict Selectnet.com? Because we have to take them down."

"That's what Price is doing. He's talking to Dan Franklin and they're designing a media campaign. He's left it to us to wrap the case. So, here's the rest of the story."

"There's more?"

"Much more. Marcus, you go. I'm getting parched."

"Okay. We backtraced the IP address for the Selectnet company. The California holdings are a front. The money trail leads right back here to Nashville. Does the name Henry Anderson ring a bell?"

Taylor felt the name go through her like a lightning bolt. The image of the man connected to the name came, vivid and sharp. A name from the past.

"Are you joking?"

They both shook their heads.

"Do you know the story behind Henry Anderson?" she asked.

"We've been familiarizing ourselves with it. He was one of your busts, that much we know. You got him into prison on child molestation charges. He charged you with brutality."

"Ha. I kicked him in the balls when he tried to run during an arrest. He deserved it. Child molestation was the only charge we managed to get to stick. And it wasn't even a felony count, it wasn't the same kind of terminology we'd use today. I think he was ultimately charged with child endangerment, actually. We couldn't do much better than that. A shame too, Henry's quite the sleazeball. He was making movies back then. He served a few years, and got out." She paused, snapped her fingers. "The movies. That's it, isn't it? Henry is Todd Wolff's benefactor."

Lincoln nodded. "That's what we think. He is definitely the owner of Selectnet, and his reach looks to be deeper than that. We're still running through all the information, but there's definitely enough to tie him directly to underage porn. Among about a thousand other violations of the law."

Taylor went to her little window, looked out across 2nd Avenue. There was dust in the air, probably from the construction site down the road, and the motes danced in the sun. Pretty. Unlike her thoughts right now. Abandoning the dust ballet, she turned back to them.

"I didn't know he was still in the state. Henry fucking Anderson. He's a mean son of a bitch. I had a difficult time with him, he came after me with both barrels, tried to have my testimony discredited, filed the charges against me. They got dismissed. I caught him red-handed with his dick in a kid's face, and he tried to make *me* look bad." She broke off again. All the little pieces fell into place.

"Tony Gorman. You said he was a member of Selectnet. He got word to Henry that I'd gotten a sniff of their enterprise. I'll bet a million dollars that's where the complaint came from, the one that Delores Norris listened to when she suspended me. I got a little cheeky with Gorman in our interview. Gorman wouldn't have had the guts to do it himself, but if he were encouraged…Henry is a master manipulator. Unbelievable."

Lincoln and Marcus were equally excited. "After we talk to Wolff this evening, hit him with all this information, that we know his role, surely we can shake his ass loose on the murder of his wife. He's facing so many different counts and so many years in jail that it shouldn't matter to him. Copping a plea to murder should be the least of his worries."

"Well, we can hope. Let's fill Page in, tell her what's happening. Then we need to go get Henry Anderson. I'm assuming you've already found him, Lincoln?"

"Yep." He flashed her a gap-toothed grin. "He's right there on the sexual offenders' database, all registered up like a good little boy."

Thirty-Six

Taylor was getting her ducks in a row.

She spent a few minutes writing up the case notes while she waited for the requisite warrants to be arranged before they took their case-breaking field trip. The evidence implicating Todd Wolff was becoming increasingly cut-and-dried. They just needed one or two more pieces of the puzzle to lock him up for life, and it seemed her team, working closely with Baldwin's FBI cohorts, was accomplishing that very nicely. The added satisfaction of bringing Henry Anderson to his knees should be quite the capper on her day.

Taylor had talked to Julia Page and they'd decided to seek separate indictments against Todd for the pornography, the cyber Peeping Tom cameras, and the murder of Corinne Wolff. No sense throwing everything into one basket, have a technicality render an acquittal and not be able to retry due to the convoluted double-jeopardy statutes.

Dan Franklin was ready to go to the media with the story as soon as Baldwin's people gave the okay sign that they'd raided the California Selectnet offices and taken possession of their physical records.

Taylor and Marcus were ready to pick up Henry Anderson. Lincoln was set up in a private office, working with one of Baldwin's forensic accountants, trying to unravel more of the Wolffs' financial trail. Considering the accountant was petite and blond, Lincoln didn't seem terribly put out.

Fitz was at the ME's office. A quick autopsy was being performed on Aiden, courtesy of one of Baldwin's calls to Quantico. Garrett Woods had sent down a staff forensic pathologist to help Sam with the evidentiary trail.

All these law enforcement folks, acting as one big happy family. They were lucky to have a good working relationship between all the jurisdictions involved. Taylor had to admit, it was nice to work with Baldwin again. His calm, cool demeanor always helped an investigation along, especially in the critical moments before they blew it wide open.

And at the moment, the man in question had his feet propped on the edge of her desk, watching her finagle a warrant for Henry Anderson. His green cat eyes were practically dancing with merriment watching her go through the elaborate machinations with the judge she'd pulled. It was the newly elected female judge, Sophia Bottelli, the former prosecutor who was adamant about *i* dotting and *t* crossing.

Promise of a signature finally secured, Taylor hung up the phone and looked at Baldwin's grinning visage.

"You look like a Halloween jack-o'-lantern. Could you smile any bigger?"

He swung his feet off her desk. "This whole week

has been unreal. You've been raked over the coals, humiliated, yelled at by your fiancé, yet here you are, unscathed, ready to swoop in and take down the bad guy. I love it when you do that."

"Funny, I was just thinking the same thing."

"Think we've got it all covered?"

"I'd still like to know why Michelle Harris went on the national news and tried to discredit me. All I've tried to do is help her and her family."

"Grief makes people do strange things."

"Well, that's true. When I first met her, I don't know, there was something off about her. I'm probably just imagining things, it was a horrible moment for that whole family. Her mom was crying in the chaplain's arms, sobbing her heart out, the dad was in shock, the other sister was blank as a slate. Michelle was the only one who had any semblance of composure about her. When she came into the room, there was this moment where she looked almost feral. She covered it up quickly, I've never seen it again, but for that instant…this is going to sound stupid."

"No, go on."

"It was like she wanted me. Sexually, I mean."

"She isn't married, is she?"

"No. She's…" She cocked her head to the side. "You know, I don't know too much about her. I was so busy focusing on Corinne that I didn't look too far into the rest of the family. Then we have the lovely moments without a badge this week. I've glossed over too much. We'll have to spend the next few weeks filling in all the pieces. Never mind about Michelle. There's nothing there. Like I said, it was probably my imagination."

Marcus knocked on her door. "Hey, I was talking to Sam, she wants to talk to you. I'm going to transfer her in, okay?"

"Sure." Taylor waited for the buzz that indicated a forwarded internal call, then picked up the receiver.

"I refuse to go to any more charity events," Taylor said.

"Then goodie for you that's not what I'm calling about. I have something you're going to love."

Taylor snickered. "Goodie for me? What are we, five? What's the big news?"

"DNA's back on Corinne Wolff."

"Ooh, you're right. That is something I want. Give it to me, sister."

"You're not going to believe this. The semen deposit was left by Henry Anderson."

"Henry Anderson, as in my video-crazy pedophile? The one who Todd Wolff was working for?"

"Todd Wolff was working for Henry Anderson?"

"Long story, but yes. In a nutshell, that's exactly what's been happening."

"There's more."

"What?"

"Henry Anderson was the father of Corinne Wolff's son."

Taylor clicked the speakerphone button, gestured at Baldwin to pay attention. "Say that again."

"Todd Wolff was not the father. The DNA on the fetus shows that Henry Anderson was the father of Corinne Wolff's child."

"Sam, you are the greatest gift a homicide detective could ever have."

"Well, thank the mayor, because if he hadn't asked

for the proof that we could streamline the system, I never would have put this case's DNA on the fast track."

"I hope this means you're getting a new lab?"

"I don't know, T. I gotta run, we've got Aiden's autopsy done and I need to write up some notes. By the way, tell Baldwin the crime scene techs found Aiden's clothes in a bin behind the McDonald's on West End. We'll get that sent to his lab, if he'd like."

Baldwin said, "Yes, please, Sam. Did you find an ID?"

"There was a wallet and a passport, both with ID in the name of Jasper Lohan. High-end stuff, they look legitimate."

"Jasper Lohan. I don't recognize that name for him. No wonder we lost him in St. Louis. Cunning bastard." He wrote a quick note, then said, "Okay. Thanks."

They hung up with promises to have dinner over the weekend. The banality of the arrangements made Taylor long for some peace and quiet, reminded her that she wasn't like everyone else. Making plans was a luxury, a formality. In most cases, either she or Sam, or Baldwin, or Sam's husband Simon, would be called to work a case. They lived in twenty-four-hour-a-day jobs, their lives cordoned off at the whim of a criminal.

Taylor toyed with a pencil. "Corinne's mother was right. Corinne *was* having an affair."

"Goes a long way toward explaining the claustrophobia that Corinne was suffering from. A psychosomatic response to infidelity. Maybe she and Henry had broken up and she found herself pregnant."

"If they'd broken up, why did she have sex with him right before she died? And why do these—" she waved the stack of love notes taken off Corinne Wolff's computer at him "—have recent dates? No, Corinne was still deep into the affair."

"Well, a better question is, did Henry Anderson kill her?"

Taylor thought about that for a moment. "I think Todd did it. That level of rage—I can see Todd finding out his wife was cheating on him, maybe even learning that the baby wasn't his child, and snapping. We have the evidence against him, the blood in his truck, on his toolbox. A stranger isn't going to know about the drawers in her closet, that's an intimate spot to stash the tennis racquet after you've beaten someone to death with it. He's been lying from the beginning, saying he was in Savannah when he was really in Nashville, or within a tank of gas to Nashville. Why did he lie if he didn't kill her? It's a helluva lot easier to prove an alibi that's real than create a false one. No, my money is still on Todd. Henry Anderson is scum, but he's a pussy. He's a manipulator, someone who knows what buttons to push to take advantage of people. Blatant violence seems a bit strong for him.

"But I may be wrong. It's been ten years since I've had this guy on my radar. He may have changed. Obviously being in jail didn't help him find the error of his ways and clean up. It's entirely possible that he did kill her."

She stopped, lost in thought again.

"You know, Baldwin, you were right. When I told you about my interview with Dr. Ricard, Corinne's therapist, and she hinted that Corinne had a lover. You hit the nail on the head about the baby not being Todd Wolff's."

"What did she say exactly?"

Taylor grabbed her notebook, flipped to the pages where she'd written down her interview with Ricard.

"Here it is. 'Instead of fighting, she acquiesced. Allowed herself to be used.' I asked about Todd using her. She said, 'By many people. Husband, family, siblings, lover. You'll hit upon the truth soon enough, Lieutenant.' Right there. *Lover*. She was helping Corinne deal with having an affair. Both Ricard and Katie Walberg, the OB/GYN, said Corinne was a serial monogamist. Maybe sleeping with two men at once was too much for her psyche."

"Not sleeping with two at once. Caring about two at once. That was the problem."

"You're probably right. Maybe she was breaking it off with Henry and he killed her. We need to go see Mr. Anderson. Maybe he can shed some light on this."

They stood.

"Bring your handcuffs," Baldwin said.

"Oh, trust me. I intend to."

Thirty-Seven

They caravanned over to 51st Avenue in northwestern Nashville, a small section of town aptly named the Nations. It was across Interstate 40 from Sylvan Park, the mirror image of the state street routes Taylor and Sam used to trace with their parents on pilgrimages to Bobbie's Dairy Dip.

The Nations was an upstanding industrial area which quickly gave way to squalor. It was another one of those bizarre Nashville disunions, a forgotten zone in the midst of splendor and plenty. A five-block area dedicated to crime. The police presence was heavy, trying to quell the rampant drug and sex trade. They were losing the battle.

Here in this little molecular oasis of misery, the residents operated in the land time forgot. Pay phones outnumbered cell phones and were still prevalent on every street corner, graffiti-painted and piss-filled. Teenagers wandered in baggy pants and cornrows, holding forty-ounce beer cans wrapped in brown paper bags. Crime, negligence, fear, all the horrors of life seeped in under the cracks of their doors in the middle of the night, carrying away their faith in humanity. These people didn't just distrust the police, they didn't acknowledge their existence. Justice was meted out behind gas stations and in dirty alleyways, business conducted under broken street lamps and in fetid, unair-conditioned living rooms.

It was the perfect place for a pedophile to hide.

The left-hand turn onto Centennial Boulevard took Taylor into what could have been a war zone. Damage from a tornado that blew through Nashville in 1998 had destroyed this area, and not much had been done to return it to its previous semi-squalor. Two patrol cars slid by, both drivers put their hands out the window with their palms down—the universal cop signal for fair sailing. All is well, be careful out there. We have your back. Taylor signaled the same back to them.

Within minutes, they pulled up to the address on record for Henry Anderson. It would be generous to call the domicile a house—it was little more than a shack, the roof sagging, the windows boarded with cardboard. They could see muffled bits of the Cumberland River beyond the property. The likes of Anderson wouldn't be accepted in a neighborhood that had expectation.

Anderson wasn't living large. The money he was pulling in from the pornography obviously went toward something else, Taylor speculated. Drugs, perhaps. The house looked like it could double as a meth lab.

Baldwin had gotten quiet as they pulled up. She put the car into park and raised an eyebrow at him.

"This place is a dump," he said. "Surely a criminal

mastermind isn't living in this hell. What's he doing with his money?"

"Funny, you read my thoughts. Let's go see."

They exited the vehicle. Marcus got out of his Caprice. All three dressed in plainclothes, sunglasses on, looking like cops, it was no surprise that there wasn't a single person in sight. Taylor knew they needed to show strength, not hesitate. She strode across the dust bowl that passed for a lawn in front of Anderson's house and banged on the door.

"Police! Open up!"

Nothing.

She pounded her fist against the door again, three times, the sound echoing. Before she could hit the door a fourth time, it opened a crack. A woman peered from the bowels of the house. Taylor smelled a unique miasma of odors—fear and old garbage predominant among them.

The door opened a little wider. The woman—check that, the girl—who stood before them wasn't smiling.

"Whaddaya want?"

Taylor could see the girl wore a uniform. She had a nametag on her left breast that read Waffle House, with *Wendy* written in crooked, childlike letters beneath the corporate logo. She wore a black golf visor with pin-on buttons affixed to the sides. Her hair was skinned back from her face in a semblance of a ponytail, blond at the ends, the roots twisted and oily, nearly black. Her eyes were dull brown, the whites slightly red as if she hadn't slept well or was indulging in some recreational drug.

"We're looking for Henry Anderson."

"Isn't here." She started to shut the door, but Taylor

stuck the toe of her cowboy boot into the crack. She stifled a yelp as the door slammed onto her toe.

"We'd like to come in. Wendy? We're with Metro homicide. We need to talk with Henry."

The girl squinted at Taylor. Her teeth were showing, small and crooked, pointed inward as if they were recoiling in horror from the life their owner had chosen. Without a word, she walked away from the door.

Taylor glanced over her shoulder at Baldwin. His hand was resting on his weapon, Marcus had his holster unsnapped and his service Glock an inch out of the leather. They nodded. Taylor pushed the door open with the toe of her boot and let it swing away.

The inside of the house was stifling. A broken fan sat on a milk crate in front of a rump sprung couch, ashtrays and empty beer cans spilled over the edge of what Taylor assumed was a kitchen counter.

"Henry's not here," Wendy repeated, lighting a cigarette. She took a deep draw, blew the smoke out with a cough.

"Don't you want to know why we want to speak with him?"

"Not my business. I rent from him. He don't live here."

Add slumlord to Anderson's list of sins.

"Where does he live, Wendy?"

"Dunno." She resumed smoking, standing warily five feet from Taylor. She held her left arm across her stomach. Taylor looked closer. The girl was slightly hunched over, and in the dim light, Taylor realized that standing was causing her pain. Coupled with the hunted, faraway look in the girl's eyes, the remnants of a bruise fading from her check, Taylor was overcome with pity.

"Why don't you sit down, Wendy. Tell us who hurt you."

Something fired in the girl's eyes, whether it was pride or fury, Taylor didn't know.

"I'm fine," she said carefully.

"You don't look fine. Did you get kicked in the stomach?"

"None of your beeswax." She stabbed out the cigarette, turned away.

The childish answer broke Taylor's heart. *There but for the grace of God go I.* Then again, maybe not. Taylor had never understood the cycles of domestic violence. She'd seen the outcomes time and time again. The plays for control, the vicious fights that escalated to beatings, the beatings that got more and more severe until they sometimes resulted in death. How hard would it be to just walk away? These men who knew how to strike without leaving visible bruises, Taylor would like to round them up and shoot them all.

She caught Baldwin's eye. He was the psychiatrist, let him try.

As Baldwin moved to talk to the girl, Marcus and Taylor took a lap around the house. Dirt-filled crevices, roaches, abandoned magazines without covers, pizza boxes. The bathroom hadn't been cleaned in weeks, and a lone plastic stick sat on the cracked vanity. A pregnancy test. Too much time had passed for the results to still be visible, whether hours or days, Taylor didn't know. There was no sign of Henry Anderson, no men's toiletries, no clothes. It seemed Wendy had been telling the truth, Anderson didn't live here. Not anymore.

They went back to the overheated living room.

Wendy sat on the decrepit couch. She was crying quietly. Baldwin was perched on the milk crate next to her, holding her hand.

Baldwin spoke without taking his eyes off the girl.

"Anderson lives in East Nashville. He holds this house as an address for the police, rents it out. Wendy hasn't seen him for weeks. I believe her," he added. A fragile trust had obviously been forged between them. Baldwin handed her something. His card, Taylor assumed, and they bid the girl goodbye.

Out in the yard, Baldwin ran his hands through his hair, making it stand on end. Taylor saw a glint of silver deep in the black, a precursor to the more salt than pepper look he'd obviously have in a few years. He had a few strands starting in his temples already; this streak was new.

"I've got the address for Anderson. She mails him a money order biweekly to cover the rent. She just lost a baby. You were right, the boyfriend kicked her in the stomach a few days ago, she miscarried yesterday. Didn't miss her shift at work though. She said she couldn't afford to skip work. Poor girl."

Marcus leaned against his car. "Are we going to go pick him up?"

"You betcha," Taylor replied. "Let's go."

Judge Sophia Bottelli was less than pleased with Taylor.

"And why didn't you know about this alternate address for this Anderson, Lieutenant?"

"I'm sorry, Your Honor. This is a breaking case, moving quickly. We only discovered Anderson's involvement less than twenty-four hours ago." *C'mon, lady, just initial the fucking amendment to the warrant and let's be done with it. Quit busting my chops, time's a-wasting.* She couldn't say that, of course, there'd be no surer way to a cell for contempt charges if she spoke aloud. *You're being bitchy to the bench, do not pass Go, do not collect two hundred dollars.* But jeez, busting her balls wasn't helping things.

"I trust that this is the last time I'll be hearing from you about this warrant, Lieutenant. I'll have it faxed with my signature. But no more. I expect to see results from you."

"Yes, ma'am. Thank you, Your Honor."

Actually, Taylor kind of liked Judge Bottelli. She was tough as nails, but so far had treated them fairly. She'd see what time brought. Obviously her fall from grace earlier in the week was still fresh on the minds of Nashville's judicial branch. Damn it. She was going to be rebuilding herself for quite some time. The Oompa's overreaction in stripping her of her badge would have lasting effects.

The fax machine spit out a single sheet of paper. "Got it," Taylor yelled. No more time to feel sorry for herself. It was time to roll.

She hustled out to the homicide office. Marcus and Lincoln were in consultation, Baldwin standing behind them, leaning in with interest.

"What's up?"

"Nothing yet," Lincoln answered. "I'm working on something, but if it doesn't pan out, I don't want to waste your time. Go snatch up Anderson before he gets wind of your imminent arrival." He nodded once at Baldwin, then left the room.

Taylor looked at Baldwin, who threw his hands up in the air. "I know nothing. Let's go."

The drive to East Nashville only took five minutes. As they turned onto Eighth Avenue North, the leafy street filled with restored Victorian homes, Taylor shook her head.

"You realize that he lives one block away from Betsy Lerner, our Lieutenant in Sex Crimes? He must be using a false name."

Baldwin shook his head. "He isn't. Marcus pulled the records while you were talking to the judge. The property rolls for this address have him listed as owner, but he had a cosigner on the loan, so that name is primary."

"What's the cosigner's name?"

"Antonio Giormanni."

Taylor expertly whipped the vehicle into a parallel spot that didn't look large enough for their sedan, then slammed the car into park and turned in her seat.

"I am going to spit nails in about two seconds."

"Why?"

"Because I've met the son of a bitch. Though he uses the name Tony Gorman in public. Baldwin, I have been played. Royally played. Tony Gorman and Henry Anderson are buddies, and hoo-boy, I have been played to the fucking hilt."

She banged her hands against the steering wheel. Marcus came to her door. She put the window down.

"Antonio Giormanni is listed as the co-owner of this house," she said. "Does that name sound familiar?"

Marcus looked at her for a long moment, then smacked his hand against the roof of the car. "Tony Gorman?"

"Exactly."

"No wonder we couldn't get anything good on him.

He's using false names. The Tony Gorman is a legit ID, that's what he's registered in Tennessee's DMV system as, the property rolls too. That's how we picked him up. Wow, they've got some kind of vendetta against you, don't they, LT?"

"Excuse me," Baldwin cut in. "Care to give me a clue what you're talking about?"

Taylor was shaking her head, a smile on her face that wasn't borne of amusement.

"Tony Gorman manhandled me at a charity dinner earlier this week. Called me Tawny. That's how we got to the sex tapes on Selectnet. This entire wild-goose chase was engineered, up to and including me getting my badge pulled. Though I'm guessing they thought their handiwork was good enough that it would be permanent, or that I'd slink away with my tail between my legs and resign from the shame. Oh, they are going to regret the day they were born."

She got out of the car with fury in the pit of her stomach. The last laugh would be hers.

Baldwin looked at Marcus. "We might want to go after her. She looks like she could burn down the whole neighborhood if we don't get her calmed down."

Marcus laughed. "Yeah, well, good luck with that. You know how she is when she's fired up. A train couldn't stop her. I wouldn't be laying money on Anderson surviving this one."

They started after her. As they crossed the street, Marcus called in to Lincoln, asked him to execute a warrant for Antonio Giormanni ASAP, and to get him picked up. Lincoln put the pieces together immediately, cursed and promised to handle things on his end. Baldwin signaled he wanted to talk to Lincoln. After a few moments, he hung up, and they caught up with Taylor.

"You ready to do this?" Baldwin asked her.

"You know it. Let's take this fucker down." She unholstered her weapon and went to the door. Banged on it like she'd done at Anderson's other house. "Police! Open the door."

Open sesame, she thought. The door was opened immediately and a familiar face stood in the doorway.

Michelle Harris looked completely and utterly shocked. Her face went white, and she moved on instinct, away from the brandished weapon Taylor had in her right hand, pointed right at her. She turned to flee. Taylor took three steps after her and got a handful of her hair, yanked her to a stop.

"Ow!" Michelle screamed.

"Shut up!" Taylor screamed right back at her. "What the hell are you doing here?"

Thirty-Eight

Baldwin was through the door now, Marcus too. Taylor looked at both of them, released Michelle's hair.

"Where is Henry Anderson?"

"He's upstairs, taking a shower. What in the world are you doing here? And why are you looking for Henry?" Though she sounded genuinely shocked, Taylor wasn't falling for it. She knew that Michelle Harris wasn't here by accident.

"I'll get him," Marcus said, charging up the oak staircase. Baldwin followed right on his heels.

Taylor steered Michelle by the arm, settled her roughly on a cinnamon-colored leather couch in what could best be described as a den. Dark wood, bookshelves lining the walls—there was a fleeting impression of beauty, but the irony of the situation was too strong. She blocked everything out but Michelle's horror-stricken face.

"Why are you here? What is your connection to Anderson?" she peppered.

"Duh. He's my boyfriend. We've been dating for

over a year. What's it to you? Why are *you* here? What do you want from Henry? He hasn't done anything wrong, has he?"

Taylor stayed standing, looming over Michelle. "You are dating Henry Anderson. You're kidding me, right?" Baldwin had sidled up beside her.

"Marcus has Anderson cuffed and in custody, has him Mirandized with me as a witness. Patrols are on their way to execute the search warrant. He's lawyered up."

"You arrested Henry? For what?"

"Oh, let's see, Baldwin, what all do we have him on? Child pornography, for starters. Libel, slander, breaking parole, falsifying information about his whereabouts to the Tennessee Bureau of Investigations, falsifying his information on the sexual offenders database. That's just for starters, I'm sure the D.A.'s office will have an indictment the length of my arm when they get done with him. Federal *and* state charges. Your Henry is going away for a long time. Oh, and there's that other pesky little thing. Your sister's murder."

Michelle shook her head, swatting her hand in front of her face like she was shooing away a bee. "Wait, wait, wait. Todd killed Corinne. You arrested him. All the evidence pointed right at him. They are working on a trial date, for God's sake. Henry has never met my sister in his life. There's no way he could be involved. And what are you talking about, the sexual offenders' database? Henry isn't a sex offender. I live here, you think I could miss it if he had a problem?"

"You're so sure about that, Michelle?"

Taylor heard the boots of the additional patrol

officers arriving. The house was quickly teeming with officers. Henry Anderson was already stashed in the back of a patrol car, awaiting a ride down to the CJC. Taylor hadn't even seen him brought out of his house. She stowed the disappointment, there was plenty of time to deal with him.

Michelle met Taylor's gaze without flinching. "Yes, I am sure. I'd like to see Henry now," she answered. She might as well have been sucking on ice cubes, the words were so cold.

Jesus. The woman didn't have a clue. How was that possible? Her lover was a full-time video pimp, running a massive, diverse organization of smut, and she didn't know? Taylor found that extremely hard to believe.

"Why don't you come downtown with us, Michelle. You can tell me more about Henry."

Taylor reached for Michelle's arm. It was one step too far. Michelle snatched her arm away and turned on Taylor so swiftly that three weapons were drawn.

"You know, I trusted you. That first day, in Mrs. Manchini's living room, when you'd just come from Corinne's house. All I saw was a kind woman, a woman I could trust to bring justice for Corinne. Now look at you. Tilting at windmills, discredited, demeaned. You're the laughingstock of Nashville, you know that? Can't even keep your own playthings off the air. Not to mention solve a predictable murder. Henry told me what you did to him. I hate you, you…you… SLUT!"

Michelle stormed out of the room, leaving Taylor stunned.

She'd only focused on one line in Michelle's tirade.

The laughingstock of Nashville?

Could that be true?

Stop it, girl. Look at the source. Michelle was obviously disturbed. First her sister is murdered, then she finds out her boyfriend is a liar. If anything, she was the sad case here. She's having an awfully tough week. Just wait until she finds out her beloved boyfriend was banging her dead sister. Might make me a little testy, too.

Taylor swallowed hard, then followed Michelle out the front door of Anderson's home. One way or another, it was time for some answers.

Thirty-Nine

Taylor was in Interrogation two, Henry Anderson across from her. He'd aged since she last saw him. The close-cropped hair was prematurely white, his skin tanned but starting to go crepey around his eyes and mouth, his teeth flashing under a still black goatee.

He still had those icy green eyes too, the ones that made her so uncomfortable all those years ago when she was putting the cuffs around his wrists the very first time. The eyes that distracted her just long enough for him to try to escape. Back then, she didn't know the difference between lust and hate. She wasn't intimately familiar with the seductiveness of evil. Now she was. And there was no question which emotion Anderson was feeling right now.

Hate was probably too gentle a word. Absolute and complete abhorrence, that was a better description of the daggers he was shooting at her.

"You know, bitch, I'm gonna be out on bail before you finish sucking your boyfriend's dick tonight."

"Henry, shut up." Miles Rose was seated next to

Anderson, looking decidedly less jovial than when he was last in the room with Todd Wolff.

Taylor's opinion of Rose had shifted one hundred and eighty degrees. Rose was on the direct retainer of The September Group, Henry Anderson's umbrella company that housed his illicit video empire. Selectnet was just one of the companies he operated, staying anonymous through multiple layers of business bullshit.

It was a damn shame Henry Anderson was such a lowlife criminal. If he were straight, he could be president.

"You still like your pussy licked, Lieutenant? I always liked watching those boys go down on you. Hard to come that way for you though, isn't it? Givin' up too much control, I expect. 'Cept for with that new boy. He's quite the *artiste*, if you know what I mean. That why you're marryin' him? He makes you cream?"

Rose had the decency to blush. "That is enough, Henry."

"No, Miles, it's fine. This is the only way Henry can get off." Taylor met the frosty eyes. "Isn't it, Henry? I should have known you'd be a watcher. Still having those impotency issues? Hit or miss, huh? Poor thing. Though I guess that works out well for Michelle Harris, doesn't it? She's not that into men anyway. Since you aren't much of a threat in the bedroom, that must be a sweet setup for you. You have a pretty woman to give you legitimacy, and you don't have to get it up for her. Did she ask you why?"

"Lieutenant, I think that's enough from you, too." Miles tapped his hand on the table, palm down. The slap echoed, but it didn't work. Taylor's and Henry's eyes were locked, pure venom shooting from his, something akin to gloating streaming back from hers.

Taylor held Henry's gaze for a heartbeat longer, then smiled. "Hope it doesn't hurt too bad, Henry. Do you have that phantom limb pain when you can't get it up? Tch. Sorry about that. I might have gotten a bit carried away way back when. Maybe I shouldn't have kicked you in the balls when you tried to run. But I see you've found new and different ways to inflict pain. Apparently you didn't need to use your prick to screw people. Too bad you blew it again."

A muscle twitched in his jaw. "I don't know what you're talking about. I am golden."

"You're shit. We have everything. The whole setup. Every company, all the records. All the videos, all the studios. Todd Wolff gave you up. And you just admitted, on tape, mind you, that you've seen the videos."

Anderson leaned back in his chair. If he wasn't cuffed to the table, he would have crossed his arms in nonchalance. "Pppft. Little pussy knows nothing. Though I will miss that little wife of his. She was quite a piece of ass. Had her every which way from Sunday, and then some."

"Too bad your son died with her."

"I have no earthly idea what you're talking about, Lieutenant. I'm impotent, remember?"

"Intermittently. You forget, I was there at the hospital after you took my boot in the crotch. The doctors specifically said that you'd have trouble getting it up and keeping it up, but that time would heal the wound. Since you'd been fucking Corinne Wolff, I assume the old adage is true."

There was finally a small degree of wariness in Anderson's eyes.

"You're saying that kid was mine?"

"DNA doesn't lie, Henry. Yes, the baby was your son. Shouldn't have killed her. You robbed yourself of a chance for an heir."

"I didn't kill her. The boy was mine?" Anderson had gotten still. My God, Taylor thought, he actually had feelings for Corinne.

"Tell me how it worked, Henry. How you slept with one sister and lived with the other. I don't understand."

"Henry," Miles warned.

"This doesn't matter, Miles. I refuse to let them try to pin Corinne's murder on me." He turned back to Taylor. "Yes, I lived with Michelle. She knows nothing about any of this. Corinne and I kept things quiet. Very quiet. I loved her."

"I didn't know that was an emotion you could feel, Henry."

"Fuck you, cop. You don't know anything about me." He turned his head away and Taylor could have sworn she'd seen a tear. But Henry was done talking. When she realized he wasn't going to be any more forthcoming, she turned off the tape recorder.

"You're right, Henry. Todd doesn't have all the details. But he had nothing to lose, testifying against you costs him nothing. He'll probably get special consideration for Corinne's murder, come to think of it. Since he's been so helpful and all. No, it wasn't all Todd."

"What are you talking about, bitch?"

This time, when she smiled, she stood up. "What, you think I'm going to lay out the whole case against you? You can worry about that all the way to court. And you'll be quite the star in prison this time, Henry. I heard they called you Henrietta last time."

She ignored him when he lunged at her, knew the shackles attached to the table would hold. Turning her back on Henry Anderson felt good. Ever since she'd gotten a little overzealous with him all those years ago, had to stomp on his private parts, she'd harbored a slight sense of guilt for hurting him so badly. That emotion was gone.

"Bye, Henry."

When the door shut behind her, she let out the breath she wasn't aware she was holding. She went two doors down the hall.

"Did we get enough?" she asked the rest of her team, who'd crowded into the observation/printer room to watch the interrogation.

Baldwin was the one who answered. "Yep. Like you said, he openly admitted to seeing your tapes. The voice prints should be perfect, you captured a range of emotions. This will seal the deal with the videotape of you and David Martin, the voice on the tape can be digitally matched to the spliced voice and we've got yet another charge to hang on him, and another example of how your good name was falsely besmirched."

"Besmirched. I like that word."

They shared a smile, then Lincoln cleared his throat. "Oh for God's sake, you two need to get a room."

Laughter rang out, which helped. Taylor felt dirty after her meeting with Anderson. He'd always known just the right things to say to get under her skin. It was the reason she'd lost her temper with him all those years ago, kicked him in the nuts so hard that they ascended and had to be surgically fixed. The odds of him fathering a child were exceptionally slim, and Taylor caught herself before she felt bad about his loss of a son. Her grief was reserved for the baby, a child that never had a chance to live because his parents were idiots.

Antonio Giormanni was being indicted as they spoke, but was cutting a sweet deal with the D.A. to testify fully against Henry Anderson. Todd Wolff, still swearing up and down that he didn't kill his wife, was also getting some consideration in exchange for his testimony. It was going to be a long, convoluted trial, but Taylor had every confidence that the state would throw Henry away for life this time.

As everyone made plans to get drinks at Mulligan's Pub, down on 2nd Avenue, she wished she had that last little bit of the puzzle. Direct causal verification of Corinne's murderer. They'd get it sooner or later, but she'd prefer it sooner.

Everyone split up to do the last-minute items that needed to be addressed before they could call this a day. A successfully solved case, on several different levels. She straightened all the papers in her office. She answered a couple of e-mails. She placed the last items in the murder book, Corinne Wolff's autopsy photos juxtaposed with a photo of her and Todd on their wedding day, lifted from the front table in their foyer. The woodsy background looked especially green tonight, Corinne a luminous wood sprite in white. What an incredible waste.

And that precious little girl, Hayden. A thought hit her. Hayden's blond hair, so different from her parents' dark. What if Anderson had fathered Hayden as well?

It was a long shot, but Taylor wrote the idea on a Post-it note and stuck it to the inside of the murder book. It didn't really matter if Anderson was Hayden's father, but it might help with the timeline. There were plenty of details to be ironed out, the case still needed to be properly prepared before going to trial. There were no guarantees in today's judicial system. She heaved a sigh.

A soft knocking made her look up. Baldwin stood in the door, Lincoln behind him.

"Come on in," she said. "I'm ready, I was just putting a couple of notes in the files so I don't forget. I could use a Guinness, I'll tell you that."

"We might have to hold off on that a moment." Lincoln had that look, that "I found something you've got to see" look that he only got when he had something explosive to tell her.

Her stomach dropped. She took her hair out of the ponytail, then put it back up. "God, don't tell me. More tapes?"

"No. Nothing bad for you." He smiled and sat in the chair opposite her. Baldwin stayed standing in the doorway.

"Spill. I'm out of patience today, Linc."

"Michelle Harris has a juvenile record. A sealed juvenile record."

Taylor's heart thumped twice, resetting its rhythm for a faster pace.

"For what? Did you get them unsealed?"

"I did, but Baldwin had to help. It was a federal case."

"Michelle Harris was charged with a federal felony when she was a kid?"

"Not exactly. She was raped. When she was fourteen. By a really bad guy who was a serial rapist, preyed on young women in Connecticut. That's why it was so hard to get, the records are tied up in a completely separate state's jurisdiction as well as with the FBI. Because this guy transported some of his victims across state lines, the FBI was able to level kidnapping charges against him. But he slipped the net. Got off in court on a bogus technicality. I could go into details, but let's fast forward to why. He slips the noose and goes out to get himself some play.

"He found them at summer camp. Tennis camp. Michelle was fourteen. We don't have all the details, but on the night he raped her, Michelle managed to kill him."

"What?"

"Yeah. It's a wild story. He raped her, left her, and instead of reporting it, she followed him. He went to a bar, she waited on him. He came out drunk, she took advantage of the situation. Lured him behind the bar, took care of business."

"How?" Taylor asked.

"With a piece of steel pipe. She beat him to death."

Forty

Taylor was tired. They were sitting outside Henry Anderson's home again. The sun had gone down. The air was cool, nippy almost. The lights in Anderson's home looked warm, inviting. She watched Michelle Harris bustle through the living room, couldn't tell if she was crying or singing with joy.

When Taylor knocked this time, it was with her knuckles. Polite. Rap, rap, rap.

Michelle came to the door, saw Taylor and Baldwin standing on her step again. Her face contorted in anger. Before she could react, Taylor held up her hands, palm forward.

"It's okay. Can we come in? We need to talk to you."

"Why would I let you in? You've completely destroyed my life in the past week." But she walked away from the door, leaving it open. With a shrug to Baldwin, Taylor went into the house.

Michelle had lit a fire and looked to be having some sort of celebration. Takeout containers and an open bottle of wine sat on the coffee table in the den. This time, Taylor did take a moment to look around, and was struck by the incongruity of the scene. Anderson was a foul creature, profited from the basest of people's emotions, yet his home was as warm and inviting as Taylor's own. It made a chill go down her spine.

Michelle sat on the leather sofa, drew her bare feet up under her. She picked up the glass of wine, toyed with the stem.

"Do you want some," she salvoed. It wasn't really a question and Taylor didn't bother answering.

"Why did you do it, Michelle? Why did you kill Corinne?"

Michelle didn't look up, just stared deep into the contents of her glass. A pinot noir, judging by the lightness of the red and the brown notes that caught in the reflection of the merrily dancing fire. Taylor glanced at the bottle. Yes, she was right. A David Bruce, decent vintage too. Jesus, was Anderson an amateur oenophile like herself as well? Dark and light, that's what they were. Two sides of the same coin. She shuddered, forced her thoughts back to Michelle.

"I loved him," Michelle said. "It was as simple as that."

"Were you with Todd that weekend? Was he with you instead of in Savannah, like he claimed?"

"Yes. We met up in Crossville, stayed the night."

God. Cold-blooded was getting a twin. Killed her sister, framed her lover. Nice girl.

"You know we have to arrest you now."

"Can I finish my wine?"

Taylor glanced at Baldwin. His green eyes had gone nearly black in the firelight. He nodded.

"If you tell us how it happened."

Michelle leaned forward, took the bottle, and poured herself a hefty dollop. With an almost apologetic smile at Taylor, she took a gulp, emptied the rest of the bottle into the glass, then sat back with a smile, as if she were going to tell a wonderful story.

"She had them both. Both of them loved her. They'd fuck me. Well, Henry couldn't do it so much, but he panted after Corinne like a dog in heat. Todd was so wrapped around her little finger, he'd do anything she told him. She ran things, you know that, don't you?"

Taylor nodded. An exhaustive search of all the records indeed showed Corinne's hand dipping into each aspect of Anderson's empire.

"She was even better at being a criminal than she was at tennis. There was nothing she couldn't do. I loved them both, and they both loved her. Gave her children. Gave her everything. I got the scraps. Always had. It wasn't fair. You know about Connecticut?"

"Yes. You beat a man to death."

She went blank, her piercing blue eyes shuttered. "He raped me. He deserved it. He promised me he'd come back the next day, rape Corinne too. I had no choice, I had to defend her."

"You killed a man to protect her. If you loved her so much, why did you kill her? Why did you frame the man you loved with your sister's blood?"

Michelle was silent, drank more of the wine. Her eyes were starting to droop; she looked a bit tipsy. Michelle knew she was caught. She had nothing to lose, not anymore.

"That was convenient. She cut her hand in his truck. I knew he'd get the blame. We always fought, but we had a horrific fight on Friday night. We'd been going through some of the tapes that we were going to sell. She made a crack about Henry not being able to get it up with me, I made a crack about Todd being able to get it up just fine. Yes." She waved her hand around. She was getting deeper into the liquor. Taylor reached for the glass, set it aside. Michelle didn't notice.

"I had such fun with Todd. She didn't know we were doing it. Right under her noshe, her *nose*. She din't like that. I said too bad, if she got to fuck my man, I got to fuck hers. One thing led to another. I couldn't stand looking at her anymore. She said I was a failure, that I'd always been the biggest disappointment in Mother and Daddy's life. She wash mean."

Michelle's eyes were clouding, and her pupils seemed huge in the soft light.

Taylor jumped to her feet. "Shit! Baldwin, call 911. She's OD'ing. God damn it. She must have taken something before we got here. Michelle!"

Taylor shook her, and Michelle smiled. "I forgot…to turn off the lights. Don't tell…Mom. She'd be…mad…if she…knew."

She stopped responding. Baldwin called the ambulance, then came and felt for a pulse. They laid her down. Her breath was short, her heartbeat thready against Taylor's fingers.

"Damn, Baldwin, what did she take?"

"I don't know. I don't see anything here."

"Maybe in the kitchen? Come on, Michelle, stay with us. Michelle?"

Baldwin left for a moment, came back with a prescription bottle. "She took lorazepam. Corinne's prescription. I don't know how many were in here though, it was refilled this afternoon. It's empty now. She wasn't kidding around."

The EMTs were banging on the front door, and Baldwin let them in, telling them what they knew.

"Will she live?" Taylor asked him.

"I don't know. Alcohol and lorazepam can be deadly, but it seems we might have caught it in time. It's going to be touch and go."

His voice was cold. They stood side by side and watched as the EMTs worked on Michelle. The urgency of the rescue effort became nearly frantic. They were forced to secure an airway and do active CPR. A few moments later, the EMTs screamed out of the house with Michelle on a gurney, not willing to let her die on their watch, headed for Baptist Hospital.

Taylor stood in the door, watched them leave. She crossed her arms and glared accusingly at Baldwin.

"You knew," she said.

He nodded.

"We could have called for help sooner," she said.

"We could have. But we know the truth now. If she didn't think she was going to die, she wouldn't have told us."

Wearily, Taylor called for a crime scene investigative team to come to the house. She didn't want to take any chances.

She felt like she was walking through mud. It was midnight when she and Baldwin got back into the car. The call came as they drove home. Michelle Harris had died at 11:56 p.m.

Saturday

Forty-One

The media was having a field day with the planted camera story.

National and local news reporters were fleshing out all the details of the past week's events. The print and online journalists were digging up some extra salacious tidbits. It felt like the whole world was focused on Nashville.

Taylor was wrapping up the report on her interview with Michelle Harris when she got a call. She was to report to the Office of Professional Accountability immediately. The Oompa wanted her.

Taylor had no idea what the problem might be, and waited a good ten minutes before finally shutting off her light and wending her way to the third-floor offices of the OPA.

Delores Norris's door was open.

"Come in," she demanded. There was no pleasantry in her tone. Taylor entered the office for the third time in a week, wishing she were anywhere but here. God, she hated this woman.

Delores looked like a very satisfied jackal, one who'd spent the previous day and night feasting on the deserted remains of an antelope. She launched in immediately, obviously thrilled.

"We have a *problem*, Lieutenant."

Taylor started to sit, and Delores tsk'ed at her. Taylor raised an eyebrow and sat anyway, crossing her arms across her chest. The Oompa was still forced to look up at her, maliciousness sparking in her eyes. Power hungry bitch, Taylor thought.

"And what problem would that be?"

"I've been looking *over* the reports on the Harris suicide. According to the EMT report on Michelle *Harris*, there *was* a chance her life could have been saved. Instead, you and your boyfriend interrogated the suspect, allowed *her* to continue drinking. Is *this* true?"

"Let me see. Yes, we interrogated her. It's called solving a case. As for whether she would have died or not, only God can tell us that."

"So you've imbued yourself *with* the power of God now?"

"Captain Norris, what do you want? I'm tired. The cases are closed. Satisfactorily to all involved, I must say."

"I have a *choice* to make, Lieutenant. Seeing as there is *yet* another complaint against you, I could *suspend* you pending the outcome of the investigation into *your* actions."

"You're kidding me. I've done nothing wrong."

"Eyes of the *beholder*, Lieutenant. Shall we review your past week? One of *your* detectives did drugs with a confidential informant, and you didn't report it. You threatened a suspect with your weapon, a *suspect* that wasn't being questioned in an official capacity. According to your *peers*, you worked on a murder investigation *while* you were on suspension, even going so far as to contact the *mother* of the murder victim. You've been *playing* extremely fast and loose with the rules. And that's not how we work things here at Metro. *Not* with me."

Wow. The Oompa had been doing her homework. Lincoln must have done his debrief and admitted he'd checked in with her. How she'd found out about Taylor's morning of interviews was beyond her. Oh, the cop who was guarding her must have talked. Or Mrs. Harris. Damn.

"I understand how some of that might look. Detective Ross confided in me. In an ordinary circumstance, I would have gone directly to Captain Price, but Detective Ross was on assignment, and we had a breaking murder investigation. As far as the suspect I questioned, I could have arrested him for assaulting an officer. He tried to detain me the evening before. I was doing him a favor by not arresting him."

"But, Lieutenant, *you* don't get to make the rules. *That* isn't how you've been trained, now is it? There is *only* one option left to me at this point. I've already *discussed* it with the chief, *and* he agrees that this is the correct course of action. You have *gone* off the reservation *one* too many times, and *we* feel a *full* psychiatric evaluation and continued monitoring would be *beneficial* to your career at the present time.

"And your team will *have* to report to *different* management while you're under evaluation. We *can't* have our team leaders on the brink, and it's become *obvious* to all involved that you're not capable of this *level* of leadership. Your team needs to be *instilled* with some discipline. They need to *learn* that they don't *get* to take the law into *their* own hands. And you need to learn that you *don't* rule this department."

Taylor let her emotions take control. She stood, forcing the chair back from the table with a rending screech. "You can't do that! That is completely unfair. I've done nothing wrong. My team has done nothing wrong. You're just pissed off that you can't fire me."

The Oompa smiled. "That's *not* true. I'm not upset with that *outcome* in the least. You'll learn that you need to *obey* your superiors. And your *superiors* have learned their lessons as well. Captain Price is going to be taking *early* retirement."

Taylor flashed back to Price, grimly challenging Delores, defending Taylor. She borrowed his words. "You bitch!" she snarled. "I'll fight you to the death on this one."

"Temper, *temper*, my dear. Wouldn't want *that* to get into the daily reports, now would we?"

"There are better ways to get at me, Delores. You don't have to punish them."

The Oompa shifted in her chair, her eyes narrowing, face tightening. "Oh, *on* the contrary. I think this is *the* finest way to get to you. I don't believe *you,* Miss Jackson. I think you *did* kill David Martin. At least you set it up so *you* could have a favorable outcome. Maybe next *time*, you'll think twice *before* you suborn and perjure yourself. Videotapes are *easily* manipulated, I believe you told me? You should be careful *what* you say, my dear. It can come *back* and bite you in the ass. If they can *be* manipulated one way, why *not* the other? Your story about Martin doesn't ring true. And too many *experts* got involved. We'll be taking the tapes to an *independent* analyst."

"I haven't lied about any of this. Not once," Taylor spit through clenched teeth. "You know that."

"Do I? Well, *all* I can say is time will tell. To top your *stellar* week off, a serial killer you allowed to escape has returned to town, has *killed* in your name. No, my dear. It's high time for this *department* to make some changes. We need a *full* accounting of the actions of your homicide team over the *past* year. Lincoln Ross *will* move to the North sector. Marcus Wade *will* be in South. And Sergeant Fitzpatrick *will* be encouraged to take early retirement along with Mitchell Price."

Taylor felt the fury rise in her gut. This woman was past power-hungry, she was giddy in her joy at Taylor's misfortune. Delores handed her the papers.

"*You* can tell them. I'm *sure* it will sting less coming from you. You've *taken* such good care of them all this time. Maybe you'll learn to keep *your* alley-cat tendencies out of their hair now so they can *try* to move on with their lives. You *will* report for your psychiatric evaluation Monday morning."

Taylor was mute. A million thoughts raced through her mind. The most prevalent was don't get yourself fired. You can fight this. Her actions are unwarranted and possibly illegal. Just don't get yourself fired.

"Oh, and *one* more thing."

Taylor dragged her eyes to the Oompa's face. The bitch had the audacity to grin.

"You will be bumped *down*. Two grades. You're a detective again." The Oompa leaned her stubby hands on the desk, leaned in toward Taylor, hissed, "You're damn *lucky* I didn't get you put back out on the street.

Maybe if you learned to think like a cop again you'd *realize* that we *all* have to follow the law."

Taylor felt her mouth open, knew if she left it open, she'd say something she'd never be able to take back. She didn't know if this was for real, if Delores Norris had enough power to make these things happen. Back to being a detective? Bumped two grades? Holy shit. She snapped her teeth together with an audible click that make the Oompa smile wider. She knew the control it was taking Taylor not to mouth herself right out of a job, was hoping Taylor's famous restraint would fail.

No. Taylor refused to let this harridan win. She took the papers, turned and left the office.

"What are you going to do?"

Baldwin was steaming mad, stalking their back deck as Taylor tried to sip a beer. The lightning bugs were putting on a show. The soft spring air glittered with humidity, the promise of a storm. The grass seemed greener in the gloaming, the bark of the trees black against the verdant lawn. A rabbit nibbled at the edges of tall grass, taking advantage of a spot where the lawn mower couldn't quite reach.

"You can't let this happen. What are you going to do?" he asked again.

Taylor shook her head. "My hands are tied. The team has been split up. Price was practically fired. Fitz is seriously considering the early retirement. I'm at a loss, Baldwin." She stood up, went to the railing. Words were failing her. She was on the verge of tears. Frustration always brought her emotions to the surface, this moment was no different. She took a few deep breaths and tried to focus.

She pointed at thin air. "Do you know this spider has been out here every night this week, trying to set up a home? He's like a camper pitching his little tent to get out of a raging storm. He runs around the edges of the web, desperate to get it built, waits and waits and waits for a gnat or moth or lightning bug to fumble their way into the sticky edges. All that work, to sit and wait, hoping for a meal."

She took a broken branch from the tree, used it to break apart the web. The spider scuttled away. "All that work," she repeated.

Baldwin crossed to her, took the branch and laid it on the railing. He turned Taylor to face him, his voice soft. "Seriously, babe, what are you going to do?"

Taylor looked into his emerald eyes and felt the despair build in the pit of her stomach. She turned away, looked out into the woods. Took a deep breath, and squared her shoulders.

"Baldwin, there's only one thing I can do. I have to fight."

* * * * *

ACKNOWLEDGEMENTS

While the execution of the words belongs to the author, we can't make the books come alive without our research, our cheering sections and our inspirations. Thanking people is truly one of the most exciting steps in writing these books. So please indulge me while I wax poetic about my team.

My incredible agent Scott Miller, of Trident Media Group, who always knows exactly what to say and when to say it, and Stephanie Sun, who makes every exchange a pleasure.

My extraordinary editor Linda McFall, the woman who makes these manuscripts into coherent books. I couldn't do it without you. And a special thanks to assistant editor Adam Wilson, who makes the business end so much fun. Between the two of them, they turn my words into magic, for which I will be forever grateful.

The entire MIRA Books team, especially Heather Foy, Don Lucey, Michelle Renaud, Adrienne Macintosh, Megan Lorius, Marianna Ricciuto, Tracey Langmuir, Kathy Lodge, Emily Ohanjanians, Alex Osuszek, Margaret Marbury, Dianne Moggy and the brilliant artists who create these fabulous covers: Tara Kelly and Gigi Lau.

My independent publicist Tom Robinson, who is truly a master at finding just the right spot to place me. Thank you for everything!

The librarians across the country who've seen fit to order my books—it warms my heart every time someone says they found me in their local library!

Detective David Achord of the Metro Nashville Homicide Department, my go-to, my first resource, my friend. He helps Taylor come to life in ways I never could.

Dr Vince Tranchida, Manhattan Medical Examiner, who makes sure Sam does everything right.

Duane Swierczynski, for not knowing Polish.

Elizabeth Fox, who stunned me with an e-mail—"I'm Taylor!"—and has since become a cherished friend.

My amazing critique group, the Bodacious Music City Wordsmiths—Del Tinsley, Janet McKeown, Mary Richards, Rai Lyn Woods, Cecelia Tichi, Peggy O'Neal Peden and J.B. Thompson, who don't ever hesitate to tell me when I've mucked it up and are the first to cheer when I get it right. I love you guys!

And an especial thanks to J.B., who always helps me get these pages ready for New York's eyes.

Laura and Linda, my goddesses at Borders—Cool Springs, who welcomed a new local author with open arms and staff recommendations! Thanks, ladies!

First reader Joan Huston needs a special thanks this time as well, for making me worry about my opening in this book. It's stronger because of her concerns.

My dear Tasha Alexander, the only woman who can actually keep me on the phone instead of at the keyboard, though many times we can do both at once. I love you, honey!

My esteemed fellow authors Brett Battles, Rob Gregory-Browne, Bill Cameron and Dave White, for the IMs; Toni Causey, Gregg Olsen, Kristy Kiernan for constantly cheering me on and making me laugh, and all my Killer Year mates for being such amazing influences on me.

My fellow Murderati bloggers, who inspire me daily, especially Pari Noskin Taichert, the best sounding board out there.

Lee Child and John Connolly, for making me think about every word, and John Sandford, who needs thanks for inspiring me every time.

My parents are the most enthusiastic cheerleaders for my novels and need to be paid a commission on their book sales. Their love and support is phenomenal. My wonderful brother Jay, and Kendall, Jason and Dillon, for putting up with their wayward aunt. My other wonderful brother Jeff, who always, always makes me laugh.

And where would I be without my darling husband to keep me grounded? Thank you, baby, for not letting me float away. You make all of this worthwhile.

Nashville is a wonderful city to write about. Though I try my best to keep things accurate, poetic licence is sometimes needed. All mistakes, exaggerations, opinions and interpretations are mine alone.

Don't miss the next Taylor Jackson novel,

THE COLD ROOM
by J.T. Ellison.

Gavin Adler jumped when a small chime sounded on his computer. He looked at the clock in surprise; it was already 6:00 p.m. During the winter months, darkness descended and reminded him to close up shop, but the daylight savings time change necessitated an alarm clock to let him know when it was time to leave. Otherwise, he'd get lost in his computer and never find his way home.

He rose from his chair, stretched, turned off the computer and reached for his messenger bag. What a day. What a long and glorious day.

He took his garbage with him; his lunch leavings. There was no reason to have leftover banana peels in his trash can overnight. He shut off the lights, locked the door, dropped the plastic Publix bag into the Dumpster, and began the two-block walk to his parking spot. His white Prius was one of the few cars left in the lot.

Gavin listened to his iPod on the way out of downtown. Traffic was testy, as always, so he waited patiently, crawling through West End, then took the exit for I-40 and headed, slowly, toward Memphis. The congestion cleared right past White Bridge, and he sailed the rest of the way.

The drive took twenty-two minutes, he clocked it. Not too bad.

He left the highway at McCrory Lane and went to his gym. The YMCA lot was full, as always. He checked in, changed clothes in the locker room, ran for forty-five minutes, worked on the elliptical for twenty, did one hundred inverted crunches and shadow boxed for ten minutes. Then he toweled himself off. He retrieved the messenger bag, left his sneakers in the locker, slipped his feet back into the fluorescent orange rubber Crocs he'd been wearing all day. He left his gym clothes on—they would go straight into the wash.

He went across the street to Publix, bought a single chicken cordon bleu and a package of instant mashed potatoes, a tube of hearty buttermilk biscuits, fresh bananas and cat food. He took his groceries, went to his car, and drove away into the night. He hadn't seen a soul. His mind was engaged with what waited for him at home.

Dark. Lonely. Empty.

Gavin pulled into the rambler-style house at 8:30 p.m. His cat, a Burmese gray named Art, met him at the door, loudly protesting his empty bowl. He spooned wet food into the cat's dish as a special treat before he did anything else. No reason for Art to be miserable. The cat ate with his tail high in the air, purring and growling softly.

He hit play on his stereo, and the strains of Dvořák spilled through his living room. He stood for a moment, letting the music wash over him, his right arm moving in concert with the bass. The music filled him, made him complete, and whole. Art came and stood beside him, winding his tail around Gavin's leg. He smiled at the interruption, bent and scratched the cat behind the ears. Art arched his back in pleasure.

Evening's ritual complete, Gavin turned on the oven,

sprinkled olive oil in a glass dish and put the chicken in to bake. It would take forty-five minutes to cook.

He showered, checked his work e-mail on his iPhone, then ate. He took his time; the chicken was especially good this evening. He sipped an icy Corona Light with a lime stuck in the neck.

He washed up. 10:00 p.m. now. He gave himself permission. He'd been a very good boy.

The padlock on the door to the basement was shiny with promise and lubricant. He inserted the key, twisting his wrist to keep it from jangling. He took the lock with him, holding it gingerly so he didn't get oil on his clothes. Oil was nearly impossible to get out. He made sure Art wasn't around; he didn't like the cat to get into the basement. He saw him sitting on the kitchen table, looking mournfully at the empty spot where Gavin's plate had rested.

Inside the door, the stairs led to blackness. He flipped a switch and light flooded the stairwell. He slipped the end of the lock in the inside latch, then clicked it home. No sense taking chances.

She was asleep. He was quiet, so he wouldn't wake her. He just wanted to look, anyway.

No, please don't

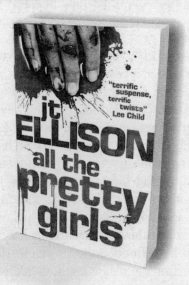

"terrific suspense, terrific twists"
Lee Child

jt ELLISON
all the pretty girls

Nashville homicide lieutenant Taylor Jackson is
pursuing a serial killer who leaves the prior
victim's severed hand at each crime scene.

TV reporter Whitney Connolly has a scoop that
could break the case, but has no idea how
close to this story she really is.

As the killer spirals out of control, everyone must
face a horrible truth: that the purest evil is
born of secrets and lies.

www.mirabooks.co.uk

MIRA

M218_ATPG

Ten victims, each with pale skin and long dark hair

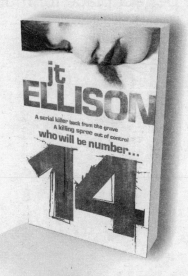

In the mid-1980s the Snow White Killer terrorised Nashville. All the victims had been slashed across the throat, the same red lipstick smeared across their lips. Then suddenly the murders stopped.

Now four more bodies are found with his fatal signature.

Homicide Lieutenant Taylor Jackson believes a copycat killer is on the loose. And this monster is even more terrifying than the original.

www.mirabooks.co.uk

A simple town
A loving community
The perfect place for murder

After a sinister case puts her life in danger, lawyer Brooke seeks sanctuary in the quiet Amish town of Maplecreek.

But when four local teenagers are slaughtered, Brooke can't abide by the community's stoic resolve to mourn the dead in private.

Daniel left his childhood home to explore the outside world. Now, returning to his Amish roots, he intends to unmask his niece's killer and he'll need Brooke's help… They could be Maplecreek's last hope as a deadly threat to their peaceful world closes in.

www.mirabooks.co.uk

MIRA

M223_TGWDT

A LONELY HIGHWAY.
A MISSING GIRL.
AND THE BIGGEST STORY
OF HIS CAREER.

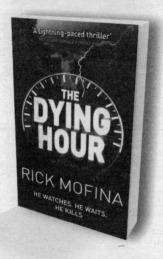

When Karen Harding ends up driving into one of
the worst storms in years, she finds herself stranded
on a desolate stretch of highway.

The next morning the police find her car, but Karen
has vanished. For rookie reporter Jason Wade, it's the
story he's been waiting for and he won't rest until
he finds Karen – dead or alive…

www.mirabooks.co.uk

You've just been jilted at the altar.
Your day is about to get a lot worse.

After Nina Cormier was left at the altar, the empty church they were in exploded. But it was when a stranger tried to run her over that Nina realised someone actually wanted to kill her.

Nina must decipher the terrifying truth: she is at the mercy of a brilliant madman, one who is playing for keeps…

www.mirabooks.co.uk

MIRA

GUILTY –
until proven innocent

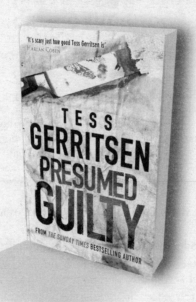

When Miranda Wood finds a man, stabbed to death,
lying in her bed, she is the obvious suspect. But as
Miranda fights to clear her name, she unearths a
murky history of blackmail, corruption and scandal.

And as she gets closer to the truth, it becomes
clear that someone else wants to kill her…

www.mirabooks.co.uk

MIRA

The mark of a good book

At MIRA we're proud of the books we publish, that's why whenever you see the MIRA star on one of our books, you can be assured of its quality and our dedication to bringing you the best books. From romance to crime to those that ask, "What would you do?" Whatever you're in the mood for and however you want to read it, we've got the book for you!

Visit **www.mirabooks.co.uk** and let us help you choose your next book.

★ **Read** extracts from our recently published titles

★ **Enter** competitions and prize draws to win signed books and more

★ **Watch** video clips of interviews and readings with our authors

★ **Download** our reading guides for your book group

★ **Sign up** to our newsletter to get helpful recommendations and **exclusive discounts** on books you might like to read next

www.mirabooks.co.uk

mira_web